HAPPY PLACE

HER PLACE

HAPPY PLACE

EMILY HENRY

THORNDIKE PRESS
A part of Gale, a Cengage Company

LIBRARY OF CONGRESS CIP DATA ON FILE.
CATALOGUING IN PUBLICATION FOR THIS BOOK
IS AVAILABLE FROM THE LIBRARY OF CONGRESS.

ISBN-13: 979-8-88578-574-7 (hardcover alk. paper).

Published in 2023 by arrangement with Berkley, an imprint of Penguin Publishing Group, a division of Penguin Random House LLC.

Printed in Mexico
Print Number: 3   Print Year: 2023

For Noosha, who made it safe to be me, and who regularly answers the question "Why not?" with "Because I don't want to." I love you, always.

1
HAPPY PLACE

Knott's Harbor, Maine

A cottage on the rocky shoreline, with knotty pine floorboards and windows that are nearly always open. The smell of evergreens and brine wafting in on the breeze, and white linen drapes lifting in a lazy dance. The burble of a coffee maker, and that first deep pull of cold ocean air as we step out onto the flagstone patio, steaming mugs in hand.

My friends: willowy, honey-haired Sabrina and wisp of a waif Cleo, with her tiny silver septum piercing and dip-dyed box braids. My two favorite people on the planet since our freshman year at Mattingly College.

It still boggles my mind that we didn't know one another before that, that a stodgy housing committee in Vermont matched the three of us up. The most important friendships in my life all came down to a decision made by strangers, chance. We used to joke

7

that our living arrangement must be some government-funded experiment. On paper, we made no sense.

Sabrina was a born-and-raised Manhattan heiress whose wardrobe was pure Audrey Hepburn and whose bookshelves were stuffed with Stephen King. Cleo was the painter daughter of a semi-famous music producer and an outright famous essayist. She'd grown up in New Orleans and showed up at Mattingly in paint-splattered overalls and vintage Doc Martens.

And me, a girl from southern Indiana, the daughter of a teacher and a dentist's receptionist, at Mattingly because the tiny, prestigious liberal arts school gave me the best financial aid, and that was important for a premed student who planned to spend the next decade in school.

By the end of our first night living together, Sabrina had us lined up on her bed watching *Clueless* on her laptop and eating a well-balanced mix of popcorn and gummy worms. By the end of the next week, she'd had custom shirts made for us, inspired by our very first inside joke.

Sabrina's read *Virgin Who Can't Drive.*

Mine read *Virgin Who CAN Drive.*

And Cleo's read *Not a Virgin but Great Driver.* We wore them all the time, just never

8

outside the dorm. I loved our musty room in the rambling white-clapboard building. I loved wandering the fields and forest around campus with the two of them, loved that first day of fall when we could do our homework with our windows open, drinking spicy chai or decaf laced with maple syrup and smelling the leaves curling up and dropping from branches. I loved the nude painting of Sabrina and me that Cleo made for her final figure drawing class project, which she'd hung over our door so it was the last thing we saw on our way out to class, and the Polaroids we taped on either side of it, the three of us at parties and picnics and coffee shops in town.

I loved knowing that Cleo had been lost in her work whenever her braids were pulled into her neon-green scrunchie and her clothes smelled like turpentine. I loved how Sabrina's head would tip back on an outright cackle whenever she read something particularly terrifying and she'd kick her Grace Kelly loafers against the foot of her bed. I loved poring over my biology textbooks, running out of highlighter as I went because *everything* seemed so important, breaking to clean the room top to bottom whenever I got stuck on an assignment.

Eventually, the silence would always crack,

and we'd end up giggling giddily over texts from Cleo's prospective new girlfriend, or outright shrieking as we hid behind our fingers from the slasher movie Sabrina had put on. We were *loud.* I'd never been loud before. I grew up in a quiet house, where shouting only ever happened when my sister came home with a questionable new piercing or a new love interest or both. The shouting always gave way to an even deeper silence after, and so I did my best to head the shouting off at the pass, because I *hated* the silence, felt every second of it as a kind of dread.

My best friends taught me a new kind of quiet, the peaceful stillness of knowing one another so well you don't need to fill the space. And a new kind of loud: noise as a celebration, as the overflow of joy at being alive, here, now.

I couldn't have imagined being any happier, loving anywhere else as much.

Not until Sabrina brought us here, to her family's summer home on the coast of Maine. Not until I met Wyn.

2
REAL LIFE

Monday
Think of your happy place, the cool voice in my ear instructs.

Picture it. Glimmering blue washes across the backs of my eyes.

How does it smell? Wet rock, brine, butter sizzling in a deep fryer, and a spritz of lemon on the tip of my tongue.

What do you hear? Laughter, the slap of water against the bluffs, the hiss of the tide drawing back over sand and stone.

What can you feel? Sunlight, everywhere. Not just on my bare shoulders or the crown of my head but *inside* me too, the irresistible warmth that comes only from being in the exact right place with the exact right people.

Mid-descent, the plane gives another sideways jolt.

I stifle a yelp, my fingernails sinking into the armrests. I'm not a nervous flier, per se.

11

But every time I come to *this* particular airport, I do so on a tiny plane that looks like it was made out of scrap metal and duct tape.

My guided meditation app has reached an inconvenient stretch of silence, so I repeat the prompt myself: *Think of your happy place, Harriet.*

I slide my window shade up. The vast, brilliant expanse of the sky makes my heart flutter, no imagination required. There are a handful of places, of memories, that I always come back to when I need to calm myself, but *this* place tops the charts.

It's psychosomatic, I'm sure, but suddenly I *can* smell it. I *hear* the echoey call of the circling gulls and *feel* the breeze riffle my hair. I taste ice-cold beer, ripe blueberries.

In mere minutes, after the longest year of my life, I'll be reunited with my favorite people in the world, in our favorite place in the world.

The plane's wheels clatter against the runway. Some passengers in the back burst into applause, and I yank out my earbuds, anxiety lifting off me like dandelion seeds. Beside me, the grizzled seatmate who'd snored through our death-defying flight blinks awake.

He looks at me from under a pair of curly

12

white eyebrows and grunts, "Here for the Lobster Festival?"

"My best friends and I go every year," I say.

He nods.

"I haven't seen them since last summer," I add.

He harrumphs.

"We all went to school together, but we live in different places now, so it's hard to get our schedules to line up."

The unimpressed look in his eye amounts to *I asked one yes or no question.*

Ordinarily, I would consider myself to be a superb seatmate. I'm more likely to get a bladder infection than to ask a person to get up so I can use the lavatory. Ordinarily, I don't even wake someone up if they're asleep on my shoulder, drooling down my chest.

I've held strangers' babies and farty therapy dogs for them. I've pulled out my earbuds to oblige middle-aged men who will perish if they can't share their life stories, and I've flagged down flight attendants for paper bags when the post–spring break teenager next to me started looking a little green.

So I'm fully aware this man in no way wants to hear about my magical upcoming week with my friends, but I'm so excited, it's hard to stop. I have to bite my bottom lip to keep myself from singing "Vacation" by the Go-Go's into this grumpy man's face as we begin the painfully slow deboarding process.

I retrieve my suitcase from the dinky airport's baggage carousel and emerge through the front doors feeling like a woman in a tampon commercial: overjoyed, gorgeous, and impossibly comfortable — ready for any highly physical activity, including but not limited to bowling with friends or getting a piggyback ride from the unobtrusively handsome guy hired by central casting to play my boyfriend.

All that to say, I am *happy.*

This is the moment that's carried me through thankless hospital shifts and the sleepless nights that often follow.

For the next week, life will be crisp white wine, creamy lobster rolls, and laughing with my friends until tears stream down our cheeks.

A short honk blasts from the parking lot. Even before I open my eyes and see her, I'm smiling.

"O Harriet, my Harriet!" Sabrina shouts, half falling out of her dad's old cherry-red Jaguar.

14

She looks, as ever, like a platinum Jackie O, with her perfectly toned olive arms and her classic black pedal pushers, not to mention the vintage silk scarf wrapped around her glossy bob. She still strikes me the same as that first day we met, like an effortlessly cool starlet plucked from another time.

The effect is somewhat tempered by the way she keeps jumping up and down with a poster board on which she's scrawled, in her god-awful serial-killer handwriting, *SAY IT'S CAROL SINGERS*, a *Love Actually* reference that could not, actually, make less contextual sense.

I break into a jog across the sunlit parking lot. She shrieks and hurls the poster at the car's open window, where it smacks the frame and flaps to the ground as she takes off running to meet me.

We collide in an impressively uncomfortable hug. Sabrina's exactly tall enough that her shoulder always finds a way to cut off my air supply, but there's still nowhere I'd rather be.

She rocks me back and forth, cooing, "You're heeeeere."

"I'm heeeeere!" I say.

"Let me look at you." She draws back to give me a stern once-over. "What's different?"

15

"New face," I say.

She snaps her fingers. "Knew it." She loops an arm around my shoulders and turns me toward the car, a cloud of Chanel No. 5 following us. It's been her signature scent since we were eighteen and I was still sporting a Bath & Body Works concoction that smelled like vodka-soaked cotton candy. "Your doctor does great work," she deadpans. "You look thirty years younger. Not a day over newborn."

"Oh, no, it wasn't a medical procedure," I say. "It was an Etsy spell."

"Well, either way, you look great."

"You too," I squeal, squeezing her around the waist.

"I can't believe this is real," she says.

"It's been too long," I agree.

We fall into that hyper-comfortable kind of silence, the quiet of two people who lived together for the better part of five years and still, after all this time, have a muscle memory for how to share space.

"I'm so happy you could make this work," she says as we reach the car. "I know how busy you are at the hospital. Hospitals? They have you move around, right?"

"Hospitals," I confirm, "and nothing could have stopped me."

"By which you mean, you ran out of there

mid–brain surgery," Sabrina says.

"Of course not," I say. "I *skipped* out of there mid–brain surgery. Still have the scalpel in my pocket."

Sabrina cackles, a sound so at odds with her composed exterior that the whole first week we lived together, I jumped every time I heard it. Now all her rough edges are my favorite parts of her.

She throws open the car's back door and tosses my suitcase in with an ease that defies her lanky frame, then stuffs the poster in after it. "How was the flight?"

"Same pilot as last time," I tell her.

Her brow lifts. "Ray? Again?"

I nod. "Of sunglasses-on-the-back-of-the-head fame."

"Never seen him without them," she muses.

"He absolutely has to have a second set of eyes in his neck," I say.

"The only explanation," she agrees. "God, I'm so sorry — ever since Ray got sober, I swear he flies like a dying bumblebee."

I ask, "How did he fly back when he was still drinking?"

"Oh, the same." She hops in behind the steering wheel, and I drop into the passenger seat beside her. "But his intercom banter was a fucking delight."

17

She digs a spare scarf out of the center console and tosses it at me, a thoughtful if ultimately meaningless gesture since my bun of chaotic dark curls is far beyond saving after three back-to-back flights and a dead sprint through both the Denver airport and Boston Logan.

"Well," I say, "there wasn't a pun to be found in those skies today."

"Tragic," she tuts. The car's engine growls to life. With a whoop, she peels out of the parking lot and points us east, toward the water, the windows down and sunlight rippling over our skin. Even here, an hour inland, yards are dotted with lobster traps, pyramids of them at the edges of lots.

Over the roar of the wind, Sabrina shouts, "HOW ARE YOU?"

My stomach does this seesawing thing, flipping from the absolute bliss of being in this car with her and the abject dread of knowing I'm about to throw a wrench into her plans.

Not yet, I think. *Let's enjoy this for a second before I ruin everything.*

"GOOD," I shout back.

"AND HOW'S THE RESIDENCY?" she asks.

"GOOD," I say again.

She glances sidelong, wisps of blond snak-

18

ing out of her scarf to slap her forehead. "WE'VE BARELY SPOKEN IN WEEKS AND THAT'S ALL I GET?"

"BLOODY?" I add.

Exhausting. Terrifying. Electrifying, though not necessarily in a good way. Sometimes nauseating. Occasionally devastating.

Not that I'm involved in much surgery. Two years into the residency, and I'm still doing plenty of scut work. But the slivers of time spent with an attending surgeon and a patient are all I think about when I clock out, as if those minutes weigh more than any of the rest.

Scut work, on the other hand, goes by in a flash. Most of my colleagues dread it, but I kind of like the mundanity. Even as a kid, cleaning, organizing, checking off little tasks on my self-made chore chart gave me a sense of peace and control.

A patient is in the hospital, and I get to discharge them. Someone needs blood drawn, and I'm there to do it. Data needs to be plugged into the computer system, and I plug it in. There's a before and an after, with a hard line between them, proof that there are millions of small things you can do to make life a little better.

"AND HOW'S WYN?" Sabrina asks.

19

The seesaw inside me jolts again. Sharp gray eyes flash across my mind, the phantom scent of pine and clove wafting over me.

Not yet, I think.

"WHAT?" I shout, pretending not to have heard.

This conversation is inevitable, but ideally it won't take place while we're going eighty miles an hour in a pop-can car from the sixties. Also, I'd rather have it when Cleo, Parth, and Kimmy are all present so I won't have to rip off the Band-Aid more than once.

I've already waited this long. What's a few more minutes?

Undeterred by the vortex of wind ripping through the car, Sabrina repeats, "WYN. HOW'S WYN?"

Electrifying, though not necessarily in a good way? Sometimes nauseating? Occasionally devastating.

"GOOD, I THINK." The *I think* part makes it feel less like a lie. He probably *is* good. The last time I saw him, he was virtually illuminated from within. Better than he had been in months.

Sabrina nods and cranks up the radio.

She shares the cottage, and its associated cars, with about twenty-five Armas cousins and siblings, but there's a strict rule about

20

returning the radio presets to her dad's stations at the end of a stay, so our trips always begin with a burst of Ella Fitzgerald; Sammy Davis, Jr.; or one of their contemporaries. Today, Frank Sinatra's "Summer Wind" carries us up the pine-dotted drive to where the cottage perches atop a rocky cliff.

It never gets any less impressive.

Not the sparkling water. Not the cliffs. Certainly not the cottage.

Really, it's more like a mansion *swallowed* a cottage, and then wore its bonnet and imitated its voice in an unconvincing falsetto, Big Bad Wolf–style. At some point, probably closer to the year 1900 than to now, it was a family home. That part of it still stands. But behind it, and on either side of it, the expansions stretch out, their exteriors perfectly matched to the original building.

Off to one side there's a four-car garage, and across the creek on the other, a guest-house sits tucked among the moss, ferns, and salt-gnarled trees.

The car glides right past the garage, and Sabrina cuts the engine in front of the front door.

Nostalgia, warmth, and happiness rush over me.

"Remember the first time you brought me

and Cleo here?" I ask. "That guy Brayden had ghosted me, and you and Cleo made a PowerPoint about his worst qualities."

"Brayden?" She unbuckles her seat belt and hops out of the car. "Are you talking about *Bryant*?"

I peel my thighs off the hot leather and climb out after her. "His name was *Bryant*?"

"You were convinced you were going to *marry* Bryant," Sabrina says, delighted. "Now you don't even remember the poor guy's name."

"It was a powerful PowerPoint," I say, wrestling my bag out of the back seat.

"Yeah, or it could have something to do with one Ms. Cleo James giving us free psychotherapy that whole week. My dad had just gotten engaged to Wife Number Three before we took that trip, remember?"

"Oh, right," I say. "She was the one with all the dogs."

"That was Number Two," Sabrina says. "And to be fair, she didn't have them all simultaneously. More like she had a revolving door that magically brought new designer puppies in as it swept her adult dogs straight back to the pound."

I shudder. "So creepy."

"She was, but at least I won the cousins' divorce betting pool that year. That's how I scored access to the cottage during Lobster Fest. Cousin Frankie's loss was our gain."

I clasp my hands together in a silent prayer of thanks. "Cousin Frankie, wherever you may be, we thank you for your sacrifice."

"Don't waste your gratitude. I think he lives on a catamaran in Ibiza these days." Sabrina yanks my bag free from the crook of my elbow, taking my hand to haul me up to the front door. "Come on. Everyone's waiting."

"I'm last?" I say.

"Parth and I got in last night," she says. "Cleo and Kimmy drove up this morning. We've all been sitting on our hands and vibrating, waiting for you to get here."

"Wow," I say, "things descended into orgy territory pretty quickly."

Another Trademark Sabrina Laugh. She jiggles the doorknob. "I guess I should've specified we were all sitting on our *own* hands."

"Now, that changes things considerably," I say.

She cracks open the door and grins at me.

"Why are you looking at me expectantly?" I ask.

"I'm not," she says.

I narrow my eyes. "Aren't lawyers supposed to be good at lying?"

"Objection!" she says. "Speculative."

"Why aren't we going inside, Sabrina?"

Wordlessly, she nudges the door wider and gestures me through.

"Okaayyyy." I creep past her. In the cool foyer, I'm hit with the smell of summer: dusty shelves, sun-warmed verbena, sunblock, the kind of salty damp that gets into the bones of old Maine houses and never quite dries out again.

From the end of the first-floor hallway, back in the open kitchen–slash–living room (part of the extension, of course), I hear Cleo's soft timbre followed by Parth's low chuckle.

Sabrina kicks off her shoes and drops the keys on the console table, calling, "Here!"

Cleo's girlfriend, Kimmy, comes bounding down the hall first, a blur of curves and strawberry blond hair. "Harryyyy!" she cries, her tattooed fingers grabbing for my face as she plants loud kisses on each of my cheeks. "Is it really *you*?" She shakes me by the shoulders. "Are my eyes deceiving me?"

"You're probably confused because she got a new face on Etsy," Sabrina tells her.

"Huh," Kimmy says. "I was wondering what Danny DeVito was doing here."

"That probably has more to do with the

24

edibles," I say.

Kimmy doesn't cackle; she guffaws. Like every one of her laughs is Heimliched out of her. Like she's constantly being caught off guard by her own joy. She's the newest addition to our little unit by years, but it's easy to forget she hasn't been there since day one.

"I missed you so much," I tell her, squeezing her wrists.

"Missed you more!" She claps her hands together, her red-gold bun wobbling like an overeager pom-pom. "Do you *know*?"

"Know what?"

She glances at Sabrina. "Does she know?"

"She does not."

"Know *what*?" I repeat.

Sabrina threads an arm through mine. "About your surprise." On my right, Kimmy catches my other elbow, and together, they perp-walk me down the hall.

"What surpri—"

I stop so hard and fast that my elbow hits Kimmy's ribs. I only dimly register her grunt of pain. My senses are fully concerned with the man rising from the marble breakfast bar.

Dark blond hair, broad shoulders, a mouth improbably soft when compared to the hard lines that make up the rest of his face, and eyes that shine steel gray from afar but, I know from experience, are ringed in mossy green once you get up close.

Like, for example, when you're tangled with him beneath a blush sheet, the diffused glow of your bedside lamp painting his skin gold and giving his whisper a texture.

His shoulders are relaxed, his face totally calm, like being in the same room as me is *not* the worst thing that could have possibly happened to either of us.

Meanwhile, I'm basically a walking, breathing bottle of soda into which a Mentos has been plopped, panic fizzing up, threatening to spew out between my cells.

Go to your happy place, Harriet, I think desperately, only to realize I'm literally *in* my happy place, and he. Is. *Here.*

The very last person I expected to see.

The very last person I *want* to see.

Wyn Connor.

My fiancé.

3
REAL LIFE

Monday

Okay, so he's not my fiancé *anymore,* but (1) our friends don't know that yet and (2) when you're engaged to a person as long as *I* was to Wyn Connor, you don't stop accidentally thinking of him as your fiancé overnight.

Or, apparently, even over the course of months.

Which is how long we've kept up this ruse.

A ruse that was supposed to end this week, while I was here. Without him.

We'd hammered out the details over a competitively cordial email exchange, how we'd take turns on trips like our friends were the children caught in our would-be divorce.

He *insisted* I get the first trip. So *why* is he here, standing between Parth and Cleo in the kitchen like the grand prize on some ill-conceived game show?

"Sur-*priiiiise!*" Sabrina sings.

I gape. Gawk. Freeze, while the seesaw in my chest swings back and forth with the force of a well-manned catapult.

His hair has grown long enough to be tucked behind his ears, a sure sign that the family furniture repair business has been swamped, and he's grown a beard too, but it doesn't soften the hard line of his jaw *or* firm up his pouty lips. I'm still painfully aware of the way the right half of his Cupid's bow sits higher than the left. At least his dimples are somewhat hidden.

"Hello, *honey.*" His smoky velvet voice makes it sound like he's feeding me lines in a salacious stage play.

This man has never once called me *honey.* He never even calls me Harry, like our friends do. Once, when I had a terrible flu, he called me *baby* in such a tender voice, my feverish brain decided it would be a good time to burst into tears. Aside from that, it's always been strictly Harriet. Whether he was laughing or frustrated, peeling off my clothes or ending our relationship in a four-minute phone call.

As in *Harriet, I think we both know where this is going.*

"Awh!" Kimmy squeals. "Look at her! She's speechless!"

28

More like my frontoparietal network is short-circuiting. "I . . ."

Before I can land on word number two, Wyn crosses the kitchen, ropes an arm around my waist, and hauls me up against him.

Stomach to stomach, ribs to ribs, nose to nose. Mouth to mouth.

Now my whole brain seems to be on fire, random pieces of data flying at me like Hitchcockian crows: The taste of cinnamon toothpaste. The quick thrum of a heartbeat. The rasp of an unshaven cheek. The soft brush of lips, once with purpose.

HE'S KISSING ME, I realize, full seconds after the kiss has ended. My legs are watery, all my joints mysteriously vanished. Wyn's arm tightens around me as he draws back, his grip very likely the only thing keeping me from face-planting onto the Armases' knotty pine floors.

"Surprise." His gray eyes communicate something more akin to *Welcome to hell; I'll be your host, the devil.*

Everyone's watching, waiting for me to say something a bit more effusive than *I . . .*

I manage to squeak out, "I thought you couldn't get away."

"Things changed." His eyes flash, his mouth twisting unhappily.

"He means Sabrina bullied him," Parth cuts in, lifting me off the ground in a bear hug so tight it makes me cough.

Sabrina tosses my bag onto the ground. "I like to think of it as problem-solving. We needed Wyn here for this. We got him here."

People like to say opposites attract, and sure, that's true — Wyn's the restless and calloused son of two ex-ranchers, and I'm a surgical resident whose most torrid fantasy of late is mopping alone in the dark.

But Parth and Sabrina are one of those couples cut from the same oddly specific cloth. Like his girlfriend, Parth's a Photoshop good-looking (thick, dark hair with a wave; strong jaw; perfect white smile), type A lawyer with a long-term signature scent (Tuscan Leather, Tom Ford). Despite all their similarities, it took the two of them a ridiculously long time to accept that they were in love with each other.

"You don't call, you don't write!" Parth teases.

"I know, I'm sorry," I say. "It's been so hectic."

"Well, you're here now." He tousles my hair. "And you look . . ."

"Tired?" I guess.

"That's just her new face," Kimmy says, popping up onto a stool and stuffing her

30

hand into a bag of Takis Fuego on the counter.

"You look *gorgeous*." Cleo squeezes past Parth to hug me, her subdued lavender scent folding around me as her head tucks neatly beneath my chin. Even the height differences between Cleo, Sabrina, and me always seemed like proof we belonged together, balanced one another out.

"Of *course* gorgeous," Parth says, "but I was going to say *hungry*. You want a sandwich or something, Har?"

"Takis?" Kimmy holds the shiny purple bag out in my direction.

"I'm good!" my mouth says.

You are VERY bad, actually, my brain argues.

Cleo frowns. "You sure? You do look sort of peaked."

Sabrina ducks her head. "They're right, Har. You're, like . . . milk colored. You okay?"

No, actually I feel like I'm going to puke and pass out, and I'm not sure in which order, and having everyone's undivided attention and *worry* on me is making things a hundred times worse, while the feeling of *his* undivided attention is pure torture.

"I'm fine!" I say.

Just furiously wishing I'd opted to put on

31

a bra before my flight, or styled my hair, or maybe even just spilled a bit less mustard down my boobs whilst eating that airport hot dog.

Oh god. He's not supposed to be here!

The next time I saw him, I was supposed to be in a sexy Reformation dress with a hot new boyfriend and a full face of makeup. (In this fantasy, I'd also learned how to apply a full face of makeup.) Most importantly, I was supposed to have no perceivable reaction to him.

Shit, shit, shit. As badly as I've wanted to avoid imploding our friend group over the past few months since the breakup, I now just as badly need to get the truth out so I can get *away* from him.

"There's something I need —"

"Honey." Wyn's back at my side, his hands catching my waist as if in preparation to throw me over his shoulder and abscond if necessary. "Sabrina and Parth have something to tell you," he says pointedly. "To tell everyone."

My skin tingles under his grip. I'm suddenly convinced I'm not wearing any shorts, but nope, I can just magically feel his calloused fingers through the denim.

When I try to extricate myself, his fingertips sink into the curves of my hips. *Don't move,* his eyes warn.

Bite me, I try to make mine reply.

The right peak of his lips twitches irritably.

Sabrina is getting a bottle of champagne out of the stainless steel and glass refrigerator, but she doesn't look celebratory. She looks downright melancholy.

Parth goes to stand behind her, setting his hands on her shoulders. "We have a couple of announcements," he says. "And Wyn already knows, because, well, we had to give him the full picture so he understood why it was so essential that he's here this week. That all of us are."

"Oh my god!" Kimmy half screams, instantly ecstatic. "Are you two having a —"

"Oh *god,* no!" Sabrina says. "No. *No!* Definitely not. It's — it's the house." She pauses for a breath, then swallows and lifts her chin. "Dad's selling it. Next month."

The kitchen goes pin-drop silent. Not comfortable quiet, shocked quiet.

Cleo wilts onto a stool at the counter. Wyn's hands scrape clear of me, and he immediately puts several feet of distance between us, no longer considering me at risk of confessing, apparently.

I stand there, an astronaut untethered

33

from her spaceship, drifting into nothingness.

I've already lost the person I expected to marry. I've already moved across the country from all my best friends. And now this house — *our house,* this pocket universe where we always belong, where no matter what else is happening, we're safe and happy — that's going away too.

All the panic I felt at finding myself trapped here with Wyn is instantly eclipsed by this new dread.

Our house.

Where, the summer after sophomore year, Cleo, Sabrina, and I slept in a row of mattresses we'd dragged to the middle of the living room floor and dubbed "super bed," staying up most nights talking and laughing until the first rays of sunrise spilled in from the patio doors.

Where Cleo whispered, as if it were a secret or a prayer, *I've never had friends like this,* and Sabrina and I nodded solemnly, the three of us holding hands until we drifted off.

The firepit out back where, in lieu of a blood pact (which struck me as dangerously unsanitary), the three of us had burned the same spot on our pointer fingers against the hot metal, then made ourselves laugh until we cried, concocting increasingly ridiculous scenarios where we could use our finger-print scars to frame one another for various heists.

The wooden staircase on which Parth once orchestrated an elaborate cardboard luge race for us, and the little wood-paneled library in front of whose hearth Cleo first told us about a girl named Kimmy. The nail that stuck up from the pier where, a year later, Kimmy cut her foot open, and the rickety staircase Wyn had carried her up afterward while she demanded the rest of us chuck grapes at her open mouth, fan her with invisible palm fronds.

And *Wyn.*

The first time I kissed him.

The first time I touched him, period. *Here.*

This house is all that's left of us.

"This will be our last trip." Sabrina tugs her scarf from her head and tosses the slip of silk across the counter. "Our last trip here, anyway."

The words hang in the air. I wonder if the others are also scrambling for a solution, like maybe if we pass around a hat and combine our spare change, we'll find six million dollars to buy a vacation home.

"Can't you —" Kimmy begins.

"No," Sabrina cuts her off. "Wife Number

Six doesn't want Dad to have it, since he bought it with my mom, I guess. Never mind that there are four more-recent wives she could fixate her jealousy on." She rolls her eyes. "Dad's already got a buyer lined up and everything. It's a done deal."

Parth rocks Sabrina's shoulders, trying to shake her out of the dark mood.

My gaze wanders toward Wyn, a subconscious part of me still expecting the sight of him to drain away my stress.

Instead, the second our eyes meet, my heart starts jackhammering. I look away.

"It's not all bad news, though," Parth says. "We actually have some good news too. Amazing news."

Sabrina looks up from the champagne she's been de-foiling. "Right. There's something else."

"*Oh, right, there's something else,*" Parth mimics, teasing. "Don't treat our engagement like a sidebar."

"Your *what*?"

At first I'm not sure who shrieked it.

Me. I shrieked it.

Well, me *and* Cleo, who shoots up from her stool so fast, she knocks it over and has to catch it against the island with her hip.

Sabrina's cackle is halfway between giddy and disbelieving.

"Your *what*?" I repeat.

"Dude, I know," she says. "I'm as surprised as you are."

Kimmy snatches Sab's hand and gasps at the gigantic emerald winking on her ring finger.

Which is approximately when I realize that someone's going to notice my missing engagement ring.

I stuff my hands in my pockets. Very natural. Just a girl with her fists in her tiny, useless women's shorts pockets.

"You said you'd *never* get married," Cleo says with a scrupulous dent between her brows, eyeing the gemstone and its white-gold mount. "Under any circumstances. You said 'not with a gun to my head.' "

And who could blame her? Even setting her father's trail of ex-wives aside, Sabrina is a divorce attorney. She spends eight hours a day, at minimum, surrounded by reasons *not* to get married.

"Tell us the story," Kimmy says as Cleo continues, "You once told me you'd rather spend five years in prison than one year as a wife."

"Babe!" Kimmy pokes Cleo in the ribs. "We're *celebrating*. Sabrina changed her mind. People do that, you know."

People do; Sabrina Armas doesn't.

Sometimes I'll go back and forth about what I want for breakfast for so long that it's already lunch. Sabrina eats the same exact yogurt and granola every day, the only variation being whatever seasonal fruit she adds.

Sabrina coils an arm around Parth's waist. "Yeah, well. Finding out we'd be saying goodbye to the cottage cleared some stuff up for me." Her voice gives the slightest waver before going steely again. "Whether Parth and I are married or not, I'm in this for the long haul, and I'm tired of trying to be smart at the expense of my own happiness. I want this to be forever, and I don't want to pretend that's not what I want."

Kimmy sets a hand across her chest. "That's beautiful."

Parth smiles down at Sabrina, rubbing her shoulder tenderly. Her eyes light on me, a grin spreading over her classic-red lips. "And honestly, we were kind of inspired . . ."

It feels like the moment before a car accident, when the tires have started to hydroplane and you know something terrible is likely coming, but there's still a chance the tread will find purchase and you'll never know what agony you narrowly avoided.

And then Sabrina goes on.

"I mean, look at Harry and Wyn. They've

been together like ten years, and they're making it work, even while they have to be long distance. Clearly love actually can conquer all."

"Eight years," Wyn corrects quietly.

Kimmy squeezes his bicep. "Eight *years*, and you're still never more than three feet apart."

By my estimation, Wyn is approximately two feet eleven and three-quarters inches from me when she says this, but at the comment, he hooks an arm around my neck and says, "Yeah, well, even after all these years, Harriet has a way of making me feel like we've just met."

Kimmy clutches her heart again, missing the irony he intended only for me.

A whoop goes up around the room as Sabrina pops the champagne's cork. I feel like I'm floating over my own body. Adrenaline is doing *weird* things to me.

Normally, I'd rather roll down a mountainside covered in broken glass and sticky traps than create conflict, but the longer this goes on, the harder it's going to be to get out of our lie.

"That's amazing." My voice lifts two and a half octaves. "But I have to tell you —"

"Harriet." And there he is again, at my side with arms coming around me from

39

behind and his chin resting atop my head, and now, when *Think of your m***** f****** happy place* flashes through my mind, all I can think is, *If only I were still on Sober Ray's death trap airplane!*

"That's not," Wyn goes on, "the end of the announcement."

Again Kimmy claps her hands together on a gasp.

"Still not pregnant," Sabrina says.

Kimmy sighs.

Parth's beaming with his very distinct *I've got an amazing surprise for you* smile. The one that preceded the New Orleans–themed birthday he threw for Cleo, or the moment he presented me with the stethoscope he'd gotten engraved as a med school graduation present.

He and Sabrina share a knowing smirk.

"Oh, come on," Cleo says.

Kimmy throws two Takis at Sabrina's head.

She swats them away. "Fine, fine! Tell them."

"We're getting married," Parth says.

Confused looks are exchanged throughout the room.

"That's . . . usually what follows an engagement," Cleo says.

"No, I mean on Saturday," he clarifies.

40

"We're getting married. Here, with the six of us. Nothing fancy. Literally a little ceremony down on the dock, with all our best friends."

My whole body goes icy cold, then blisteringly hot. My face and hands are numb.

Wyn releases his hold on me *again,* and when my gaze slices up toward his, I see my own misery reflected on his face.

We're trapped here.

My ears ring, my friends' voices becoming a muffled warble. A blue Estelle champagne flute is forced into my tingling fingers for a toast, and my hearing clears enough to catch Parth crying, "To everlasting love!"

And Sabrina adding, "And our best friends forever! There's no other way we'd want to spend this last week at the cottage."

GO TO YOUR G.D. HAPPY PLACE, HARRIET, I think, followed by, *NO, NOT THAT ONE.*

Too late.

41

4
Happy Place

Mattingly, Vermont

A street downtown lined in old redbrick buildings. An apartment over the Maple Bar, our favorite coffee shop, for our junior year. Cleo and I have met our new roommate Parth only once, but Sabrina had a class on international law with him last spring, and when he told her rooms were opening up in his place, we jumped.

He's a year ahead of us, a senior, and two of his roommates have already graduated, while the third, a business major, is spending the fall semester abroad in Australia. I'll take *his* room, because in the spring I'm doing a term in London. The other roommate and I can easily switch places over winter break.

Mattingly's a small school, so even though we don't *know* Parth Nayak, we know his reputation: the Party King of Paxton Avenue. Called such partly because he throws amazing themed parties but also because he has a habit of showing up at *other* people's parties with top-shelf liquor, a dozen beautiful friends, and an incredible playlist. He is a Mattingly legend.

And living with him is great. Though he and Sabrina — both natural leaders — occasionally butt heads. The real Parth is better than the myth. It's not just that he's fun. He *loves* people. Loves throwing them parties, picking out perfect gifts, making introductions between people he thinks should meet, finding the quietest person in the room and bringing them into the thick of things. The world has never felt so kind, so positive. Like everyone is a potential friend, with something fascinating and brilliant to offer.

By the time I leave for London, I almost wish I were staying.

The city is gorgeous, of course, all that old stone and ivy blending seamlessly into sleek steel and glass. And thanks to the last semester, I'm more prepared than ever to socialize with strangers. Most nights, at least a handful of people from the study-abroad program go out for pints in one of Westminster's endless supply of pubs, or grab crispy fish-and-chips wrapped in newspaper and eat it as we walk along the Thames. On weekends, there are champagne picnics in sprawling gardens and day trips to art galleries, hours of browsing as many iconic London bookshops as possible — Foyles and Daunt Books and a whole slew of others on Cecil Court.

As time wears on, people couple off into friendships and relationships. That's how I escape the constant pining for my friends and our corner apartment overlooking Mattingly's redbrick downtown: I start spending more and more time with another American, named Hudson, and in those hours when we're studying — or *not* studying — I stop, if only for a while, imagining the seasons passing outside Parth, Cleo, Sabrina, and Mystery Roommate's bay window, the heaps of snow melting away to reveal a quilt of springy pale green and bursts of trout lily, wild geranium, bishop's-cap.

The closer summer gets, though, the less of a distraction Hudson offers. Partly because we're both obsessively studying for exams, and partly because the thing between us — this romance of necessity — is approaching its sell-by date, and we both know it.

My parents text me roughly five hundred

times more than usual as my flight home nears.

Can't wait to hear all about the London program in a few weeks, Dad says.

Mom writes, The ladies at Dr. Sherburg's office want to take you out to lunch while you're here. Cindy's son is considering Mattingly.

Dad says, Saved a ten-part documentary on dinosaurs.

Mom says, Think you'll have time to help me get the yard cleaned up? It's a disaster, and I've been so swamped.

I'd hoped to have a quick trip to see them before flying back to Vermont, but they're so excited. I end up spending two months counting down the seconds in Indiana, and then fly directly to Maine to meet my friends for Lobster Fest.

My flight gets in late. It's already dark, the heat of the day long since replaced by a cold, damp wind. There are a couple of cars idling in the lot, headlights off, and it takes me a second to find the cherry-red sports car. Sabrina specifically got her driver's license so we could cruise around in it this summer.

But it's not Sabrina standing against the hood, face illuminated by the glow of a cell phone. He looks up. A square jaw, narrow

45

waist, messy golden hair pushed up off his forehead except for one lock that falls across his brow the second our eyes meet.

"Harriet?" His voice is velvety. It sends a zing of surprise down my spine, like a zipper undone.

I've seen him in pictures of my friends over the last semester, and before that, on campus, but always from a distance, always on the move. This close, something about him seems different. Less handsome, maybe, but more striking. His eyes look paler in the cell phone's glow. There are premature crow's-feet forming at their corners. He looks like he's mostly made out of granite, except for his mouth, which is pure quicksand. Soft, full, one side of his Cupid's bow noticeably higher.

"A whole semester apart," I say, "and you look exactly the same, Sabrina."

Symmetrical dimples appear on either side of his mouth. "Really? Because I cut my hair, got colored contacts, and grew four inches."

I narrow my eyes. "Hm. I'm not seeing it."

"Sabrina and Cleo had one too many boxes of wine," he says. "Apiece."

"Oh." I shiver as a breeze slips down the collar of my shirt. "Sorry you got stuck with pickup duty. I could've scheduled a cab."

He shrugs. "I didn't mind. Been dying to see if the famous Harriet Kilpatrick lives up to the hype."

Being the object of his full focus makes me feel like a deer in headlights.

Or maybe like I'm a deer being stalked by a coyote. If he were an animal, that's what he'd be, with those strange flashing eyes and that physical ease. The kind of confidence reserved for those who skipped their awkward phases entirely.

Whereas any confidence *I* have is the hard-won spoils from spending the bulk of my childhood with braces and the haircut of an unfortunate poodle.

"Sabrina," I say, "tends to embellish." Weirdly, though, her descriptions of *him* didn't come close to capturing the man. Or maybe it was that because I knew she had a crush on him, I'd expected something different. Someone more polished, suave. Someone more like Parth, his best friend.

The corners of his mouth twitch as he ambles forward. My heart whirs as he reaches out, as if planning to catch my chin and turn it side to side for his inspection to prove that I've been oversold.

But he's only taking my bag from my shoulder. "They said you were a brunette."

My own snort-laugh surprises me. "I'm glad they spoke so highly of me."

"They did," he says, "but the only thing I can corroborate so far is whether you're a brunette. Which you're not."

"I am definitely a brunette."

He tosses my bag into the back seat, then faces me again, his hips sinking against the door. His head tilts thoughtfully. "Your hair's almost black. In the moonlight it looks blue."

"Blue?" I say. "You think my hair is *blue*?"

"Not, like, Smurf blue," he says. "Blue black. You can't tell in pictures. You look different."

"It's true," I say. "In real life, I'm three-dimensional."

"The painting," he says thoughtfully. "That looks like you."

I instantly know which painting he must be referring to. The one of me and Sabrina strewn out like God and Adam: Cleo's old figure drawing final. It hung in Mattingly's art building for weeks, dozens of strangers passing it daily, and I never felt so naked then as I do now.

"Very discreet way of letting me know you've seen my boobs," I say.

"Shit." He glances away, rubbing the back of his neck. "I sort of forgot it was a nude."

"Words most women only ever dream of hearing," I say.

"I in no way forgot you were naked in the painting," he clarifies. "I just forgot it might be weird to tell someone they look exactly the same as they do in a painting where they're not wearing clothes."

"This is going really well," I say.

He groans and drags a hand down his face. "I swear I'm normally better at this."

And normally, *I* do my best to put people at ease, but there's something rewarding about throwing him off-balance. Rewarding and charming.

"Better at what?" I say through laughter.

He rakes one hand through his hair. "First impressions."

"You should try sending a big-ass nude painting of yourself ahead when you're going to meet someone new," I say. "It's always worked for me."

"I'll take that into consideration," he says.

"You don't look like a Wyndham Connor."

His brow arches. "How am I supposed to look?"

"I don't know," I say. "Navy-blue jacket with gold buttons. Captain's hat. A big white beard and a huge cigar?"

"So Santa, on a yacht," he says.

"Mr. Monopoly, on vacation," I say.

49

"For what it's worth, you're not the stereotypical image of a Harry Kilpatrick either."

"I know," I say. "I'm not a Dickensian street orphan in a newsboy hat."

His laugh makes his eyes flash again. They look more pale green than gray now, like water under fog rather than the fog itself.

He rounds the front of the car and pulls the passenger door open.

"So, Harriet." He looks up, and my heart stutters from the surprise of his full attention back on me. "You ready?"

For some reason, it feels like a lie when I say, "Yes."

Wyn makes driving the Jaguar along those dark, curving roads seem like a sport or an art form. One corded arm drapes over the wheel, and his right hand sits loose atop the gearshift, his knee bobbing in a restless rhythm that never disrupts his control over the gas pedal. As we get closer to the water, I crank the window down and breathe in the familiar brine. He follows suit, the wind ruffling his hair against his cut-glass profile. That one chaotic strand always finds its way back to the right side of his forehead, as if connected by an invisible string to the peak of his Cupid's bow.

When he catches me studying him, his

brow lifts in tandem with his lips.

Quicksand, I think again. An old predator-prey instinct seems to agree, my limbic system sending out marching orders to my muscles: *Be ready to flee; if he gets any closer, you'll never get away.*

"You're staring," he says. "Suspiciously."

"Just calculating the odds that you are in fact my friends' roommate and not a murderer who steals his victims' cars," I tell him.

"And then picks their friends up from the airport, exactly on time?" he asks.

"I'm sure plenty of murderers are punctual."

"Why do you think our entire generation expects everyone to turn out to be a murderer?" he asks with a laugh. "As far as I know, I've never met a single one."

"That just means you've never met a bad one," I say.

He glances at me as a bar of moonlight passes over him. "So I hear you're some kind of genius, Harriet Kilpatrick."

"What did I tell you about Sabrina and embellishment?"

"So you're *not* an aspiring brain surgeon?"

"*Aspiring*'s the operative word," I say. "What about you? What's your major?"

He ignores my question. "I would've assumed *surgeon* was the operative word."

51

This coaxes another snort of laughter out of me. Eyes back on the road, he smiles to himself, and my bones seem to fill up with helium.

I look out the window. "What about you?"

After several seconds of silence, he says, "What about me?" He sounds vaguely displeased by the question.

"Is what I've been told about *you* accurate?" I ask.

He checks the mirror again, teeth scraping over his full bottom lip. "Depends what you've been told."

"What do you think I've been told?" I say.

"I'd rather not guess, Harriet."

He uses my name a lot. Every time, it's like his voice plucks a too-tight string in a piano deep in my stomach.

What's actually happening is my sympathetic nervous system has decided to reroute the path of my blood to my muscles. There are no butterflies fluttering through my gut. Just blood vessels constricting and contracting around my organs.

"Why not?" I ask. "Do you think they said something bad?"

His jaw squares, eyes back on the headlights slicing through the dark. "Never mind. I don't want to know."

He's gone back to bouncing his knee, like

there's too much energy in his body and he's siphoning it out.

"They told me it would be impossible to tell whether you were flirting or not."

He laughs. "Now you're *trying* to embarrass me."

"Maybe." Definitely. I'm not sure what's come over me. "But they did say that." In actuality, Sabrina had bemoaned not being able to tell, even while adamantly proclaiming that she liked him too much to make any kind of move anyway. It would've disrupted their living situation too much.

"Either way," Wyn says, "I'm *much* better at flirting than that makes me sound."

"Have you ever considered," I say, leaning over to insert myself into his frame of view, "that that might be the problem?"

He smiles. "Flirting never killed anybody, Harriet."

"Clearly you're unfamiliar with the concept of the Regency-era duel," I say.

"Oh, I'm familiar, but since I rarely find myself flirting with the unwed daughters of powerful dukes, I figure I'm okay."

"You think we're just going to skate over you being well versed in Regency customs?"

"Harriet, I don't get the feeling you skate over *anything*," he says.

I give another involuntary snort of laughter, and his dimples deepen. "Speaking of highborn ladies," he says, "they teach you how to laugh like that at etiquette school?"

"No," I say, "that has to be bred into you across centuries."

"I'm sure," he says. "I'm not like that, by the way."

"Gently bred to laugh through your nose?"

His chin tips, his gaze knowing. "The impression you have of me. I don't play with people's feelings. I have rules."

"Rules?" I say. "Such as?"

"Such as, never tell the rules to someone you've just met."

"Oh, come on," I say. "We're stepfriends now. You might as well tell me."

"Well, for one thing, Parth and I made a pact to never date our friends. Or each other's friends." He casts me a sidelong glance. "As for stepfriends, I'm not sure what the policy is."

"Wait, wait, wait," I say. "You don't date your *friends*? Who do you date, Wyn? Enemies? Strangers? Malevolent spirits who died in your apartment building?"

"It's a good policy," he says. "It keeps things from getting messy."

"It's dating, Wyn, not an all-you-can-eat barbecue buffet," I say. "Although, from what I've heard, maybe for you they're the

54

same thing."

He looks at me through his lashes and tuts. "Are you slut-shaming me, Harriet?"

"Not at all," I say. "I love sluts! Some of my best friends are sluts. I've dabbled in sluttery myself."

Another bar of moonlight briefly lights his eyes, paling them to smoky silver.

"Didn't suit you?" he guesses.

"Never got the chance to find out," I say.

"Because you fell in love," he says.

"Because men never really picked me up."

He laughs. "Okay."

"I'm not being self-deprecating," I say. "Once men get to know me, they're sometimes interested, but I'm not the one their eyes go to first. I've made peace with it."

His gaze slides down me and back up. "So you're saying you're slow-release hot."

I nod. "That's right. I'm slow-release hot."

He considers me for a moment. "You're not what I expected."

"Three-dimensional and blue-haired," I say.

"Among other things," he says.

"I expected you to be Parth 2.0," I admit.

His eyes narrow. "You thought I'd be better dressed."

"Than a torn sweatshirt and jeans?" I say. "No such thing."

He doesn't seem to hear me, instead studying me with a furrowed brow. "You're not slow-release hot."

I look away, fumble the radio on as heat scintillates across my chest. "Yeah, well," I say, "most people don't start by seeing me naked before we've spoken."

"It's not about that," he says.

I *feel* the moment his gaze lifts off me and returns to the windshield, but he's left a mark: from now on, dark cliffs, wind racing through hair, cinnamon paired with clove and pine — all of it will only mean *Wyn Connor* to me. A door has opened, and I know I'll never get it shut again.

Regency era or not, in a lot of ways, he ruins me.

5
REAL LIFE

Monday

We're trapped in the kitchen for the length of three more toasts to undying love before Wyn finally asks our friends to excuse us and pulls me away to "settle in."

Kimmy purrs throatily, and Parth high-fives her for it, which makes Cleo shudder because high fives are her personal fingernails-on-a-chalkboard.

As Wyn and I are all but *running* up the steps, we silently struggle for control of my suitcase.

By which I mean, I'm carrying it until he pulls it easily out of my hand and shifts it to his opposite hand, where I can't reach it.

"I've got it," he says.

"Stop trying to be charming," I hiss. "No one's watching."

"I'm not," he says.

"Are too," I say.

"No." He jerks my bag further out of

reach as I lunge for it. "I'm doing this for the sheer pleasure of annoying you."

"If that's all," I say, "then you don't have to try so hard. Your mere presence is doing the trick."

"Yeah, well," he says, "you've always made me want to aim a little higher, Harriet."

We're nearly home free when Sabrina appears behind us at the top of the stairs. "I forgot to tell you. We put you in the big bedroom this time."

Wyn and I not only screech to a halt, cartoon-style, but he snatches my hand, like if he doesn't, Sabrina might scream and drop her champagne in shock at discovering us in a strange reversed flagrante delicto, everyone fully clothed and no one touching.

At least he didn't go straight for a handful of ass.

"The big bedroom," he repeats, his hand relocating to the small of my back. I lean into him so hard he has to catch the wall with his shoulder so we both don't topple over.

I wonder if we look even one percent like a couple in love, or if we're fully projecting "rivals in a spaghetti western showdown."

"We're always in the kids' room," I say.

That's what Sabrina's family calls it, because it has two twin beds, rather than one king, like each of the other two bedrooms.

"Cleo and Kimmy offered to take it this time," Sabrina says. "You two only get to see each other like once a month — we're not going to make you spend your visit in separate beds."

As long as Wyn and I have been together, we've pushed the twins together.

"We don't mind," I say.

Sabrina rolls her eyes. "You never mind. You're the queen of *not minding*. But in this case, we do. It's a done deal. Clee and Kim already unpacked."

"But —"

Wyn cuts me off: "Thanks, Sabrina. That was thoughtful of you all."

Before I can feebly protest, he herds me into the largest bedroom, like he's a cattle dog and I'm a particularly difficult sheep.

The second the door snicks shut, I whirl on him, prepared to attack, only to be hit with the full force of his closeness, the strange intensity of being behind a closed door together.

I can feel my heart beating in the back of my throat. We're close enough that I can see his pupils dilating. His body has decided I'm a threat he needs to analyze as quickly as possible. The feeling is mutual.

It was easy to be angry when we were downstairs, surrounded by our friends. Now I feel like I'm standing naked on a spot-lighted platform for his inspection.

He finds his voice first, a low rasp. "I know this isn't ideal."

The ludicrousness of the statement jump-starts my brain. "Yes, Wyn. Spending a week locked in a bedroom with my ex-boyfriend is *not ideal.*"

"Ex-fiancé," he says.

I stare at him.

He looks away, scratching his forehead. "I'm sorry," he says. "I didn't know what to do." His eyes come back to mine, too soft now, too familiar. "She called me with a speech. About how this was the end of an era. About how she'd never asked me for anything and she never would again. I tried calling you. It only rang once, but I left a voicemail."

There was a very good reason I hadn't gotten the message.

"I blocked your number," I say. I got tired of lying awake late into the night with my thumb hovering over his contact number, practically aching from wishing he'd call, tell me the whole thing had been a mistake. I needed to take the possibility away, to free myself from waiting for it.

His eyes go stormy. His lips part. He looks toward the balcony, grooves rising between his eyebrows. He just has one of those vaguely tortured faces, I remind myself.

He can't help it, and he certainly doesn't need my comfort.

He's the one who derailed our life together in a four-minute phone call.

His jaw muscles leap as his pale-fog eyes retrain on me. "What should I have done, Harriet?"

Found an excuse.

Simply told her no.

Not have broken my heart like it was a last-minute dinner plan.

Not have made me love you in the first place.

I shake my head.

He steps closer until he's a question mark, hanging over me. "I'm really asking."

On a sigh, I drop my eyes and massage my temples. "I don't know. But now there's nothing we *can* do. You can't break up *at* a wedding. Especially when the guest list is four people."

"Maybe we give them tonight," he says. "Celebrate everything, tell them tomorrow."

I look up at the ceiling, buying some time. Maybe in the next four seconds the world

61

will end, and I'll be spared making this decision.

"Harriet," he presses.

"Fine," I bite out. "I'm sure we can stomach each other for one more night."

His gaze narrows, limiting the intake of light to his eyes and sharpening their focus to better suss out my expression. "Are you sure?"

No.

"I'm fine," I say. "It's fine." I slump against the edge of the bed.

After a beat, he shakes himself. "I'm glad we're on the same page."

"Sure."

He nods. "Fine."

"Fine." I push off the bed.

He retreats a step, keeping the space between us. "We can tell them things have been rocky for a while, and seeing how happy they were made us realize we've grown apart."

My chest stings. It's not the exact phrasing, but it's close enough to what he said to me, months ago: *We were kids when we got together, and things are different now, and it's time we accepted that.*

"You honestly think they won't suspect anything?"

"Harriet." His eyes flash. "They didn't

62

even know we'd been *hooking up* for a whole year."

I step backward, only to collide with the bed so hard I rebound right into him.

We snap apart like each of us is convinced the other is made of wasps, but the faintly spicy scent of him has already hit my bloodstream.

"This might be harder than that," I say stiffly.

Wyn's hand rakes back through his hair, his T-shirt riding up to expose a sliver of his waist so sensually you'd think there was an art director in the corner barking orders.

I force my eyes back to his face.

"We can handle one night."

He's trying to make *one night* sound like a mere accumulation of minutes. I know better. When we're together, time never moves at a normal pace.

I rub my eyes with the heels of my hands. "We should've told everyone months ago."

"But we didn't," he says.

At first, it wasn't intentional. I was just too stunned, hurt, and — yes — in denial. Then, a few days after the breakup, a box of my stuff had arrived on my doorstep. No note, so abrupt I half wondered whether he'd dumped me while en route to the nearest UPS.

Then I was angry. So I mailed *his* stuff back to *him* on the same day. Even tossed my engagement ring in loose when I realized I couldn't find the blue velvet box it came in.

Three days after that, a second package, a small lump of brown paper, arrived. He'd sent the ring back. I knew him well enough to know he was *trying* to do the right thing, which only made me angrier, so I'd immediately mailed it back to him. When he got it, he texted me for the first time in two weeks: You should keep the ring. It belongs to you.

I don't want it, I replied. More like, I couldn't bear it.

You could sell it, he said.

So could you, I said.

Five minutes passed before he messaged again. He asked if I'd told Cleo and Sabrina. The thought nauseated me. Telling them was going to destroy our friend group, ten years of history down the drain.

Waiting until I can catch them both at the same time, I said. It was only halfway a lie.

I'd told a couple of coworkers at the hospital but barely texted with Cleo and Sabrina. We were all so busy.

Sabrina and Parth worked late for their respective law firms most nights, and because running a farm meant lots of four a.m. wake-up calls, Cleo and Kimmy went to bed early.

Out in Montana, Wyn has the Connor family furniture repair business to run, and his mom to help out.

And then there's me, in my own time zone out in San Francisco, two years deep into my training at UCSF. Most days I'm operating at a level of tired that goes beyond yawns and eyelid twitches to reach straight to my core. My *organs* are tired. My *bones* are exhausted.

My time off is usually spent at the pottery studio down the block, or watching old episodes of *Murder, She Wrote* while cleaning the apartment Wyn and I picked out together two years ago, before things went south with his mom's Parkinson's and he went back to Montana.

The long-distance arrangement was supposed to be temporary, only as long as it took for Wyn's younger sister to finish grad school and move back, take over Gloria's care. So Wyn left, and we made it work, until we didn't.

I didn't have to ask whether Wyn had told Parth about the breakup. I would've heard from everyone if he had. So instead I'd asked about Wyn's mom. Does Gloria know?

Not the right time, he said. After a minute he added, She's been trying to get me to go back to SF. She already feels so guilty I'm here. Tried to check herself into an assisted-living home without telling me. If I tell her now that we broke up, she'll blame herself.

I loved Gloria, and I *hated* the idea of upsetting her. Still, I thought about suggesting Wyn tell her the truth. That as far as he was concerned, it was all *my* fault.

He messaged me once more: Can we wait to tell everyone? Just a little while?

And I'd not only agreed, I'd been immensely relieved to put off those conversations, to relegate them to the realm of Problems for Future Harriet. After two months, on a night that I found myself perilously close to calling him, I finally blocked his number. Though I'd occasionally unblock long enough to engage with him in the group chat; I'd always been a sporadic texter, so I figured the others wouldn't notice. A month after that, I'd initiated the email conversation over how to handle the yearly trip, and we'd settled on the plan. The plan that currently lay in shambles somewhere in the kitchen.

That was two months ago, and now Future Harriet has some choice words for Past Harriet about her shitty decision-making abilities.

She's the reason we're in this situation.

I focus on the thin ring of green around Wyn's irises rather than the entirely too overwhelming totality of him. "How will it work?"

He shrugs. "We just pretend we're together a little longer, then come clean."

I start to cross my arms, but Wyn's standing too close, so rather than wedge my arms between our stomachs, I awkwardly return them to my sides. "Yeah, I got that. I'm talking about the rules." I brace myself so I can say, nearly evenly, "Do we touch? Do we kiss?"

He glances sidelong, a little embarrassed, guilty. "They know what I'm like with you."

A very diplomatic way of saying they'll expect him to be touching me, constantly. Pulling me into his lap or hooking me under his arm or wrapping my hair around his hand and kissing me at the dinner table as if we're entirely alone, burrowing his face into my neck while I'm talking, or tracing my bottom lip when I'm not, and —

The point is, some people live the bulk of their lives in their minds (me), and some are highly physical beings (Wyn).

Briefly I fantasize about pitching myself out the window, over the cliffs, and into the ocean, swimming until I reach Europe. I'd happily take Nova Scotia.

But as someone who's *not* a highly physical being, I'd probably knock myself unconscious on the way down and awake to a shirtless Wyn performing mouth-to-mouth.

"No touching when no one's around to see it," I say quickly. "When we're with the others, we'll . . . do whatever we have to do."

His head cocks. "I'm going to need more specific guidelines than that."

"You know what I mean," I say.

He stares, waits. I stare back.

"Holding hands?" he asks.

I'm not sure why *that* of all things makes my heart shoot up into my esophagus. "Acceptable."

His chin dips in confirmation. "What can I touch? Lower back, hips, arms?"

"Do you want me to draw you a diagram," I say.

"Desperately."

"It was a joke," I say.

"I know," he says. "And yet that doesn't make me any less curious."

"Back, hips, arms, stomach are fine," I say, stomach warming ten degrees for every word.

"Mouth?" he says.

68

I glance over at the side table. A black leather folder sits propped up there, like a dinner check waiting to be collected. "Are you talking about *touching* my mouth or kissing it?"

"Either," he says. "Both."

I grab the folder and flip through it, pretending to read while I wait for my synapses to stop screaming.

"Itinerary."

At my evident confusion, Wyn juts his chin toward the document I've been "reading." "We've got personalized itineraries."

"But . . . we do the same thing every year," I say.

"I think that's the point," he says. "It's a keepsake. Plus, Sabrina planned some individual surprises for us for Saturday, so she and Parth can have a little alone time before the wedding."

"Oh my god." I study the page in earnest. "She's got *bathroom* breaks on here, Wyn."

When I look up, he's caught off guard.

A memory flares bright, swelling from the back of my mind until it overtakes the present: Wyn and I hopscotching across the wet rocks at the bottom of the cliffs behind the house. Yelping and leaping aside as the tide's icy fingers raced toward us. From down the beach, the sound of our friends' laughter

69

spiraled up into the night sky, carried by the smoke of our bonfire.

I'd volunteered to run up to the house for another six-pack, and Wyn, who never sat still if he could help it, came along. We raced each other up the rickety stairs to the cottage's back patio, choking over laughter.

You're a six-foot-tall block of muscle, Wyn. How am I beating you?

His hand caught mine as we reached the patio, the flagstone aglow with the strange green light of the heated saltwater pool. It was the first time he'd touched my fingers. We'd known each other only a few days then, on our first group trip here, and my whole body hummed from the simple contact. He murmured, *You hardly ever say my name.*

I must've shivered, because his brow pinched, and he peeled his sweatshirt, the Mattingly one with the tear in the neck, over his shoulders.

I told him I was fine, through chattering teeth. He stepped in closer, slowly, and pulled his sweatshirt down over my head, pinning my arms to my sides and making my hair wild with static.

Better? he asked. It terrified and thrilled me how, with that one quiet word, he could make my insides shimmer, shake me up like a snow globe.

When we were with the others, I could still barely look at him.

But because Wyn and I had been the last to arrive, or maybe because the others had decided our friendship should begin with a trial by fire, we'd been sharing the kids' room all week, and every night, when we turned off the lights, we'd trade whispers back and forth from our beds on opposite sides of the room. Talk for hours.

I rarely said his name, though. It felt too much like an incantation. As if it would light me up from the inside, and he'd see how much I wanted him, how all day long my mind caught on him like a scar in a record. How, without even trying, I knew exactly where he was at all times, could likely cover my eyes, get spun around, and still point to him on the first try.

And I couldn't want him. Because my best friend did. Because he'd become an important part of Sabrina's and Cleo's lives, and I wouldn't mess that up.

Besides, I told myself, my reaction to him didn't mean anything. Just a biological imperative to procreate, setting off little fireworks through my nervous system. Not the kind of thing you could build any kind of lasting relationship on. I told myself I was too smart to think I was falling in love with him. Because I couldn't. I wouldn't.

If only I'd been right.

Now Wyn pulls the itinerary out of my hands, his gaze traveling across the open page.

"I genuinely love how organized Sabrina is," I say. "But there *is* such a thing as too much of a good thing. And when you're mentioning bowel movements on your group vacation schedule, I think you've hit it."

Wyn returns the folder to the end table. "You think this is bad, but it's nothing compared to the packing list Parth sent me. He told me how many pairs of underwear to bring. So either my 'personalized surprise' on Saturday is going to end badly, or he thinks I'm incapable of counting my own underwear."

"Don't sell yourself short," I say. "I'm sure it's a little of both."

As he laughs, his dimples flash, little dark pricks in his scruffy jaw. For a second, it's like we've come unglued from the timeline, tumbled back a year.

Then he steps back from me. "The next fifteen minutes are scheduled for *relaxing* before lunch," he says, "so I'll leave you to it."

72

I nod.

He nods.

He moves toward the door, hesitates there for a second.

And then he's gone, and I'm still frozen where he left me. I do *not* relax.

6
REAL LIFE

Monday

The "big bedroom" is a disaster. A beautiful, amazing, nightmarish disaster. The kids' room is at the front of the hallway and thus is part of the original house. This is at the back, in the behemoth extension. There are no wonky doors that get stuck, or windows you have to prop open with books, or floorboards that snap and groan when no one's even touching them.

This room is pure luxury. The king-sized bed has four-zillion-thread-count sheets. A set of double doors opens onto a balcony that overlooks both the saltwater pool and the bluffs beyond it, and there's both a massive stone tub and a two-person shower made of dark slate and glass.

However, if I could make one minor interior design suggestion, it would be to put one or both of the aforementioned amenities behind a door. As it stands, they're out in the open.

Sure, the *toilet* gets to hide in a shameful little cabinet, but if I plan on changing my clothes at any point during this week, my options are (1) accept that I'll be doing so with an audience of one, namely my ex-fiancé; (2) stuff myself into the shit-closet and pray for good balance; or (3) find a discreet way to sneak down to the infamous outdoor shower stall over by the guesthouse.

All this to say, I spend my fifteen minutes of "relaxation" taking a *private* shower while I can. Then I pull on a pair of jeans and a clean white T-shirt. One of Wyn's and my few areas of overlap is our complete absence of personal style.

His work has always required him to dress practically, and most of his clothes quickly get beaten up, so there's no point in having anything too nice to begin with.

For me, though, the overreliance on tight Levi's and T-shirts has more to do with the fact that I hate making decisions. It took me years to figure out what kind of clothes I like on my body, and now I'm sticking with it.

Another solar flare–bright memory: Wyn and me lying in bed, lamplight spilling over us, his hair a mess, that one obstinate lock on his forehead. His mouth presses to the curve of my belly, then the crease of my hip. He whispers against all my softest parts, *Perfect.*

A shiver crawls down my spine.

Quite enough of *that.*

I knot my hair atop my head and trudge back downstairs.

Everyone's moved out to the wooden table on the back patio. Four feet worth of charcuterie runs down its center, and because Sabrina is Sabrina, there are place cards, ensuring that Cleo and Kimmy are seated in front of the vegan offerings, while I'll be face-to-face with a Brie wheel so big it could be fixed to a wheelbarrow in a pinch.

Wyn looks up from his phone as I step onto the patio. I can't tell if the momentary splash of anxiety across his face is wishful thinking on my part, because as soon as I clock it, he puts his phone away, breaks into a smile, and reaches out to collect me around the waist, pulling me in against his side.

Rigidly, I drop into the wrought iron chair next to his, and his arm rearranges, loosely crooking around my shoulders.

Sabrina rises from her seat at the head of the table. "I'm not sure if you had a chance to look at your itineraries yet . . ."

"Is that what that was?" Cleo says. "I've

76

been using it as a doorstop."

Kimmy, with two gherkins sticking out of her mouth like walrus tusks, adds, "So much of it was redacted, I assumed it was a deposition."

"Those are just a couple of surprises," Sabrina says. "The rest of the week will be our usual fare."

Wyn takes a hard chomp of carrot, the force of which rattles down my body. I can't get a good breath without hundreds of the nerve endings along my rib cage and chest pressing into him, which means I'm barely getting any oxygen.

"Grocery Gladiators?" Kimmy squeals right as Cleo says hopefully, "Murder, She Read?"

"Yes and yes," Sabrina says, confirming we will be doing two of our usual — and most diametrically opposite — Maine activities: a trip to the local bookstore (Cleo's and my favorite) and a very ridiculous way of grocery shopping, which has been Parth and Kimmy's great passion ever since they teamed up three years ago and started a "winning streak," insomuch as one can "win" at grocery shopping.

Wyn and I used to debate whether Sabrina concocted the game of Grocery Gladiators because she got tired of how long our trips to the market were. There's a heavenly bakery in one corner, and a whole local snacks section, and between the six of us, it's like shopping with very bougie, somewhat drunk toddlers, one person wandering off every time the rest of us are ready to go.

"But tonight I figured we'd swim, do our usual cookout and all that," Sabrina says. "I just want to bask in the togetherness."

"To togetherness," Parth cries, initiating the fifth toast of the day. As soon as Wyn removes his arm from around my shoulders, I scooch my chair sideways under the pretense of grabbing the open prosecco to refill my glass.

"To Grocery Gladiators," Kimmy joins in.

To drinking your body weight in wine and hoping you wake up and realize this was all a dream, I think.

Across the table, Cleo's looking at me thoughtfully, a little divot between her delicate brows. I force a smile and lift my flute in her direction. "To that one guy at Murder, She Read who still gives us the student discount."

Cleo's mouth quirks faintly, like she's not fully convinced by my display, but she clinks her glass — water; Cleo gave up alcohol years ago because it irritated her stomach — to mine anyway. "May we always be so lucky, and so youthful."

"Shoot, bottle's empty," Sabrina says from the end of the table.

I lurch to my feet before Wyn can volunteer. He starts to rise anyway, and I shove him back down in his chair. "You stay here and relax, *honey,*" I say, acidly sweet. "I'll get the wine."

"Thanks, Har," Sab calls as I beeline for the back doors. "Door should be open!"

Another facet of Mr. Armas's upgrade to the cottage: he had the old stone cellar converted to a top-of-the-line vault for his immense and immensely expensive wine collection. It's password protected and everything, though Sabrina always leaves it open so any of us can run down and grab something.

Too quickly I find a bottle whose label matches the one on the table. I'm guessing that means it's *not* a thousand-dollar prosecco, but with Sabrina, you never know. She might've pulled out all the stops for us, regardless of whether our unrefined palates are able to appreciate said pulled stops.

It makes my heart twinge, thinking of this perfect final week she's planned for us and my utter inability to enjoy it.

One day. Let them have one perfect day, and tomorrow we'll come clean.

By the time I get back upstairs, everyone's laughing, the very picture of a laid-back best friends' trip. Wyn's gaze snags on mine, and his dimpled smile doesn't fall or even falter.

He's fine! No big deal that his ex-fiancée's here, or that we're essentially staying in a honeymoon suite with an extreme every-surface-here-is-specifically-designed-with-fucking-in-mind vibe!

No discernible reaction to my presence.

This time, the zing that goes down my spine feels less like a zipper undone and more like angry flame on a streak of gasoline.

It's not fair that he's fine. It's not fair that being here with me doesn't feel like having his heart roasted on a spit, like it does for me.

You can do this, Harriet. If he's fine, you can be too. For your friends.

I set the wine bottle on the table as I round it and come to stand behind Wyn, sliding my hands down his shoulders to his chest, until my face is beside his and I can feel his heartbeat in my hands, even and unbothered.

Not good enough. If I'm going to be tormented, so is he.

I burrow my face into the side of his neck, all warm pine and clove. "So," I say, "who's up for a swim?"

Goose bumps rise from his skin. This time, the zing feels like victory.

"I'm starting to suspect," Kimmy says, "that we might be a wee bit in-*bree*-biated. In-*bee-biatred.*"

"Who? Us?" I say, slowly trying to push myself to my feet on the slippery stand-up paddle mat as Kimmy crouches on the far end. Wife Number Five bought the mats for "aqua yoga" a couple of years back, and I'd forgotten all about them until tonight.

Kimmy screams, and Parth dives out of the way as the mat flips over, dumping us back into the pool for easily the sixth time.

The three of us pop out of the water. Kimmy flicks her head back to get her matted red-gold hair out of her face. "Us," she confirms. "All of us."

"Well," I say, jerking my head toward the patio table, where Cleo, Sabrina, and Wyn are deep in a game of poker, "maybe not them."

"Oh, no," Parth says. "Sabrina absolutely is. But competition sobers her up, and her big goal of the week is to finally beat Cleo."

"And to get married," I point out.

"And that," Parth agrees, swimming toward the side of the glowing pool. Kimmy's already trying to wrangle her way back upright on the paddle mat, but I kick my way over to follow Parth.

"How did it happen?" I ask.

"Don't you want to hear it from her?" he asks.

"No, I want to hear the detailed version," I say. "Sabrina's terrible at telling stories."

"I heard that!" she cries from over at the table, then lays her hand down. "And I'm not terrible. I'm succinct. Straight flush."

Beside her, Cleo grimaces a little and says, almost guiltily, "Royal flush."

Sabrina groans and drops her forehead to the table. From behind us comes the unmistakable sound of another Kimmy belly flop.

Conspiratorially, Parth says, "I asked her a year ago," and I'm so surprised, I accidentally smack him.

"A year?" I cry. "You've been engaged a year?"

He shakes his head. "Back then, she was still saying she never wanted to get married! Wouldn't even take the ring. And then, a few weeks back, she found out about the house, and . . ." He glances toward the poker match. Sabrina's absorbed in shuffling. "She asked me."

"What?"

He grimaces and rubs the back of his

neck. "And I said no. Because I thought it was, like, this knee-jerk reaction. You know how it is for her. This house was the last place she felt like she had a family, before her parents split. And then once she brought you and Cleo here — and then the rest of us — this cottage is the place she considers home. So when her dad told her he was selling it, I figured she was scrambling to put some kind of anchor down. That wasn't a good enough reason for me to say yes."

"So you proposed and she said no," I reply, "and then *she* proposed and *you* said no?"

He nods. "But that was a month and a half ago, and I thought she was mad at me for it. Until a couple weeks ago. She asked me again, with this for-real proposal. Like, planned an elaborate scavenger hunt and everything."

"Wow," I say. "Parth vibes."

"I know," he agrees. "Anyway, at the end, she got down on one knee in Central Park, like a bona fide romantic, and told me that she's always known she wanted to be with me forever, but she was so scared that was impossible, she'd never let herself say it aloud. Because of her parents, you know. And Cleo's." He gives me an apologetic look as he adds, "And yours."

It was something she and I bonded over early on: her dad, who burned through marriages like they were limited-series thrillers, and my parents, who stayed together but rarely seemed happy about it.

Sabrina had never wanted to get married, lest she have to go through a vicious divorce. I was more scared of marrying someone who couldn't bring himself to leave me or to keep loving me.

It was why I hadn't let myself cry when Wyn dumped me, or ask for answers or a second chance. I knew the only thing more painful than being without him would be being together knowing I no longer truly had him.

Parth, Wyn, and Kimmy were all the product of loving, lasting marriages, and Cleo's parents had split when she was little but stayed on excellent terms. They still lived a block apart in New Orleans and had regular family dinners with each other and their respective spouses.

"Anyway," Parth says. "Sabrina decided she'd been letting her dad have too much impact on her life. She didn't want to make any more decisions just for the sake of *not* doing what he'd do. So I said yes and then planned my own proposal."

"Well, naturally," I say. "You're the Party

King of Paxton Avenue."

He laughs, flicks back his wet hair. "I needed her to know I wanted it too, you know. Maybe it's weird to combine the wedding with this goodbye trip, but I don't know. I just need this week to be absolutely perfect for her."

My chest aches. My palms itch.

"I'm really, really happy for you," I tell him.

He grins crookedly, plants a loud smooch atop my head. "Thanks, Har. We really couldn't have figured our shit out without you and Wyn. I hope you know that."

"Oh, come on," I say.

"I'm serious," he replies. "You were the first ones to cross that friendship line, and to prove it could work. Sab says all the time that she spent way too much time worrying that going after what she wanted could jeopardize what the six of us already had, and watching you two keep loving each other for all these years, that really helped her believe we could do this."

My throat squeezes, and my eyes go straight to the poker match. Wyn's not looking, is focused on his phone, but heat unfurls from my hairline to my collarbone anyway.

Behind us, Kimmy cries, "I did it! I'm a

god!" right before she topples again.

"I think I need to pee," I tell Parth, hauling myself from the pool. "Or drink water. One of those."

"If you can't tell the difference between those, Harry," Parth calls after me, "I think you need to see a doctor!"

"Parth," I say, pausing in the doorway. "I am a doctor."

"Seems like a conflict of interest." He flips backward, away from the wall, and strokes toward Kimmy.

I towel off as I make my way through the cool, silent house. The kitchen is a mess, so I wipe down the counters, add the empty bottles to the recycling, and then head toward the powder room tucked back by the laundry. No one ever uses this one, because it's been here in some form since the early 1900s and thus is approximately two feet wide.

I take hold of the sink as I try to catch my breath. In the mirror, my face is already sunburnt, my hair a salty, tangled mess. So much for that shower. Maybe I can sneak away for a quick rinse while everyone's still out back.

Maybe I can throw all my clothes back into my bag and run away and, I don't know, *not* ruin my best friends' wedding.

Oh *god.* This is a disaster.

I pee, wash my hands with the luxurious grapefruit-scented soap Mr. Armas stocks all his hotels with, take one last deep inhale, and open the door.

My first instinct when I see Wyn waiting in the narrow hall is to slam the door shut in his face. Like this is a bad dream, and if I close it and open it again, he'll have disappeared.

But as usual, my body is two and a half steps behind my brain, so by the time I've registered him *and* the sound of overlapping voices down the hall in the kitchen, he's already pushing me back and shutting us in together.

My heart is hammering. My limbs feel hot and unsteady. I'd already turned off the light, and for some reason he doesn't reach to switch it back on, so we're cast in the dim, candle-like glow of the sensor-operated night-light mounted beside the mirror.

"What are you doing?" I ask.

"Relax." The dark makes his voice sound too close. Or maybe that's the six inches between us.

"You can't shove a woman into a dark room and tell her to relax!" I hiss.

"I couldn't figure out how to get you alone," he says.

87

"Have you considered that might be intentional?" I say.

He huffs. "Our plan isn't going to work."

"I know," I say.

His brow lifts. "You do?"

"I may have just mentioned that," I say.

He sinks back against the door, chin lifting, a deep inhale filling his lungs to the point that our chests brush. I try to step backward and am met with a towel rack.

"We'll have to stick it out five more days," I say.

He rebounds from the door. Our chests press together, a current of angry electricity leaping from his skin into mine, or maybe the other way around. "You *just* agreed with me that we couldn't do this."

"No, I said we can't follow through with our plan. They need this week to be perfect, Wyn. Sabrina's already a bundle of nerves. This could mess up everything."

"Oh, it's going to mess up *something*," he growls.

"Talk to Parth," I say. "If *you* leave that conversation feeling good about blowing up this week, then I can't stop you. But you're not going to."

He sighs. "This is so unbelievably messed up."

"It's certainly *not ideal*," I say, parroting

his phrasing from earlier.

His eyes flash. "Hilarious."

"I thought so." I lift my chin like I am not at all intimidated by his closeness. Like there definitely *aren't* hundreds of hornets batting around in my chest trying to get to him.

Our glares hold for several seconds. I'm not sure he's ever glared at me. As a categorically conflict-averse person, I'm surprised how powerful the glare makes me feel. I'm finally getting a rise out of him, getting past that granite facade he used to shut me out.

"Fine," he says. "Then I guess we have to do *this.*" He catches my hand. My whole body feels like it's made of live wires, even before I register the cool white-gold loop slipping over my finger.

I jerk back before he can get the ring on. *He* lets me, but again, the towel rack doesn't.

"Someone's going to notice if you're not wearing it," he says.

"They haven't so far," I say.

"It's only been a couple of hours," he says. "And Kimmy was dancing and singing into a wooden spoon to that one Crash Test Dummies song for the vast majority of that. People were busy."

"So we commandeer the playlist," I say. "I

can easily think of at least twenty-six songs that will put Kimmy into show mode."

Wyn's eyebrow arches. It tugs on his mouth, revealing a sliver of glow-in-the-dark smile. That snow globe feeling hits, where up is down and down is up and everything is either glitter or corn syrup.

"Why do you even have this?" I demand.

"Because," he says, "I knew I was going to see you, and it's yours."

"I gave it back," I remind him.

"Well aware of that," he says. "Now are you going to put it on, or should we go tell them it's over now?"

I shove my hand out, palm up. I'm sure as hell not letting him slide my old engagement ring onto my finger.

He hesitates, like he's debating saying something, then sets it in my palm. I put it on and hold my hand up. "Happy?"

He laughs, shakes his head, and starts to leave. He turns back, leaning into the door. "How long should we say it's been? Since we last saw each other, if anyone asks."

"They won't ask," I say.

My vision's adjusted to the dark enough that I can see, in detail, the creases at the corners of his eyes deepening. "Why not?"

"Because it's a boring question."

"I don't think it's a boring question," he

says. "I'm desperate to know the answer. I'm on pins and needles, Harriet."

I roll my eyes. "A month."

His eyes close for a moment. If I knew they would stay closed, I wouldn't be able to help myself: I'd trace a finger down his nose, around the curve of his mouth, not touching him but relishing in the *almost*. I hate how entangled we still feel on a quantum level. Like my body will never stop trying to find its way back to his.

His eyes slit open. "Did I come to San Francisco, or did you come to Montana?"

I snort.

His eyes flash.

"I haven't had time to do laundry in the last month," I say. "I definitely didn't fly to Montana and walk around a ranch in a ten-gallon hat."

Somberly, he asks, "How many pairs of underwear do you own?"

"Now, *that* I'm sure no one will ask you," I say.

"You haven't done laundry in a month," he replies. "I'm just doing that math, Harriet."

"Well, if I run out, at least Parth's packing list for you has me covered."

"And if you visited me," he says, "no part of your visit would have been me marching you around a ranch in a ten-gallon hat. What exactly do you think I do all day?"

"Furniture repair," I say with a shrug. "Rodeo clowning. Maybe that one senior water aerobics class Gloria was always trying to get us to go to when we used to visit."

Date beautiful women, breathe in the Montana air, and feel whole-body relief to have left San Francisco, and me, behind.

"How *is* Gloria?" I ask.

Wyn's head falls back against the door. "Good." He doesn't go on.

It stings like he meant for it to, this reminder that I'm not entitled to any more information about his mother, his whole family, than this one-word reply.

Then his face softens, mouth quirking. "I did try the water aerobics class with her."

"Yeah, right."

He sets a hand across his heart. "I swear."

My snort of laughter catches me off guard. Even stranger, it doesn't stop after one, instead devolving until it's like popcorn is exploding through my chest, until I feel — *almost* — like I'm crying instead of laughing.

All the while Wyn stands there, leaned against the door, watching me, bemused. "Are you quite finished, Harriet?"

"For now."

He nods. "So *I* visited *you* in San Francisco. Last month."

Any trace of humor evaporates from the air. "That's the story."

He studies me for a beat too long. My face prickles. My blood hums.

We both jump at a sudden, high-pitched blast of sound from down the hall.

Wyn sighs. "Parth got an air horn app."

"God save us," I say.

"He used it like fifteen times before you got here. As you can imagine, it hasn't gotten old."

I bite my lip before any hint of a smile can surface. I refuse to let myself be charmed by him. Not again.

"Well." He pushes away from the door. "I'll leave you to . . ."

He waves toward me, as if to wordlessly communicate *Standing alone in this dark bathroom.*

"That would be great," I say, and then he's gone.

I count to twenty, then let myself out, heart still pounding. After pausing in the kitchen long enough to fill my abandoned wineglass to the very brim, I step back out into the brisk chill of night. Everyone's bundled up now, a fire burning in the stone pit, my friends crowded around and

93

wrapped in a mishmash of towels, sweat-shirts, and blankets. I take a seat beside Cleo and she pulls me into a side hug, rear-ranging her flannel blanket over my bare legs too. "Everything good?" she asks.

"Of course it is," I insist, snuggling closer. "I'm in my happy place."

7
HAPPY PLACE

Knott's Harbor, Maine

The kids' room. Warped floorboards and crooked windows, creamy drapes, and twin beds topped in matching blue-gray quilts on either wall. My first week back with my friends after my London semester, and I'm sharing a room with a virtual stranger.

A pleasantly musty smell, tempered by lemon verbena furniture polish.

By cinnamon toothpaste. By pine, clove, woodsmoke, and strange pale eyes that wink and flash like some nocturnal animal. Not that I'm looking at him.

I *can't* keep looking at him. But within hours of meeting Wyn Connor, it's obvious he has his own gravity. I can't bring myself to look at him straight on in the full light of day, always start loading dishes or drawing a net through the pool when he's too close.

From the early mornings curtained in mist to late at night, my subconscious tracks him.

95

I'm living two separate weeks. One of them is bliss, the other torture. Sometimes they're indistinguishable.

I laze in the pool with Cleo while she reads some artist's memoir or encyclopedia exclusively about mushrooms. I wander the antique shops, junk shops, fudge shops in town with Sabrina. Parth and I walk up to the coffee place and the little red lobster roll stand with the constant hour-long line.

We play chicken in the pool, Never Have I Ever around the firepit. We pass around bottles of sauvignon blanc, rosé, chardonnay.

"Will your dad mind that we're drinking his wine?" Wyn asks.

I wonder if he's worried, like I was the first time Sabrina brought Cleo and me here, if he's realizing she'd have every right to present us with bills at the end of the week, bills that the rest of us couldn't afford.

"Of course he'd mind," Sabrina replies, "if he ever noticed. But he's incapable of noticing anything that's not inside a Swiss bank account."

"He has no idea what he's missing," Cleo says.

"All of my favorite things happen outside of Swiss bank accounts," Parth agrees.

96

"All my favorite things are here," I say.

In the hottest part of the day, we take turns leaping off the end of the pier below the bluff, making a game out of *not* reacting to the icy shock of the Atlantic, then lie on the sun-warmed platform watching the clouds stampede past.

Sabrina plans our drinks and meals to perfection. Parth finds ways to turn everything into an elaborate game or competition, as in the case of the pier-jumping game we name DON'T FUCKING SCREAM. And Cleo, almost out of nowhere, asks questions like, "Are there any places you go back to again and again in your dreams?" or "Would you redo high school if you could?" Parth says he would, because he had a great high school experience; Cleo says she would, because she had a *horrible* time and would like the chance to correct it; and the rest of us agree it would take a many-dollared offer to tempt us to relive our own mediocre experiences.

After that, Cleo asks, "If you could have another life entirely, separate from this one, what would you do?"

Parth says, right away, he'd join a band. Sabrina takes a minute to decide she'd be a chef.

"Back when my parents were still to-

97

gether," she says, "when we'd come out here for the summer, Mom and I would cook these elaborate meals. It was a whole-day thing. Like we had nowhere to be, nothing to do but be together."

While she's always shared blunt observations and flippantly self-aware comments about her family life and her past — like *Sorry if that came out too strong. It's my child-of-a-narcissist complex. I still think I have thirty seconds to make my case before everyone gets bored* — it's rarer for her to share happy memories.

It's a gift, this bit of tenderness she's brought out to show us. It's an honor to be trusted with something so sacred and rare as Sabrina's softness.

With Cleo's extra life, she tells us, she'd farm, which makes everyone laugh so hard the wooden pier trembles under us. "I'm serious!" she insists. "I think it'd be fun."

"Yeah, right," Sabrina says. "You're going to be a famous painter, with landscapes in every celebrity's LA mansion."

When she turns the question to me, my mind blanks. I've wanted to become a surgeon since I was fourteen. I've never considered anything else.

"You can do *anything*, Harry," Sabrina presses. "Don't overthink it."

"Overthinking is the thing I'm best at, though," I say.

She cackles. "Maybe in your other life you figure out how to monetize that."

"Or maybe," Cleo says, "in our other lives, we don't *have* to figure out how to monetize anything. We can just be."

Without sitting up, Parth reaches over to high five her.

"I love you," Cleo says, "but I do not high-five."

He lets his hand drop to his stomach, unbothered. He asks Wyn what he'd do with his second life. I don't look over, but I feel him stretched out under the sun on my left, a second star, a thing with its own gravity, light, warmth.

He sighs sleepily. "I'd live in Montana."

"You've already done that," Parth says. "You're supposed to say you'd go to the South Pole and rehabilitate penguins or something."

"Fine, Parth," Wyn says. "I'd go to the South Pole, for the penguins."

"There's no right answer," Cleo says. "Why would you move back to Montana, Wyn?"

"Because in this life, I decided not to stay there," he says. "I decided to do something different than my parents did, be someone different. But if I had another one to live, I'd want the one where I stayed too."

I chance a glance at him. He turns his cheek flat against the wooden pier, and our gazes hold for the span of four breaths, his damp arm and mine barely touching.

A silent conversation passes between us: *Hi* and *Hi back* and *You're smiling at me* and *No, you're smiling at me.*

I turn my eyes back to the sky and shut them tight.

By the time we crawl into our beds on opposite sides of the kids' room, the buzzing in my veins still hasn't let up.

Wyn, however, is so still that I assume he's instantly fallen asleep. After some time, his voice breaks the quiet. "Why do you always start cleaning when I come into the room?"

My laugh is part surprise, part embarrassment. "What?"

"If everyone's out back and you're in the kitchen, the second I come inside, you go for a sponge."

"I do not," I say.

"You do." The blankets rustle as he rolls onto his side.

"Well, if I do, it's a coincidence," I say. "I love cleaning."

"They told me that," he says.

I laugh. "How did that come up? Did you

ask for the least interesting thing about me?"

"A few weeks after I moved in, the apartment was completely disgusting," he says. "And I'm not even that clean of a guy. I finally asked Sabrina about it, and she said they must've gotten used to you always scrubbing everything. I think I'm the only person who's taken out the trash in the last six months. Cleo picks up after herself, but she won't touch Sabrina's mess."

I smile at the dark ceiling, my heart swelling with affection for both of them. "Cleo's great at boundaries. She probably thinks if she lets Sabrina's toothpaste splatter accumulate long enough, she'll notice."

"Yeah, well, if I didn't intervene, the counter would be more toothpaste than porcelain by now."

"You're being unrealistic," I say. "The entire apartment would be toothpaste."

"You don't seem to mind that our friend is a disgusting slob."

"I've always liked cleaning," I say. "Even when I was little."

"Really?"

"Yeah," I say. "Both my parents had to work a lot, and they were always stressed out about money, but they were also good about making sure my sister and I had everything we needed. There wasn't a ton I could do to help, except cleaning. And I like how it's so measurable, like you immediately see that what you're doing is making a difference. Whenever I get anxious, I clean, and it relaxes me."

A long silence. "Do I make you anxious?"

"What? Of course not," I say.

His blankets rustle again. "When I came into the room tonight, you started rearranging the drawers."

"Coincidence," I insist.

"So you're not anxious," he says.

"I'm never anxious here," I say.

Another pause. "What are they like?"

"Who?"

"Your family," he says. "You don't talk about them all that much. Are they like you?"

I prop my head up in my hand and squint through the dark. "What am I like?"

"I don't know how to explain it," he says. "I'm not good with words."

"If you'd rather, you can act it out," I say.

He turns onto his back again, waves his arms in a circle.

"A gigantic orb," I guess.

He laughs. "I guess I'm not good at charades either. I mean it in a good way."

"A gigantic orb in a good way," I say.

"So." He faces me once more. It's easier

to meet his eyes in the dark. "Are they gigantic orbs too?"

"It's impossible to say, since I still have no idea what that means. But my parents are nice. Dad's a science teacher, and Mom works at a dentist's office. They always made sure my sister and I had what we needed."

"You said that already," he says.

Reading my hesitation, he says, "Sorry. You don't have to talk about it."

"There's not a lot to say." We fall back into silence, but after a while, it bubbles over: "They don't love each other."

The words hang there. He waits, and it doesn't matter that I've decided not to talk about this. It comes out anyway: "They barely knew each other when they got married. They were in college still, and my mom got pregnant with my older sister. Mom was supposed to go to medical school, and Dad was supposed to go to grad school for astrophysics — but they needed money, so she dropped out to raise Eloise, and he got a job substitute teaching. By the time I was born, it was already like this weird late-twentieth-century marriage of convenience."

"Do they fight?" he asks.

"Not really," I say. "My sister's six years older than me, and she was kind of a wild

103

child, so they used to argue with her, but not with each other."

About her dropping AP classes without talking to them, or coming home with a belly button ring, or announcing her plans to take a backpacking gap year.

Mom and Dad never screamed, but Eloise did, and when, inevitably, they sent her to her room or she stormed out of the house, everything would always seem somehow quieter than before. A dangerous quiet, like one tiny peep might make the cracks spread, the house collapse.

My parents weren't cruel, but they were strict, and they were tired. Sometimes one or both of them had to get a weekend job to fill in the financial gaps if the minivan broke down, or Eloise chipped a tooth, or I got a virus that led to pneumonia, which dovetailed nicely with a need for chest X-rays. By the time I was nine, I might not have known what *deductible* meant, but I knew it was one of those words trotted out when Mom and Dad were bent over paper bills at the kitchen table, massaging their eyebrows and sighing to themselves.

I also knew that my dad hated when my mom sighed. And that, conversely, my *mom* hated when my *dad* sighed. Like both of them were hoping that the other would be fine, wouldn't need comforting.

All the quiet made me strain for hints and clues until I became an expert in my parents' moods. Eloise had been out of the house a long time, since the blowup fight when she'd told them she wouldn't be going to college, and things were a lot better now, but they'd never fully forgiven her, and I didn't think she'd forgiven them either.

"They're good parents," I say. "They came to every single thing I was a part of. In fifth grade, for a talent show, I did this series of 'magic tricks' that were actually little science experiments, and you'd think they'd watched me give a lecture at NASA.

"We only ever ate out for special occasions, but that night they took me for ice cream at Big Pauly's Cone Shop."

Talking to Wyn like this feels like whispering my secrets into a box and shutting it tight.

A sliver of a grin appears through the dark. "So you've always had a sweet tooth."

"All of us do. We ordered *multiple* rounds," I say. "Like we were doing birthday shots."

We stayed until the place was closed, well after my normal bedtime. One of my most vivid memories was falling asleep against the back seat, feeling so happy, glowy with their pride.

I lived for those rare nights when everything clicked and we were all happy together, when they weren't worried about anything and could just have fun.

When I won the high school science fair my sophomore year, and Dad and I spent the night making s'mores over the stovetop and binge-watching a documentary on jellyfish. Or when I graduated salutatorian, and the front-office team from Dr. Sherburg's dental practice threw me a mini party, complete with a truly hideous brain cake Mom had baked. Or when I got the letter about my scholarship to Mattingly, and the three of us stayed up late, poring over the online course catalog.

You, my girl, I remember Mom saying, *are going to do great things.*

We always knew it, Dad had agreed.

"What about your parents?" I ask Wyn. "They come from ranching families, right? And now they run a furniture repair business? What are they like?"

"Loud." He doesn't elaborate.

My first impression of him has proven true: Wyn doesn't like talking about himself.

But I feel greedy for more of him, the real Wyn, the parts under the smoky-sultry eyes.

"Happy loud," I say, "or angry loud?"

His smile lights up the dark. "Happy

loud." He pauses. "Plus, my dad's deaf in one ear but insists on always asking questions from the other room, so sometimes just *loud* loud. And I've got an older sister and a younger one. Michael and Lou. They're loud loud too. They'd love you."

"Because I'm loud?"

"Because they're brilliant like you," he says. "And also because you laugh like a helicopter."

Unfortunately, that causes me to prove his point. "Wow. Stop hitting on me."

"It's cute," he adds.

Another full-body flush. "Okay, now you *really* need to stop flirting with me."

"You make it sound so easy," he says.

"I believe in you," I say.

"And you have no idea how much that means to me," he replies.

I turn over and bury my face in my pillow, mumbling through a grin, "Good *night,* Wyn."

"Sleep tight, Harriet."

The next night follows the same pattern: We climb into bed. We fall into silence. And then Wyn turns onto his side and asks, "Why brain surgery, specifically?"

And I say, "Maybe I thought it sounded the most impressive. Now I can constantly respond to things with *Well, it's* not *brain*

107

surgery."

"You don't need to be any more impressive," he says. "You're already . . ." In the corner of my eye, he waves his arms in that huge circle again.

"A freakishly large watermelon," I say.

He lets out a low laugh, his voice gone all raspy. "So was that it? You chose the hardest, most impressive thing you could think of?"

"You ask a lot of questions, but you don't like answering them," I say.

He sits up against the wall, the corner of his mouth curling, dimples sinking. "What do you want to know?"

I sit up. "Why didn't you want to guess what our friends told me about you?"

He stills. No hand running through his hair, no jogging knee. A very still Wyn Connor is an almost lewdly beautiful thing.

"Because," he says eventually, "my best guess would be they told you I'm a nice guy who barely got into Mattingly and didn't get my credits in time to graduate, and honestly might never manage to."

"They love you," I say. "They'd never say anything like that."

"It's the truth. Parth's off to law school next year, and I was supposed to be moving to New York with him, but I failed the same gen ed math class for the second time. I'm hanging on by a thread."

"Who needs math?" I say.

"Mathematicians, probably," he says.

"Are you planning to become a mathematician?" I ask.

"No," he says.

"That's good, because they're all going to be put out of business once this calculator thing catches on. Who cares if you're bad at math, Wyn?"

His gaze lifts. "Maybe I hoped to make a better first impression than that."

"No part of me believes," I say, "that you struggle with first impressions."

He brushes his thick hair up off his forehead, and it stays there, all except that one strand, of course, which is determined to fall sensually across his eyebrow. "Maybe you make me a little nervous."

"Yeah, right," I say, spine tingling.

"Just because you don't see me grabbing a mop every time you walk into a room doesn't mean I don't notice you're there."

It feels like a bowling ball has landed in my stomach, a sudden drop. Then come the butterflies.

Blood rerouting, vessels constricting, I tell myself. *Meaningless.*

"Why?" I ask.

"I don't know how to explain it," he says, "and please don't ask me to act it out."

"You make me a little nervous too," I admit.

He's waiting for me to say more, the weight of his focus on me. An ache starts behind my ribs. Like having this small bit of him has transformed all the pieces I can *never* have into a kind of phantom limb, a pain where there should be more Wyn.

"Why?" he says finally.

"Too handsome," I say.

A strange look flits across his face, something like disappointment. He averts his gaze. "Well. That has nothing to do with me."

"I know that," I say. "That's the thing. Abnormally good-looking people aren't supposed to also be so . . ."

"So . . . ?" He arches a brow.

I wave my arms in a circle.

He cracks a smile. "Spherical?"

I latch on to the closest word I can find. "Vast."

"Vast," he repeats.

"Funny," I say. "Interesting. It's like, pick a lane, buddy."

He laughs, tosses a pillow across the room at me. "I never would have pegged you for a snob, Harriet."

"Huge snob. *Huge.*" I toss the pillow back with another circular wave of my arms. It lands about three feet shy of his bed.

"What was that?"

"The pillow you threw at me," I say, "perhaps you remember it."

"I know it's a pillow," he says. "I'm talking about the throw."

"Now who's a snob?" I say. "Just because I'm not an athlete —"

"It's a pillow, Harriet," he says, "not an Olympic throwing hammer, and we're four feet apart."

"We're like ten feet apart," I counter.

"Absolutely not." He stands and starts across the room, counting each step. I catch myself cataloging his arms and stomach, the juts of his hip bones above his gym shorts.

"Three . . . four . . . five . . ."

"You are taking *massive* strides right now." I jump up to measure the distance myself. Our elbows graze as we pass, and every fine hair down my arm rises.

"One, two, three, four, five, six, seven, eight, nine."

When I turn, he's standing right behind me. The dark quivers between us. My nipples pinch, and I'm terrified he'll notice, and desperate for him to notice, to feel his

111

eyes all over me.

He clears his throat. "Tomorrow."

My voice comes out thin. "Tomorrow what?"

"We'll measure the distance," he says. "Whoever's guess is closest wins."

"Wins what?" I ask.

His lips twitch. One of his perfectly curved shoulders lifts. "I don't know, Harriet. What do you want?"

"You say my name a lot," I say.

"You hardly ever say mine," he replies. "That's why I had to get you to say *Wins what.*"

I smile at the floor, which underscores how close we're standing. "Wins what, *Wyn?*"

When I look up, his lips are pressed tight, his dimples out full force. "I honestly forget what we were talking about."

Another head rush. A belly flutter. Warning bells clanging through my nervous system.

"We were talking about how badly we both need to go to sleep," I say. He pretends to believe me. We climb back into our respective beds.

We talk through the next night too. I tell him I'm still not used to all the casual physical affection between our friends. How Cleo

112

snuggles into my side like a cat nestling into towels fresh from the dryer, and Sabrina hugs me hello and goodbye, and Parth tousles my hair as he's passing through a room.

"Would you rather I didn't touch you?" Wyn asks quietly.

As quietly, I say, "You don't ever touch me."

"Because I haven't known," he says, "if you want me to."

Everything in me twists and tightens.

He tucks a pillow under his ear and shifts onto his side, his bare chest and long, lean torso tinged with the first bit of morning, the freckles on his sculpted shoulders visible in the streaks of light.

My train of thought is disappearing around a corner, leaving me alone with a half-naked Wyn Connor, when he says, "Just to be clear, you're always welcome to touch me."

I become acutely aware of every place the cool silk sheets skim my legs. I shake the blankets out. "What an extremely generous offer."

"Not generous at all," he says. "I'm voracious for physical touch. Can't get enough."

"So I've gathered," I say. "If I ever meet someone in need of casual physical touch,

113

I'll give them your business card."

The corner of his mouth tugs downward. "Remember what you told me about Sabrina?"

"No, what?"

"That she exaggerates," he says. "So does Parth."

I pitch myself higher on my elbow. "So which were the exaggerations, Wyn? The hot TA who left her phone number on your last essay of the term? The flight attendant who bought all your drinks? The identical triplet Russian acrobats?"

"The triplets," he says, "were literally just some girls I met in a bar and talked to for thirty minutes. And for the record, they were gymnasts, not acrobats, and they were very nice."

"One can't help but notice you didn't protest about the TA and the flight attendant."

He sits up against the wall. The man cannot stay in one position for longer than forty or so seconds. "How about we discuss *your* romantic history?"

"What about it?" I say.

"Sabrina said you were dating another American while you were in London."

"Hudson," I supply.

"You never bring him up," Wyn says.

I don't bring him up because he and I agreed our relationship was temporary, right from the start. We knew when we went home, we'd be too busy, too focused, for each other. *Focus* was the second biggest thing Hudson and I had in common. The first was a love of the same chip shop in London. Not the stuff of romantic legend, but it worked out okay, and no one got hurt.

"I'm an open book," I say. "What do you want to know?"

Wyn's teeth scrape over his bottom lip. "Is he a genius like you?"

"I'm not a genius," I say.

"Fine," Wyn says, "is he brilliant like you? Is he going to be a surgeon?"

Brilliant. The word fizzes through me.

"He wants to be a thoracic surgeon," I say. "He goes to Harvard."

Wyn scoffs.

"Tickle in your throat?" I say.

"What's he look like?" Wyn asks. As I consider, his grin twitches. "Can't remember?"

"Dark hair, blue eyes," I say.

"Like you," he says.

"Identical." I sit up too. "Side by side, you couldn't tell us apart."

Wyn's eyes slink down me, then climb back to my face. "You're a very lucky

115

woman."

"The luckiest," I say. "Once, when I was sick, he went to class as me."

"Can I see a picture?" Wyn asks.

"Seriously?"

"I'm curious," he says.

I lean over the bed and feel around for my phone on the ground, then carry it over to him, swiping through my camera roll.

I choose a picture of Hudson that shows off his high cheekbones, his pointed chin, his glossy dark hair. When I hold it out, Wyn grabs my wrist to steady it and squints at the screen. Then he slides my phone from my hand and brings it closer to his eyes. "Why isn't he smiling?"

"He is," I say. "That's how he smiles. It's subtle."

"*This* guy," Wyn says, "only smiles when he's looking in the mirror. Which is also how he masturbates. While wearing his Harvard sweatshirt."

"Oh my god, Wyn. *You* are officially the snob among us." I reach for my phone, but he rolls onto his stomach, taking it with him.

Slowly, he swipes back through my pictures, taking each in before moving to the next. I flop down next to him and peer over his shoulder as he pauses on a shot of me in the library, hunched over a notebook,

116

several towers of textbooks lined up in front of me.

"Cute." He glances over his shoulder at me, then back to the phone before I can react.

He spreads his thumb and finger over the image to zoom in on my face. I watch him in profile, his face lit up, his dimples shadowing. "So fucking cute," he repeats quietly.

Heat blooms in every nook and cranny of my body. This time when I reach for my phone, Wyn lets me take it. He sits up. Only a handful of inches separate our faces. I can smell his clove deodorant. His gaze is heavy on my mouth.

"I told you," I manage, "you need to stop flirting with me."

His eyes lift. "Why?"

Because my best friend has a crush on you.

Because this group of friends matters too much to risk ruining it.

Because I don't like how out of control I feel around you, how whenever you're nearby, you're the only thing I can focus on.

I say, "You don't date your friends."

"You're not my friend, Harriet," he says quietly.

"What am I, then?" I ask.

"I don't know," he says. "But not that."

Our gazes lash together, a heady pressure

building between us; his want and mine have started to overlap, two halves of a Venn diagram drawing together on the twin bed.

"We can't," I murmur.

"Because of Sabrina?" he asks.

My heart spikes. "No." It comes out thin, unconvincing.

"I don't see her like that," he says.

"You see everyone like that," I say.

"I don't," he says, voice firm. "I really don't."

"Wyn," I say quietly. "This is . . ." What word did he use earlier this week? "Messy."

"I know," he says. "Trust me, I'm trying not to — feel like this."

"Try harder." I want to sound light and teasing. Instead, I sound as angsty as I feel.

"Is that what you want?"

I can't bring myself to lie, so I just stand. "We should get at least a little sleep."

After several seconds, he says, "Good night, Harriet."

8
REAL LIFE

Tuesday

The first thing I register is a heaviness across my stomach, a bar of gentle pressure, like a weighted blanket, only concentrated. A cold breeze wriggles through the sheets. I nestle back into the delicious warmth behind me. My head spins from the motion. My stomach roils. Something stiff rocks against the backs of my thighs, and a bolt of heat, of want, goes down my center.

Holy shit!

I scramble upward, eyes snapping open on the pewter gray of morning, blankets snared around my thighs. I'm on the floor.

Why am I on the floor?

Why am I on the floor with *him*?

I search my immediate surroundings for clues.

King-sized bed. Window open above it, a damp wind wisping in. Bare legs, covered with goose bumps. And the shirt I'm wear-

119

ing — *No!*

Shit. Shit. Shit.

Tissue-paper thin. Faded to near transparency, long enough to reach a third of the way down the fronts of my thighs but somehow not long enough to cover my whole ass. A cartoon horse barrel racing with a cartoon cowboy on its back, yellow serifed font superimposed over it: *THIS AIN'T MY FIRST RODEO.*

No, no, no, no, no, absolutely not. This is not my shirt.

Sure, it *used* to be my favorite shirt to sleep in, but once that UPS box of my stuff showed up (a whole two days after our breakup), I'd stuffed this shirt — along with every other trace of Wyn I could find — into the Crate & Barrel box from our first set of shared dishes and shipped it right back to him.

Why am I fixating on the shirt?

Surely, I should be panicking about the fact that my ex-fiancé is lying on the floor beside me, bare chested, face half buried in a pillow, his arm still a deadweight across my lap and his erection wedged against me.

"Psst!" I shove him. He rocks right back into the same position. I've always been a terrible sleeper, whereas Wyn — who *never* stops moving while awake — sleeps so hard that I used to check his pulse in the night.

"Get up!" I shove his shoulder harder. His eyes flutter open, slitting against the half-light of morning.

"What?" he grumbles, one eye closing to better focus on me. "What's wrong?"

"What's wrong?" I hiss back. "How did this happen? How could I let this happen? How could *you* let this happen?"

"Hold up." He pushes himself up, scrubs his hair back. "Tell me what happened."

"What happened?" My whisper pitches up to a teakettle whistle. "We slept together, Wyn!"

His eyes widen. "Slept together?" He laughs hoarsely. "When would we have slept together, Harriet? In between you and Kimmy doing body shots and me — literally — carrying you up the stairs?"

"But . . ." I look around for all that evidence I'd cataloged. "I'm wearing your shirt."

"Because you puked on yours," he says. "And when I went to get you another one, you demanded, quite vehemently, the *I've been to so many fucking rodeos* shirt."

I gawk at him, trying to recall the night he's describing. "That doesn't sound like me."

"Are you kidding?" he says. "You once

121

told me you wanted to be buried in that shirt. And then that you didn't want to be buried, so I'd have to cremate you in it."

"I don't *demand* things," I say.

"Yeah," he says. "That part was a pleasant surprise."

"Wait." The front of my head throbs. I push my hands against it, hard. "Why am I on the floor?"

"Because you refused to take the bed," he says.

"And why are *you* on the floor?"

"Because," he says, "I refused to take the bed first. I think you were trying to make a point, but you passed out pretty fast, and then I was worried you might get sick again and choke on your own vomit."

"Oh." Another nail pounds into the spot above my right eye. My stomach makes a noise like a possum who's both dying and in heat.

I remember chugging the glass of wine in the kitchen and going back onto the patio.

I remember Parth playing one of his famous party playlists through the fancy outdoor speakers hidden in fake rocks, and everyone dancing, except Cleo and Wyn, who hung back by the fire, deep in conversation, and I remember how despicably beautiful he looked, backlit by the flames.

Then Parth hauled him and Sabrina bodily over to the rest of us, and I remember telling Wyn that sitting by the fire, he'd looked like the devil, and him saying, *Stop flirting with me, Harriet,* and me feeling angry and something else entirely. Things get fuzzy after that. Probably for the best, if that last little flicker is anything to go on.

"Why don't you feel like complete shit right now?" I ask.

"Probably," he says, "because I drank half as much wine as you, and one hundred percent fewer shots than you took off Kimmy's stomach."

"That was *true*?" I say. "I did a body shot?"

"No, you didn't do a body shot," he says.

My shoulders relax.

"You did *four* body shots."

"Why didn't anyone stop us?" I ask.

"Probably because Cleo went to bed early, Sabrina and Parth were having the time of their lives, and every time *I* came near you, you'd rub your ass on my crotch until I left you alone."

I scoot abruptly back from him. "There is absolutely no way I did that."

"Don't worry," he says. "It was clearly vengeful grinding."

I rub the heels of my hands over my

eyebrows.

Wyn reaches back for the glass on the nightstand behind us. "Drink some water."

"I don't need water," I say. "I need a time machine."

"I'm not made of money, Harriet. Water's all I've got."

I swipe the glass from him. As soon as I've drained it, he plucks it from my hand and stands, padding into the bathroom portion of our fuck-palace and turning on the faucet. I crawl toward the balcony and push up onto my knees to open the door, dragging the blanket outside with me to swallow some big gulps of fresh sea air.

The sun's barely come up. There's too much mist to see much of anything. Everything's a shimmering gray.

"Here."

I flinch at the sound of his voice. Wyn's stepped out beside me and holds the refilled glass out, along with a couple of ibuprofen. Begrudgingly, I down the pills.

"I don't need you to take care of me," I say.

"You've always made that clear." He lowers himself to sit beside me on the damp wood, his arms coiled around his knees, his gaze out on the water. Or where the water must be, hidden behind the silver curtain.

"Since when do you drink like that?"

"I don't." At his look, I add, "Under usual circumstances. But as you'll recall, *these* circumstances are *less than ideal.*"

He pushes his hair out of his face. "Can I ask you something?"

"No," I say.

He nods, his gaze steady on the invisible horizon.

My curiosity bubbles up until I can't ignore it. "Fine. What?"

"You're happy, aren't you?" He looks at me sidelong, the corners of his mouth tense, thoughtful ridges between his brows.

That exaggerated seesawing sensation rocks through me, only with the added benefit of there being a turbulent ocean of alcohol in my stomach.

There's no right answer. Tell him he did the right thing, and he gets absolution. Tell him I'm not happy, and I'm admitting that even now, a part of me wants him. That he's gone back to being my phantom limb, an unstoppable ache where something's missing.

I'm saved by the bell. Except the bell is an air horn app at top volume, blasting through the hallway, followed by a muffled shriek — Kimmy — of "GROCERY. GLADIATORS.

BITCHES!" Parth lays on the air horn again.

Wyn lumbers to his feet, his question forgotten, my answer avoided. "At least *someone* remembered to hydrate before bed."

9
REAL LIFE

Tuesday

"I have never loved a grocery store," I say, "like I love this grocery store."

"I love all grocery stores." Sabrina wheels our cart around an endcap toward the Crayola-bright produce section.

"Honestly, I have a hard time with grocery stores now," Cleo says. "Once you start growing your own fruits and veggies, everything else pales in comparison."

"Oh, is that so?" Sabrina pauses to feel a couple of mangoes. "I wouldn't know."

Something about the way she says it makes it clear it's a barb. Or it at least suggests that, and then the way Cleo's eyes flick up but don't fully roll confirms it.

"I've told you," Cleo says. "You can visit in the winter. Things are too busy now." She shoots me a look. "Open invitation, Harry: if you and Wyn want to come up to the farm then too, we'd love to have you."

I focus on checking a box of strawberries for mold. Because this adorable coastal market has been blessed by angels, there isn't the tiniest bit of fuzz. I check three more boxes, all of them mold-free. "Seriously," I say. "This is the best grocery store on the planet."

"You like this grocery store because you don't have to make any decisions because you're always with us, and I'm good at making lists," Sabrina says. "And you hate every other grocery store because I'm not there to meal plan for you. If you moved back in with us, we could fix that." She turns to Cleo. "And Parth and I are amazing houseguests, by the way. We always bring chocolate babka from Zabar's."

She says it flatly, in her unbothered Sabrina way, but I can tell by Cleo's expression that the little jabs are landing with some force. "We didn't cancel your visit because we think you're bad houseguests," she says. "Things just got hectic."

Before Sabrina can reply to that, I jump in: "Well, I'm so glad you and Kim could still make the trip work. That means a lot."

Cleo's mouth softens into a smile. "I'm glad too." She brushes a hand over Sabrina's elbow. "I mean, how often do two of your best friends get married?"

128

Sabrina grins now too, irritation apparently forgotten. "Well, in this case, at least twice, since we'll still have to do a big family wedding next year. Plus, if Parth has his way, there will probably be three or four more sprinkled in there somewhere."

"Well, of course," I say. "You've got to make sure it sticks."

From the far end of the shop, I can hear Kimmy barking orders at Wyn and Parth like she's a musher. Their strategy in this pseudo-game is always to go as fast as possible, which means they end up having to circle the whole store like three times, while Cleo, Sabrina, and I lazily meander, testing fruit and sorting through the *impressive* imported cheese fridge. There are usually even a couple of Cleo's favorite nut cheeses.

The game's gotten more elaborate over the years. We are now to the point where Sabrina makes the list, cuts it into tiny one-line strips, folds the strips, puts them in a bowl, and has each of us take turns pulling random grocery items out until both "teams" have an even number.

Another reason I know this is not a real game: Sabrina clearly does not give one single shit about winning, and she is *always* hypercompetitive.

"Hold on a sec." Cleo ducks down the row

of fridges and returns with three large coconut waters. She drops two into our cart and pushes the other at me. "You're green."

Sabrina examines me. "More like chartreuse."

A flash of memory: Parth shoving green drinks with paper umbrellas into our sweaty hands as we danced around the patio.

I wince. "Don't say that word."

Sabrina cackles. "What about *puce*?"

"Puce is more like a dark red," Cleo puts in helpfully.

"Like if one were to puke up red wine?" Sabrina asks.

I grab a loose Maine blueberry and throw it at her. At the front of the store, someone is whooping. "We Are the Champions" starts to play over phone speakers.

"Wow," Sabrina says, tossing a couple of blueberries into her mouth. "They win again. Who would've thought?"

"How is Kimmy even alive," I ask, "let alone whooping and cheering?"

"I don't know, dude. She's superhuman," Cleo says. "Plus, she woke me up to tell me about the body shots, and I took the opportunity to pour three gallons of water into her mouth." Her brow arches. "Kind of surprised Wyn didn't think to do that for

130

you. He was totally sober when I went to bed."

I busy myself with another package of blueberries. "Aha!" I spin back. "See that? Mold."

"Every rose has its thorn," Sabrina says, angling our cart back toward the front of the shop. "Just like every cowboy sings a sad, sad song."

Another flash of memory: me, kneeling on the ground, atop the comforter Wyn's dragged to the floor. *Arms up, baby,* he says gently. He peels the ruined white T-shirt over my head, runs a cool washcloth over my collarbones, collecting what's left of my mess. I can barely keep my eyes open. *Did you get me the shirt about the rodeos? The I've been to so many fucking rodeos shirt?*

I got it, he says. *Arms back up.* I must not lift them high enough, because his rough palms catch the undersides of my biceps and ease them over my head. Then the butter-soft fabric is being tugged down around me, pooling against the tops of my thighs.

I love this shirt, I grumble.

I know, he says, sliding my hair out from under the collar. *That's why I brought it. Now go to sleep.*

"Har?" Cleo jolts me out of the memory.

131

"You actually are puce now."

"That word." I press my hand over my mouth and bolt for the bathroom.

The instant I step under the jangling bells and into Murder, She Read, I feel five hundred thousand times better.

Which is to say, I still feel like utter shit, but shit ensconced in books and sun-warmed windows. Shit with sugary iced latte flowing through its veins.

I've never finished a chapter on one of these trips, let alone a book, but I've always loved coming here, picking out my next read.

Wyn and Cleo split off for Nonfiction, and Kimmy darts to Romance. Parth heads for General Fiction, and Sabrina veers toward Horror. I alone head for the black coffin mounted to the wall, door ajar and waiting, *Mysteries* painted in gold letters at the top of the box.

I step through it to the room beyond, a space nearly as large as all other genres combined.

I'd never been a big reader until the summer before I started at Mattingly, when all my high school extracurriculars and AP summer work abruptly ended. My acceptance to (and funding for!) the school of my dreams was already assured, and I was bored for the first time in my life.

I found the dime-store mystery in Eloise's old room, now the family office, when I went in to look for packing tape. I sat on the windowsill to read the first page and didn't look up until I'd finished the book. Afterward, I went straight to the library for another. I probably read twenty cozy mysteries that summer.

I run my fingers along the paperback spines, each title featuring a worse pun than the last. As I pull one out, Cleo appears at my side. "I thought you'd read that one."

"This?" I hold it up. "Maybe you're thinking of *Dying to Give.* The one about the auctioneer murdered at the fundraiser. This one's *Dying to Sieve,* about a baker who finds a body inside a bag of flour."

"A whole body?" she says.

"It's a really big bag," I say. "Or a really small body, I'm not sure, but for a mere six dollars and ninety-nine cents, I could find out. Did you find something already?"

She holds up a dictionary-sized tome with a giant illustration of a mushroom on its pale green cover.

"Didn't *you* already read *that* one?" I say.

Her mouth curls. "You're thinking of *Fabulous Fungi.* This is *Miraculous Mushrooms.*"

"How silly of me," I say.

She leans away from me to peer through the doorway to the rest of the store. "So what do you think about all this?"

"All what?"

"Sabrina and Parth," she says. "Getting married. In like four days."

"I guess when you know, you know." I slide the book back onto the shelf and keep skimming.

"Yeah." A moment later, she says, "I guess things have just felt a little off with her."

"Really?" I haven't noticed anything, but then again, I haven't been exceptionally present the last few months. I've known that the next time we talked — *really* talked — I'd have to talk about the breakup.

"Maybe I'm reading into it too much," Cleo says, swirling her raspberry iced tea. "But last month, she texts me out of the blue that she and Parth were going to come up for a visit. And I said yes, because she seemed set on it. Only later I realized we were way too swamped, so I asked to re-schedule, and I've barely heard from her since then. When we got in yesterday, I tried to talk to her about it, but she brushed it off, and then today she seems mad about it again."

My fingers stop, hooked over a spine:

134

Murder in the Maternity Ward. "I think she's just taking this cottage thing hard," I say. "I don't think it's personal."

Cleo screws up her mouth. "Maybe." She lifts her braids off her shoulder, shaking them to fan her neck. There's no airflow in here, and the humidity is dense. "I guess I'll try to talk to her again tonight. I just wanted to see if you'd noticed anything . . . different with her."

"Nope!" I say, probably a bit too chipper. "I think everything seems totally normal."

Cleo's head cocks. I'm fully expecting her to cry *You and Wyn broke up, didn't you?* at any second. Instead, she tucks her arm through mine and rests her head on my shoulder. "I'm probably just tired," she says. "I always worry more when I'm tired."

I frown. I've been so self-absorbed (and/or drunk) that somehow I missed the way her face has thinned, and the faint purple blots beneath her eyes. "Hey," I say. "Are *you* okay?"

"Why wouldn't I be?" That's a weirdly evasive reply for Cleo.

"Because you run a whole-ass farm," I say. "And you are but one dainty five-foot-two-inch woman."

Her smile brightens her whole face. "Yes, but you forget: my girlfriend is a five-foot-

135

ten-inch Scandinavian American goddess who can drink four barrels of moonshine and still win a grocery store race."

"Clee," I say.

She checks over her shoulder, then drops her voice. "Okay, yes, I'm stressed," she says. "The truth is, Kimmy and I went back and forth about bowing out of this year's trip for the last three weeks. When I told Sabrina we might have to miss it, it did *not* go well, so we decided we'd come for a couple of days. Only now we can't head back early after all, so we're scrambling to have neighbors go take care of things for us at home."

"I'm so sorry," I say. "How can I help?"

"It's okay. It's one week of stress. Well, and the full week it will take us to catch up on the time away."

"Hey!"

For some reason — quite possibly all the subterfuge I'm currently engaged in — I jump when Sabrina pops her head in between us.

Cleo does too. "Don't sneak up on us."

"Um, I literally just walked up," Sabrina says. "Did I catch you two in the middle of a drug deal or something?" She reaches between us to grab Cleo's book, scrutinizing the cover. "Mushrooms? Again?"

Cleo's lips thin. "They're fascinating."

"What about you, Sab?" I cut in. "Did you find anything?"

"Oh my god, yeah," she says. "This book is a fictional take on the Donner Party."

"How . . . nice," I say.

She cackles, grabs the book out of my hand. I didn't realize I was holding one — I must've yanked it out when she surprised us. "Harry," she says, reading the back of it. "This book is every bit as fucked as mine."

"I guarantee it's not," I say.

"An interior designer finds a hand behind a wall," she says.

"Yes, but it's *cozy*." I take the book back.

"How is that cozy," she asks.

"It's a cozy mystery," I say. "It's hard to explain."

"Oh-kay." Her voice wrenches up into a wordless yip of surprise as Kimmy appears at her shoulder. Beside me, Cleo grabs for the edge of the bookshelf, as if for support.

"Why is everyone so jumpy?" Kim asks.

"Sabrina's reading about the Donners again," Cleo says.

"It's fiction," Sabrina says.

Cleo asks, "Where are Parth and Wyn? Are they finished?"

Kimmy shrugs. "I passed Parth by the fancy books."

"What are the fancy books?" I ask.

"She means he's looking for something the *New York Times* has described as 'revelatory,' " Sabrina says.

"Actually . . ." Parth walks up with a paper bag already in hand. "I picked this because the *Wall Street Journal* gave it such a cranky review I needed to read it myself. It's by this married couple who usually publish separately. One of them writes literary doorstop novels and the other writes romance."

"What!" Kimmy snatches the book. "I know them!"

"Seriously?" Parth asks.

"I went to college with them in Michigan," she says. "They weren't together yet, though. Her books are *really* horny. Is this one horny?"

"The *Wall Street Journal* review didn't touch on the horniness," Parth says.

"Is Wyn done?" Sabrina asks.

"Checking out now," Parth confirms

"What'd he get, a Steinbeck novel?" she asks.

Parth shrugs. "Dunno."

There's no way Wyn's getting a Steinbeck novel. I'm surprised he's buying a book, period, since we never have time to read on these trips and he's cautious with his spending. But if he *was* going to get a book, it wouldn't be about the American West. He would've felt like too much of a caricature.

Parth and Sabrina herd us toward the register. Cleo gets her mushroom book and I buy *Death by Design,* and then we step out onto the cobbled street. The sun is high in the sky, no trace of mist left, only dazzling blue. Across the street, Kimmy spots a flower cart in front of the florist and, with a squeal of delight, pulls Cleo after her.

"Parth and I are gonna grab more coffee." Sabrina tilts her head toward the Warm Cup, the café next door with the awning-sheltered walk-up window. We've already been twice today. Once before the market, once after.

"Want anything?" she asks.

"I'm good, thanks," I tell her.

"Wyn?"

He shakes his head. As they wander off, we stand in silence, avoiding gazes. "I meant to tell you," he says finally. "I talked to Parth last night."

"And?"

He clears his throat a little. "You're right. We'll have to tell them after this week."

I'm not sure why that floods me with relief. The rest of my week is now guaranteed to be torturous. But at least Parth and

139

Sabrina will get their perfect day.

Wyn gets a text. He's not usually so attentive to his phone. While he's checking it, I lean toward him a little, trying to peer into his paper Murder, She Read bag.

He stuffs his phone back into his pocket. "You can just ask."

"Ask what?" I say.

His brow lifts. I stare back at him, impassive. Slowly, he slides his purchase from the bag and holds it out to me. It's huge.

The Eames Way: The Life and Love Behind the Iconic Chair.

"This is a coffee-table book," I say.

"Is it?" He leans over to look at it. "Shit. I thought it was an airplane."

"Since when do you buy coffee-table books?" I ask.

"Is this some kind of trick question, Harriet?" he says. "You know these don't require a special license, right?"

"Yes, but they require a coffee table," I say. "And Gloria's won't have room for this." Wyn's mother is a pack rat. Not in a gross way, just in a sentimental one. Or rather his father was, and Gloria hasn't changed much about the Connor family home since her husband passed.

The last time I was there, there was hardly an inch of space on the refrigerator. She

140

had a printout of a group picture we'd all taken at the cottage on our first trip taped up there, right next to a Save the Date for one of Wyn's cousins, who'd already gotten married, divorced, and remarried since then. His older sister Michael's engineering degree sat on the mantel, right next to a framed one-page short story his younger sister, Lou, wrote when she was nine, beside a framed photo of Wyn's high school soccer team.

Aside from the lack of space in his childhood home, this book had to have cost at least sixty dollars, and Wyn's never been one to spend money. Not on himself, and not on anything whose value is primarily aesthetic. In our first apartment together, he used a tower of shoeboxes as a side table until he found a broken one on the street that he could fix.

He slides the coffee-table book out of my hand and drops it back into his bag. I'm still staring, puzzled, trying to make sense of all the tiny differences between the Wyn of five months ago and the Wyn in front of me, but he's gone back to checking his phone.

Kimmy comes bounding up with a bundle of sunflowers. "Where are Parth and Sabrina?" she asks, shielding her eyes against the sun.

"Sabrina needed more coffee," Wyn says. "And Parth needed more Sabrina."

"Awh." She clutches her heart. "They're so cute. Terrifying, but cute."

I catch Wyn peeking into the bag again, sort of smiling to himself.

In my chest, a metric ton drops onto the proverbial seesaw.

Oh my god.

The beard, the slight softening of his body, the sixty-dollar coffee-table book. *All of the texting.*

Is he . . . *nesting?*

Is he *dating someone?*

The seesaw jolts back in the other direction. A burst of cold air-conditioning and roasted espresso beans wafts toward us as Sabrina and Parth emerge from the coffee shop's lesser-used interior. "I don't know about y'all," Sabrina says after a loud slurp on her paper straw, "but I could use some popovers."

Ordinarily, the thought would make my mouth water.

Right now, the idea of dumping fried egg and jam into my seething stomach is worse than hearing *puce* a thousand times in rapid succession.

I smile so hard my molars twinge. "Sounds great."

"Awh. Sunflowers. Sab loves those." Parth leans over to smell them.

Kimmy thrusts the bundle toward him. "These are for you and Sabrina."

"They're just a sample," Cleo puts in. "We went ahead and ordered some bouquets for Saturday. I know you want it to be simple, but it's not a wedding without flowers."

Sabrina goes from eyeing the bouquet like it might be some kind of Trojan horse, sneakily stuffed with tiny mushroom encyclopedias, to clapping her hands together on a gasp. "Cleo! You didn't have to do that." She hooks an arm around Cleo's head, pulling her in for a hug. "They're gorgeous."

"*You're* gorgeous," Cleo says, starting down the street, the rest of us following like baby ducks.

"No, you guys," Parth says, "*I'm* gorgeous."

Wyn hangs back beside me, asks tersely, "What just happened in there?"

"In where?" I say.

"Your brain," he says.

"Body shots," I say. "My brain is full of body shots."

143

"Both a surgeon and a medical anomaly," he says.

"What can I say," I reply flatly. "I'm —"

"I know." He waves his arm in a circle. *"Vast."*

My stomach lurches at the years-old inside joke. "I was going to say *hungover.*"

10
HAPPY PLACE

Mattingly, Vermont

A new apartment for our senior year, the first floor of a peeling white Victorian at the edge of town. Windows that rattle whenever the wind blows, a half-collapsed porch where Sabrina and I intend to spend the fall sipping brandy-spiked hot cider, and a patch of side yard where I promise to help Cleo plant a vegetable garden: broccoli, cauliflower, kohlrabi — things that can withstand the frost that will arrive in a few short months.

Wyn was supposed to be in New York right now, sharing a loft with Parth, making his way in a new city while his best friend studies law at Fordham. If he hadn't failed that math class a second time or overlooked his history gen ed requirement, everything might be different.

Instead, he's living with us. To save money, Cleo and I share the biggest room. Sabrina

145

gets the next one. Wyn has the shoebox originally intended for me.

The morning after move-in day, Parth has donuts delivered for us. The note reads, *If you don't all come to grad school in New York next year, I will be pressing charges.*

Realistically, I'll have to go to whatever medical school will take me. Likewise, Sabrina will have to choose her next city based on her own law school admission, and Cleo will do the same with an MFA program. But the idea is alluring — all of us together in a new city — even as I'm unsure how I'll survive *one* year as Wyn Connor's roommate.

Our whole first week in the place, we manage not to be alone together. Finally, though, we bump into each other early one morning in the stuffy kitchen. The sun's started to come up, and he's making coffee. He fills a mug with the Montana state flag printed on one side and passes it to me. "I want you to know I understood what you said," he murmurs. "Back in Maine."

His voice, still husky with sleep, pulls all the tiny hairs on the back of my neck to eager attention. His closeness, here in the quiet morning, is overpowering.

"I don't want you to worry about this

146

year," he tells me. "I won't make things weird."

I manage something that sounds sort of like "Oh . . . good" and sort of like someone with both stage fright and strep throat has taken a crack at public yodeling.

And then he's nodding curtly, letting himself out the back door to cut our grass before the day gets too hot, and once again, I'm left waiting for a spell to break.

He's true to his word all year. A couple of times a week, he goes out with women the rest of us never meet. Then, in winter, he starts seeing one woman, again and again, a dancer named Alison. She's beautiful. She's nice. But she never stops by for longer than a few minutes before the two of them leave for the night. I try to be happy for him. That's what a friend would do.

You're not my friend, Harriet sometimes replays in my mind.

He struggles with his math class, so I volunteer to help him. On Tuesdays, we study late into the night in Mattingly's dusty golden library. He moans, groans, says his brain wasn't made for this kind of thing.

"What's it made for, then?" I ask, and he says, "Tumbleweeds. They like to just roll through." I've noticed that he does that, talks himself down, self-deprecates, and he

147

does it like it's a joke he's in on, but I think he might mean it, and I hate it.

While we're studying for finals, he brings me vending machine coffee and chocolate chip mini muffins, Snickers bars, and Skittles, and even with all that caffeine and sugar and the rush of being close to him, I drift off to sleep, facedown on a textbook, and wake to him nudging my shoulder from across the table.

When I lift my face, he grins and smudges the transferred ink away from my cheek.

"Thanks," I say sleepily.

"What are friends for?" he says.

You're not my friend, Harriet.

The four of us cook elaborate dinners together in our cramped kitchen, Sabrina acting as sous-chef. We sit on the front porch while Cleo sketches us in a hundred different poses, and when it snows, Wyn and I take long walks through town to get hot chocolate or maple lattes, despite the fact that he hardly touches sweets.

When one of us goes to Hannaford for groceries, we double-check whether the other needs anything, and even if I say no, when Wyn walks into the apartment, he'll set a pint of blueberry ice cream on my desk in front of me, without a word.

And when Sabrina and I get our respec-

tive acceptance emails from Columbia —
her from their law school and me from their
medical school — and in a shocking twist,
Cleo announces she's going to work on an
urban farm in New York City rather than
getting her MFA, I don't even resist the
prospect of the four of us finding a new
place with Parth in New York, of sharing yet
another set of walls with Wyn Connor.

He's become my best friend the way the
others did: bit by bit, sand passing through
an hourglass so slowly, it's impossible to pin
down the moment it happens. When suddenly more of my heart belongs to him than
doesn't, and I know I'll never get a single
grain back.

He's a golden boy. I'm a girl whose life
has been drawn in shades of gray.

I try not to love him.

I really try.

11
REAL LIFE

Tuesday

Usually on Tuesday we take a day trip to Acadia National Park, the most beautiful place I've ever seen and, perhaps more importantly, the location of our favorite popover restaurant.

I've been dreaming about fluffy, strawberry-slathered rolls for weeks, but now all I want is to climb into a cool, dark hole with a barrel full of Tums and a two-liter bottle of ginger ale.

After a quick stop home to change, hydrate, and pee, we repack the cars with picnic supplies. The process of getting everyone and everything out the door is like herding cats on acid. Like the cats are on acid, and the cat shepherd is also on acid.

Right as Parth returns from using the restroom, Kimmy realizes she forgot her sunglasses and darts back inside.

Sabrina says, "Do you think the first two

hours of their days on the farm are Cleo sending Kimmy back into the house for every individual item of clothing she's forgotten to put on?"

"And once more when she accidentally puts her pants on her head," Cleo calls from down by the cars.

"That's not an accident, babe," Kimmy says, barreling back outside. "I'm just waiting for the day you finally embrace my forward-thinking approach to fashion."

"Wear whatever you want," Cleo says. "I'm more concerned with what's underneath."

"Awh!" Kimmy kisses the side of Cleo's neck. "I don't know if you're being lascivious or sentimental, but either way I'll take it."

Sabrina slaps her forehead. "The wine. Can you run down to the cellar and grab it?"

"Pick anything pink or white?" I guess.

She shakes her head. "It's the Didier Dagueneau Silex from 2018. You mind?"

"It's not that I mind," I say. "It's just that I recognized very few of those words."

"Silex," she repeats, jogging her multiple tote bags up her shoulders. "It says that on the label, followed by Didier Dagueneau,

151

and you're looking for the 2018. It's a white."

I drop my own bag inside the door as I double back. The door to the wine cellar sits ajar, the lights already on. Allegedly, there are bottles worth twenty thousand dollars down there. Hopefully none of those *also* starts with *Silex* and ends with *eau*.

As I descend, a faint rustling rises to meet me.

At the bottom of the steps, I round the corner and stop short at the sight of Wyn, limned in the soft golden overhead lighting like some tortured fallen angel as played by James Dean.

"Silex something-something?" he says.

"Sabrina must've forgotten she'd already sent you to get it." I turn to go.

"I've been staring at this spot for like ten minutes. It's not here."

I hesitate. When I pictured retreating to a cool, dark cave, this wasn't what I had in mind, but if Sabrina has her heart on this particular wine, we're not leaving until we find it. I mean that literally. When she gets an idea into her head, there's little room for deviation. *See also* her reaction to Cleo canceling her and Parth's visit to the farm.

I let out a breath and cross toward him, crouching in front of the shelf to run my fingers across the labels.

"I've checked everywhere," he says, grumpy.

"It's basically a universal law that if one person looks for something for an extended period of time, then the next person to walk up to it will spot it immediately."

"How's that going?" he asks.

Among the dozens of chardonnays, Rieslings, sauvignon blancs, gewürztraminers: no Silex.

"Satisfied?" he says.

The hair at the nape of my neck tugs upward at his bemused tone. My brain wanders to the absolute worst place it could possibly go in this particular room.

The cellar, for us, is full of ghosts. Not the scary kind. Sexy ghosts.

I straighten up. "Just grab a white that doesn't look too expensive."

His eyes flash. "You want me to look for a Big Lots clearance sticker, Harriet?"

"Choose something they have more than one of," I say, practically running for the stairs, like he's a riptide I need to claw free from.

Halfway up the steps, I notice the door's shut. Then I reach the top, and the knob won't twist. Won't even budge.

I knock on the door. "Sab?"

At the bottom of the steps, Wyn steps into view, a bottle of wine in hand.

"The door must've locked," I explain.

"Why'd you shut it?" he asks.

"Well, I was hoping it would automatically lock, *from the outside,* and I'd be trapped down here with *you,*" I deadpan.

He ignores the sarcasm and climbs up, brushing me aside to try the knob himself.

"Seems to be locked," he says, probably to annoy me.

He pounds on the door. "Cleo? Parth? Anyone?"

I can feel heat rising off his skin. I descend a couple of steps, check my pockets for my phone as I go. Once again, my pockets are tiny, and my phone must be in my bag, in the foyer.

"Call someone," I say.

Wyn shakes his head. "I left my phone in the car. You don't have yours?"

"Upstairs," I say. "We'll have to wait until they get sick of waiting and send someone to hurry us up."

Wyn groans and drops onto the top step, setting the bottle down by his ankle. He bows his head and knots his fingers together against the back of his neck.

At least I'm not the only one panicking.

Of course, I'm freaking out about being

154

here with *him,* and *he's* freaking out because he's claustrophobic. He has been ever since he was a kid and a broken armoire fell on him in his parents' workshop while no one else was home. He was trapped for hours.

As soon as the door's open, he'll be fine. Whereas I'll still be reeling from the purchase of a stupid coffee-table book.

The whole stairwell sways as an awful realization hits me. I latch on to the banister to keep from falling over.

"What? What's wrong?" Wyn leaps up, steadying me by the elbows. His drawn mouth is visible in bits under the black splotches swimming across my vision.

"We were taking two cars," I squeak out. "We were taking two cars, so all four of them could've left in the Rover."

His eyes darken, clouds creeping across the green. "They wouldn't."

"They might," I say.

"We don't need to assume that's what happened. They could be back any second." He stares at the ceiling, doing some kind of mental calculation.

I descend the rest of the steps, trying to regain the space between us. But he follows. "This isn't my fault, Harriet."

"Did I say it was?" I ask.

"You stormed off," he says. "There's an

155

implication there."

I spin back to him. "Wyn. We're in a twelve-foot box. That wasn't storming. There isn't room for storming. But if your point is to remind me that *I* shut the door, point received."

"I'm not blaming you. I just — who the hell has a door that locks from the *outside*?"

"It's a panic room," I point out. "That's what the little panel on the wall does. We could unlock it if we knew the code."

His gaze clears. He climbs the stairs in three long strides to examine the panel. "There's a button to call 911."

How long will it take for them to realize something's wrong? Will they drive all the way out to pick up the pre-hike popovers without trying to call us?

If they do call, will they assume we don't answer because we're driving?

My stomach resumes its roiling nausea.

"You want to call or wait?" Wyn asks.

Now I'm doing the math of how expensive it might be to replace this door if the fire department has to ax it down or blow it up or something.

"I think . . ." I take a steadying breath, try to find a grip on *some* version of my mental happy place that has nothing to do with this house or this man. "I think we have to wait, for at least a while."

It's obviously not the answer he wanted. "Unless you don't think you can —"

"I'm fine," he says tersely, perching on the bottom step. He sets the wine aside and yanks his hiking boot off.

"Oh my god, Wyn," I say. "It's been five minutes. How long until you're dropping your pants and designating a pee corner?"

He tears the foil from around the wine bottle's cork. "*I* won't need a pee corner. I'll use this bottle when we're done drinking it. You, on the other hand . . . you're going to be out of luck unless you learn to aim, fast."

I unfold my arms only to recross them when his gaze tracks the movement straight to my chest. "Are you walking around with a corkscrew in your pocket at ten thirty in the morning?"

"No," he says, "I'm just happy to see you."

"Hilarious."

His eyes steadily hold mine as he sets the wine bottle into his boot and smacks the whole arrangement against the wall.

I yelp. "What are you doing?"

He drives the boot against the wall again three more times. On the last hit, the cork leaps up the bottle's neck a half inch. With another two quick snaps against the wall, the cork pops out entirely. Wyn lifts the open bottle toward me.

"I'm concerned that you know how to do that," I say.

"So you don't want any." He takes a swig. As the bottle lowers, his eyes dart over his shoulder, toward the alcove under the stairs.

Heat swiftly rises from my clavicles to my hairline.

Don't go there. Don't think about that.

I know it's ill-advised, but a part of me is desperately hoping there's something to the whole hair-of-the-dog school of treating hangovers when I grab the bottle and take a sip.

Nope. My stomach does not want that. I pass it back to him.

"Parth taught me that trick," he says. "I've never needed to use it before now."

"Oh, you haven't found yourself imprisoned with any other jilted lovers in the last five months?"

He snorts. "Jilted? Not exactly how I remember it, Harriet."

"Maybe you have amnesia," I suggest.

"My memory's fine, Dr. Kilpatrick, though I do appreciate the concern." As if to prove his point, his eyes dart toward the nook under the stairs again.

He *can't* be seeing someone. He'd never

go along with this act if he was. Wyn may be a flirt, but he's not disloyal.

Unless he's in something brand-new? Not officially exclusive?

But if it were brand-new, then would he have already reached comfortable-relationship status?

The little so-called clues could just as easily be random bits of information I'm jamming together to tell a story.

But that doesn't mean he isn't *seeing anyone.*

The bottom line is, I have no idea what's going on in his life. I'm not supposed to.

He takes a few more sips. I guess it doesn't do the trick for him either, because within minutes, he's pacing. He rakes his hands through his hair as he walks in circles around the space, sweat brimming along his forehead.

"If only you'd brought your coffee-table book."

Wyn looks abruptly back at me, eyes sharply appraising.

"Then we'd have something to look at," I say.

His brow arches, tugging on his lip. "What do you have against my coffee-table book, Harriet?"

"Nothing."

"Did you suffer some kind of coffee-table-book-related trauma in the last five months?"

"That thing cost sixty dollars," I say.

He shakes his head, goes back to pacing.

"Is it a gift?" I say.

"Why would it be a gift?" he says. Not an answer.

"Because you never spend that kind of money on yourself," I say.

The tops of his cheeks flush a little, and I really, really regret asking now. We go back to sitting in silence. Well, I'm sitting. He's power walking in tiny rectangles.

Even after everything, it's hard to see him like this.

When the defense of his charm gets peeled back, he's always so expressive. It's partly what made me pour out so many secrets to him all those years ago, the feeling that he absorbed some piece of whatever I gave him, *felt* what *I* felt. Unfortunately, the reverse was also true.

"You've been crammed in much smaller spaces," I remind him as he's passing me on his ninetieth lap (best guess; I haven't been counting).

His gaze flashes toward the space under the stairs again.

Not what I meant. My face flames. "Like

every single car you've ever been in," I clarify.

"Buses are bigger than this," he says.

"True," I say. "But they also smell worse. It smells great down here."

"It smells damp."

"It's Maine," I say. "It *is* damp."

He tips his head back. "I'm freaking out, Harriet."

I stand up. "It's okay. They'll be here soon."

"You don't know that." His eyes flicker back to me, the tension around his mouth revealing his dimples. "They might think we decided to hang back . . ."

I swallow. "Sabrina wouldn't stand for that. We're supposed to all be together."

He shakes his head. He sees all the holes in that logic just like I do.

Sabrina might be *annoyed* if she thought we stayed back to score some alone time, but she's already shaken up the natural order of things on our behalf, with giving us the nicest bedroom. Aside from that, if she tried to call and we didn't answer, it's not like she'd speed back here and storm upstairs to try to catch us in the act.

I try a different tack. "You come down here all the time. And you've probably been down here much longer than this, honestly."

161

I try not to go back there.

I try not to revisit the memory.

The summer after he, Cleo, Sabrina, and I all graduated. Before we moved to New York to join Parth.

We'd driven down from Vermont, with all our stuff packed and ready for the big move. Parth had flown in from the city, fresh off finishing his time as a Fordham 1L.

It was his idea to play sardines, a kind of reverse hide-and-seek.

We turned off all the lights, then rolled dice to see who'd hide first.

Wyn lost. We gave him five minutes to hide before we spread out to search through the dark for him.

Somehow I knew, the same way I always seemed to, exactly where he was.

I found him in the cellar. Under the stairs, there was a waist-high rack of wine, but behind it there was a dark nook, empty space, and he was tucked inside it. I almost missed him, but on a double take, I spotted a shifting shadow.

We'd lived together all year but were never truly alone, not like that. For walks, sure, or in the library, where there was always someone around the corner at the reference desk.

I'd almost convinced myself we'd truly

made it to the level of *platonic friends* until, per the game's rules, I climbed over that wine rack to curl up in the dark with him, and my thumping heart and flipping stomach proved they'd never stopped waiting for this moment, this closeness.

I clear my throat, but the memory seems to stick in my windpipe. "We must've been down here for at least an hour."

I have no idea if that's true. I just know every second before we touched felt like a century. Then once we did, time lost all meaning. I think of the black hole documentary I watched with my dad a few years ago, how astrophysicists speculated that there were places in our universe where the rules of time and space inverted, moments becoming a place where you could stay indefinitely.

"I had a good distraction then," Wyn says. No flirtation, no charm. Earnest Wyn. Matter-of-fact Wyn.

"You had the exact same distraction." I hold my arms out to my sides, shimmering my hands.

He looks skeptical. "Fine, then distract me, Harriet."

I tut. "Where are the famous Wyn Connor manners?"

His eyes glint, only the left dimple wink-

163

ing into being. "Distract me *please*, Harriet." His voice drops a little.

I suppress the shiver that sizzles down my spine.

He takes another sip of wine and goes back to pacing, clenching and unclenching his fists. His hands, I know, go numb when his claustrophobia kicks in.

I have to do *something*. I have only one idea.

I stand, brush past him, and swing one leg over the rack under the stairs.

"What are you doing?" he asks.

"Helping." Careful not to topple the thirty or so bottles slotted through the rack, I swing my other leg over, hunching so as not to hit my head on the underside of the stairs.

"Yes, the extra one square foot of space is a huge relief."

"If you put yourself into a smaller space, inside this room," I say, "then you'll know you can get out of that space whenever you want."

"But we still can't get out of the room," he says.

"It's not a perfect science," I say. "But it's something. And honestly, no matter what, we're not trapped. Worst case, we call the fire department. But let's try this first — I can't afford an Armas-approved door, and I don't want you to have to return that coffee-table book."

A huff of laughter as he swings his leg over. That's a good sign.

I sidestep to make room for him, but with the angle of the stairs, stooping isn't enough this far back. I lower myself to the ground and scoot into the corner.

"Now what?" he grumbles.

"Now? Now we put our heads together and try to solve the Zodiac murders," I say. "Sit down, Wyn."

He promptly obeys. At this point, I think he's in the exact right headspace that I could tell him to stand on his hands and sing "Ave Maria" and he might do it.

"Pretend you're playing the game," I say. "Pretend we need to be as quiet and still as possible until they find us."

Raggedly, he says, "That's not going to work."

"Wyn."

His neck bows, his shoulders rising and falling with his shallow breaths.

"Wyn."

"I'm sorry," he says. "I'm trying not to freak out."

"Don't apologize." Without thinking, I reach for his hand. After the initial spark of surprise, of recognition, I realize his fingers

165

are ice-cold and shaking.

I flatten his palm between mine. "Look at me. Talk to me."

He keeps his head down.

"Talk to me," I press again.

"About what?" he asks.

"Anything," I say. "The first thing that comes to mind."

"Getting trapped under the armoire," he says. "That's all I can think about. Being sure I was going to die before anyone found me. Losing feeling in my leg, and then the pain coming back worse when the shock wore off."

"Okay, anything other than that," I amend. I think about my meditation app, the visualization exercise I've been relying on these past five months. "Tell me about a place you love."

He gives one firm shake of his head. "I'm sorry."

"Hey." I scoot closer. Our knees bump. "You don't have to apologize. Not for this."

"I thought I was over this shit," he huffs. "I'm doing so much better. Everything is so much better — I thought this would be better too."

It stings, hearing that: *Everything is so much better.* I brush the thought aside, clear my throat again. "Tell me about when we

166

played that game."

I don't mean to say it. Or I don't know, maybe I do. Maybe I need to know that he remembers, that he hasn't totally forgotten what it felt like to love me, while I'm trapped with him burned onto my heart, my brain, my lungs, my skin.

Finally, his gaze lifts. There's a beat of perfect stillness. "I was hiding," he says thickly. "And you came down first. You almost missed me."

"And then what?"

"And then I moved," he says.

I blink. "You moved?"

"So you'd see me," he explains. "And you did. I scared the shit out of you, and I felt bad."

"You never told me that," I say.

"Well, I did," he says. "I hadn't been alone with you, not really, in a year, and you came down the stairs, and I wanted to touch you so badly. But you didn't see me, and you started to turn, so I moved."

My sternum heats. My thighs heat. Even the backs of my knees melt a little, wax too near to a flame.

"And then we heard footsteps," he goes on, "and you were going to be completely visible, so I pulled you back into the corner with me, where you'd be hidden." His

167

fingers twitch between mine. Some of the warmth is returning to them.

"I pulled you into my lap," he says hoarsely. "And I prayed Parth would go back upstairs without finding us, and he did. I could feel your heart racing, so I knew you must be able to feel mine too, and then I realized I was hard. I was so fucking embarrassed. I expected you to get out of my lap once we were alone."

His eyes return to mine, his pupils dilated from fighting the dark. "But you didn't."

My heart races, the liquid warmth rushing out from my center as it replays in my mind.

How I stayed there, in his lap, with his arms around me, terrified that any movement would break the spell. Finally, one of my ankles started to go numb, so I shifted the slightest bit, and he let out an uneven breath at the motion that made me feel like I'd swallowed a hot ember.

Hungry, and desperate, and brave all at once.

How he always made me feel.

"Then you touched my jaw." He lifts my hand slowly, sets it against his scratchy jaw.

"I didn't mean to," I get out, almost defensively.

I don't even know if I mean *way back then* or now. My pulse is screaming through my palm and fingertips into his skin. The memory of that fevered first kiss in the dark presses in on us from all sides.

"I thought I made you." He tips his head so that my hand slides back toward his ear. "Just by wishing."

"Wishing for things doesn't make them happen, Wyn," I say.

His hand circles my wrist, his thumb gentle on the tender underside of it. "Oh?" he says, his voice softly teasing. "Then what was it that made you finally kiss me, Harriet?"

Eight years have passed, and still my nerve endings light up with the memory of how our breath caught in an uneven back-and-forth, each of us waiting, debating what would come next, until I couldn't take another second not knowing what it was like to kiss him.

"I didn't kiss you," I say. "You kissed me."

He smiles unevenly. "Now which of us has amnesia?"

The rest of the memory crashes over me. How I tipped my chin up until our mouths brushed, not quite a kiss. How his lips parted and his tongue slipped into my mouth, and a full-body sigh, the pure undiluted sound of relief, slipped out of me. At the noise, he hauled me further up into

169

his lap, any hesitancy dissolving into a fever, a need.

My skin erupts with goose bumps at the memory of his whisper against my ear — *You're so soft, Harriet* — as his hands stole up my shirt to find more of me: *The others won't like this.*

I'd whispered back, *I like it,* and his laugh shifted into a groan, and then a promise: *I do too. I'm not sure I've ever liked anything more.*

Sabrina had wanted to bring her boyfriend Demetrios on the trip, but Parth had argued that it would transform the vacation into a couples' trip, which would ruin it altogether. In the end, everyone agreed it was best for the trip to stay friends-only.

I doubted they'd be any happier to hear that two of those *friends* were secretly going at it in the wine cellar. I couldn't bring myself to care. Not until the second set of footsteps sounded on the stairs. That had snapped us back to reality. We'd jolted apart, put ourselves to rights, by the time Cleo found our hiding spot and joined it, per sardines' rules.

I'd spent the whole rest of the night bracing myself for it to never happen again. But when we shut ourselves into the bedroom that night, Wyn picked me up and set me

170

on the dresser, kissing me like not even thirty seconds had passed.

That was then. The *mystery* was the thrill.

Now I know how he'd taste, how he'd touch me, how quickly he'd become the foremost need in my personal Maslow's hierarchy of needs. Which is why I need to put distance between us again. His gravity's too strong. I should probably just be grateful it hasn't pulled all my clothes off me and dragged me into his lap.

"Harriet," he murmurs, like it's a question. His hand slides up along my cheek, the calluses on his fingers so familiar. I find myself leaning into his palm, letting him take some of my weight.

"Tell me about San Francisco," he says softly.

My veins fill with ice. Logic regains a foothold in me.

"You know what San Francisco's like," I say, straightening away from him, cold air rushing in to kiss my skin as his hand falls away. "There's a big-ass Ghirardelli store, and it's always a little cold and wet."

His nose drops, his mouth close enough that I can taste the wine on his breath. "The Ghirardelli store?"

"The whole city," I say.

"Tell me about your residency," he says.

A flare hits my solar plexus. Warning bells jangle. I know what he's getting at — or rather *whom* he's getting at — and a mix of anger and nausea squirms through my gut.

"What about the coffee-table book," I say.

His lips curve in uncertain amusement. "What?"

My ears roar. My throat tightens. "Who's the coffee-table book for?"

He stares at me.

If he won't say it outright to me, then I guess I'm going to have to be the one to ask.

"Are you dating someone?" I bite out.

The amusement melts off his face. "What the fuck, Harriet. Are you serious right now?"

"That's not an answer," I say.

His gaze wavers across my face. "What about you?" he rasps. "Are you with *him*?"

There it is. Acid rises through my stomach. A cleaving goes through my chest.

I refuse to cry. Not over something that happened five months ago. Not over someone who's already told me he doesn't want me.

"That's what you think of me?" I scoot back from him until the wall meets my back. "You still honestly believe I *cheated* on you, and beyond that, you think I'd turn around and do it to someone else too."

"That's not what I'm saying," Wyn says, his voice gravelly. "I'm not accusing you of anything! I'm trying to ask . . ."

"Trying to ask *what,* Wyn?" I demand.

"If you're happy," he says. "I want to know that you're happy too."

Now it's my turn to stare at him in disbelief. He still wants absolution.

And what can I say? That I'm not happy? That I've tried dating someone else and it was the emotional equivalent of bingeing on saltines when all I wanted was a real meal? Or that there are whole parts of the city I avoid because they remind me of those first few months in California, when he still lived with me. That when I wake up too early to my screaming alarm, I still reach toward his side of the bed, like if I can hold on to him for a minute, it won't be so hard to make it through another grueling day at the hospital, in a never-ending series of grueling days.

That I still wake from dreams of his head between my thighs, and reach for my phone whenever something particularly ridiculous happens in the cozy mystery I'm reading, only to remember I can't tell him. That I spend more time trying *not* to think about him than actually *thinking* about anything. All that heady nostalgia and sweltering lust

173

has become combustible, erupting into anger.

"Yes, Wyn," I say. "I'm happy."

He starts to reply. Overhead, a rapid series of beeps sounds, followed by the door bursting open and Sabrina's voice: "HARRIET!? WYN?! ARE YOU OKAY?"

I call, "We're fine."

If he can be *happy,* surely I can be *fine.*

12
REAL LIFE

Tuesday

Before dinner, Wyn "goes for a run." I'm reasonably certain this is an excuse for him to use the outdoor shower by the guesthouse, so I take the opportunity to fume while I lather up in the shower in our bedroom. Afterward, I riffle through my assortment of T-shirts, tanks, jeans, and sundresses. Basically I packed a blob of white, black, and blue.

And then there's the lone splash of red, which I'd thrown in more to please Sabrina than because I actually planned to wear it. She'd sent the dress to me on my last birthday, without even knowing my size — she'd always had an eye for that sort of thing — and I'd tentatively thought of it as my Getting Back Out There Dress, though in my few depressing attempts to Get Back Out There, I hadn't been able to bring myself to wear it.

175

Now it strikes me more as the kind of too-short, too-tight, too-red dress you'd wear to the wedding of a man who jilted you, with plans to tip over his cake and set his tie on fire.

In brief, it's perfect. I stuff myself into it, twist my hair into a clip, slip the one pair of hoops I brought through my ears, and grab my heels on my way out the door.

Downstairs, Sabrina's watching the progress of our approaching cab on the phone while plying everyone with water. Well, everyone except Wyn, who isn't in the kitchen.

"Hydrate, hydrate, hydrate," she chants. "Tonight, we're going full twenty-one-year-olds on spring break."

Kimmy guffaws, her strawberry blond waves jouncing with the motion. "You all should be very glad you didn't know me when we were twenty-one. Four Loko still had caffeine in it then."

"I got great pictures of the body shots, by the way," Parth says. "Those will be perfect for the photo wall."

"Photo wall?" I repeat.

The back of my neck tingles in the second before I hear his voice: "For the wedding."

I turn toward the patio door he's stepped through, his hair damp and that one lock

176

curled toward his brow.

He's wearing a gray T-shirt, half tucked into slate-blue chinos, and the color combination brings out all the green in his eyes as they rove over what I now must rename my Vengeance Dress. He misses a half step in the process but recovers quickly, averting his eyes as he heads to the fridge and starts filling his water bottle.

I wonder if my cheeks are nearing the color of the skintight chiffon yet. It takes me a second to retrace the conversation to where we left off. "So what's this about a photo wall for Saturday?" I manage. "Something I can help with?"

"No, it's not for *our* wedding," Sabrina says. "The photo wall is for yours."

"Remember?" Parth says. "We got your parents' contact info so we could get your baby pictures? We've been slowly accumulating a wall of humiliation for years."

The flush in my face is downright itchy now. "This isn't ringing any bells whatsoever."

"You weren't part of the conversation. You were TAing that semester," Wyn says, without looking over.

Sabrina glances up from her phone and clocks the dress for the first time, her face lighting up. "Harry! Va-va-*voom*. I *told* you red was your color."

I force a smile. "You were right. This has become my go-to Date Night Dress."

The sound of water splatting against the floor draws all of our attention to the fridge. "Shit!" Wyn's gaze snaps away from me like a whip to the water spilling out over his full water bottle onto the floor.

Cleo yelps as she lurches off her stool at the marble island, out of the water's path. Her new mushroom book (or maybe her old one) goes flying out of her hand.

"Sorry," Wyn says under his breath, grabbing a lobster-print tea towel off the dishwasher handle so Cleo can sop up some of the water that hit her clingy black midi dress and boots. In this outfit, she could easily be the gorgeous front woman of a famous nineties grunge band.

As Wyn stands from soaking up the rest of the water on the floor, Parth claps a hand on his shoulder. "You okay, man? You seem kind of out of it."

"Fine," Wyn says, tossing the now drenched towel onto the counter. "Fine."

The second *fine* sounds even less convincing than the first. Now we're getting somewhere. I slide past the marble island to pull his water bottle from his hand, holding eye contact as I take a long sip.

"Thirsty?" he says dryly.

I shove the bottle back toward him. "Not anymore."

"Cab's here!" Sabrina announces, jumping up from her own stool. "Book down, Cleo. Finish that water, Kimberly. We're out of here."

As I'm climbing into the passenger van, I take zero care to keep my barely covered ass out of Wyn's face. I feel a *smidge* less bold once I'm smooshed into the back seat between him and Sabrina, but at least I'm spared from small talk by the early 2000s Pump Up playlist that Parth blasts from the front passenger seat. Plus, Wyn's on his phone the entire ride over anyway.

A handful of minutes later, we pull up in front of our old haunt, the Lobster Hut. It's a ramshackle dive with no sign and no indicator of its moniker on either its cocktail napkins or its sticky laminated menus, though somehow everyone knows what to call it.

The first time I came here, I was nineteen years old, fresh off my first breakup. Sabrina knew they didn't card, and that was back when Cleo could knock back six tequila shots and still be on her feet, fending off frat boy advances with diatribes about

Modigliani paintings.

We sang, we danced, we downed the steady stream of Fireball that kept appearing at our high-top in the corner, and I finally stopped checking my phone compulsively for some word from Bryant. When we got home, and Sabrina and Cleo both flounced off to shower, the loneliness crept back in, and the booze had filed down all my defenses.

I beelined toward the powder room no one ever used, nudged on the faucet, sat atop the toilet, and cried.

Not about Bryant. From the loneliness, from the fear that I would never escape it. Because feelings were changeable, and people were unpredictable. You couldn't hold on to them through the force of will.

Cleo and Sabrina found me there, and Sab insisted she'd break down the door if I didn't let them in. *Then I'll have to, like, go to a polo match with my dad as an apology,* she said, *and I won't let you forget that until one of us dies.*

As soon as I unlocked the door, the tears dried up, but the knot in my throat made it hard to speak. I tried to apologize, to convince them I was fine, just embarrassed, as they wrapped their arms around me.

You don't have to be fine, Cleo said.

180

Or embarrassed, Sabrina said.

I stood in that tiny bathroom, letting them hold me until the heavy feeling, the unbearable weight of loneliness, eased.

We're here, they promised. And the loneliness never found such a foothold again. No matter what, I'd always have the two of them. At least I used to think that.

After this week, things will change between all of us. They'll have to.

Don't think about it, I tell myself. *Don't go there yet. Be here, on the sidewalk in front of your favorite dive ever.* Sabrina, Parth, Cleo, and Kimmy are already at the front door.

I take one step to follow them, only for my heel to catch in a crack between two cobblestones. Wyn appears at my side, dutifully steadying me by the elbow before I can break my ankle. "Careful," he says in a low murmur. "You're not used to wearing shoes like that."

Anger shoots through me like an emergency flare, the only thing bright and hot enough to be seen through the fog of nostalgia.

"At this point, Wyn," I say, jerking my arm free, "you have no idea what I am or am not used to."

I stalk off through the portholed front doors into the dark bar, a karaoke version of "Love Is a Battlefield" folding around me at full volume. The smell of fried haddock and paprika-dusted potato wedges hangs thick in the air, right alongside the tang of beer and vinegar, and the year-round Christmas lights strung back and forth over the ceiling dust the crowd in every color of glitter.

As I catch up with Cleo, she looks over, the lights accentuating the bits of gold in her eyes and the matching gold undertones in her deep brown skin. Leaning in, she says, "This place never changes, does it?"

"Everything changes eventually," I say, and then, at her odd expression, force a smile and thread my arm through hers. "Remember when the lobster rolls here used to be like six dollars?"

She's not falling for the false cheeriness. A divot forms between her winged brows. "You okay?"

"Hard to breathe in this dress without worrying about the seams splitting," I say, "but otherwise good."

She still looks unconvinced. Cleo's always been able to see through me. When we lived together, I used to watch her paint for hours and think, *How does she always see things so clearly?* She knew what colors to start with and where, and none of it made sense to me until, suddenly, it all looked exactly right.

Wyn brushes past us, swims through the crowd toward the too-small table Sabrina's already claimed at the back of the room. Cleo catches me watching him.

"We had a little argument," I admit, surprised by the relief I feel at sharing this tiny sliver of truth with her.

"You want to talk about it?" she asks. "Let me rephrase that: maybe you should talk about it."

"It's fine," I say. "I don't even know what it was about, really."

"Oh, yeah." Cleo nods. "The *am I hungry/ tired/stressed or are you actually being the worst* fight. I know it well."

I snort. "You and Kimmy don't fight."

She drops her head against my shoulder. "Harriet. I'm a sober introvert homebody, and my girlfriend is a human party bus, complete with flashing lights and spinning dance poles. Of course we fight."

Across the bar, Sabrina waves us over.

"Well, whatever's going on between you and Wyn," Cleo says as we start across the packed bar together, "you'll figure it out. You always do."

My stomach sinks guiltily. "Anyway, how are you? I feel like we haven't had a single second to talk yet."

"I'm good," she says. "Tired. Not used to this schedule. Kim and I usually get up between four thirty and five."

"Excuse me," I say. "That just brought my hangover back."

She laughs. "It's not that bad. I actually mostly love it. I love being up before anyone else and seeing the sunrise every day, being outside with the vegetables and the sunshine."

"Sometimes I still can't believe you're a farmer," I say. "I mean, it's so cool, don't get me wrong. I just really did think you'd have art in the Met someday."

She shrugs. "It could still happen. Life's long."

That makes me snort with laughter. "I don't think anyone says that."

"Maybe not," she says, "but if they were truly present, maybe they would."

"So wise," I say. "So deep."

"Read it on the inside of a Dove chocolate wrapper," she jokes. "What about you, Har? How's the residency?"

"Good!" I know I've said it too brightly from the way her brow lifts. I forge ahead anyway, with the spiel I give my parents every time we talk. "It's busy. Long hours and a lot of work that has nothing to do

184

with surgery. But the other interns are nice, and one of the fifth-years has kind of taken me under her wing. It could be a lot worse. I mean, I'm helping people."

Thinking of the hospital always floods my body with adrenaline as if I'm there, scrubbed in, someone's skull open on a table in front of me.

Happy place, I remind myself. *That's where you are. The Lobster Hut. Knott's Harbor.*

"I always knew our girl was going to save the world," Cleo says. "I'm so proud of you, Harry. We all are."

I glance away, chest cramping. "Same goes for you," I say. "A whole-ass farm."

"And we maxed out our CSA." She clarifies, "The crop-sharing subscription we do for locals? We officially can't grow enough for everyone who wants in."

"In three years!" I cry. "You're incredible."

"And to think," she says, "a mere decade ago, we were dancing on these tables to that one MGMT song that played every fifteen minutes."

"You," I say, *"never* danced on those tables. I distinctly remember Sabrina commanding us to get up on them, and you calmly saying, *No thanks.*"

Cleo laughs. "There is nothing my parents

185

drilled into me like good boundaries."

"God, that must be terrible," I say. "Miles and Deandra must lie awake every night, in their matching houses, wishing they could do it all over again."

"Oh, I'm sure," she agrees. "It probably kills them, knowing how many baby showers I've had to miss, simply because I had no interest in going to them."

"Brave," I say. "I spent my last day off at my new hairdresser's daughter's bat mitzvah, so I don't relate."

"Oh, Harry," she says, wincing. "You deserve to honor yourself."

"Well, I toasted myself at the bat mitzvah," I say.

She grins, but her brow remains lifted skeptically. I don't think she's ever totally understood why I find it easier to fulfill other people's expectations than to set my own.

Underneath her tiny frame and button nose, Cleo's always had a spine of steel. Back in college, she could drink the better part of a bottle of Tanqueray, and you still wouldn't convince her to do anything stupider than continuing an in-depth conversation about nihilism with a wasted field hockey player.

And then one day, she decided she didn't

like how she felt when she drank, so she just stopped. It was the same way when she changed her mind about going to an MFA program and announced she found a job on an urban farm instead.

When Cleo knows her mind, she knows her mind.

As we reach the table, I ask Sabrina, "Did you know Cleo and Kimmy's co-op maxed out?"

"I did," she says. "Not that I've been able to see it in action."

Cleo slides onto a chair beside Kimmy. "We'll find a time this winter."

"You name the date," Sabrina replies, almost like a challenge.

"We live too close to each other to go this long without hanging out," Parth puts in. Cleo doesn't reply, and Kimmy casts her a quick sidelong look, the kind of temperature check that passes between two people who know each other inside and out. Cleo's getting irritated.

"Remember coming here with Kimmy for the first time?" I pipe up.

Cleo lifts her girlfriend's hand to kiss the back of it.

"That's right," Sabrina says. "This is where we fell in love with you, Kimberly."

"To be clear," Cleo tells Kimmy, "*I* was in

love with you well before that."

"Awwh! You guys!" Kimmy *instantly* tears up. "You've always made me feel like I belong."

"Of *course* you belong," I say.

"You were our missing link." Parth settles into the chair beside Sabrina's. "We needed a redhead to round us out."

"Keep your eye on those blue-haired ladies, by the way," Sabrina says, looking toward the women nursing sodas at the next table over. "When they go, we'll grab one of their chairs."

"I'm fine to stand," Wyn says, pulling the final available chair out for me. He meets my eyes. "Go ahead, honey. Give yourself a break from those heels."

I wonder if my fake smile is doing anything to soften my very real glare.

"Well, *someone* sit," Parth says. "You're making me nervous."

"You know what?" I touch Wyn's bicep. "I'll sit in your lap."

He balks, and I push him toward the chair. With the air of one resigned to his grisly fate, Wyn sinks into it, and I drape myself across his thighs like a living toga.

His arm comes around my back, a highly impersonal touch, but it's all it takes for my body to remember, replay, relive that moment in the cellar.

A server stops by, and Sabrina puts in an order for a pitcher of margaritas, a truckload of fries, and Cleo's usual soda with lime.

"Could I get one of those as well?" I call as he's walking away. As badly as I want some alcohol to disrupt the electrical impulses firing through my neurons, I need to stay clearheaded.

The memory of Wyn's velvety murmur: *Arms up, baby.*

My drunken warble: *Did you get me the shirt about the rodeos?*

My spine prickles. The backs of my thighs warm.

The crowd is roaring along to Shania Twain now, a bachelorette party tipsily leading the charge from the karaoke stage at the back wall.

Before Kimmy, Cleo mostly dated ultra-hip people who were completely uninterested in hanging out with us. Laura, who rode a motorcycle and had the bridge of her nose pierced. Giselle, who always wore red lipstick and never laughed. Trace, who joined a punk band that got huge, and then dumped Cleo for the famous model daughter of another famous model.

Then Cleo met Kimmy, a gorgeous and affectionate goofball who never stopped

189

laughing, while working on an organic farm in Quebec.

The first time she came on the trip, Kimmy, Sabrina, and I smoked the best joint of our lives in the Lobster Hut bathroom, then performed "Goodbye Earl" together.

From the beginning, she *belonged.* With Cleo. With us.

An uneasiness needles between my ribs. Again, I find myself wondering what *we'll* be, exactly, after this week, when the trip is over and the cottage is sold. When Wyn and I come clean.

Sabrina has started filling salt-rimmed glasses from the margarita pitcher, and I fight the urge to throw one back. Instead, I lean across the table to grab one of the sodas the server dropped off and, in so doing, inadvertently shove my ass back into Wyn's crotch.

Wyn shifts uncomfortably. What did he call it? Vindictive grinding?

I drain my soda like it's my last shot of moonshine before an 1800s doctor pries a bullet from my arm, and then lean forward exaggeratedly again to return my glass to the table.

While the others are busy pouring their drinks, Wyn drops his lips beside my ear.

"Can we step outside for a minute?" he asks stiffly. "I need to speak with you."

So did I, I think. *Five months ago.*

It's too late to talk. It's too late for him to ask if I'm happy, or how my residency's going, or whether I'm dating the man he pinned our breakup on. I didn't sign up for that. I signed up to play this game, and now I'm going to play it.

I sift my hand through his hair, winding the ends around my knuckles. "Don't you just *love* Wyn's hair like this?" I shout to the others over the music.

Over the sweating lip of his margarita glass, Parth says, "He looks like he's the tormented leader of a motorcycle gang."

Wyn clenches my hips, a warning that I'm playing with fire. "Just haven't had time to cut it, *honey.*"

"I think it looks great, Wynnie," Kimmy says. "And the beard."

"I'm going to shave that too," he says.

I turn into him with an exaggerated pout, slinging an arm around his neck. "But I like it."

The skin above his collar prickles, and our gazes lock in a game of chicken, his hand sliding across my stomach, his palm almost preternaturally warm.

On a laugh, Parth says, "Hey, remember

191

when we swore this would never become a couples' trip?"

Sabrina takes a sip. "Pretty sure you were the only one who cared."

"Pretty sure you only said it because you didn't want Sabrina to bring her boyfriend," Cleo puts in.

"That was just an added bonus," Parth says. "The main thing was, I wanted to stay young forever. Couples' trips seemed like such an old-person thing. My parents would go to Florida with my aunties and uncles all the time, and then they'd make us look through one hundred separate pictures of them inside a Margaritaville."

As long as I've known him, Parth's been morally opposed to chain restaurants. Probably because, like me, he grew up in the suburban Midwest and those were the only offerings at hand. Personally, I find chains comforting. You know exactly what to expect, no huge surprises. Chain restaurants are the *Murder, She Wrote* reruns of the food industry.

Wyn leans past me to plop his half-downed margarita onto the table. "You'll have to excuse us," he says, hoisting me out of his lap. "This is Harriet's and my song."

I'm sure I look baffled. Our friends certainly do.

He gives me no chance to argue, just grabs my hand and pulls me into the crowd, Sabrina's voice trailing after us, "How the fuck is Vitamin C's 'Graduation' their song?"

13
REAL LIFE

Tuesday

We settle on the dance floor, in front of the stage. Stiffly, I ring my arms around his neck and let him draw me in close, partly because Cleo's watching us and partly because at least this way, I don't have to look at his face.

"You're playing dirty," I say.

"Me?" he replies. "You just gave me a lap dance."

"I did not," I say, "and I will never."

"Doesn't Wyn's hair look sexy like this?" he parrots in a breathy voice.

"I didn't say *sexy*. When did I say *sexy*?"

"You did the voice. I knew what you meant."

I roll my eyes. "I'm playing my part."

"What part is that? Marilyn Monroe singing 'Happy birthday, Mr. President'?"

"The part where I'm supposed to be in love with you," I say.

He stiffens slightly. "Yeah, well, maybe you don't remember this all that well, but back when you *were* in love with me, you didn't often straddle me in public."

"Well, considering I haven't straddled you tonight either," I say, "one can only assume you're employing reverse psychology right now. Sorry, Wyn. It's not going to happen."

He scoffs but has no comeback.

We angrily sway to the music for a few more seconds.

"We're really not going to talk about what happened in the cellar?" he says.

"Nothing happened in the cellar," I remind him.

"So you don't have any thoughts about what *almost* happened."

Something he said a long time ago pops into my mind. "Tumbleweeds," I say. "Rolling through my brain."

He shakes his head once, the side of his mouth brushing my temple.

"Graduation" has ended. Someone's singing "Wicked Game" now, someone who can actually sing. Not as well as Chris Isaak, but well enough to make the song appropriately devastating and inappropriately sexy. It's the kind of auditory hard-right turn common to karaoke nights but *less than ideal* for these specific circumstances.

195

Kimmy and Cleo have moved onto the dance floor, only a few feet away from us. Wyn takes the opportunity to twirl me; I take the opportunity to get a deep breath of air that smells a *little* less like his heady mix of pine and clove. Then he brings me back closer, stomach to stomach and chest to chest, so he can murmur in my ear: "So. The heels, the dress, the Etsy-spell face, the new appreciation for facial hair — any other big changes I should be aware of?"

My fingers catch the ends of his hair, and once again, goose bumps rise up along his top few vertebrae. I thrill at having the power to stir at least *some* reaction in him. He might've shaken me up in the cellar — and his life may be *so much better* without me in it — but that doesn't mean he's any more immune to this thing between us than I am.

"The coffee-table book," I say evenly. "The beard, the hair, the constant texting. Anything else *I* should know?"

As soon as I say it, I want to take it back. I know how quickly he scrubbed me out of his life; I don't want to know how fast he got the shrapnel out of his heart.

His gaze darkens, prying into mine, searching for the answer to some unspoken question. His grip on my waist loosens, his palms gliding down a few inches to settle on my hips. His lips press together. "I guess not," he says.

When the song ends, we stay locked together for a few seconds, unspeaking, unmoving. Finally, we let go.

When we get back to the table, Sabrina has claimed another chair. Before I can take it, Wyn sits and hauls me across his lap without hesitation.

The message is clear: if I keep upping the ante, he'll keep matching the bet.

I'm in no mood to fold. I press myself against his chest and let my fingers find their way back into his silky hair.

He responds by sliding one hand up the outside of my thigh, the heat of his palm burning through the red chiffon. My pulse seems to drop straight down between my thighs. He nuzzles into the side of my neck, not quite kissing me but letting his lips drag over the sensitive skin on a slow inhale and exhale.

"Could I get a glass of white wine?" I yelp as our server appears with the six orders of fries Sabrina put in.

"Sure thing," he says, mostly avoiding looking at my and Wyn's ridiculous display

197

before turning to scurry back toward the bar.

When he brings the wine back, I drink it in one go, because now slowing my brain down seems like the better of two fairly terrible options.

"You all right there, Harriet?" Wyn asks in his own husky equivalent of the happy-birthday-Mr.-President voice.

I turn back toward him, leaning in until his firm chest meets mine and our mouths are close. My arms lock tight across the back of his neck, and his gaze slinks down me and back up, the muscles in his jaw flexing.

His deep breath presses us closer, his pulse thrumming against my breast. His hands move to my hips, adjusting me in his lap.

Drunk on the power, plus five months of repressed anger, plus one glass of wine, I lean even further into him, feeling my nipples pinch between us as I lower my mouth, like he did, to the spot beneath his ear. "Never better," I say. His fingers unconsciously tighten against my hips, glide down the sides of my thighs until they pass the chiffon and reach bare skin.

We may be playing our parts, but that's not all this is. I can feel him stiffening beneath me. It makes every soft place on my body feel like magma: incendiary, volatile. But I'm not going to be the one to back down.

"Dartboard's open," Sabrina says from the far side of the table. "Anyone want to play?"

"I'm in," Kimmy chirps, jumping up.

I hold Wyn's gaze, waiting for him to break. Finally he flicks a look toward Sabrina. "Maybe later." His eyes come back to mine, hard and steely. "I'm pretty comfortable right now."

Sabrina beats four locals, plus Kimmy, at a game of darts, and Parth and Cleo get into a long conversation with the bachelorette party about gerrymandering and how Parth's organization works to fight it.

The bachelorette partygoers are impressively accepting of the turn their night of debauchery has taken. No one knows how to hold court quite like Parth Nayak. Plus, Sabrina keeps having shots of Fireball sent over.

By the end of the night, both she *and* Parth have exchanged literal, physical business cards (Who knew they even had these? Not me.) with a couple of people in the party, and Cleo, Wyn, and I have to basically mop the two of them and Kimmy out

199

of the Lobster Hut and into the cab.

Still, Parth finds the wherewithal to play his traditional end-of-the-night soundtrack, the eerily beautiful Julee Cruise song from the opening of *Twin Peaks.*

In the back seat, Sabrina slumps against me, half asleep, a domino effect that forces me into Wyn's chest. He holds on to my knee, and I wonder whether it's his pulse or mine thundering between us.

Back at the cottage, the sober among us herd the others into the kitchen and ply them with water. Upstairs we hug each other good night, and then, with my heart clanging wildly in my throat, I trail Wyn into the bedroom. I'm suddenly too nervous to close the door and be truly alone with him.

He reaches over my shoulder and shuts it himself. His hand stays there, to the left of my head.

There's a foot of space between us, but it feels like friction. Like straddling him in a dark alcove under the stairs. Like draping myself across his lap in a crowded bar.

His eyes move back and forth over my face, and his tongue sweeps absently across his bottom lip. In a rasp, he asks, "Are we done yet?"

I lift my chin. "I don't know what you're talking about."

Somehow we've gotten closer. The corner of his mouth hitches, but his eyes stay dark, focused. His breath feathers over my mouth. One more strong inhale, from him or me, would close the gap. "Why are you punishing me?"

I try for an angry laugh. It doesn't come. He looks too earnest, too lost, like he's desperately trying to understand.

Like he can't fathom that all my love for him didn't just vanish, the way his did for me. That it had to go *somewhere,* and funneling it into anger is how I've managed to make it through these last two days.

It makes me feel alone. It makes me feel defeated.

He swallows. "Can't we . . . call a truce?" he asks. "Be friends for the next few days?"

Friends. The irony, the sterility of the word, stings. It's pouring alcohol over my wounded heart. But I can't quite grasp on to my anger.

"Fine," I say. "Truce."

Wyn's hand slides clear of the door. He steps back and, after a moment, nods. "You take the bed."

I can't help but think he doesn't look any happier than I feel.

14
HAPPY PLACE

Morningside Heights, New York City

A four-bedroom apartment that the five of us can barely afford. One full bathroom, with a rigid shower schedule (organized by Sabrina), and a half bathroom we call the "emergency can" because there's nothing but a toilet and a lightbulb with a chain in it, and it's creepy as hell.

Original hardwood floors that bow in the middle, tired of holding up grad students' thrift store furniture for generations. Windows that get stuck for days at a time and must simply be left, tried again later. When it's hot or when it's raining, the smell of cigarettes past seeps faintly out of the walls, reminding us that we're passing through, that this building has stood here since long before we came to this city, and will be here long after we leave.

After Wyn's and my first kiss, in the cellar over the summer, I'd expected that to be it:

our curiosity satisfied, our crush squashed. Instead, the moment the door to our shared room at the cottage closed, he'd lifted me against him, kissed me like only seconds had passed.

Still, we took it slow that first night, kissing for hours before finally taking off each other's clothes. *Are you sure,* he'd whispered, and I was.

Will we still be friends after this, I'd whispered, and he'd smiled as he told me, *You've never been just a friend to me.*

He'd laid me gently in his twin bed, and when the creak of the bed frame threatened to give us away, we moved to the floor, hands tangling, and whispered into each other's mouths and hands and throats, trying not to call out each other's names to the dark.

Every night after had been the same. We were friendly until the door closed, and then we were something else entirely.

Still, when we moved into the new place with the others — so I could start medical school, and Sabrina could begin 1L at Columbia Law, and Cleo could take up her post at an urban farm in Brooklyn — I expected this delicate thing to fizzle.

Instead, it heightens. When everyone's around, we find seconds of privacy, steal brushes of each other's shoulders and hips, the bare skin just beneath our shirts. And when we're alone, the minute the front door snicks shut, he tugs me into his closet-sized room — since I share one with Cleo — and for a few minutes, we don't have to be quiet. I tell him what I want. He tells me how it feels. And this thing between us isn't a secret.

Though maybe the secret is what makes it fun for him.

One night, while everyone else is out, we lie in his bed, his hand tugging at each of my curls in turn. "If we aren't friends," I ask, "what is this?"

He studies me through the dark, smoothing my hair back from my forehead so tenderly. "I don't know. I just need more of it."

He kisses me again, slow and languid, like for once we have all the time in the world. He pulls me on top of him, his hands soft on my waist, our eyes holding. Our breaths rise and break together, our hands knotting against his headboard as he murmurs into my mouth, "Harriet, *finally*."

Finally. The word pumps through my veins: *Finally. You. Finally.*

I'm on the verge of crying, and I'm not sure why, except that this is so intense. So different than it's ever been.

"I changed my mind," he tells me. "I think you're my best friend."

I laugh against his cheek. "Better than Parth?"

"Oh, much better," he teases. "After tonight, he can't compete."

"I think you should know," I say, "Cleo and Sabrina are my best friends. But you're my favorite man I've ever met."

He turns his smile in to kiss the inside of my elbow. "I can live with that."

We don't talk about what it means or how it will end, but we talk about everything else, text all day, every day, even from the same room.

He sends pictures of the new mystery releases during his shifts at Freeman's to see if I want them. Or samples of fabric from the upscale reupholstery job he goes to *after* his bookstore shifts, especially the more abstract textiles that inevitably look extremely and only like vaginas or penises.

I fire back illustrations from the medical journals I'm poring over, or give the textiles informal diagnoses, or send screenshots of Google image searches for cowboys and ask him, *Are any of these your relatives?* to which he always has an answer, like, *Only the one with all the gold teeth. When he dies,*

I'm actually going to inherit those.

When he goes to Montana to visit his family, he comes back with a stack of ten-cent Goodwill paperbacks for me: *She'll Be Dying Around the Mountain, Purple Mountain Tragedy, Big Rock Candy Murder,* and *Cowboy Stake Me Away,* the last of which is actually about vampires and was misshelved.

When he stops by Trader Joe's on his way home from work, he brings me cartons of ice cream, Maine blueberry or Vermont maple.

So much of life is waiting for more of him, and even that torture is bliss.

One night, after months of sneaking around, while everyone is home, he offers me a spare movie ticket — a work friend of his canceled — and we leave the apartment together. Outside, he takes my hand and holds it tightly, his pulse tapping into my palm: *you, you, you.*

I ask what movie we're seeing. "There is no movie," he says. "I just wanted to take you on a date."

Date, I think. *That's new.* I hadn't even known to want a date with Wyn Connor, but now that it's been spoken, I feel a kind of breathless happy-sad. Like I'm missing this night before it's even begun. Every time he offers me more of him, it gets harder not to have it all.

We traipse around Little Italy for hours, stuffing ourselves with cannoli and gelato and cappuccinos — or rather I stuff *myself* while he tries bites. He's not big on sweets.

He tells me he didn't grow up eating them, that the Connors were a "meat, potatoes, and Miracle Whip family," and then he says, "Did you always love sugar this much?"

"Always," I say. "And you just did that thing again."

"What thing?"

"The thing where you give me the tiniest kernel of Wyn, then turn things back to me."

He rubs the back of his head, frowning.

I ask, "Why don't you like talking about yourself?"

He says, "Remember when you told me you thought you were slow-release hot?"

"I finally stopped falling asleep to that humiliating memory one month ago," I tell him, "and now I have to start all over."

He pulls me closer, hooks his arm around my shoulder as we make our way down the frosty, light-strewn sidewalk. After several seconds, he says, "I think I'm slow-release boring."

"What are you talking about?"

He shrugs one shoulder. "I don't know."

207

I wrap my arms around his waist, beneath his coat. "Tell me," I say. "Please."

He hesitates. "It's just," he says, "I'm the kind of guy people are always more interested in *before* they get to know me."

"Says *who*," I ask.

"Take your pick, Harriet."

My brow knits. He laughs, but it's shallow.

"I've had like ten years to come to terms with this," he says. "People are interested right up front, but it never lasts. I told you I don't date friends, and that's why. Because once I get together with someone, really let them in, the novelty wears off fast. It's been that way since high school, when girls would come from out of town for the summer, and it's still that way. I'm not all that interesting."

"Stop," I say. "That's bullshit, and you know it."

"It's not," he says. "Even with Alison. I thought it would work with her, I really did. I figured I'd been going for the wrong people, so I went for someone more like me, who didn't have all these huge aspirations, so she wouldn't get bored so fast. Then she broke up with me for her yoga teacher. Said they connected on a deeper level than I was capable of. I'm . . . I don't know. Simple?"

He sounds self-conscious. My chest aches, like I feel the little sore spot in him, the thorn deep in between layers of muscle. I'd do anything to get it out.

I grab the lapels of his coat and look up into his face. "First of all," I say, "simple isn't bad. Second of all, simple isn't stupid, and you're *not* stupid, and I don't know why you're always trying to convince yourself you are, but it really is bullshit, Wyn. And lastly, you're the opposite of slow-release boring. I like you so much more than when we first met. Partly because you actually answer my questions now, instead of turning everything around to flirt."

His brow lifts. "And what's the other part?"

"Everything," I say.

He laughs. "Everything?"

"Yes, Wyn," I say. "I like your body and your face and your hair and your skin, and I like how you're always warmer than me, and how you never sit still except when you're really trying to concentrate on what someone's saying, and I like how you always fix things without being asked. You're the only one of us who will actually take out the trash before it's spilling over. And every time you're doing *anything* — going to the store or doing laundry or making yourself breakfast — you'll always ask if anyone else needs anything, and I like how I know when you're about to text me from the other side of the room because you make this really specific face."

He laughs against my cheek. I wish I could swallow the sound, that it would put down roots in my stomach and grow through me like a seed.

He says, "The *I want to go down on you* face?"

I hug him closer as we pause at a **DO NOT WALK** sign. "I didn't have a name for it until now."

The light changes, but instead of crossing, he draws me around the corner into an alleyway and kisses me against a brick wall until I lose track of time, of *space*. We become the only two people in the world.

Until a group of fratty drunk guys hollers at us from the street, and even then we don't stop kissing, our smiles colliding, our hands twisted in each other's clothes.

When we draw apart, he rests his brow against mine, breathing hard in the cold. "I think I love you, Harriet," he says.

Love, I think. *That's new.* And I'll never be happy without it again.

Without any forethought, any worry, I tell him the truth. "I know I love you, Wyn."

He touches my chin, his hand shaking a little, and slides his nose down along mine. "I love you so much, Harriet."

At home, we gather our friends at the dining room table Wyn rebuilt from scraps for us, all our favorite people looking various degrees of terrified to hear what we have to say. Wyn and I terrified for them to hear it.

"We're together," Wyn says, and when no one reacts, he adds, *"Together.* Harriet and I."

Sabrina runs to the fridge like she's planning to vomit in it, only when she throws the door shut, she's holding a bottle of prosecco, then grabbing mismatched coupes from the shelf over the stove. And Parth is on his feet, pulling Wyn into a hug, then squeezing me tight next, lifting me off the ground. He shakes me back and forth before setting me back down. "About time our boy finally told you how he felt."

Sabrina pops the cork and starts filling glasses. "You know that now that you're *finally* together, you can't *ever* break up, right?"

"Don't put that kind of pressure on them," Cleo says.

"The pressure's on whether we admit it or not," Sabrina says. "If they break up, this" — she waves the bottle between us —

"implodes."

"Lots of people stay friends if they break up," Cleo says, then quickly to me, "not that you're going to break up!"

"I'm with Sabrina on this one," Parth says.

She holds the bottle up as she tries to cup a hand around her ear. "What's that? Is that just global warming I'm feeling, or has hell frozen over and Parth is actually *agreeing* with me on something?"

"I'm agreeing with you," Parth says, "because this time, you're right. It was bound to happen eventually."

She rolls her eyes, goes back to filling glasses.

"Harry, I'm serious," Parth says, setting his hands on my shoulders. "Don't you dare break my delicate angel's heart."

Sabrina snorts. "Oh, come on. *Wyn* better not break *her* heart."

Cleo says, "There's no need for all this pressure."

"He would never in a million years hurt her," Parth says to Sabrina, passing Wyn and me each a glass of champagne. Just like that, they're back to their old squabbling selves.

"And she's been secretly obsessed with him for years," Sabrina argues.

"Speaking of unspoken sexual tension,"

Wyn grumbles, waving his glass in their direction. "You two want us to leave you alone for this argument, or can we be done now?"

"Ew!" Sabrina says.

Parth pulls a face. "Thank you, Sabrina."

"I'm not saying *you're* gross," she says. "I'm saying the idea of *us* is gross. Can you imagine? And also, the last thing this friend group needs is *another* romantic entanglement. We're already playing with fire here, and I really, really cannot lose this. This" — she waves the bottle between us again — "is my family."

It's mine too, but I'm not worried. I already know: I will love Wyn Connor until I die.

That night, for the first time, I sleep in Wyn's room. We lie awake late, with the sheets kicked off us, our sweat drying, and he plays with my hair.

"It's always a complete mystery to me," he murmurs, "what you're thinking."

"I'll help you out," I say. "Eighty percent of it is picturing you naked."

He kisses my sticky forehead. "I'm serious."

"I am too," I say.

"You're a mystery to me, Harriet Kilpatrick."

My smile falters. "I'm a mystery to me too," I say. "I didn't realize how little I understood myself until I met Cleo and Sabrina. They're both so sure of how they feel about things."

He pulls another curl straight, and the gentle tug sends a current down my center. "Well, we should get to know you," he says.

"I wouldn't know where to start."

"Something small," he says.

"Like what?"

He smiles unevenly. "Like why do you love cozy mysteries?"

I shrug. "I don't know. They're so . . . mild."

His kiss against the side of my head melts into a laugh. "Mild?"

"The worst thing that can happen to a person happens, right at the start of the story," I explain. "And it's like . . . this feeling of safety. You know exactly what's going to happen by the end. So many things are unpredictable in life. I like things you can trust."

He frowns, his golden hair mussed up off his forehead. I'm suddenly sure I've found the one unacceptable answer to his question, the one that makes him realize I am not the cool, sexy, mysterious woman he has confused me with.

His teeth scrape over the fullest part of his lip. "You can trust me, Harriet."

In that moment, he pierces a little deeper into my heart, opens another door, finds an entire walled-off room I didn't realize was there.

He pulls me into his chest, and our heartbeats sync. I've never felt so certain of anything, so right, so safe.

15
REAL LIFE

Wednesday

Someone is jackhammering inside my skull.

I roll over, press my face into the downy mattress.

THUNK-THUNK-THUNK.

A voice breaks the bodiless dark: "Everybody decent?"

My eyes snap open on a bedroom washed in the dim gray of morning. The smell of wet stone and brine wafts in from the open window, and rain pummels the roof.

"I'm coming in!"

Sabrina. She's calling through the door.

My eyes zigzag around the room, my scrambled egg of a brain piecing together my surroundings. I'm sprawled in the middle of a king-sized bed, wearing only my underwear and *Virgin Who CAN Drive* T-shirt.

"In three . . ." Sabrina says.

My gaze finds the jumble of spare sheets

216

on the floor, the golden-brown leg extending beyond it, the arm tucked under the mess of sun-streaked golden hair.

"Two . . ."

I hurl a pillow at Wyn's face, and he jolts upright.

"One," Sabrina says. "That's it. I'm coming in. Cover up your" — I wave frantically at Wyn — "goods if you don't want me to see them."

His gaze clears, widens. He gathers the bundle of bedding around him and launches himself onto the bed, a trail of sheets spilling out behind him.

"Good morning," Sabrina says, swinging the door open.

"What's going on?" I jerk the blankets up over Wyn's lap and mine.

Sabrina's mouth curves when she notices the bedding half draped on the bed and half bunched on the floor, as if carelessly thrown there in a moment of passion.

"Breakfast was supposed to be twenty minutes ago," she says. "Didn't anyone read their itineraries?"

"Our *novelty* itineraries?" Wyn says. "For the rough schedule we *always* keep?"

Parth's head pops into the doorway, still damp from a shower. "Come on. We've got a schedule to keep."

Wyn pushes his hair off his forehead. "Are you two on steroids?"

"Back-alley Adderall?" I guess.

"Cocaine," Wyn says.

"Pixy Stix and Robitussin."

"Up, up, up." Sabrina punctuates her words with impatient claps that I feel behind my eyeballs.

"Is it possible to be hungover on one glass of wine?" I grumble.

"Once you hit thirty, anything's possible," Parth calls, and the swell that carried the two of them in takes them right back out.

Wyn exhales, his shoulders relaxing.

The folds in the blankets and pillowcase left little indentations all over his stomach and face. As he stands and ambles toward the bathroom, rubbing his hands over his face, I catch myself studying them like there's going to be a test later. He looks over his shoulder at me, his voice gruff: "You want to shower?"

Any remaining haze of sleep zooms off me, cartoon-roadrunner style. "Shower?"

He looks puzzled, possibly by the sudden lack of blood in my face. "Do you need the shower, or can I use it?"

Right. As in, *Do you want to shower by yourself.* Not *Do you want to take a shower together.* Obviously.

"I'm good!" I squeak. "Give me a minute to get my stuff and get out of here."

He laughs as he leans into the shower, the water sputtering on. "It's nothing you haven't seen before, Harriet."

I slide off the bed and start digging through my suitcase for a pair of jeans.

"I mean, aside from the new tattoo," he says.

I turn around before I can tease out the obvious jest in his voice. He's starting to pull off his shorts, and I yelp and spin back to my suitcase.

"You could wait thirty seconds to start your stripping," I say.

Another gravelly, fresh-from-sleep laugh. "If it bothers you so much, close your eyes."

I step into my jeans and hop to get them over my butt. He still hasn't turned the fan on, and the steam is building behind me. I can imagine how it's making the ends of his hair curl.

"What if I close *my* eyes?" he says.

"How would *that* help?" I grab a fresh T-shirt.

"I don't know. Maybe it would make you . . ."

He trails off as I shuck my sleep shirt off and toss it onto the bed. I hold the fresh T-shirt against my chest and look over my shoulder at him. "Make me what?"

Wyn clears his throat and turns back to the shower. "Feel like I'm not here."

"Not necessary." I pull my shirt over my head. "I think I'm done here."

He doesn't turn around again until I'm out of the room.

In the hallway, a groan of "Haaaarrryyy" reaches me, and I backtrack to peer through the open door to the kids' room.

Cleo and Kimmy lie in the pushed-together twin beds in the center of the room, the same way Wyn and I used to. While Cleo looks tidy and well rested, her braids tucked in a russet-colored bonnet and her skin luminous, Kimmy is starfished out beside her, freckled limbs strewn in every direction, last night's sparkly eyeliner smeared and her hair in a nest atop her head. At least she remembered to take out her contacts, I guess, because she's wearing her dark-framed glasses.

"Saaaaave us," Kimmy moans.

"You," Cleo gently corrects her. "I feel great."

"Save meeeee," Kimmy amends.

Cleo pats the sliver of space between them, and I flop into it like they're my parents and it's Christmas morning.

I mean, not *my* parents. I had one of those

220

upbringings where my parents' bedroom was treated like an FBI safe house: don't go in it, don't look at it, don't even speak of it. Probably because it was the only room in the house that was allowed to accumulate mess (if clean laundry in the process of being folded can be considered mess), and I'm pretty sure if given only the two options, Mom would rather join the witness protection program than let anyone see our laundry.

Wyn's family was different. When he and Lou and Michael were small, the Connors had a rule that they couldn't start Christmas morning before the sun was up. So Wyn and his sisters would sit in front of the tinseled tree waiting until the *minute* the sun rose, then run into Gloria and Hank's room and pile onto their bed, shrieking until they got up.

Thinking about Gloria and Hank always gives me a *homesick* ache, or something like it. I used to feel that pang a lot as a kid, which never made sense, because I mostly felt it at home.

"I'm hiring a hit man to take out Sabrina for buying that last round of Fireball last night," Kimmy says, flinging her forearm over her face. "Feel free to Venmo me your contribution."

"I was starting to doubt you were capable of being hungover," I say.

"It's all the half drinks," Cleo says. "She tries to drink less that way, and then loses track."

"I didn't lose track. I smeared." She holds her arm out to reveal a row of lipstick tallies that run together.

"Ah," Cleo says, fighting a smile. "My mistake."

"I need nine more hours of sleep," Kimmy grumbles.

"Aren't you two hippie farmers used to getting up way earlier than . . ." I lean over Cleo to see the clock on her bedside table. It's unplugged and on the ground a yard away, as if ripped from the wall and thrown there. "Whatever time it is."

"And do you know what time we usually go to bed on those nights before our early mornings?" Cleo says. "Nine. And I'm not saying we get into bed at nine. I'm saying we're fully unconscious by then. Deep REM sleep."

"I didn't notice REM anywhere on this week's schedule," I say.

"Oh my god." Kimmy lurches upright so fast I expect her to vomit over the side of the bed. Instead, she turns an expression of horror on us. "Did I . . . do the worm on a

222

table last night?"

Cleo and I both burst into laughter.

"No," I say. "You did not."

"But you certainly *thought* you did," Cleo adds.

Kimmy gasps in mock offense. Cleo sits up and leans over me to kiss her. "Babe, I love you too much to ever lie to you," she says. "You could not do the worm if *my* life depended on it. Some of your other moves weren't too shabby, though."

"HEY," Sabrina screams from downstairs. "GET. YOUR. BODIES. DOWN. HERE. OR. ELSE."

"Hit man," Kimmy grumbles.

Cleo pops up onto her feet, balanced in a wide second position on either side of the bed frame. "Babe, who am I?" She presses her hands to her knees and gyrates nonsensically.

"Okay, if I looked that good," Kimmy says, "I feel a lot better."

From somewhere beneath us — perhaps deep in the bowels of the earth — an air horn blasts.

Normally when we eat at Bernadette's, we take advantage of the outdoor patio, with its gorgeous view of the harbor and its wide variety of rude, fry-stealing seabirds, even if the temperature requires us to be bundled in fleeces.

But by the time we get downtown to the red-shingled greasy spoon, the storm has blown back in. In the span of our run from the car to the front doors, we get soaked. We score a table at the back, where the windows look out on the faded gray patio, the striped umbrellas shut tight and wobbling in the wind, lightning streaking down to touch the waves in the distance.

Bernie's is packed with summer visitors like us, here for the Lobster Festival's grand opening tonight, and the locals having their morning cups of coffee and reading the *Knott's Harbor Register* while tolerating the people "from away," as they call us.

At the counter, I spot my seatmate from the flight over and wave. He harrumphs and looks back to his newspaper.

"Friend of yours?" Wyn murmurs against my ear as everyone's peeling off their drenched outermost layers. His cool breath against my damp skin makes me shiver.

I drop into my chair and look up at him. "That would depend on which of us you asked."

"What," Wyn says, "has he been bugging you to define the relationship?"

"Other way around," I say. "I'm head over

heels, but he's married to the sea."

"Ah, well, it happens," Wyn says.

The eye contact goes on a fraction of a second too long, then Wyn's phone buzzes, and his brow furrows as he checks it. "I'll be back in a minute," he announces and slides away. I watch him back by the host stand, phone to his ear, his face brightening on a laugh.

The expression makes my heart feel like it's blooming and then withering just as fast. It always surprised me, how quickly the ratio of his face could change. In a second, he can go from that broody, tender look to almost boyish delight. Every time his expression changed, I used to think the new one was my favorite. Until it changed again and I had to accept that whichever Wyn was directly in front of me, that was the one I loved most.

The server comes up to take our order, bringing with her a wave of maple syrup, coffee, and pine — Bernie's signature scent. If I could walk around smelling like this restaurant for all time, I would.

I would also have to start wearing a fanny pack stuffed with blueberry pancakes, though, and that could make things awkward at the hospital. People get all up in arms if their surgeon has a partially zipped knapsack of food strung around their waist.

Sabrina puts in our usual drink order. Coffee for everyone but Cleo, who gets a decaf, plus a cup of ice to mellow out Bernie's famously (dangerously) hot and strong brew. "We should go ahead and order food too," Parth says, and when the server gets to me, I order my pancakes along with Wyn's usual, the egg white omelet with sriracha.

"Gloria?" I ask when he gets back to the table and wriggles out of his canvas jacket.

He looks vaguely surprised, like he'd forgotten I was even here. "Ah, no," he recovers, avoiding my gaze. "Work thing."

Wyn's not a liar, but the way he said it feels distinctly like a dodge.

Cleo pushes back from her vegan hash, groaning as she massages her stomach. "I'm having some kind of Pavlovian response to this place. Three bites into this meal, and I feel the ghost of all my past hangovers."

Parth says, "I feel it too."

"Yeah, but you, Kimmy, and I *also* drank shots of something that was on fire last night," Sabrina reminds him. "Don't think blaming Bernie is appropriate here."

I swallow my laugh, which somehow makes it louder, and Parth spins toward me and thwacks me, hard, between my shoulder blades.

"What the hell, Parth!" I cry.

"You were choking!" he says.

"I was not," I say.

"Okay, well, I'm not the doctor here, so."

"And is WebMD now telling people that if someone's choking the best thing to do is punch them in the back of the head?" Wyn says.

"It wasn't the back of her head," Parth objects. "It was more like . . . mid-spine."

"Ah, yes, the lesser-known cousin to the Heimlich maneuver," I say. "The right hook."

"I'm sorry, Harry," Parth cries. "Instinct took over!"

"You have the instincts of a Victorian women's hospital orderly," Cleo says.

"Next time, stick with the leeches," I say.

Parth frowns. "I left those at the cottage. Are you okay?"

"I'm fine," I say.

"Trust me," Wyn says. "She's quietly plotting revenge."

"Our Harry?" Parth scoffs. "Never."

"You think that . . ." Wyn sips from his steaming mug. "But she knows how to bring a person to their knees when she wants to."

I angle myself abruptly back toward Sabrina. "So, what is there still to do for the wedding?"

Sabrina waves a hand. "Nothing. Like I said, it's just the six of us and an ordained unitarian universalist minister I found online. I wasn't even planning on having flowers until Cleo and Kimmy stepped in."

"We don't mind helping," Cleo says.

"You'll get to when we have the big wedding for family next year," Sabrina says, squirting maple syrup into her mug. "This week, I just want to be in my favorite place with my favorite people. I want every second to count, and I don't want to miss anything."

At the clap of thunder and flash of lightning outside, she gestures toward the window. "I mean, what is *this*? We were supposed to go sailing today."

I check my phone's weather app. "It'll be sunny and hot tomorrow. We could sail then?"

"Just because the house is selling," Cleo says, "doesn't mean this has to be the last time the six of us come here."

I try to smile encouragingly at Sabrina, but guilt spirals through me. I want so badly for this week to be perfect, to be good enough to compensate for the fact that it will be the last. Not just in this house but as a sixsome. Truce or not, I can't be Wyn Connor's friend.

Sabrina's gone quiet and sullen, and I know she's already thinking about next week too.

I clear my throat. "I have an idea."

"Matching tattoos," Parth says.

"So close," I say. "It's this thing I used to do as a kid because I hated my birthday."

Sabrina, a woman deeply devoted to the concept of a *birthday month,* audibly gasps.

"It was hard to manage my expectations," I explain. "And it seemed like something always went wrong."

A pipe burst and my parents had to put repairs on a credit card.

Or Eloise was failing a class and needed a tutor. Or Dad's second job called him in for a shift the night we were supposed to go out. No matter how much I told myself I didn't need any big celebration, I always felt disappointed when things fell through, and then guilty because I knew how hard my parents were working to keep things going.

"A couple days before I turned ten, I had this idea," I say. "If I chose one thing I really wanted — and knew I could actually *get* — on my birthday, then no matter what else happened or didn't, it'd be a good day. So I told my parents I wanted this Oreo cheesecake, and they got it for me, and my birthday was great."

This earns me crickets from the audience.

"That," Sabrina says, "is so incredibly sad."

"It's nice!" I say. "It's practical. I had a great birthday."

"Honey, it's tragic," Sabrina says, right as Parth says, "I'm emotionally scarred."

"I think you're missing the point here," I say.

Sabrina sets her mug down. "Is the point that all parents invariably fuck up their children for life, and there's no avoiding it, so we should really stop procreating rather than continuing to make one another miserable?"

Cleo rolls her eyes. "Neither the point *nor* accurate."

"We can't control how every little thing goes this week," I say. "But it's been amazing, and it's going to keep being amazing. So maybe if each of us can choose one thing — one thing we *must* do or have or see or eat this week — then no matter what else, we'll have that. The one thing that we really needed out of this week. And the week will be a success."

There's a beat of silence as everyone considers.

"It's a good idea," Wyn says. Across the table, his eyes meet mine. His overgrown hair is damp from the rain, tucked behind his ears. So many of his details are slightly different, but my heart still sees him and whispers into my veins, *You.*

Hearts can be so stupid.

"I like it too," Cleo says.

Parth shrugs. "I'm down."

"Do we say what our goals are, or do we have to keep them secret?" Kimmy asks.

"Why would you have to keep it a secret?" I ask.

"So it comes true," she says.

"It's not a birthday wish," Sabrina says.

"No, I like that." Wyn's eyes dart toward Kimmy. "It's less pressure if it's private."

Parth nods. "So no one tells one another their goals until *after* we've met it."

"You all love rules too much," Kimmy says.

"This started with *you,* Kimberly Carmichael," Sabrina reminds her.

"Lots of things start with me. That doesn't make them good ideas."

Cleo puts her hands on the tabletop and gyrates in another stunning approximation of Kimmy's dance moves.

Sabrina narrows her eyes. "What am I

231

looking at, and why do I feel like I had a nightmare about it last night?"

16
REAL LIFE

***

Wednesday

While everyone else in town is packed into coffee shops and restaurants, sipping tea or eating clam chowder, the six of us brave the rain to tromp between candy stores and home decor boutiques filled with snarky hand towels about loving wine, our arms uselessly folded over our heads in lieu of umbrellas.

"Maybe we should go back to the house and chill," Cleo suggests after one particularly loud crack of thunder and jarringly close bolt of lightning.

"What? No!" Sabrina cries.

Kimmy squints at the roiling sky. "I don't think this rain's going to let up."

"Then we'll go to a Roxy double feature," Sabrina says.

"Do you even know what's playing?" Cleo asks.

The Roxy has only two screens. At night,

each is devoted to a new release, but in summer, the matinees are reserved for double features of movies set in Maine. Ninety percent of these are Stephen King adaptations, which works for Sabrina but is *less than ideal* for Cleo.

"Who cares what's playing?" Sabrina says. "We always used to do this when we got rained out. It's tradition."

We follow her down the block toward the bored teen in the ticket booth out front.

Cleo eyes the marquee skeptically. "*Salem's Lot* and *Return to Salem's Lot.* Weren't those miniseries?"

"Um, no," Sabrina says. "*Salem's Lot* was a two-part miniseries, and *Return* was a feature, and combined, they are glorious. You're gonna love it."

"I'm not sure I'm up for four hours of vampires?" Cleo says.

Kimmy pokes her ribs. "What if they *glitter,* though?"

"Oh, come on, Cleo," Sabrina says. "Don't be a wet blanket."

"Please don't call me that," Cleo says.

Sabrina lifts her hands in supplication. "I'm just saying, this is the last time we'll ever get to do one of these."

I glance between them. We're headed for a standoff. "Maybe you just come for the first movie," I suggest.

"Miniseries," Cleo reminds me.

"And then you can go to the Warm Cup and we'll meet you after?"

Kimmy touches Cleo's elbow. "I'll go back to the house with you if you want, babe."

Cleo's delicate point of a chin lifts. "No, it's okay. I don't want to miss out. I'll come to the first movie."

Sabrina squeals, wheeling back to face the booth. "Tickets on me!"

At some point in the last thirty seconds, the attendant has donned a top hat, and it takes Sabrina a beat to remember what she's even doing, face-to-face with this somber freckly teenager in Victorian headwear. "Six for the double feature?" she says.

"Yes, milady," the teenager says.

On our way inside, Wyn hangs back. "You don't have to do that, you know."

"Do what?" I ask.

"Find some crafty compromise to their disagreements. They'll work it out on their own if you let them."

"I have no idea what you're talking about," I say.

His brows flick upward in amusement. "None?"

"Zero," I say.

"They're having a great trip," he says.

"Try not to worry."

My stomach flips. As much as has changed between us, he still knows me a little too well. "I'm fine."

We take up the whole first row of the tiny theater, and since it's otherwise empty, we stretch our wet outer layers on the seats behind us to dry. I'm trying to find a way to sneak in between Sabrina and Cleo; I wind up at the end of the row, with no one to talk to but Wyn, who fumbles with his phone — angled pointedly away from me — until the house lights come down.

At the first minor jump scare, I fight the impulse to burrow into his side. It's not helping that it's freezing in here, and every time I unthinkingly put my arm on the armrest, it brushes his arm, which is scalding in comparison to the meat-locker temperature of the room at large.

Sabrina leans forward and flashes a thumbs-up at us from the far end of the row. As if by instinct, Wyn snatches my hand against my thigh, and my heart leaps into my throat.

Our pulses bat back and forth between our palms, a human Newton's cradle. It's all I can focus on, this lone point of contact between us. I notice every minute twitch of his fingers.

I wonder if *he's* thinking about last night, me perched on his lap with my arms slung around his neck, wriggling against him like a cat in heat, the tension between us building.

Because it's suddenly *all* I can think about. Having the lights this low gives us too much privacy for this to feel like an act, yet not enough that we can completely avoid each other.

I'm so thoroughly *not* following the movie that when someone on-screen is impaled by a wall of antlers, it's genuinely jarring.

"Oh, come on, Harriet," he whispers as I yelp and thrust my face into his chest. "I'm sure that wasn't your first antler impalement. I've seen your library books."

"It's different," I hiss, drawing back to peer at him through the dark. "Those are *cozy.*"

"That just means whoever finds the body has a boring job and wears sweater-vests."

"You know," I say, "some would think your insistence on holding my hand suggests *you're* a bit unnerved too."

"I'm unnerved," he says. "Just not by the movie." He doesn't sound flirtatious so much as resigned. Like this thing between us, this last ember of *want,* is an undesirable truth he's accepted. As our gazes hold, the pressure builds between us, heady, potent.

I think about our four-minute breakup. Curt, sterile, almost *surgical.* I think about scrubbing our apartment top to bottom afterward, cleaning the grout with a toothbrush until sweat dripped into my eyes and never feeling any better, never managing to get my head above the waves of shock and grief.

I think of all the ways he let me down and of his most annoying habits. (I've never seen a dishwasher loaded so inefficiently.) But that's not where my mind wants to go.

I need space. I need air. I need hours of hypnotherapy to erase him from my nerve endings.

"I need to use the bathroom," I blurt, and slip out into the aisle.

17
HAPPY PLACE

An hour outside Bozeman, Montana

A snowy driveway and a frigid rental car, struggling to keep purchase on the iced asphalt.

Wyn's warm hand tight on mine. He lifts the backs of my fingers to his mouth, lets his breath warm them. "They're going to love you."

I wasn't even this nervous before my MCAT. No moment in these first two years of medical school has induced this kind of anxiety. In school, I know what it takes to succeed, how to win approval. It's something you can earn with work, but this is different.

They might not like me. I might not like them.

I might talk too much or not enough. I might keep them up with my middle-of-the-night trips to the bathroom, or put their dishes away in the wrong place, or get in their way in any of the millions of highly specific ways you can only *learn* to avoid with time.

The windows are lit yellow gold, and the snow looks purple in the dark. It's so beautiful it makes me wish I were a painter or a photographer, someone whose lifework was capturing the ungraspable. Cleo would be able to bottle this moment if she were here.

Before Wyn's even put the car in park, the front door flies open. His parents come running in flannel pajamas and untied bathrobes, the hems of their pants stuffed into snow boots. Gloria is wordlessly whooping. Hank hugs me before we're even introduced.

Wyn's mother is taller than I'd expected, nearly as tall as Hank, with ice-blond hair and permanently rosy cheeks. Hank has thick sandy-brown waves heavily laced with gray, and a more deeply grooved version of Wyn's face behind a pair of wire-rimmed glasses.

His sisters, tiny platinum Lou and even tinier dark-haired Michael, are already inside, sipping brandy in front of the fireplace, and after insisting on getting our bags himself, Hank ushers us inside, straight into a wall of noise.

Even in front of his family, Wyn keeps his

hands on me — at my waist or the curve of my back or resting against the base of my neck, his thumb moving restlessly as he answers the dozens of questions thrown at us rapid fire.

The drive wasn't too bad.

The flights from New York were long and cramped.

We aren't hungry. (As Gloria asks this, she shoves plates of pumpkin pie toward us.)

We've been together (openly) for ten months now. "I've been in love with her since we met, though," Wyn says.

"Of course you have," Gloria says, squeezing my knee. "She's sweet as pie!"

"You just think that because of the curly hair," Wyn says. "She's actually extremely feisty." My face goes beet red, but everyone is laughing, talking over one another, and Wyn is kissing the side of my head again, squeezing me against him on the couch, and I feel like I'm finally *there,* that place I've always wanted to be, the other side of the lit kitchen windows I could see from my childhood street, where rooms are filled with love and noise and squabbling.

"He needs a stern hand," Michael says.

"He's not a workhorse," Lou says with an eye roll.

"No, of course not," Michael says. "Much more of a mule."

Wyn pulls me across his lap, looping his arms around my waist. "How do you know Harriet isn't even more stubborn than I am?"

"He's right," I tell them. "Between the two of us, I'm the mule."

"Well, if you're the mule," Michael says, "then Wyn's the ass."

"If I'm going to be an ass," he says, "I'm glad to be yours."

When Hank comes back to the cramped little den with its raging fire, he says, "Put you in Wyn's room, Har," and I think, *Har. I've been here ten minutes and I'm already "Har,"* and there's a sensation like an inflating balloon in my chest, a pleasant pain, like stretching a stiff muscle.

Wyn had warned me that his parents wouldn't let us share a room, even though we live together back in the city. In some ways, they're eccentric and freethinking, and in others, they're surprisingly traditional.

Later, while his parents finish washing the dishes, Wyn takes me to his room to settle in. For hours he lets me go through his stuff, picking things up, asking questions, while he acts as the docent for this museum dedicated to my favorite subject.

I hold things up; he tells me about them. I'm gluttonous for all these bits of him.

Plastic MVP trophies from his soccer days; washed-out disposable-camera shots of him as a teenager, surrounded by girls with the sperm-shaped eyebrows and bleached-to-death hair of our youth. Pictures of him with friends at football games, their faces painted, and walking in summer parades, and even, in a couple of cases, at the rodeo.

Every time I point to someone, he tells me her name (most of his friends, it seems, were girls), how they met, where she is now. "You keep in touch with all these people?"

"It's a small town," he says. "We were all friends, and so were our parents. I hear stuff through the grapevine. Some of them try to sell me multi-level marketing smoothies on occasion."

At my request, he shows me all the girls he's kissed, and the ones who came for the summer and broke his heart before heading home.

I stop on a framed professional photo of him on his dresser and snort in delight. "You were *prom* king? And you never mentioned it?"

Wyn peers over my shoulder. In the photograph, he wears a black suit and crooked plastic crown, his arms wrapped around the waist of a pretty brunette in a silver mini-dress and matching tiara. The backdrop behind them reads BRIGHT LIGHTS, BIG CITY over a sparkling skyline that somehow contains both the Empire State Building and Seattle's Space Needle.

Wyn groans. "I swear to you that's not even normally in here. Pretty sure my mom put it out for the occasion."

"Oh? She wanted to make me jealous of your teenage flame?" I tease.

He rubs his forehead. His cheeks go adorably pink. "She thinks she's showing me off."

"I can't believe I've known you for like three and a half years and you never mentioned you were prom king."

"Yes, my finest accomplishment." He shakes his head. "So embarrassing."

"What are you talking about?" I face him. "How is *this* embarrassing? When I was this age, I still had braces and a pixie cut that made me look like I'd been electrocuted. Meanwhile, you were crowned prom king while on a date with a teen model."

I lift the picture, offering him cold, hard evidence.

He returns the frame to the dresser. "I

wouldn't expect you to know this as a former teen brainiac and current brilliant medical student, but prom king is the consolation prize they give guys they think have already peaked and probably will be staying in town to be a spokesman for the local car dealerships."

"Hold on, let me write this down." I start to turn. He pulls me back, winding his arms around my ribs.

"See, you don't know this because everyone in your town expected big things of you," he says, grinning.

"I didn't know this," I reply, "because I went to a four-thousand-student school where no one knew my name and because I've never followed car-dealership culture very closely."

"Ah," he says. "Your first mistake."

"Wyndham Connor," I say. "Don't you think this whole theory of yours is a teensy bit . . . narcissistic?"

His smile splits open, and my heart follows suit. "Because I think car dealerships would use me as a spokesperson? They've done it with like eighty percent of the town's prom kings."

"Not that," I say. "The idea that all your classmates voted you prom king . . . because they felt sorry for you."

He shrugs.

I wrap my arms around his neck. "Yeah, that was probably it." I kiss him and he pulls me closer, lifting me up and into him as if to absorb me. "Surely it had nothing to do with how hot and kind and funny you are. It was sheer pity." I kiss him again, deeper.

"And that?" he asks.

"*Extreme* pity." I grab his ass. "This too."

"Wow. Being a washed-up former golden boy isn't so bad after all."

Someone knocks on the doorframe. I pull back, but Wyn's arms stay around me as he angles his head toward the hall.

His parents stand at the door, smiling, Gloria's head resting on Hank's shoulder.

"We're headed to bed, you two," Hank says.

"You need anything?" Gloria asks.

Wyn shakes his head. "Just saying good night."

Gloria's eyes shrink when she smiles, like Wyn's. "Sleep tight."

When they're gone, Wyn walks me back against the dresser and we make out for a handful of minutes before he kisses the top of my head and leaves my room.

For the next four days in Montana, we barely do anything. We go cross-country skiing once, eat twice at an all-day pancake

246

house that Wyn's parents describe as "a haunt for old silver tails like us," and take nightly walks with the whole family through the snow. We bundle up like astronauts, and Hank insists we wear headband lamps so we don't "get hit by cars or attacked by wild animals" in the solid black of a Montana night.

Mostly, though, we lounge around the fireplace, an endless supply of food and drink cycling through the room. In the mornings, Hank makes each of us individual pour-over coffees, a process that takes so long that by the time he finishes the last one, we're all ready for our second cups, and he lunges to his feet, without anyone asking, to start all over again.

"Dad, we're fine with the Keurig," Wyn tries to reason.

His dad wrinkles his nose and shuffles in his flannel slippers toward the kitchen. "That stuff's for emergencies, *not* for guests."

Most meals are casseroles. Hank doesn't have the same affinity for food that he has for drinks, and Gloria's cooking leaves me feeling like a walking balloon after every meal.

After dinner our second night in town, Lou and Michael lie on their backs on the rug, groaning and massaging their tummies.

"Mom, you and Dad need to consider eating, like, even a single vegetable per week," Lou says.

To which Gloria replies, "Potatoes are a vegetable."

"No," Michael, Lou, and Wyn all say in unison.

Vegetables or not, the potatoes at least *are* helpful for soaking up the bourbons and scotches Hank lines up at their old wooden dining table for us to sample every night.

"Dad's the Beverage King," Michael says to me.

"I see why you gravitated toward Parth when you got to Mattingly," I tell Wyn.

"That's not why I gravitated toward Parth." Wyn hauls me against him as he nestles back into the squashy couch. "I gravitated toward Parth because he had the prettiest friends."

Lou snorts from where she lies on the rug in front of the hearth. "Thank you, Harriet, for saving him from himself."

"I think you have too high an opinion of me," I tell her. "I also befriended Parth for his hot friends."

Wyn kisses the top of my head. Michael and Lou exchange a look I can't read.

Maybe they've seen this before, I think.

Maybe he's always like this with his girlfriends.

But I don't really believe it. I am in that phase of love where you're sure no two people have ever felt this way before.

And over those four days, I fall in love again. With Wyn's family, with all the new pieces of him.

I want to stay up late, digging through his old closet, where his mom stored his home-made stormtrooper costume. I want to sit for five hours in the woodshop, sawdust drifting in the air, while he recounts the fights hc got into with Lou's middle school bullies. I want to know where every single little white scar and divot carved into his permanently sunned skin came from.

The one from when he braked too hard on his bike and went skidding down the road. The white specks on his elbow from the agitated horse that threw him on his grandfather's now-defunct ranch. The thin line where he split his lip on the corner of the fireplace as a toddler.

I want to stockpile these pieces of him: the quilt his grandmother made him before he was born, his embarrassing preteen journals, his horrifying childhood drawings, the dent in his mom's truck from when he hit a patch of ice and slid into a split rail at sixteen.

He takes me to see it, the stretch where the beams are less dingy, having been replaced after his accident. He and Hank had done it themselves without being asked.

Wyn ran wild here, and this place carved him into the man I love.

With my hand on the wooden post he'd worked into the ground all those years ago, I ask, "Why'd you leave?"

"It's hard to explain," he says, grimacing.

"Can you try?" I ask. "You seem so happy here."

He lets out a breath and searches the horizon for an answer. "They had money from selling my dad's family's land. And they always wanted my sisters to go to college, because Mom and Dad didn't get to."

"Your sisters?" I say. "But not you?"

His mouth quirks into a crooked half smile. "Told you, they're little geniuses, like you. Big dreams. I guess my parents assumed I'd want to stay. Keep working with my dad."

"Because you love this place," I say.

He runs his hand over his jaw. "I do. But I don't know. I was watching all these people with dreams and goals leaving, going other places. And I didn't know what I wanted. I got scouted by Mattingly's soccer coach, and it seemed like a sign, I guess."

"But you didn't stick with the soccer team."

"I never loved it," he says. "And I couldn't keep up with it *and* school at the same time. It was all harder than I expected. The schoolwork, the social stuff."

"Everyone loved you, Wyn," I say.

He looks at me through his lashes, his mouth curling. "No, Harriet. They wanted to hook up with me. That's not the same thing. I never fit there."

I pull my fingers away from the icy fence and touch the spot where his dimple belongs. The corners of his mouth twitch, and the dip appears under my middle finger. "You fit with me, and I was there."

"I know," he says. "I think that's really why I went. To find you."

"That's a very expensive dating app," I say.

"You get what you pay for," he replies.

My hands fall to the collar of his coat, the tops of my fingers tucking in against his hot skin. "Did you at least figure out what you wanted too?"

In the dying light, the green ridges in his eyes glitter like bits of mica underwater. His work-coarsened hands circle my wrists, his thumbs gentle on the delicate skin there.

"This," he says. "Just this."

Me too, I think. I can't bring myself to say it, to admit that the rest of my life, everything I've worked for, has started to feel like set dressing. Like loving him is the only essential, and everything else is garnish.

He shows me the workshop too, the exact place where the heavy armoire fell on him one New Year's Eve while his parents were out, where he lay for four and a half hours in the cold, waiting to be found.

It makes my heart ache. Not just the memory but the smell, the cedar and sawdust and that touch of something that's all Wyn to me. "You don't mind being out here?" I ask, walking along the table in-process, its top sanded down to be refinished.

"I always loved it out here," he says. "So after the accident, my parents were adamant about getting me back out before I started fixating. It worked, mostly."

I pause, fingers stilling on the table, and look back at him. "I like seeing you here."

He crosses toward me, gently takes my hips in his hands. "I like seeing *you* here," he says, voice low, a little hoarse. "It makes me feel like this is real."

"Wyn." I look up into his face, searching his stormy eyes, the rigid lines between his

252

brows and framing his jaw. "Of course it's real."

He folds his fingers through mine and brings my hands to the back of his neck, our foreheads resting together, our hearts whirring. "I mean," he says, "like I can make you happy."

"This is me, happy," I promise.

On our last night in town, we sample more of Hank's scotch and play a highly competitive game of dominoes, and then sit in front of the hearth and watch the fire crackle and pop.

On a sigh, Hank says, "We're gonna miss you, kiddos."

"We'll come home again soon," Wyn promises, lifting my hand, brushing the back of it absently across his lips.

Home, I think. *That's new.*

But it's not. It's been growing there for a while, this new room in my heart, this space just for Wyn that I carry with me everywhere I go.

18
REAL LIFE

Wednesday

I take my time in the movie theater's neon green bathroom.

I wash my hands, then wipe down the sink area and wash my hands again.

On my way back through the burgundy-carpeted arcade in which the bathrooms are tucked, I nearly collide with Wyn.

"Sorry," we both huff, stopping short.

My eyes drop to the smorgasbord of paper cartons he's carrying: Twizzlers, Nerds, Red Hots, Whoppers, and Milk Duds.

"Going to a slumber party?" I ask.

"I was thirsty," he says.

"Which explains the cup of water and nothing else," I say. "You think shortbread's too sweet."

"Thought you might want something," he says.

His eyes look more green than gray right now. I'm finding it hard to look at them, so

I train my gaze on the candy. "It looks like you thought I might want *everything.*"

His eyes flash. "Was I wrong?"

"No," I say, "but you didn't have to do that."

"Trust me, it wasn't intentional," he says. "I walked up for the water, and next thing I know I've got a wagon filled with corn syrup."

"Well, that's the Connor family thriftiness. If you buy a wagon, refills are free."

His laugh turns into a groan. He runs the back of his hand up his forehead. "I'm so hungover."

"Didn't you have *one* drink last night?"

"If we're ignoring the half bottle I drank in the cellar," he says.

"We should probably ignore everything that happened in the cellar," I say.

He studies me for a second. "Anyway, I have no tolerance anymore. I drink less than ever these days."

"Wow, *humblebrag,*" I say.

He laughs. "Actually, it's just that I've been using edibles."

At my surprise, he says, "They've been really helping my mom, but she gets kind of embarrassed. About taking them on her own. So a couple times a week, I'll split a brownie with her. She's funny. She'd never

255

even tried weed before, and she gets super giggly. I sort of think it's a placebo effect, but it doesn't matter."

I suppress a grin. "Moved back in with your mom and get high with her twice a week."

"Living the dream," he says.

"You are, though," I say. "I'm actually jealous."

"It is fun," he says. "But she gets so munchy. I've probably gained like fifteen pounds."

"It suits you." I quickly add, "How is she, really?"

He glances at me askance. "You haven't talked to her?"

I'm sure he knows I still text regularly with Gloria. I even field the odd text or two from his sisters. Mostly when his little sister, Lou, wants my opinion on a potential present for Wyn, invariably a gag gift that requires no special insight whatsoever, or when his older sister, Michael, wants an opinion on a medical ailment that invariably has nothing to do with neurosurgery. As far as his family knows, he and I are still engaged.

"I do talk to her," I say. "But I figure she's mostly lying."

Wyn's laugh is low. "I'm sure she is."

His gaze drops. I let mine linger on the

dark fringe of his lashes, the curve of his full upper lip, until his eyes lift. "It really does help. The weed. Just . . . not enough."

Emotions tangle in my esophagus. *Globus sensation,* my mind supplies, as if naming it will take away the ache. It doesn't. "I'm glad you're there with her," I say.

His lips part, come together, part again. "I, um . . ." He sets the boxes of candy and cup atop the air hockey table beside us and shifts between his feet. He takes a deep breath. "I know you don't want to talk about it all," he says in a low, husky voice, "and I respect that. But you said something yesterday, and . . ."

Heat creeps all the way up my neck to my ears. "I was having a bad day, Wyn."

"No, no — it's not . . ." He shakes his head, then tries again. "Something you said in the cellar made me realize you thought he was why I ended it."

He. It lands with a violent impact.

Wyn swallows. "That you thought I *blamed* you for what happened with him."

"Of course you blamed me." My spine stiffens as I will myself not to crack, or rather not to let the cracks show. The truth is, they're already there.

"I didn't," he says roughly. "And I don't. I swear. Okay?"

My chest pinches. "So sheer coincidence that I told you about him and you immediately dumped me."

I have no idea what to make of his look of surprise and hurt. I have no idea what to make of any of this. I went into the bathroom in one universe and walked out into another.

"Harriet," he rasps, shaking his head. "It was more complicated than that."

More complicated than thinking I'd betrayed him. It wasn't that he was angry. It wasn't that he didn't trust me.

He just didn't want me anymore. It feels like my body is turning to sand, like in a minute I'll be nothing but a shapeless heap on the floor.

"I was in a dark place," he goes on.

I turn from him because I feel the cracks spreading, my eyes stinging. "I know."

I *did* know. Every second of every day. "I just didn't know how to fix it," I choke out.

"You couldn't have," he says.

I close my eyes as I try to gather myself, stuff all these messy feelings back down.

The truth is, I knew he hated San Francisco. I felt guilty that he'd followed me there. Guilty about keeping him there, even as it was killing me not being able to make him happy.

His hand slides through mine, tentatively lacing our fingers and tugging me back to him.

"It wasn't just that," he says. "My dad . . ."

I nod, the ache in my throat too severe to speak.

Hank's passing was so sudden. I don't know if that made it any worse. There never would have been an okay time to lose him. Not for Wyn. Not for anyone who knew Hank.

Everything combusted at once, and somehow I still thought we'd make it. When he promised to love me forever, I believed him. That was what made me the angriest, with both of us.

"I didn't think that I . . ." His eyes hold mine, his jaw muscles working. "I never wanted to hurt you."

"I know." But it changes nothing.

"All I want," he says, "is for you to be happy."

There it is again, that word.

"That's what I was trying to say, down in the cellar," he goes on. "That I don't want to do anything this week that messes anything else up for you. And I'm sorry I almost did."

The pieces click together.

"I'm not with him," I say. "There's nothing to mess up."

His lips part.

I wish I could roll the words back into my mouth and down my throat. "If that's what you were getting at."

"Okay," he says.

Okay? What kind of response is that?

After a beat of awkward silence, he says, "I'm not either."

I suppress a smile. "You're not in a long-distance relationship with my coworker you've met once?"

An irresistible blush hits the tops of his cheekbones. He knocks his foot against the leg of the air hockey table. "I can hardly believe it myself. The chemistry was undeniable, but it wasn't enough."

I swallow the second half of a laugh, and he looks up at me from under that one lock of his. "There's no one else," he says.

It doesn't matter, I tell myself.

It can't matter.

He wasn't happy with you.

He broke your heart.

He was never yours to keep, and deep down you knew that.

I *watched* him fade from me, bit by bit, day by day, a mirage receding into nothingness.

But the way he's looking at me threatens

to obliterate logic, to erase history. If he's a black hole, I've reached his event horizon.

My chest aches, but I don't want it to stop. I want to lean into the feeling, this wholeness. My heart and body and mind are all finally in the same time and place. Here, with him.

I don't want to go back into the theater, but something has to give. We can't keep walking out along this tightrope, or someone's going to get hurt. *I'm* going to get hurt.

I clear my throat. "How's the furniture repair business?"

His Cupid's bow twitches. "Still a furniture repair business."

"Oh?" I say. "Not using it to run drugs and host illegal gambling nights yet?"

His lips split into a smile. "Still in the same apartment?"

Our apartment. It still manages to hold traces of him. Or maybe that's me, carrying his ghost around wherever I go. "Mhm."

"How's your sister?" he asks.

"Good, I think," I say. "She and her hairdresser friend went into business together. They mostly do weddings and dances. Still Face-Times me twice a month, makes about five minutes of small talk, then says goodbye."

His teeth skate over his bottom lip. "I'm sorry."

He's the only person who knows how much it bothers me that I barely know Eloise, that despite having a sister, I always felt acutely alone in our childhood home. Between our six-year age gap and her constant disagreements with our parents, we didn't have much time to bond.

I shrug. "Some things never change, and the best thing is to stop hoping they will."

"Other things do, though," he says.

I break eye contact. "What about your sisters? How are they?"

"Good," he replies, half smiling. "Lou's with my mom this week. Said to tell you hi."

I smile despite the twinge in my chest. "And Michael? Still in Colorado?"

He nods. "She's dating another aerospace engineer, who works for a competing company. They moved in together, but they're both under NDAs, so neither of them even lets the other into their home office."

I laugh. "That," I say, "is so unbelievably on-brand."

"I know," he says. "And Lou finished at the Iowa Writers' Workshop in May."

"That's amazing," I say.

Together, the three of them could be loud

and rude and competitive. They argued over everything — what to have for dinner, who got first use of the shower, who really understood the rules of dominoes and who was totally off — as if as soon as a thought or feeling occurred to them, it spewed out.

But nothing ever blew up. Little arguments flared and extinguished; small insults casually faded. And everyone went back to joking, hugging, kicking, acting like siblings do in movies.

I wonder but don't ask whether his younger sister, Lou, is just visiting their mom or if she ended up moving home after grad school like she'd been planning, back when Wyn's stay out there was supposed to be temporary. She was going to take over Gloria's care.

"I miss them," I admit.

"They miss you too," he says.

I ask, "Do they wonder why I never visit?"

"I go out of town sometimes," he says. "For work stuff."

"Work stuff?" I ask.

He nods but doesn't clarify. "They think we're seeing each other then."

I nod. I don't have anything to say to that.

He clears his throat. "My mom said you were taking a pottery class."

"Oh," I say. "Yeah."

"I pretended I already knew about it," he says.

"Right. That's good."

"But she mentioned that she thinks you're getting better. And your newest bowl looked way less like a butt."

The laugh rockets out of me as if shot from a cannon. "That's funny, because you should have *seen* the rapturous text she sent me about that butt-bowl. She pretended it was *very* good."

"Nah." He grins. "She wasn't pretending. She told me it *was* really good. It just also looked like a butt. You know how she is."

"Remember how nice she was about that painting we gave her as a joke?" I ask. "The fucked-up Velvet Elvis that looked more like Biff from *Back to the Future*?"

His smile widens. "She kept saying how unique it was."

"But fully making *unique* sound like a good thing. So much nuance to Gloria's opinions."

"The nuance being that she can know something's objectively terrible," he says, "but if it's even loosely connected to one of her family members, then it's got to also be groundbreakingly special."

The idea of being one of Gloria's family members, of being *groundbreakingly* special, pricks at my heart.

"It's been weirdly fun, living with her," he says.

"Nothing weird about it," I say. "Gloria's a blast."

He smiles to himself. "It's just funny. I spent all those years convincing myself I needed to get away. I saw my sisters finding their things and talking about leaving, and my parents being so proud of how they were going to make something of themselves, chart their own path or whatever. And I thought I needed to do that too."

I think back all those years to the day the five of us, sans Kimmy, lay on the Armases' dock, charting our alternative paths, how even then, Wyn used his hypothetical *other life* to go back to the one he'd left behind. A part of him knew he belonged there.

Once I went home with him for the first time, met Hank and Gloria and Lou and Michael, saw the woodshop and the child-hood bedroom filled with proof of a happy, love-filled childhood, a part of *me* knew he belonged there too.

I tried to hold on to him anyway. Watched, those months in San Francisco, as the walls closed in around him — and it killed me to see him so broken, so hunted, but I hadn't been brave enough to cut him loose. Maybe that was part of the anger that burned in me too: disappointment that I hadn't loved him well enough to make him happy nor well enough to let him go.

"Anyway," he says, "if someone had told me, at twenty-two, that I'd end up living in my childhood bedroom and doing crosswords with my mom over breakfast every morning, I *would* have believed them, but I'd be shocked to hear I'm actually happy in this scenario."

"You do crosswords?" I say. "You *never* wanted to do crosswords when we lived together. I used to try to get you to, every time it rained."

"And I always said yes," he says.

"And we *never* finished them," I say.

"Harriet." His eyes settle on mine, a knowing glint in them. "That's because I could never sit still that long across from you without touching you."

Blood rises to my cheeks and chest, thrums down into my thighs.

Without my realizing it, we've moved closer together. Maybe it's like Cleo's Bernie's-induced hangover: a Pavlovian response that will always draw us together.

I say, "And here I thought it was the crosswords themselves getting you riled up."

"As it turns out," he replies, "it's not writing letters in tiny boxes that gets me *riled up.*"

"That's good," I manage. "That would make breakfast with Gloria pretty awkward."

The fan blows a wisp of hair across my face, and he catches it, twisting it between his calloused fingertips. My heart pounds, my every cell tugging toward him.

Behind us, the door to the theater swings open. Our friends stream out in a flurry of chatter and laughter. Intermission has begun.

I start toward them, but Wyn catches my wrist.

"I like the bowl," he says. "She showed me a picture. I thought it was beautiful."

267

19
REAL LIFE

Wednesday

"I thought you weren't staying for the second movie," I whisper to Cleo as we settle back into our seats. This time, Wyn and I are in the middle, and I can't help but wonder if Sabrina nudged us into this position so we wouldn't run out again.

Cleo shrugs. "This clearly means a lot to Sab. Plus, I don't want her hanging it over me that I left early."

"Pssst." Kimmy leans forward around Cleo. She holds a plastic sandwich bag out to me.

I squint at the contents. "Are you trying to sell me drugs?"

"Of course not," she says. "I'm trying to *give* you drugs." She swings the little red gummy bears in front of Cleo's face and tosses them into my lap.

"You are," I say, "so discreet."

"I don't have to be discreet," she says. "It's

268

legal here."

Wyn leans in. "Is Kimmy selling drugs?"

"Want some?" she asks.

Sabrina shushes us, eyes glued to the screen as she shovels popcorn into her mouth.

Wyn looks at me, then back to Kimmy. "If Harriet's in, I am."

"How strong are they?" I whisper.

Kimmy shrugs. "Not too strong."

"Not too strong for *you* or not too strong for *me*?" I say.

"Let's put it this way," she says. "You'll have a great time, but you won't make me call the hospital and ask them if you're going to die. Again."

What the hell. When in Rome.

Each of us takes one. We tap them together in a toast before throwing them back.

"Hey," Sabrina says at full volume, "are you guys doing drugs down there?"

"We're taking tiny weed gummies," I say.

"Got any more?" Sabrina asks. "I haven't gotten high in forever."

Kimmy passes the bag down the line. Parth and Sabrina each take one. Cleo waves off the offer. "I don't smoke anymore, really."

"And I'm cutting back too," Kimmy says. "So whatever we don't finish this week, you all can fight over."

"Okay, is it possible this is already making me hungry," Sabrina asks.

"No," Cleo, Wyn, and I all say in unison. From the back of the theater, someone shushes us. We all duck down in our seats.

"Holy shit," Kimmy hisses. "Did anyone know there was someone else back there?"

Parth sneaks a look over his shoulder. "I think he's a ghost."

"He's not a ghost," I whisper.

"How can you be sure?" Parth says.

"Because," I say, "he's wearing his sunglasses backward. That's Ray. He's a pilot."

"Just because he's a pilot doesn't mean he's *not* a ghost," Kimmy says sagely.

The gray-shingled buildings on Commercial Street steadily drip, but the downpour has ended, and everyone is out for the first night of Lobster Fest. The concerts, contests, and parade of red-gowned former Lobster Ladies don't start until Friday, but the food trucks and carnival games are open, their lights flashing not quite in time with the Billy Joel hit piping through the speakers. Kids in lobster and mermaid face paint dart through the crowd, couples in matching windbreakers dance in front of the wine-slushie stand, and glassy-eyed teenagers

270

pass around suspicious water bottles.

"Do you smell that?" Sabrina literally skips ahead of us. "If there's a heaven, this is what it smells like."

Salt water and burnt sugar, garlic simmering in butter and clams frying in oil.

"I want a cup of extremely foamy beer," she says dreamily.

"I want french fries covered in Old Bay," Kimmy says.

Cleo's nose wrinkles on a laugh. "I want a video camera so tomorrow you can see how high you all are."

"I want to win at Whack-a-Lobster," Parth says, peeling off toward the game's flashing lights like a hypnotized magic show volunteer, and Wyn follows in a daze.

I hook an arm around Cleo's shoulders. "Now aren't you glad you didn't miss out on all *this*?"

"It wasn't *this* I wanted to miss," Cleo says. The others have moved on to a milk-bottle toss game. She jerks her head toward the lobster beanbags and the bottles painted to look like nervous lobstermen. "What do you think the narrative is here? The lobsters fighting back?"

"Let's hope it's not prophetic, or this town's the first to go," I say.

She turns back to me. "I guess I feel

like . . . this week's already half-over, and we've all barely gotten to catch up. And I know how important this is to her — to everyone. Doing all these things one last time, and I get that.

"But it's also been a long time since we've been together, and today just felt like kind of a bummer. Sitting through hours of movies when we could be talking."

I grab her hand. "I'm sorry. That makes complete sense."

She glances back, to where Sabrina and Parth are taunting each other in front of the game, and smiles a little. "I just want this week to be perfect for them."

"Me too." I squeeze her hand. "But hey, the night is young and so are we. What do *you* want to do? I'll go on any ride or play any game. I'll even let you monologue about mushrooms."

She laughs and tucks her head against my shoulder. "I just want to be here with you, Har."

The weed must be hitting me hard, because I instantly tear up a little.

It's that happy-sad feeling, that intense homesick ache. It makes me think of my semester abroad. Not the old cobbled streets or tiny pubs overstuffed with drunk university students, but Sabrina and Cleo

FaceTiming me at midnight to sing me "Happy Birthday." The feeling of being so grateful to have something worth missing.

We walk, we talk, we sweat and frizz and eat. Funnel cakes and lobster rolls, over-stuffed whoopie pies and battered-and-fried fiddlehead ferns, caramel corn and salted popcorn.

"Does anyone else feel like time's moving really fast?" I ask when I realize it's full dark.

Cleo and Sabrina look at each other and burst into laughter.

"You're so high," Sabrina says.

"Says the woman who spent like nine minutes making us stand in one place while she googled whether corn is a nut or a vegetable," I say.

"I wanted to know!" Sabrina cries, eyes shrunken.

"A *nut,* babe," Cleo says. "You thought corn was a *nut.*"

"Well, they look like little nuts before you pop them," Parth says, coming to Sabrina's defense. Cleo is now laughing so hard she's doubled over.

Wyn is wandering toward the Ferris wheel, saucer-eyed.

"Dude, Wyn's about to be beamed up," Kimmy says, and I have no idea what she's talking about, but it makes me laugh anyway.

Wyn looks over his shoulder and says, "Look at it. It's beautiful." Sabrina stares at him for one second, then throws her head back and cackles.

But he — and his not-quite-tiny gummy — is right.

Everything looks soft around the edges, dreamy.

Parth leads us into the Ferris wheel line. I try to pair up with Sabrina, but she sidesteps me in the queue, switching places so she's with Parth and I'm with Wyn.

"Okay, okay," Parth says. "Raise your hand if you're high."

"What if we all close our eyes first?" Kimmy says. "Just so no one's embarrassed."

Wyn's head droops against my shoulder, his laughter spilling across my skin, dripping down my spine, lighting up my nerve endings as it goes. A mixed metaphor, sure, but when are you *supposed* to mix your metaphors if not at thirty years old, high as a satellite?

"I feel young!" I cry, which makes Sabrina cackle again, throw her arms out to her sides, and spin twice.

Parth grabs my shoulders and says urgently, "We *are* young, Harry. We'll always be young. It's a state of mind."

"Now seems like a good time to tell you," Cleo says, "Kim buys this shit from a neighbor who makes it at home. It's not regulated. Hope you're all prepared to go to the fucking moon."

Kimmy's eyes have essentially disappeared at this point. "Listen," she says, "you're gonna have a great time. Moon's beautiful this time of year."

Normally the idea of unregulated weed gummies might make me a tad anxious. Or, like, have a full-blown panic attack. But the way Kimmy says it and the goofy look on her face make me snort-laugh some more.

"Wait," Wyn says, face stern and serious, "how do you make gummies at home?"

"Listen," Kimmy says. "It's a mystery."

"Listen," Sabrina says. "I love it."

The very unimpressed twentysomething Ferris wheel attendant waves us up the metal steps to the loading platform.

Sabrina and Parth take the frontmost open bench, and Wyn steadies me as we climb in the next one, my breath still coming in giggly gasps.

"These," he says, "are not my mother's weed gummies."

I chortle into his shoulder, then pull back

quickly. Well, in all honesty, I doubt I'm doing *anything* quickly, but I do remember to remove my face from his neck region, and that's not nothing at this point.

We lift our arms as the attendant checks our lap bar, then drop them again as he moves to the bench behind us to latch Kimmy and Cleo in.

"Remember the maritime museum?" he says.

I wipe my laugh-tears away with the back of my hand. "*Remember* might not be accurate. I have bits and pieces floating around inside my hippocampus like little soap bubbles."

"It was the trip right before your last year of medical school," he says.

"Seriously?" My hand flops onto his on the lap bar. I pull it back. "It was that long ago?"

He nods. "It was the same trip where Sabrina and Parth first hooked up."

The memory feels like it's being broadcast from another life. Sabrina and Parth had stayed up later than all of us, caught in a viciously competitive game of gin rummy, wherein they took turns winning. Late the next morning, they'd come down to the kitchen together, cranky but glowing. "Don't say a single word," Sabrina warned.

"We aren't going to speak of it." And we'd all nodded and hid our smirks, but that night, they'd shared a room again.

"Later that day we all shared *one* joint," Wyn goes on, "then went to the museum, and you watched that boat-making presentation for like thirty-five minutes without blinking."

"He was an artist!" I cry.

"He was," Wyn agrees. "And for like two hours, you were convinced you were going to quit medical school to make boats."

"I'd never even been on a boat at that point," I say.

"I don't think that's strictly required," he says.

"I was probably just scared I wasn't going to match with any residencies," I say.

"You told me you wouldn't even care," he replies. "You said it would be a sign from the universe."

My chest pinches with guilt. As if I'd *cheated* on my future, had an emotional affair with *boat making*. I'd devoted my entire adult life to this one thing, and all it took was one puff of the right joint for me to contemplate throwing it all away.

"It was fucking adorable," he says. "I high-texted my dad to ask what we'd need to get for you to be able to make a boat in the shop."

"Seriously?"

"He was extremely excited," Wyn says. "He was going to ask around to see if someone could come show you how to get started."

"You never told me that," I say.

"Well," he says, "you never mentioned boat making again, so I kind of figured it was the weed talking."

"It was exceptionally talkative weed," I muse.

"What about the gummy?" he asks. "Is it telling you we should impulse-buy some heavy machinery?"

We. Hearing him say it is like biting into a Maine blueberry, the way you taste the salt water and the cold sky and the damp earth and the sun all at once. When *we* lands on my tongue, I see everything:

His moonlit shoulders leaned against the Jaguar.

The moment he pulled his hoodie down over my shoulders, my hair pushing out around my face.

A kiss in the wine cellar.

Falling asleep crammed in one twin bed, his sweat still clinging to me.

The night he asked me to marry him.

"Harriet?" he says. "What do you think? Should we invest in your boat-making dream or not?"

The morning we found out Hank was gone.

The deep, painful silence in our San Francisco apartment.

The night he broke my heart.

I shake myself. "What have we got to lose except for thousands of dollars we don't have and limbs we're fairly accustomed to and —" I scrabble for his arm as the Ferris wheel lurches to life, sweeping forward along the loading dock and then shooting us skyward.

As the ground drops away, Wyn's face lights in alternating hues of neon, colors pulsing in a nonsensical rhythm.

For a few seconds, I'm hypnotized.

Okay, realistically, I have no concept of how long I'm hypnotized. The weed is still making time stretchy as taffy. Some colors paint his face for eons, and others flash so fast I hardly have time to register them.

The bitter salty breeze runs through his hair as we lift higher into the night, the smell of burnt sugar still clinging to his clothes.

"You're staring, Harriet," he says, the corner of his mouth twitching.

"Am I?" I say. "Or are you just high?"

When he laughs, I become intensely aware of my fingers, still clutching his forearm, and of the smooth, dry texture of his skin. Up close, whenever he's been out in the sun, there are millions of tiny dark freckles, small as sand grains, scattered over his skin. I want to touch all of them. In my current state, that could take days.

Wedged together like this, I feel his breath moving in and out of his lungs, his heartbeat tapping out messages in Morse code.

"Why are you looking at me like that?" he asks.

"Like what?" I say, a bit thickly.

He tucks his chin. "Like you want to eat me."

"Because," I say, "I want to eat you."

He touches his thumb against the middle of my chin, the air taking on an electrical charge. "Is that the weed talking," he teases gently, "or is it that I've still got powdered sugar on my mouth?"

For someone who's spent a lifetime living inside her own mind, I become nothing but a body alarmingly fast, all buzzing nerve endings and tingling skin.

"This is confusing," I whisper.

"I don't feel confused," he says.

"You must not be as high as me."

His smile unfurls from one corner of his mouth, never quite making it to the other. "I *know* I'm not as high as you. You look like you ate a trash bag full of catnip."

"I can *feel* my blood," I say. "And these colors have *tastes.*"

"You're not wrong," he says.

"What do they taste like to you?" I ask.

He closes his eyes, his nose tipping up, the breeze ruffling his T-shirt. When he opens his eyes, his pupils have overtaken his irises. "Red gummy."

I snort. "How astute."

His eyes flash, lightning crackling in the pre-tornado green of them. "Okay, fine," he says. "You want the truth?"

"About what these lights taste like?" I say. "Dying for it."

His hand slides off the lap bar, the tips of his fingers dragging up the outside of my thigh all the way to my hip, his eyes watching their progress. "They taste like this fabric."

I'm trying my best not to shiver, not to nuzzle into him, because the light pressure of his fingers against the satin of my sundress *does* in fact have a taste right now, and it's delicious.

"Soft," he says. The backs of his fingernails drag back down my thigh, sliding past the hem of my dress to the bare skin above my knee. My head falls back of its own volition. "Delicate. So fucking light it dissolves on your tongue."

His eyes meet mine. His nails drag back up, a little heavier. For several seconds, or minutes, or hours, we hold on to each other's gazes while his hand makes slow passes, up, down, up a little higher.

"Can I see more pictures?" he says.

I startle from my lust haze. "What?"

"Of your pottery," he says.

"It's not good," I say.

"I don't care," he says. "Can I see it?"

Our gazes hold again. I'm really struggling to move at a normal pace. Every time I look at him, everything else stops, like we're floating outside time and space.

I fumble my phone out and flip through my pictures.

Aside from a handful of targeted ads for murder mystery TV shows I wanted to remember to watch, there isn't much to get through before I make it to shots of my last few projects. A mug, two different vases, another bowl that doesn't really look butt-like at all. Or hardly, anyway.

I pass him my phone. He studies it, his tongue tracing over his bottom lip as he slowly flips through the pictures. We've done at least one full rotation on the Ferris wheel by the time he reaches the last one and starts flipping back the other way, pausing on each, zooming in to see the details of the glazes.

"This one." He's staring at the smaller of the vases, streaked with shades of green, blue, purple, and brown, a horizon of earthy colors.

My heart squeezes. "That one's called Hank."

He looks up, face open, with the expression that used to make me think of quicksand, a face that could pull you in and never let you go.

"You named it?" he says. "After my dad?"

"Isn't that humiliating?" I try to pull my phone away.

He doesn't let go. "Why would it be humiliating?"

"Because I'm not Michelangelo," I say. "My vases don't need names."

He holds the phone up. "This one needs a fucking name, and that name is Hank." I reach for it again, but he yanks it out of reach, goes back to staring at the screen, creases rising from the insides of his brows. Quietly, he says, "It looks like him."

"You don't have to say that, Wyn," I reply. "It's a vase, by an amateur."

"It looks like Montana," he says. "The colors are exactly right."

"Or maybe you're just really high," I say.

"I am definitely really high," he says. "But I'm also right."

Our eyes snag, warmth gathering at my core. I hold my hand out. He sets my phone in it.

"Did you show this to my mom?" he asks.

I shake my head. "I was thinking about giving it to her."

"Let me buy it," he says.

I laugh. "What? Definitely not."

"Why not?"

"Because it's not worth anything," I say.

"It is to me," he says.

"Then you can pay for shipping," I say. "It will be from both of us."

"Okay. I'll pay for shipping." After a pause, he says, "How'd you get into it?"

"Ceramics?"

He nods.

I let out a breath. "It was about a week after we broke up. I was walking home from a shift, and I was a couple blocks from ou— my apartment." I correct myself at the last second, but my face flames anyway.

I hadn't wanted to go home that day. I'd scrubbed in on another rough surgery. The patient pulled through, but I'd felt sick ever since.

All I wanted was to be wrapped up in Wyn's arms, and I knew if I walked into our apartment, there'd be shadows of him everywhere but no trace of the real thing.

I swallow the lump burgeoning in my throat. "And I saw this shop. And it reminded me of being here, because, you know . . ."

"You can't go four feet without hitting a ceramic nautilus shell vase?" he guesses.

"Exactly," I say. "And I've never been super interested in all those pottery shops while we're *here,* you know? But when I saw this place, I felt like . . . like it was a little piece of home. Or, you know, whatever the cottage is for us."

"So you just went in?" he asks.

"I just went in."

A smile teases at the edges of his mouth. "That's not like you."

"I know," I say. "But I was having a bad day. And there was an ice cream shop next door, so I got a scoop there, and by the time I was leaving, people were showing up at the studio for a beginners' class, and the alternative was to go home and watch more *Murder, She Wrote,* so I just went in."

Softly, he says, "And you liked it."

"I really liked it," I admit.

"You're good at it," he says.

"Not really," I say. "But that's the thing. Nothing's riding on it. If I mess it up, it doesn't matter. I can start over, and honestly, I don't even mind. Because when I'm working on it, I feel good. I'm not muscling through to see how it turns out. I like *doing* it. I don't have to stay hyperfocused. I don't have to do *anything* but stick my hands in some mud and be. I zone out and let my mind wander."

He must see something in my expression, because he says, "What do you think about?"

My cheeks tingle. "I don't know. Places, mostly."

"Which places?"

I look down to the festival stretched out beneath us, watching a little boy and girl zigzag through the crowd with cotton candy bouquets twice as big as their heads. "Anywhere I've been happy," I say.

There's a long pause. "Montana?"

My throat twists. I nod.

"That bowl that looked like a butt — I was thinking about the water here in Knott's Harbor," I say. "About the waves, and how weird it is that they don't really exist. Like the water is just the water, but the tide

286

moves through them and the wind moves over them and they change shape, but they're always just water."

"So I guess," he says, "some things change *and* stay the same."

I know we're high. I *know* he hasn't actually said anything profound, but when his pale coyote eyes lift to mine, my heart seems to flip over, everything inside me turning a full one hundred and eighty degrees. It's like I've been upside down all this time, and the motion has finally righted me.

"Is there one that looks like us?" he asks.

They all do, I think. *You are in all of my happiest places.*

You are where my mind goes when it needs to be soothed.

I shift on the bench. His fingertips graze my thigh. His focus homes in on the contact.

His lips knit together as he traces the fold of fabric, and while he's not exactly touching me, the nerves along my hip still whir to life, heat, fizz.

"You have to feel this, Harriet," he says dreamily.

I break into giggles. "That gummy was not tiny."

"On the plus side," he says, "it's making this fabric feel amazing."

"You mean *taste* amazing," I say.

"Like red gummy," he agrees, dropping his mouth toward my shoulder, running his parted lips over the strap. My breath catches. I set my hands against the lap bar, where I can be reasonably sure they won't spontaneously climb up the inside of Wyn's shirt.

"Is this what silk is?" he asks, lifting his face, eyes sparkling earnestly beneath the flashing purple lights.

"Satin," I tell him. "A poor man's silk."

"A poor but lucky man's silk," Wyn says. "It feels like . . . damp skin. Here." He takes my hand from the lap bar and brings it to my own thigh, watching for my reaction as he lets our hands drift over the hem until the very ends of our fingers are on skin. "See?"

I nod, breathless.

His eyes darken, pure black now except the outermost edge of silvery green.

"Do you remember what you told me," I say, "about your brain?"

His hand pauses.

"You said it felt like a Ferris wheel," I say. "Like all your thoughts were constantly circling, and you'd reach out for one, but it was hard to stay on it for too long because they kept spinning."

The lines of his face soften. His fingers curl, the backs of his nails pressing into my skin. "Except with you. You're like gravity."

I couldn't have pulled myself away from him then if he'd burst into flames.

"Everything keeps spinning," he says in a low, hoarse voice. "But my mind's always got one hand on you."

The night air warms between us until it crackles. We're about to break the rule. We're about to kiss with no one looking, and I don't care. Or I do care, in that I need it. I need *his* gravity. I need his mouth and hips to pin me in place, to anchor me in this moment, to slow time even further, like he always has, until *this* becomes my real life, and everything else — the shoebox apartment, the aching back and knees, the sweat pooling under my gown and mask, the nights staring up at a ceiling that has nothing to say to me — is the memory.

"HAR!" someone shouts above us. The moment snaps.

We both look up.

"CATCH!"

I don't see which of them shouts it. All I see is Kimmy and Cleo — now above us as we're descending the back of the Ferris wheel — leaned out over their lap bar, laughing hysterically, and then something

289

flamingo pink fluttering, flapping, twirling down toward us.

It lands squarely in my lap.

"Hold on to that, would you?" Kimmy shouts. Cleo doubles over, her shoulders twitching with laughter.

Wyn takes hold of the pink thing and lifts it, spreading it out so the hot-pink bra cups jut from his chest.

Above us, Cleo and Kimmy are shrieking now.

"This," Wyn says, "is exactly why I hate getting clothes as presents. Nothing ever fits."

"At least it's your color," I say.

He tuts, laughing, and shakes his head. "Thanks, Kim."

Kimmy hurls herself forward, squawking something through her guffaws, but Cleo yanks her back against the bench.

"Excuse me, Wyn." I pull the tiny bra out of his hands, holding it in front of me. "In which universe does *this* fit on Kimmy's boobs?"

He gapes, looks up at Cleo and Kimmy, who are still falling all over each other in fits of laughter, then back at me. "Damn," he says. "Didn't see that one coming."

"Me neither," I say. "I always assumed Cleo was die-hard Free the Nipple."

"What's going on up there?" Parth calls from below us.

They're starting to level out on the loading platform. "We have to act fast," Wyn says, expecting me to read his mind.

I do. "You've got better aim than me."

"I'm not even going to politely argue," he says, and takes the bra.

We lean forward, and as Sabrina and Parth are about to dock, Wyn tosses the bra straight onto Sabrina's head.

"WHAT THE —" she screams, her words cut short when Parth pulls the bra off her head and holds it aloft for examination in the neon light, right as they're drawing to a stop beside the long-suffering Ferris wheel attendant.

Even from here, his grumble sounds like "millennials," which makes Wyn and me burst into laughter so forceful that tears are literally sliding off my chin.

"It happened!" I squeal. "We've replaced our parents as the drunk-mom-on-vacation generation."

"Excuse you," he says, "I think you mean the high-dad-on-vacation generation."

Below us, Sabrina climbs out of her seat, head held high and dignified. She hands the bra over to the attendant and, loudly and clearly enough for all of us and everyone in line to hear, says, "Do you have a lost and found? Someone seems to have dropped this on the ride."

"Are we about to get kicked out of Lobster Fest?" I ask Wyn.

His head falls back with another wave of laughter. "It was bound to happen eventually."

"End of an era," I say.

"Nah." His eyes slice sideways. "Another beginning."

We're still giggly when we spill out of the Rover in front of the cottage, Sabrina leaning heavily on me, Kimmy leaning even more heavily on Wyn behind us. We're almost to the front steps when our fearless (braless) designated driver takes off toward the side of the house.

"Where are you going?" Parth throws his arms out. "You have the keys!"

Sabrina and I exchange a look, then take off after her, around the dark side of the house. Cleo throws the gate to the patio open, kicking her shoes off as she runs through, unbuttoning her pants.

Sabrina thumps my arm to get me to run faster, and we round the bend in time to see Cleo, now pantsless, leap into the pool. The others come around the bend, and

Sabrina spins toward Parth, uses her full weight to shove him in.

Without hesitation, Kimmy cannonballs in after him, one shoe still on. Sabrina whirls on me. I shriek and swat her hands away. "We're too old!" I cry. "Don't make me do this!"

I get hold of her wrists. Her yelp turns into laughter as we struggle at the water's edge.

I'm swept off my feet from behind. An arm tight around my rib cage, a clovey smell, as I'm pitched off-balance.

We fall together, tangled, breathless. The water folds around us, and I open my eyes beneath the surface, turning in his arms. Everything is glitter, shimmering bits of silver blue at first, and then there he is, paled by the pool's strange light. His hair waves out, dancing around his face, and bubbles slip from his nose and the corners of his mouth.

He catches my hands and draws me closer. I don't even think about holding myself back. I'd like to blame the weed, but I can't. It's him and me.

My thighs skate over his, nesting loose against his hips. He brings my hands to the back of his neck, and we sink like that, descending from the glowing legs treading water. He pulls me flush to him, his heart pumping against my collarbone.

And then we've reached the bottom of the pool. We can't go any deeper. He pushes off against the tile, sending us back to the surface.

Cold air, laughter, screeching from the edge of the pool, where Kimmy and Cleo have now teamed up to get Sabrina into the water.

And I don't feel young. I feel alive. Jolted awake. My skin, muscles, organs, bones, all somehow more concrete here. Wyn's face and eyelashes glisten, his shirt plastered to him. His fingers are gentle on my jaw, his thumb tracing over my bottom lip as his eyes watch it drop open, as if to breathe him into me. Our lungs expand, pushing into each other, and his gaze lifts to mine, and here, with everyone to see it, where the rule I set won't be broken — where I can *act* like it's an *act* — I tip my mouth up under his.

20
NOT QUITE REAL LIFE

But still Wednesday

His tongue brushes my bottom lip first, like he's just tasting. Like he doesn't plan to kiss me at all. But my lips part for him anyway, and he sighs as his mouth sweeps upward, catching mine in full.

He captures my face in his hands and angles me up to deepen the kiss, the heat of his mouth scorching compared to the mild warmth of the water.

There's no thought, no logic, no feeling other than *him.* My hands slip up the back of his shirt, nails sinking into his shoulder blades, and his hands sweep down my body, barely touching, leaving trails of goose bumps. My breath catches, spine curving into him, and his grip tightens against my thighs, scraping up beneath my hem to press me flush to him. His erection rocks against me, sending sparks showering across the backs of my eyes, and my nipples pinch as I arch into him.

My back meets the corner of the pool. Our hips angle together as his mouth glides down my neck, kissing me, biting wherever shivers erupt.

My skin burns everywhere it wants him.

The saving grace of this situation is that we're not alone. That I can't take this as far as I want to.

Behind us, Cleo and Kimmy finally manage to shove Sabrina into the pool. The splash carries a torrent of swear words up to the night sky. Wyn pulls back from me, his forehead resting against my temple, his heart slamming into me.

All I want now is to go to bed. I'm vaguely aware that there are reasons this is a terrible idea, but I'm having trouble pulling any of them to the forefront of my mind.

"You're full of surprises tonight, Clee," Parth shouts.

Cleo backstrokes past us, grinning up at the visible sliver of moon overhead. "Then I guess I've met my goal for the week."

Still sputtering over the water and pushing fistfuls of honey-blond out of her face, Sabrina says, "Your goal for the week was to throw your bra off a Ferris wheel and bodycheck me into a pool?"

Cleo sits up, treading water. "More or less."

Kimmy spikes a beach ball right at us, and I dive away from Wyn, my face tingling, my smile aching, my whole body buzzing.

Try as I might to bring myself back to reality, to the world outside the bubble of Knott's Harbor, I am fully, terrifyingly *here*, where nothing else seems to matter.

After we've toweled off, climbed the stairs, and said our good nights, my bravery flags a little. Wyn holds tight to my hand as we make our way down the hall and into our dark bedroom.

He presses me back into the door the moment it's closed. We've barely taken our hands off each other since that first kiss in the pool, but now that we're alone, we're both so much less certain. He's trembling, or else I am — it's always been hard to tell where one of us ends and the other begins — and our hands twist together, our breaths shallow.

It's not that I think what happened downstairs was an act. But it was part of an agreement.

This isn't. And neither of us seems to have decided what happens next.

My body has one idea. My brain isn't a

fan of the plan.

You've spent months trying to forget what you're missing, I tell myself. *How will you survive being reminded? Living the loss of it all over again?*

His pulse is drumming into my chest. My weight shifts into him, my breasts brushing against his soaked T-shirt, and he lets out an unsteady breath.

I'm starved of him. I've been stranded in a Wyn-less desert, my throat bone-dry, and that first sip downstairs has made the thirst worse. My nervous system doesn't care that this is a mirage. The violent kinetic thrumming is back, the air particles between us sparking.

"Is this okay," he asks thickly.

I lift toward him like a charmed snake, my knees buckling a little when his palms touch my stomach through the damp satin, start to glide heavily up me. His lips skirt along my collarbone, his breath diffusing over my skin.

His dark eyes lift as his palms settle against my chest. I rock into his touch. His hands move to cup me more fully. When his thumbs graze my nipples, he groans, catches them between his fingers, watching the way my breath staggers and my body bows upward.

He slips one of my straps down my shoulder, kisses the bare skin where it used to be. His fingers find the other strap and tug it away too. My head tips back as I try to get a good breath, and he slips a hand into the now loose top of my bodice, his fingers curling against me.

He steps in close, his knee batting my thighs apart. I wrap my hand around his neck to keep from collapsing when his mouth drops to my chest, his lips closing over me. My existence narrows to that point, to the gentle pressure and fierce heat of his lips. He yanks my dress down until I'm bare to the waist, kisses his way across me, his palm moving to roll heavily against me.

"Tell me to kiss you, Harriet," he rasps.

I don't know if it's wounded pride or fear of this all-consuming want or something else, but I can't stand to ask for more of him.

"Tell me to kiss you," he says again, nudging my thighs wider to ease in between my hips.

I rake my hands down his back, take hold of his waist, keeping us pinned together. I feel his pulse in his groin, or maybe it's mine. The lines between him and me have become fuzzy, insubstantial.

"What are we doing?" he asks.

"I thought that was obvious," I say.

His hips rock into me, and god help me, my hands go straight to his ass. He lifts me against the door, my thighs around his hips, my arms hooked behind his head, his erection hard against me.

I want him on top of me, beneath me, behind me. I want him in my mouth, his clothes in a pile on the floor, his sweat on my stomach, his voice rough against my ear. I want anything other than to stop.

"What does this mean," he asks raggedly, still cupping me, kissing me.

"I don't know," I say.

A low, frustrated sound dies in the back of his throat, and he stills, holding me firmly against the door.

"This is a bad idea, Harriet," he says hoarsely after a few seconds, lowering me but not stepping back. "We can't be together."

The words knock the wind out of me.

"I know that," I say.

And I do. He broke my heart, destroyed it. And even if I *could* forgive him, he's *happy* in his new life. I know there's no going back.

So why does hearing it make my chest feel like a split log?

I push against Wyn's shoulders, pull my straps back up.

He steps back, murmuring, "I'm sorry. I wasn't thinking."

"I'm not sure you started it," I get out.

He runs a hand up the back of his head, his brow deeply grooved. "I'm not sure that I *didn't* either."

"Then I guess I should say I'm sorry too," I say.

His mouth twitches, a smile that's anything but happy. He sighs. "This place."

This place, indeed. It's too easy to forget about the real world here, our circumstances, the things that broke us.

All the reasons there's no finding our way back.

I flatten my palms against the door's smooth wood. "We got swept up in it. That's all."

After a beat, he says, "I don't want to do anything else that hurts you."

"You didn't," I say.

I hurt myself, I think.

He looks over my shoulder at the door, almost guiltily.

"I think I should take a walk. Cool down."

The thought of being any farther away from him than this is torment. I nod.

His eyes scrape down me and back up

301

once more, heat washing from my head to my toes, a heavy pulse of need between my thighs.

"The bed's all yours," he says, and stalks past me. I slide out of the way so he can open the door. "Don't feel like you need to wait up."

It's not that I wait up for him. It's that as soon as I climb under the sheets, it's like he hasn't left at all, only multiplied. Every breeze from the cracked window is his mouth. Every brush of the sheets is his hand, moving across my thigh, over the curve of my stomach. Every creak of the settling house is his voice: *Tell me to kiss you.*

I try to think about anything else. My mind is caught on him.

Earlier tonight, as Cleo and I rested our chins atop our folded arms at the pool's edge, legs sweeping in slow, luxurious kicks through the water, she asked, *Any progress on your goal for the week?*

And my eyes went straight for Wyn.

Not yet, I told her.

I don't even know what I need from this week. To make it to the end without coming apart? Or without ruining Sabrina and Parth's wedding?

My life has been on one set of rails since I

decided to go into medicine. It's been easy to make decisions with that as the governing force. Outside of that, I've rarely had to.

But I don't want to regret anything at the end of this week. I want to feel like I used this time, even in a small way, how I wanted to.

And that's what I fall asleep thinking over and over again: *What do you want, Harriet?*

I dream he climbs into bed with me. *Arms up, baby,* he says, and peels away my *Virgin Who CAN Drive* T-shirt.

There's no one else, he whispers into the curve of my belly, the underside of my arm. *Perfect,* he says.

When I wake before sunrise, I'm still alone.

21
HAPPY PLACE

West Village, New York City

Wyn's and my first place, just the two of us. A hissing radiator. A ghost who never does much, other than open a window when it's cool out or knock a book off a shelf. Sitting on the floor, eating noodles straight from the take-out boxes because we don't have a couch yet.

Side tables found on curbs and repaired to perfection by Wyn. A shelf installed above our bed, lined with the James Herriot paperbacks Hank used to read Wyn and his sisters when they were small. Plus one particular romance novel, whose origins neither of us even recall. (Wyn says it probably belongs to the ghost.) Our first place together, just the two of us, and it's bittersweet.

Weeks ago, as the end of the lease on the Morningside Heights apartment drew closer, Cleo sat us down in a row on Parth's squashy couch to announce she was moving.

Not just out of the apartment, or even New York.

To Belize, to work on an organic farm.

It's called WWOOFing, she explained. *You live there for free in exchange for some work.*

And at first no one said anything. Until then, we'd been in a suspended reality. It had felt as if we'd stay like this, together forever, and nothing would change.

It's only temporary, Cleo said, *a six-month contract,* but she was crying.

We all knew: this was the end of an era.

So we sat on the rug, our arms wrapped around her like we were a giant artichoke, her as our heart.

The night before she left, Parth organized a slideshow send-off, putting our favorite memories from the last three years up on the wall, and we cried some more, but in the morning, we put on brave faces and hugged goodbye outside JFK. *See you soon,* we promised.

We tried to find a new place to accommodate the remaining four of us.

We couldn't.

Instead, Parth moved in with a friend from Fordham, Sabrina took over an Armas cousin's vacant Chelsea loft, and Wyn and I scrounged up enough to rent the tiny apartment over the bookstore he'd been working at.

The whole first night we were there, I had to keep shutting myself in the bathroom for crying jags. I missed Cleo so much it hurt. I was afraid this was the end. That my friends would prove to be passing figures in my life, family becoming strangers.

After my last crying fit, I came out of the bathroom to a cry of "SURPRISE!"

Wyn had called Parth and Sabrina. They came, with pizza and champagne. "We had to christen the place," Parth said.

"Plus, I want to see if this place is as haunted as it looks," Sabrina added.

After that night, the apartment becomes home.

We're happy here.

Parth and Sabrina come over once a week for dinner, and even though we're alleged Real Adults, sometimes they sleep over on the couch and air mattress, and in the morning we get diner breakfast before heading to our separate programs or, in Wyn's case, down to the bookstore.

And it doesn't get boring, just the two of us. Every bit of Wyn he gives me is something to treasure, to examine from every angle.

The last words I hear every night are *I love you so much*. Sometimes he gets to say it last, but sometimes I do too. Sometimes we compete, saying it back and forth like we're fourteen-year-olds: *No, you hang up first*.

Medical school ramps up. I start TAing for my favorite professor. The sex slows down, but not the touching, not the affection. His love is steady, constant. Easier than breathing, because *breathing* is something you can overthink, to the point that you forget how your lungs work and get yourself into a panic.

I could never forget how to love Wyn.

Sometimes, lying beside him in our bed, my ice-cold feet tucked between his warm calves, the words flit through my mind, like they're coming from somewhere else, like my soul hears his whispering in its sleep, *You belong here.*

On Saturday mornings, we drink coffee on the sofa next to the window and do crossword puzzles. Or we start crossword puzzles. It becomes something of a tradition, starting and abandoning them.

Every week I try to make it through at least one more clue than the week prior, while Wyn tries to derail us earlier and earlier.

"Eight across," I tell him, while he's kissing his way down my neck, "is *The Weakest Link.*"

"Isn't that the one where they dropped people through a trapdoor when they got eliminated?" he hums against my collarbone.

"I never watched that," I say, "but I swear, the moment I said it, that's what I pictured. But that seems impossible, right? It's too ridiculous."

He shrugs, pulls me over his lap, but I keep my hold on my laptop, type *weakest link trapdoor* into a Google search.

The first few hits are from message boards. People who remember the show exactly how we do, though everything else online confirms there was never a trapdoor.

"How is it possible we *all* remember it wrong?" Wyn asks.

I tell him about the Mandela effect, the idea that sometimes huge swaths of the population misremember something precisely the same way. Scientists explain the shared false memories as confabulations, or examples of fuzzy-trace theory, where memories are malleable and unreliable, while others wonder if the Mandela effect proves we live in a multiverse.

Grinning, Wyn twines one of my curls around his hand. "I like how you talk to me like you expect me to understand what you're saying."

I frown. "I *don't* like how you always downplay your own intelligence."

"I don't," he says.

"You do," I say. "And not knowing something doesn't make a person stupid, Wyn."

"Oh," he says, amused. "Then what does?"

After a moment's thought, I say, "An unwillingness to learn."

"I'm willing." He sets my laptop aside and pulls me closer, hands settling on my thighs. "Tell me about this multiverse and what it has to do with *The Weakest Link.*"

"Well, if there are multiple universes, then maybe our consciousnesses move through them sometimes. Maybe we spend years in one reality, then jump to another where only one tiny thing is different. Like a certain reality show used a trapdoor to eliminate contestants. And there are infinite universes, where everything that ever could happen has and will."

Wyn brings one of my hands to his mouth, his expression serious. "How many universes do you think we're together in?"

"Higher than either of us can count."

His mouth quirks. "And you can count *very* high."

"It's true," I say. "That's how they decide

who gets into medical school. You stand in front of a committee of doctors and count as high as you can."

His lips twitch. "Do they let you use your fingers?"

"None of the *good* schools do."

He flattens my hand between his palms. "I'm glad I'm in one of those," he says. "I feel bad for all the Wyns in universes where you're with guys like Harvard Hudson. They're so miserable right now, Harriet."

"Or the Harriets in universes where you're with the Dancers Named Alison of the world," I say.

"No," he says quietly. "In every universe, it's you for me. Even if it's not me for you."

That isn't how it works.

I don't care.

Wyn — *my* Wyn — means it.

I am happier than I've ever been. Don't yet know that there is a level of happiness even deeper, one so intense it hurts, almost like loss or grief. A happiness so bright and hot you feel like it could incinerate you. That comes later that night, when Wyn goes out to pick up Chinese food, comes back drenched from the rain.

At the sound of the door clicking shut, I look up from the crossword I've gone back to, jump up from the couch, and pad over to help him with the rain-speckled paper bags. I flick the stove on to make tea and take the bags from his arms, and as I'm setting them on the counter, he catches me by the wrist and looks down at me with such softness and vulnerability that I'm afraid, sure something terrible has happened. Quietly, then, a murmur, he says, "Marry me, Harriet."

"Yes," I say on a breath.

He stills. He blinks, like he's trying to puzzle out what I just said. The teakettle has started to whistle. I catch his jaw. "Wyn, *yes.*"

His brow tenses. "Wait."

"I don't want to wait," I say.

He fumbles in his jacket. "Shit. Give me a second. Don't move."

He turns and runs back to the bedroom, and I stand there shivering, listening to the scrape of dresser drawers. When he comes back, he's holding out a blue velvet box, his hand quivering.

It's an old white gold ring with a square sapphire mounted in its center. "I thought it looked like you," he says hesitantly, "but it wasn't expensive. So if you don't like it, we'll replace it, as soon as I can afford —"

His face blurs behind my tears. "You just had this?"

"I was trying to wait for the perfect moment," he says, almost apologetic.

"Now," I say. "Now is the perfect moment."

"I just couldn't keep waiting," he says, still a little rueful.

The tiniest bit of doubt creeps in. I whisper, "What if you get sick of me?"

"Harriet," he says, gently chiding and tender all at once. "What if you get bored with me?"

My laugh is so teary it sounds like a sob. "Never."

He cradles my face in his hands, his mouth soft and brow stern. "Then marry me."

"Done," I say.

He kisses me, all teeth and tongue and raw emotion, our hands scraping over each other in eager fits, bodies pulling together, determined to become one thing.

I never pictured my proposal, but if I had, it would've looked nothing like this.

It wouldn't have ended with us eating the same Chinese takeout we get once a week and making love on the rickety Ikea couch, laughing every time his head collided with the wall but not moving to the bed.

This is better. Everything is better with him.

When we go back to Maine that summer, Sabrina, Parth, and Cleo — who's managed to get back from Belize — throw us an engagement party, complete with a slide-show covering our relationship (largely illustrated by stick figures Parth drew in MS Paint).

It doesn't matter how busy life's been, how long the five of us have gone without seeing one another: meeting at the cottage is like pulling on a favorite sweatshirt, worn to perfection.

Time doesn't move the same way when we're there.

Things change, but we stretch and grow and make room for one another.

Our love is a place we can always come back to, and it will be waiting, the same as it ever was.

You belong here.

22
REAL LIFE

Thursday

Sabrina practically skips down the dock toward the sleek white rental boat.

Wyn brushes past me to follow Parth down the pier, and my legs fully forget what we're doing at his sudden closeness, stopping abruptly.

When I got downstairs this morning, he was already eating fruit and toast on the back deck, his hair damp and clothes changed. He must've sneaked in at some point in the night and out again before I woke up. Ever since then, we've been politely dodging each other.

Cleo pauses to dig a tube of motion sickness pills out of her backpack. "Want one?"

"Did you just happen to bring these with you?" I say. "And here I was, proud of myself for remembering *floss.*"

Cleo's shoulders hitch. "For the drive down. I can't read in the car without get-

314

ting sick."

Wyn climbs in, then turns to offer his hand to Cleo as she makes the hop down. He moves to help me too, but I pretend not to notice and jump down.

Right then, some traffic in the harbor sends a wave under the boat, and my knees buckle. Wyn has to catch me around the hips, and the pressure of his body against mine from chest to hips is, oh, three trillion times worse than accepting his hand would have been.

"You okay?" he asks.

To which I reply, "Mm!"

Cleo settles onto one of the marshmallowy benches. "Where exactly are we going?"

Sabrina has already taken her station at the chrome steering wheel, and Parth is zigzagging around the little vessel, loosening lines. At least I assume that's what he's doing. Everything I know about boats I learned while high out of my mind, so it's hard to say.

"Wherever the wind takes us," Parth cries over his shoulder.

"So we're going to die," Cleo says.

"Possibly," Sabrina says. "But first we're going to see some puffins and harbor seals."

Parth undoes the final knot, and the

breeze nudges us away from the dock as Sabrina spins the wheel to point us toward the open water, the smell of brine thickening as the wind brushes salt over our skin.

At the back of the boat, Wyn watches the harbor shrink, his shirt rippling to show off slices of his low back and upper arms, only to hide them again.

Overhead, the clouds part, Sabrina's hair and the white knit of her matching halter and shorts gleaming in the sun against her olive skin. Parth joins her at the wheel, in his own white linen combo, the top and bottom buttons of his shirt casually undone in a way that truly makes him look like he's filming a Tom Ford commercial, or like the two of them are Hollywood A-listers off the coast of Ibiza.

I, meanwhile, look like a frazzled camp counselor holding on for dear life through the end of the summer. Not so different from how I feel.

"I think the itinerary's prompt to *dress comfortably* could have been a little more specific," I say to Cleo.

Sabrina beams over her shoulder. "You actually read the itinerary!"

Cleo leans into me, the light glancing off her septum ring, and says, "Oh, Harriet. Sabrina can't help it that she's most comfortable in Gucci."

Sabrina scoffs. "Don't be ridiculous. This is Chanel."

"Oh my god, are you kidding?" Kimmy flops onto the bench opposite us. "You're wearing Chanel? On a boat?"

Wyn takes the seat beside her, and I tip my head toward him. "So is Wyn."

It's our first moment of direct eye contact of the day. It makes me feel like my bathing suit is disintegrating beneath my clothes.

"Really, Wyn? Chanel?" Kimmy says. "I had no idea you were so fancy."

His gaze snags on mine for a second before dragging to hers. "Only my briefs."

"Well, I think you're *all* overdressed," Kimmy says. "The itinerary said *comfortable,* and if you wanted to be comfortable, then you, like me, would not be wearing underwear."

"Hard agree," Parth says.

Sabrina looks nonplussed. "Are you seriously not wearing any underwear?"

Parth drops into the seat beside Wyn. "What, it's fine for Kimmy but not for me?"

"Kimmy isn't wearing white pants made out of tissue paper," Wyn points out.

Parth's hands go protectively toward his crotch, then he sighs, resigned. "Whatever. Everyone in this boat has seen me naked at

317

some point or another."

"I actually haven't," Kimmy says thoughtfully.

"Well, Kimberly," Parth replies, "it might just be your lucky day."

Wyn's eyes catch mine for a second again. In my chest, an engine turns over.

We cruise through the smattering of islands that dot the coast, sail past two separate lighthouses, and pause for giddy pictures when we spot the first slew of plump seals sunbathing on the rocks. Pretty quickly, we realize the water is brimming with them. A horde of them, an embarrassment of seals.

"Quick," Kimmy says to Cleo, "help me grab one to take home."

"This isn't my exact area of expertise," Parth says, "but I'm guessing there *are* laws against that."

"Yes, and there are higher divine laws about little whiskered faces needing kisses," Kimmy says, leaning out over the edge of the boat toward a seal who's either scratching his back on the rock or possibly trying to roll upright. "Plus, taking a seal home was my secret goal for this week."

"Sometimes when you love something," Cleo says, squeezing Kimmy's shoulders, "you have to let it go."

I have to work not to look over at Wyn.

"You're a good boy!" Kimmy shouts at the seal as we pull away. "Or girl! Or whatever!"

Around lunchtime, we dock on one of the summer community islands and climb over the jagged shoreline, watching horseshoe crabs dart and scuttle through the murky shallows.

"These things freak me out," Parth says.

"They look like something out of *Jurassic Park*," Wyn says, lightly touching my elbows as he leans over me to see. The breeze swirls his scent around me like a length of silk.

"I love them," Cleo says.

"I'll let you take one home," Kimmy says, "*if* we go back for my seal."

"I'm sorry, babe, I just don't think we've got room for that kind of responsibility in our lives."

"If life's too hectic for your best friends to visit," Sabrina says, "then you don't have time to start a horseshoe crab preserve."

"Would you quit picking at me," Cleo says.

Sabrina's eyes widen. "I was kidding."

"Well, it's not funny," Cleo says.

"Okay, okay," Sabrina replies. "I'm *sorry!*"

Cleo turns away, hiking up the shore toward the gnarled woods, and Sabrina looks at Kimmy.

She shakes her head. "She's under a lot of pressure right now. Give her a break."

It's as close to an admonishment as I've ever heard Kimmy give, and she doesn't wait around for Sabrina's reply before striding up the path after Cleo.

Sabrina turns away, looking out at the water, shoulders square and arms folded. She gives one firm shake of her head on a laugh that rides the line between exhausted and hurt.

"Maybe we should eat," I suggest.

"Great idea," Parth chimes in, clearly as eager as I am to smooth things over.

"I'll go grab the picnic basket," I call, already picking my way back over the kelp-strewn rocks toward the docked boat. I kick off my sandals and hop in.

"What was that about?" comes Wyn's voice.

I turn to find him walking up the dock. I look back toward the others. Sabrina and Parth are having an animated conversation on the shore, and Cleo and Kimmy are ambling through the woods, partially obscured by twisted branches of thick dark pine needles and yellow-green leaves.

"From what I've gathered," I say, looking away before his closeness can hit my bloodstream, "Sabrina's jockeying for an invitation to the farm, and Cleo's annoyed that she's jockeying."

"And Kimmy?" Wyn asks.

"Annoyed with Sabrina for being annoyed with Cleo."

The boat rocks under my feet as he steps down. "So where do we fit into this?"

"I don't know, I guess I could be annoyed with Kimmy about being annoyed, and then that could potentially annoy you?"

"You never annoy me," he says.

I look up, catch him watching me.

My laugh is breathless, woozy. "We both know that's not true."

He studies me for a second, brow furrowed. "Frustrate, maybe. Not annoy."

"What's the difference?" I ask.

His eyes drop to my legs and back up. "When you're annoyed, you don't want to be around a person." His chin shifts to the left, not quite a shake of his head. "I always want to be around you."

I want to call him out, to trot out those key moments from our history that decidedly disprove this. But I can't. I can remember what the arcuate fasciculus does for the human brain but not exactly how to use it to make words.

"Here," he says, reaching for the cooler. "I can get that."

"So can I," I say, lifting it against my shins.

"Harriet."

I shuffle sideways.

He laughs. "So we're back to this?"

"Back to what?" I say.

His brow scrunches against the sun, his full upper lip inching up like there's a string tied to his Cupid's bow. "Fighting about every tiny thing."

"Is this fighting?" I say.

"Harriet," he says. "Compared to the rest of our relationship, this is a brawl."

I glance down the shore. Parth has his arm around Sabrina and they're climbing the rotting wooden steps from the beach to the forested hill, catching up with Kimmy and Cleo now. I fight an urge to sprint after them, to take up the role of buffer or referee.

"Don't," Wyn says gently.

I look back at him, my low back aching. "Don't what?"

"Go after them," he says, drifting closer.

I swallow. "Why not?"

He pulls the cooler out of my hands and sets it on the bench. "Because we're talking."

"You mean *brawling*," I say.

His lips twitch.

"Shouldn't we be done fighting," I say, "now that we're broken up?"

The corners of his mouth twist downward now. "Harriet, we never fought when we were together. If we had . . ."

He trails off, doesn't land that final blow. I feel it all the same, a knife twist in my heart.

From the shore, an air horn blasts, three times in rapid succession.

Neither of us moves, or even looks away. The wanting is palpable.

"Shit," Wyn says, shaking his head. "I don't like not touching you."

I look away. Now my heart feels like one giant blister, too tender, too delicate. If only he'd felt that way sooner. If only I had any clue what went wrong, how I lost him. If only I believed there were some way to fix it. But he's not the only one who's done things he can't take back. And revisiting what's happened will only make the pain worse.

The air horn blows again. I clear my throat. "You get the cooler, and I'll grab the picnic basket."

He nods for several seconds, then hoists the ice chest into his arms and turns away.

23
UNHAPPY PLACE

An Hour Outside Indianapolis, Indiana
A quiet bi-level at the end of a quiet cul-de-sac. A place where everything is familiar but nothing belongs to me. Trees standing too still in the stiff humidity. Mosquitoes buzzing, moths gathering around the streetlights, the screech of cicadas emanating from the woods.

I managed to put this off for a long time, but I couldn't anymore. It meant too much to him.

At the doorstep, I ask, "What if we leave? We can pretend our flight got delayed."

"Delayed for what?" Wyn says. "It's June."

"Too sunny," I say. "The pilots couldn't see with all that light."

He cradles my face in his hands, his brow knitting. "I'm great with parents, Harriet. Talking to old people is one of my very few God-given skills."

I'm too anxious to call out the self-deprecation. "It's not you I'm worried about."

His fingers thread into my hair. "If you want to run, we can run. But I'm not scared."

"I'm making them seem terrible," I whisper, "and they're not. I don't know why I get so anxious just being here."

His mouth nestles into my temple. "I'm here too. I've got you."

The words dissolve into my skin, fast-acting relief. "Just . . . please still like me after this."

He draws back, looks down the plane of his face at me. "Are you planning to stab me or something?"

"Only if there's no better way to put you out of your misery."

"Harriet." His mouth moves to the peak of one of my eyebrows and then to the other. "If it was possible to stop loving you, I would've managed it in that first year of desperately trying to. I'm here. For good."

"Well, if I'd known you needed help getting over me, I would've brought you to Indiana much sooner."

Holding my gaze, he reaches one hand over my shoulder and rings the doorbell.

My parents answer the door looking like a tired Norman Rockwell painting. Mom's wearing an apron, and Dad's got a David Baldacci book in hand, an immediate confirmation that they were in separate rooms until three seconds ago.

They take turns stiffly shaking Wyn's hand, and despite having braced myself for an awkward reception, I'm still embarrassed by the stark contrast between a weekend with the Connors and a Kilpatrick family welcome.

After several seconds in the doorway, I ask, "Did Eloise make it?"

"In the kitchen," Mom says, our cue to go inside.

In the dining room, Eloise shakes Wyn's hand from so far away they both have to lean forward to make it work, and then we all sit right down to eat. There's a lot of fork and knife action, unpleasant scratches and squeaks against the plates. I imagine Wyn is wondering whether this is actually a group of strangers I hired over the internet to pose as a family.

But somehow he's convincingly enthusiastic about everything: the sweet-tart-flavored Ohio Riesling, the very tame stroganoff, and even the conversation.

He tells my family how he and I met, as if they asked, and about our favorite park back in the city. He talks about how much we've missed Cleo since we last visited her up near her new farming job north of Montreal.

I probably *did* tell them about Cleo's international farming adventure at some point, but they've never met my friends, so I doubt they remember who Cleo is. Still, they nod along.

"And you're a cosmetologist, right?" Wyn asks Eloise, who stares at him for a second like she's trying to remember who he is and how either of them got here.

"That's right."

"Well, she's in cosmetology *school*," Mom says.

Eloise picks her fork up and goes back to eating.

"She's really good," I say. "When I was in high school, she always did my makeup for dances." Those were some of the few sisterly moments to pass between us. We'd barely speak, but they were nice memories all the same, having her tip my chin back and forth as she dusted bronzer on my cheeks and taught me how to use shadow to make my small almond eyes pop.

It was the only time I ever really felt like I had a sister.

"This girl was smart as they come," Dad says, jerking his noodle-laced fork in Eloise's direction. "Even skipped the third grade.

Wanted to be an astronaut, same as I did when I was a kid. But she fell in with the wrong crowd in high school."

Eloise doesn't even roll her eyes. She is perfectly unflappable as she drags her steak knife through her stroganoff and stuffs another bite in her mouth. My hairline is sweating.

"I was never good at school," Wyn says. "And I can't blame the crowd, because there were like forty people in my grade."

"But you got into Mattingly," Mom says. "You're clearly very intelligent."

"He is," I say, right as he says, "I was a student athlete."

"Well, to get into medical school, anyway," Dad says.

I full-body wince, but Wyn squeezes my knee reassuringly. "I'm actually not a med student," he says.

"He's in *law* school, Phil," Mom says, irritable.

"That's Sabrina and Parth," I say. "Wyn works at the bookstore and does furniture repair." *You know,* I think, *the one I'm* engaged *to.* But I think it with a smile that hopefully says, *No big deal that you don't remember the slightest thing about the love of my life.*

"Oh." Mom tries to smile pleasantly. She

328

and my dad exchange the briefest of looks, allies for a second.

"Have you thought about the wedding at all?" Eloise asks.

"Oh, I'm sure it's way too early for that," Mom says. "Harriet's still got a couple of years of medical school. And then she'll have to do a long residency."

Anxiety gurgles through my gut. "We're figuring it out."

Under the table, Wyn's hand finds mine, and he laces our fingers together. He drags the pad of his thumb over the callus where I burnt my index finger with Sabrina and Cleo on our first trip to the cottage. *I got you.*

"We're not in a rush," Wyn says. "I don't want to do anything that gets in the way of Harriet's career."

It's the perfect answer for my parents. My chest relaxes at my mom's pleased smile. Eloise downs her glass of wine and sets her napkin on the table. "I should get going," she says. "I've got work early in the morning."

"Who gets their makeup done early in the morning?" Mom asks, like it's an entirely innocent question and not a thinly veiled expression of two decades' worth of disappointment.

"Brides." Eloise pulls her denim jacket off the back of her chair. "Like Harriet."

Mom starts to stand. "At least let me put some leftovers together for you."

Eloise holds her off, insists she's too busy the next couple of days and won't get around to eating them, and Mom sags a little but relents. After quick waves and *nice to meet you*s, Eloise sees herself out.

"More wine?" Mom says.

We have another glass, sitting around the cleared table. Some of the awkwardness and tension fades as we sip, largely because Wyn brings up the research position I've scored for the summer, how proud he is of me.

"You know," Dad says, "we never had to worry about Harriet. Never even had a rebellious phase."

"Never got a detention," Mom says, "had perfect grades, got plenty of scholarships. No matter how stressful anything else was, we always knew Harriet was fine."

Wyn gives me a look I can't read, a tenderness around his mouth but concern in his brow.

He's good at getting them talking about themselves too: Mom talks about her receptionist job at the dentist's office — "Of course it's not brain surgery," she says brightly, "but it's fast-paced work, and it keeps me busy; I don't do well with boredom" — and Dad tells Wyn about teaching eighth-grade science.

"It wasn't the plan," Dad says, "but it's all been worth it. Our girl Harriet is going to change the world."

It makes me beam. It makes me ache.

It's this feeling like the universe is compacting around me, while something in my rib cage is expanding. I'm the culmination of their lost dreams, their missed other lives, and at the same time, they're proud of me.

Before they shuffle to bed at nine forty-five — the same time they've gone to sleep my entire life — I follow my mom into the kitchen to finish the dishes.

"So," I say. "What do you think?"

"About what?" she says.

"About Wyn," I say.

"He's a very nice young man," she says.

I wait for her to go on. For a minute, we're both drying plates and putting them away. Finally she faces me and smiles wanly. "Just don't rush anything. You've got your whole life, your career, ahead of you. And you know, *feelings* come and go. Your career won't. That's something you can rely on."

I make myself smile. "But you like him?"

She sighs and sets the hand towel aside, facing me with a creased brow. "He's sweet, honey," she says in a low voice, eyes darting toward the doorway, "but frankly, I don't see it."

My heart jitters. "See what?"

"Him making you happy," she says. "You making *him* happy."

"I *am* happy," I say.

"Now." She nods, glances toward the dining room again. "But that's the kind of boy who's going to want to move home and start having kids. He's going to want someone who's at home, who has a life that matches his. I pictured you with someone who had a bit more going on, who wouldn't expect more from you than you were able to give."

I blink against the stinging sensation in my eyes, the whole front of my face.

She softens a little. "Maybe I'm wrong." She picks up the towel and goes back to drying dishes. "It's our first time meeting him. Just be careful, Harriet." She hands me another dish, and I robotically towel it off.

Inside, I feel like I'm a log she's split with one swift swing of an ax.

I miss Wyn from the other room. I miss our apartment with its hissing radiator and its friendly book-moving ghost. I miss sitting on the rocks in Maine, shivering in the cold with Cleo's arms wrapped around me, both of us bundled up in old Mattingly sweatshirts while Parth and Sabrina argue over the best way to make a s'more.

Perfectly golden, according to Parth. *Utterly burnt,* if you ask Sabrina.

The four of us say good night in the living room, and then, when they close their bedroom door and it's just Wyn and me, I slump against his chest, and he holds me for a long time, kissing my head, rocking me back and forth.

"I missed you," I tell him.

He cups my face. "From the kitchen?"

I nod in his hands.

"Me too."

"I want to go home," I say.

His arms tighten across my back. "We will," he says. "You and me. In two days. But first I want to see everything."

"My boobs?" I joke.

"Those too," he says. "But I was thinking more like your boy band posters and embarrassing diaries."

"Joke's on you," I say. "The periodic table was my boy band poster."

He groans. "God, you're such a nerd."

I lace my fingers against the back of his preternaturally warm neck. "But you still like me?"

"You," he says, "are my periodic table."

I laugh into his chest. "I don't know what that means."

"It means when we get home," he says, "I'm covering our walls in lewd posters of you."

"It's always fun to have a home improvement project."

Circling the first floor, examining the minutiae of my home with him, is a funhouse version of our trip to Montana. Instead of a fridge crammed with out-of-date holiday cards and time-yellowed crayon drawings, there's a smooth stainless steel surface with a whiteboard mounted to it, a grocery list tidily written in Mom's handwriting. "Yogurt," Wyn reads, tapping the list. "Fascinating."

"Well, you didn't think all of *this*," I say, gesturing toward myself, "could come from a home without yogurt."

He kisses the back of my hand. "I still have no idea where *this* came from."

He tugs me back into the lamplit living room. Instead of washed-out pictures in macaroni frames of me and Eloise in home-made Halloween costumes, like I'd seen of Wyn, Michael, and Lou, my degree sits in a frame, off to one side rather than centered. There was already an empty frame on the other side, waiting for my medical degree.

They'd bought it as soon as I called them to tell them I got into Columbia.

"Where are the baby pictures?" Wyn asks.

"There's a box of albums in the basement," I tell him.

"Can we get them out?" he wants to know. So we go down and click on the overhead bulb, dig around until we find the right box, and carry a couple of albums back to my room.

My parents' story has never been much more than a corkboard of haphazard mental snapshots, and the photo album does little to fill in the gaps. There are a smattering of photographs to capture their whirlwind courtship in college, and a couple over the course of Mom's surprise pregnancy. Five pages' worth of pictures to capture the shotgun wedding, where Mom's belly was straining at her dress's seams, and a few more covering Eloise's infancy. My parents look tired but happy. In love. If not with each other, then at least with Eloise.

But then the pictures get more sporadic — a couple of birthdays and Christmases, a trip with my aunt and her first husband — and my parents' tiredness has transformed.

Not staying-up-all-night-with-a-crying-baby exhausted, but bored-beyond-belief-chafing-at-their-new-roles fatigued. You can

335

practically see their deferred dreams reflected back in their eyes.

There's a fairly large gap in time where there are no pictures at all, and then I'm born. And my parents do look happy again, in love again, cradling my wrinkly little baby body in my much-too-large pink onesie. Maybe not *quite* as overjoyed as the first time around. In six years, Mom's transformed from a cherub-cheeked near teenager to a full-fledged and stern-jawed adult. Dad's gained some weight, along with a vague terseness in the corners of his mouth. Even when he's holding me on his hip at the zoo, Eloise dangling from his other hand, smiling in front of the giraffes, he looks distracted.

Not miserable. Just like it's not enough. Like he and Mom both know there are other universes where they're *more,* bigger, happier.

As we flip forward through pages and times, Eloise becomes increasingly sulky, always standing a ways off, whereas I start to smile like my life depends on how visible my teeth are.

Wyn pauses on a picture of me with my first-place science fair trophy, grinning despite my missing front tooth. "My little genius." He touches the edge of the picture.

"I hope our kids have your hair."

Kids, I think. It knocks the wind out of me. The way he says it — so easily, so lovingly. That familiar homesickness, that longing, roars awake. But what my mom said sneaks in too, a quiet whisper at the fringes of my mind.

"What if I'm bad at it?" I ask. "Being a parent."

He sweeps my hair back from my neck. "You won't be."

"You don't know that," I say.

"I do," he says.

"How?" I say.

"Because you're good at loving," he says. "And that's all you have to do."

My throat tightens. My eyes burn.

"When I was a kid," I say, "I always felt like I was balanced on the edge of something. Like everything was so . . . tenuous, and it could all crumble at any second."

"What could?" he asks softly.

"Everything," I say. "My family."

His hand runs down my spine, turning soothing circles at the curve at its base.

"There was never enough money," I say. "And my parents were always exhausted from their jobs. I mean, tonight was the most positive I've *ever* heard them be about their work. And then when Eloise got older, they'd get into these huge fights with her, and they'd tell her she had no idea what they'd sacrificed for her, and how she was throwing it all away. And then she'd storm out, and they'd go to separate rooms, and I would be *so* sure that was it. That Eloise wouldn't come back. Or my parents would split up. I was always waiting for something terrible to happen."

Wyn's fingers graze back up my spine, settling at the base of my neck. He listens, waits, and like it always has, his presence pulls the truth out of me. *Like whispering secrets into a box and shutting it tight,* I used to think.

"I used to make these bargains with the universe," I say, smiling a little at the ridiculousness of it. "Like if I got straight As, then everything would be okay. Or if I won the science fair a second time. Or if I was never late to school, or if I always did the dishes before Mom got home from work, or I got her the perfect birthday gift, or whatever. And I know my parents love me. I've *always* known that," I say tightly. "But the truth is . . ."

Wyn squeezes the back of my neck: *I've got you.*

"I've spent my whole life trying to make it up to them."

Wyn tucks a curl behind my ear, ever patient and calm, warm and safe.

"That we cost them so much," I go on. "That they didn't get the lives they wanted, because of us. But if I could be good enough . . ."

"Harriet," he says, crushing me in against his chest, tightening his arms against me, a human barricade. *"No."*

His voice takes on a throatiness. "Sometimes when things go wrong, it's easy to blame someone else. Because it simplifies things. It takes any responsibility out of your hands. And I don't know if your parents did that to you and your sister or if somewhere along the way you took that blame on yourself, but it's *not* your fault. None of it. Your parents made their decisions, and I'm not saying their situation was easy, or that they didn't do the best they could. But it wasn't enough, Harriet. If you could even think that, if you could ever even fucking wonder if they regretted you, then they didn't do enough."

But he doesn't understand. They've done *everything.* Shelled out for tutors, paid the fees for every club I signed up for, chauffeured me back and forth, helped me study when they were dead tired from work, cosigned my med school loans.

My parents aren't people of words, but they sacrificed so much. *That's* love, and I *hate* that I want more from them. That I can't just feel grateful for all they've given me, because at all times I'm aware of what it cost them.

"You," Wyn says roughly, "are the very best thing that's ever happened to me. And they were lucky to have you as their kid. Even if you hadn't bent over backward to make them proud, they still would have been lucky, because you're smart and you're funny and you care about the people around you, and you make *everything* better, okay?"

When I don't answer, he says again, *"Okay?"*

"How can love end up like that?" I ask thickly. "How is it possible to love someone so much and have it all just go away?"

The thought of resenting Wyn like that is torture. The thought of him resenting me is even worse. Of holding him back, keeping him from what he wants.

"Maybe it never goes all the way away," he says. "Maybe it feels easier to ignore it, or turn it into a different feeling, but it's still there. Deep down."

He takes my face in his hands and kisses my tears as they break. "Do you want me to promise I'll love you forever, Harriet?" he whispers. "Because I will."

An ice-cold rush of adrenaline, a spurt of terror, a whole-body bracing, every muscle drawing tight to keep the words from sinking into my heart.

Because it won't matter.

Because he can promise me anything, but in the end, feelings could come and go, and we'll be powerless to stop the change.

"Just promise," I say, "we'll end things before we ever let them get like that."

Hurt flashes across his face. I want to take it back, but I don't.

This is all I can give him, all I can give myself: some tiny measure of protection.

The only way I can bear loving anyone this much is knowing it will never turn to poison. Knowing we'll give each other up before we can destroy each other.

"If we're making each other unhappy," I say as evenly as I can, "we can't keep going. I couldn't stand living every day knowing you resent me."

"I won't," he says softly. "I couldn't."

"Please, Wyn." I touch the muscles along his jaw. "I need to know we're never going to hurt each other like this."

His eyes travel back and forth across my face. "I'm not going to stop fighting for you, Harriet."

My vision blurs behind tears. He pulls me in, holds me tight. "I'm not going to stop loving you."

It's not the answer I asked for. It's the one I desperately want.

Years later, when it's late and I can't sleep for the phantom ache in my chest, I pull this memory out and turn it over. I think, *We did the right thing. We let each other go.* That too is a kind of comfort.

24
REAL LIFE

Thursday

We sit with our toes in the icy water and eat the cheese, fruit, and bread we brought from home. We doze in the sun and watch the clouds drift. Afterward we hike along the pine-needle-dusted trail in the woods, moss and ferns all glistening with dew, the ground soft and hollow.

Cleo seems to have entirely let the moment of tension go, but Sabrina's uncommonly quiet and keeps stalling toward the back of the pack as we walk. Every time I slow down to walk with her, though, she seems to speed up and chime in on whatever conversation the others are having.

When we get back to the shore, we're not ready to leave, so we stretch out along the red-brown rocks, watching birds dive toward the whitecaps in the distance.

"What's one tiny thing you'll miss about these trips?" Cleo asks.

"The Warm Cup," Parth says. "I love walking down to get coffee while it's still cool and gray out and the streets are empty. And Sab and I are both totally silent because we haven't had caffeine yet, but it's nice. At home we're always rushing in the morning."

"I'll miss that too," Kimmy says. "And sitting on the bench next to the walk-up window, petting all the dogs that come past. And all the junk shops and yard sales. Every time I come here, I end up trying to convince Cleo to rent a U-Haul to drive back."

"A garden filled with lobster traps has a different aesthetic effect in upstate New York," Cleo says.

"Yeah, but we could at *least* cover our walls with wood-burned signs that say *Wicked Pissah.*"

"Well, now we know what to get you for your birthday," I say.

"Should we all get *wicked pissah* tattoos?" Parth jokes.

"We can do better than that," Sabrina says.

"Giant lobsters," Wyn puts in.

"Mermaids that look like Bratz dolls," I suggest.

"I'll come up with something." Sabrina props her chin in one hand, the other fluttering through the shallow water.

"What's something you'll miss, Harry?" Cleo asks. "Something small."

I say, "Seeing everyone so happy together."

Cleo bats her hand against my leg. "Something for you."

I think some more. "I guess . . . going to sleep."

Parth bursts into laughter.

"I'm serious!" I cry.

"Your favorite part," Sabrina says, "of this amazing trip I planned for us . . . is going to sleep."

"No." I toss a seashell shard toward the sparkling lip of the tide. "It's going to sleep so tired, in a good way. Feeling content and exhausted and relaxed, but also excited to wake up and still be here."

I catch Wyn's eyes and look away. "It feels like nothing can go too wrong here. At least once you're off Ray's airplane."

Sabrina grabs my hand a little too hard, then lets go on a sigh. "I'll miss that too. Hell, I'll even miss Ray."

"I'll miss Bernie's," Cleo says.

"Even though it gave you a phantom hangover?" Wyn asks.

"For all I know," Cleo says, "that was the last hangover I'll ever have. The least I can do is appreciate it."

We get back onto the boat as the sun is

345

beginning its descent. The water is diamond edged, the air cooling and the spray lifting off the sides of the boat positively freezing, despite the sun beating against the crowns of our heads.

At the helm, Sabrina glows. She's where she's meant to be, doing what she was born to do, and no matter how complicated this week has been, I now realize how worth it it all was.

Parth passes out a round of Coronas with lime wedges — and soda for Cleo — and Sabrina cranks up the radio, Bruce Springsteen's "Dancing in the Dark" crackling out. It feels like time has been canceled, thrown out, suspended indefinitely.

As long as we stay out here on the water, salt spray flecking our skin, nothing else exists.

Kimmy wrangles Cleo into a slow dance, and Parth and I heckle them from our benches until the combination of the setting sun and beer has me heavy eyed and yawning.

Beside me, Wyn lifts his arm in invitation, and either because everyone's watching or because I simply want to, I curl against his side, his warm arm settling over me, his sweat and detergent and deodorant and toothpaste knitting together to cloak me in my favorite smell.

Even now, I'd buy Wyn-scented candles in bulk if I could, keep them long after the wicks had burned down, until every last vapor faded from the glass.

At a particularly cold gust, I turn my face into his chest to hide from the chill, let myself breathe him in and feel the rush of dopamine it brings.

I've only drunk half my beer, but I feel very nearly intoxicated. His hand slides from my stomach to my hip and lightly squeezes, and my breath rushes out against his neck, a coil of heat dropping from my low belly to the point between my thighs.

"This would be the song for our first dance," Kimmy says dreamily to Cleo, "if we ever got married."

If we ever got married.

My muscles go taut. I *feel* Wyn's heart speed, his hand slackening against me. Ahead, the harbor draws closer, and with it, reality.

Through laughter, Cleo says, "Based on *what,* Kimmy?"

"This magical moment we're having!" Kimmy says. "Do we need a better reason?"

"I guess not," Cleo allows. "Since this wedding is entirely hypothetical, why don't we have Bruce Springsteen *play* the reception?"

"You really don't want to get married?" Parth asks her, clearly unconvinced.

"Cleo has conflicting feelings about the institution of marriage," Kimmy says, "and I don't care that much either way as long as we're in it for the long haul. But I think a wedding could be fun. It's just a big-ass expensive party. No offense."

I sit up, pulling away and keeping my eyes fixed on a gaggle of circling gulls.

"No, you're right," Parth says. "It's an excuse for the best party you'll ever throw, with everyone you love in one place."

"All six of us," Wyn says.

Sabrina shrugs, steering us nearer to the harbor. "That's how it was with my parents, and it was perfect."

"I didn't realize you were there," I say. I know a decent amount about her parents' relationship, but mostly concerning the end of it. Like my own parents, hers were barely together when Sabrina's mother got pregnant. Unlike my own parents, once their initial happiness faded, they quickly divorced.

Sabrina's mom was a wreck after that, largely because Mr. Armas wasted no time before marrying a Norwegian model. Sa-

348

brina quickly became her mom's confidante, support system, and therapist all in one, until the former Mrs. Armas started dating herself.

From what I could tell, Sabrina's summers in Knott's Harbor were the lone bright spot in a lonely childhood, the only place either of her parents truly had time for her.

"I was four when they got married," she says. "We were here for the summer, and we'd driven down the coast a bit." A sliver of her perfect white smile appears, as if even after everything, this memory has been guarded deep in her heart, where nothing could mar it.

"There's this big farm," she says. "And it has a chapel, down a trail in the woods. I mean, maybe *chapel* isn't the right word. It's outside, looks out toward the coast. You can see the water through the trees. Anyway, it was a random Tuesday, and my parents decided they were going to get married. So they found a priest, and it was him, them, and me, out in the woods. For all I know, that guy wasn't even a real priest. He could've been a very somber stripper Dad found in the Yellow Pages. But whatever. We were happy. For three years, anyway."

She lets out a half-formed Sabrina cackle, and Parth joins her at the wheel, winding an arm around her waist.

"Have you two figured out your perfect wedding yet?" Cleo asks me, and my pulse spikes from the guilt.

But Wyn says easily, "The courthouse."

"No way." Kimmy shakes her head. "You're too much of a romantic. You have some perfect time and place picked out. Probably the exact minute you first told Harry you loved her, in a field full of her favorite flower."

"Nah," Wyn says. "Maybe I used to think there'd be a perfect time or place. But now I think, if you really want to be with someone, you don't wait for things to be perfect." His eyes come to mine. "I would have married Harriet at a drive-through chapel in Vegas the day after I proposed, if she wanted."

His eyes look dark in the dying daylight, the kind of gaze that falls like a heavy curtain, shutting out everything else.

Would have. The past tense of it slices through me.

"Then shit," Parth says, "what's stopping you? I'll find you an Elvis online *today*. We can have this whole thing taken care of in forty-five minutes. Back-to-back weddings."

Wyn casts his eyes back to the dock. "Because. That's not what she wants."

You, you, you, my heart cries.
We pull into the harbor.

25
REAL LIFE

Thursday

When we get back to the cottage, everyone disperses to wash the day's grit and sunburn away before dinner. It's Taco Thursday, a tradition in which Sabrina makes a much-too-large meal while the rest of us bumble around, acting as her semi-inept sous-chefs.

"Tonight," Sabrina says, ticking her menu items off as we walk up to the front door, "we're doing a grapefruit and avocado salad, doused in citrus dressing and fennel. Zucchini fritters and grilled corn. And then fried fish tacos for the meat eaters among us, and pulled jackfruit ones for Kimmy and Cleo."

The side dishes change, as do the taco toppings, but Sabrina's always been adamant that the worst thing about vacationing in Knott's Harbor is the absence of a good taco place, and she cannot abide that. I linger downstairs while everyone else goes up, waiting until Wyn comes back with clean clothes, headed to the outdoor shower, as I knew he would be.

"It's all yours," he says, tipping his head back toward the stairs at the front of the house.

"Thanks." We both root to the spot for a few seconds.

He cracks first, heading for the back door.

Upstairs, I rifle through my luggage for something comfy and warm enough to sit out on a cool night like this, and then head toward the bathroom portion of the suite. My phone lights up on the side table, and I stop to pick it up.

Mom's texted me, and I have no idea what she's talking about.

> I know you're scared, but you can't keep putting this off. The longer you wait, the worse it will be. You have to tell her, Wynnie —

I drop the phone like it's a live snake.

His phone, not mine. Mine's on the other side of the bed.

I step back, heart beating furiously. I'm unsure if I'm more afraid of being caught with Wyn's phone or of what else I might see on it. Scratch that, it's the second one.

For a minute I don't know what to do. My mind is cycling through all the worst possibilities, the things Gloria might want Wyn to tell me.

Something about her health. Something about his.

Or maybe he's started introducing the idea of the breakup to her, slowly guiding her toward the expectation that we don't belong together and that it has nothing to do with the physical distance caring for her requires.

It doesn't. Not anymore. The thought pings through me, a drunken, angry pinball rebounding back and forth between my ribs. He's happy. He might've gone to Montana for his mom, but he's there for himself now.

She must see how happy he is. She must know he's ready to let go of me.

I sink onto the edge of the bed, tears pouring down my cheeks out of nowhere. I don't know why, but it feels like a whole separate breakup. Accepting, now, the truth: That he's moved on. That all these moments I cling to, like little mental life rafts, are just memories for him.

The truth is, I don't know what this text means.

I can talk myself in and out of worrying about it all day, but it's not my business.

Just like I told him my life wasn't *his* business.

I won't ask. I can't. If he wants to tell me, he will, but it's been a long time since Wyn has given me any answers. Much longer than five months.

I take a shuddering breath, square my shoulders, and get into the shower.

Where I cry some more.

Stupid, stupid, stupid heart. Don't you know he hasn't been yours to cry over for a long time?

26
DARK PLACE

San Francisco, California

A graying one-bedroom apartment we talk about painting robin's-egg blue. The one we found online and, despite its cramped kitchen and small windows, believed we could turn into a home. The one where we will finally plan our wedding, after years of putting it off.

He'd hardly batted an eye when, after that first trip to my parents' house, I'd broached the possibility of waiting to get married until I finished school. It wasn't about what my mom said in the kitchen the night she met him, except inasmuch as I wanted her to see she was wrong.

I wanted her to see how well Wyn loved me, how patient and kind and good he was.

We can take our time, he promised, and when things didn't come together, wedding-wise, during my final year at Columbia, it was obvious we'd have to plan it *after* we moved out to my residency.

It takes a few months to find my footing at the hospital. Or hospitals, rather. They have us bounce around, get experience in a lot of different environments. I'd thrived in medical school, like I'd always thrived in college and high school, but this is different. Things move too quickly, and I'm always trying to catch up. My feet and knees hurt from standing all day, and my brain can't seem to store a map of any one hospital floor without blending it into another, so I'm always the tiniest bit late. Four weeks in, a fourth-year named Taye, with big dark curls and a model-esque stature, catches me by the shoulders as I'm hurrying past. "Breathe for a second," she says. "Rushing makes you clumsy, and we can't afford to be clumsy."

I nod my understanding, but the conviction is somewhat dampened when I immediately knock a jar of pens off the reception desk as we're parting ways.

Wyn's the one who finds the wedding venue: a renovated warehouse overlooking the bay, with an opening this coming winter. "If you like it," I say, "I like it."

We put down the deposit. In the month that follows, though, we make little progress on the rest of the plan. There are too many decisions to be made, and everything costs too much, and despite his business degree, Wyn's struggling to find work that pays above minimum wage.

"I'm terrible at interviews," he says late one night, rubbing the stress from his face after yet another we've-decided-to-go-in-a-different-direction email.

"Only because you talk yourself down," I promise, climbing into his lap, wreathing my arms around his neck. "Next time you're in one, just answer every question like you're answering for me."

He nods somberly. "So when they ask for my best qualities, I tell them I'm amazing in bed."

I snort into his neck, inhale his scent. "I mean, it worked for me getting my residency."

He smooths my hair back, kisses the corner of my mouth.

"Answer how the people who love you would answer for you, Wyn," I say.

He keeps trying. We keep trying.

He finds another bookstore job, but it's barely over minimum wage, not enough to cover the rest of the rent, so after a couple more weeks, he takes another part-time gig, doing upholstery repair.

Then one morning, I come home from a

graveyard shift and find him sitting at the table, still in his clothes from the day before, his phone on the ground with a crack through its screen.

"Wyn?" I say, heart in my throat.

He looks at me and breaks, descends into sobs. I go to him, kneel on the floor, take his weight as he slumps into me, his forehead against my shoulder, his hands wringing my scrubs so hard I think they might tear.

It takes him a long time to get out the words.

To tell me that Hank is gone.

27
REAL LIFE

Friday

"I think we should give you a proper wedding tomorrow," I announce over breakfast.

"Oh, thank god, someone said it," Kimmy says, dropping her spoon into her acai bowl.

Parth casts a quick glance over at Sabrina, who dusts her hands off on her cloth napkin.

We're sitting at a white wrought iron table in the Bluebell Inn's overgrown garden, tucked up in one of the hills that overlook the harbor. Our server stops by to drop off fresh cappuccinos, then moves off to another table.

"We don't need anything fancy," Sabrina says. "*This,* the six of us, is all that matters."

"I'm not saying *fancy,*" I reply. Lying awake, late into the night, it became apparent that the only way to make it through these last two days without crumbling was to give my brain something else to focus on. "I'm just saying, like, a cake. A photog-

360

rapher. Maybe something old, new, and blue, or whatever the saying is?"

Wyn softly snorts beside me.

"Could be nice," Parth says, eyeing Sabrina again.

"It's tomorrow," she reminds me.

"It would only take a few hours," Cleo says.

"We can split up tasks and knock it all out," I add. A completable chore *and* alone time: the perfect combo.

Sabrina's head tilts as she sips the foam from her cappuccino. "Okay." She nods to herself. "Okay, sure. You and Wyn handle the cake."

I balk. "Wouldn't it be faster if we all divided up? Covered twice as much ground?"

"No, it would be chaotic. We'd end up with six cakes."

"Probably why Harriet suggested it," Wyn says.

I ignore him, regroup, and face Sabrina again. "If we're teaming up, then you and I should be on cake duty. I want to be sure I get something you like."

Her head slightly cocks, and something flits behind her eyes.

She and I have barely had a second alone together since the ride from the airport, and for the first time, I'm wondering if that's because *I've* been afraid she'd find Wyn and me out or if *she's* been avoiding *me*.

She gives a little shake of her head. "I don't care about the cake. If I care about absolutely anything other than the ceremony, it's the bachelorette-slash-bachelor party, so I'll figure that out."

"*I* want to plan that," Parth says.

"Duh," she says. "We'll do it together, and Cleo and Kim can try to find a photographer, if they're up for it."

"We'd love to," Cleo says.

"But a hard out in two hours, okay?" Sabrina says. "No matter what progress you have or haven't made, in two hours, we meet back at the house."

Wyn's gaze darts my way, and I look at the floor.

It's only two hours, I think.

What have I done, I think.

I don't know if he's picking up my discomfort and mirroring it back to me or if he's really in his head. Maybe about the text from Gloria or maybe something else entirely. But as we drive from bakery to bakery, we barely even make small talk.

The afternoon flies by. We've reached the ninety-minute mark of our allotted two

362

hours when the fifth local bakery tells us they don't touch weddings. "No one gets quite so litigious as the parents of a newlywed," the red-faced baker tells us.

"Did we say wedding?" Wyn laughs, looks at me, and claps a hand to his forehead, shaking himself. He faces the baker again, leaning across the counter with a devastating smile, the kind that looks like a hook has snagged under his lip. "I meant *birthday*. We've been planning this wedding of ours for, like, four years, so I guess that's why *that* came out. This cake is for a birthday."

The baker narrows her eyes. "All our birthday cakes say *Happy Birthday* on them."

"Okay, then what about a regular cake," I say.

"Those say *Happy Birthday* on them too," the woman says, determined not to sell us a black market wedding cake, I guess.

"Great," Wyn says. "We'll do a red velvet one of those."

The baker's lips purse. "Who should it be addressed to?"

It's not enough that she's forcing us to buy a cake with *Happy Birthday* on it when she *knows* it's for a wedding.

"*Happy birthday, wicked pissah,*" Wyn suggests.

"That's not how you use *wicked pissah* in

a sentence," the baker tells us.

The rules surrounding this cake are getting more specific by the second.

A smile blossoms from one corner of Wyn's mouth. "Inside joke."

The baker does not smile, but she turns to inscribe our not-wedding cake all the same.

In the Rover, we fall back into silence. We're halfway up the wildflower-covered hill to the cottage when Wyn suddenly pulls over onto the gravel shoulder that overlooks the ocean. "Okay," he says, looking at me.

"Okay, what?" I say.

"What's going on?" he asks.

"Nothing," I lie.

His head tips back on a frustrated laugh. "Please don't do this."

"Do *what*?" I demand.

"Pretend you're fine," he says. "Act like I'm imagining that you're pulling away from me."

"Pulling away?" The words squeeze out of my tightening windpipe. I'm suddenly so frustrated it becomes a kind of claustrophobia. I undo my seat belt and throw open my door, stumbling out into the harsh midday sun.

He gets out too, rounding the hood of the car toward me. "This isn't fair."

I throw my arms out to my sides. "*What isn't fair?*"

"We were getting along," he says. "We were acting like friends, and now —"

"*Friends?*" The word tears out of me on a laugh. "I don't want to be your friend, Wyn!"

"I don't want to be yours either!" he cries.

I turn up the hill, but he catches my hand and pulls me back to face him. I don't know how it happens: I'm confident I don't *trip* into his mouth, but that's how it feels, because I'm *positive* he didn't initiate it — Wyn would *never* — and it makes no sense that *I* would do this, but I have.

I am.

My hands are twisted into his shirt, and his are flat against my back, and we're kissing, hard, hurried, like this is a timed activity and we're in our final seconds.

"What was the text," I hiss out as our lips draw apart.

"What text," he asks, turning me back to the car, the warm metal of the hood meeting my back.

"From your mom," I say. "I saw a text from your mom."

"Nothing," he says, lifting me onto the hood.

"*Wyn.*"

"It's about work, Harriet," he says, squeezing my thighs, pulling them around his hips.

"That doesn't make any sense," I say as he kisses his way down my throat, hand curling against my ear.

"I can explain it to you right now," he says, "or we can have sex in the car."

A plumb line of heat drops through my center, my thighs tightening against him as he kisses me more deeply. "The *car*? We're like a mile from the house."

"I don't have a mile in me right now, Harriet."

I push against his shoulders even as the rest of my body strains toward him. "Tell me," I say.

He steps back. A car flies by our spot on the shoulder, and he blinks as if emerging from a trance. Then obvious anxiety torques his brow and mouth, and I am positive I made the right decision, that there's something I need to know.

With a resigned sigh, he pulls his phone out of his back pocket and taps on it for several seconds, teeth worrying at his lower lip, while the suspense pummels my nerves.

Finally, he hands the phone to me.

There's a web browser open to some hip minimalistic shop. A white backdrop. Soft serifed headings: *Gallery, Contact, Social Me-*

dia. Beneath them, a photograph of a massive oak pedestal table out in a green-gold meadow. Mismatched wooden chairs line it, wildflowers bursting up around their legs. Behind the meadow, periwinkle mountains jut up into a cloudless sky.

It's so beautiful it makes me ache. I feel the same brand of longing I used to get when I rode my bike home at dusk as a kid, past lit kitchen windows, saw the people inside laughing while they set their tables or washed their dishes.

I tap the image. An option to purchase the table pops up. "Fifteen thousand *dollars*? American dollars?"

"It's the cheapest one," Wyn says.

I look up, stunned. "Wyn. Are you buying a *fifteen-thousand-dollar* table? Here I was freaking out about a coffee-table book, and you're buying a millionaire's table?"

"What?" He laughs uncomfortably. "No. Harriet. It's not — I'm not buying it . . . I made it."

I stare at him. "You . . ." I look back down to the table, then up at him. "You *made* this? Or you fixed it?"

Color rises along his cheeks. "I made it. For that home goods store in Bozeman. Juniper and Sage?"

Juniper and Sage. I went once with Wyn's

367

parents, and Hank joked that we shouldn't touch any of their vases, because if we broke them, we'd have to mortgage the house.

"They're selling them on consignment," Wyn says. "The first two they bought are already gone. I kind of hate that one, and apparently the Bozeman millionaires agree, because it's been sitting for weeks. But I've started doing commissions too. Mostly for people's summer homes, but I've also got this sixty-thousand-dollar order for a resort. I'm getting requests every few days. Tourists want something locally made — I'll have to hire someone to help soon if it keeps up — and . . . what?"

"Nothing." I look away, toward the water, bat my eyelashes against the welling emotion.

"Harriet?"

"You're . . ." I shake my head. "You're amazing, Wyn. This is amazing."

The corner of his mouth twitches, his gaze dropping to the water below us. "Yeah, well, turns out that business degree wasn't a complete waste."

I flip through the pictures on the home page, and he watches me out of the corner of his eye, like he can't bear to see it straight on.

A dark walnut table sitting in a sparkling

creek, vases filled with prairie coneflowers and common chokecherry and Rocky Mountain penstemon. And then a cedar table with a live edge, sitting in a pine forest, like an altar in a cathedral made of trees.

The photograph sends an imprecise ache through my limbs. To *be* there, maybe, or maybe to be standing behind the camera with the man who built that table.

"In their natural habitat," I say.

What I mean is, *In* your *natural habitat.*

I think back to those phone calls when he went home to Montana, how even over video, I could see that the colors of Wyn had leached back into him, after months of fading under the fog and drizzle of San Francisco.

"I mean, it's a table." He reaches for the phone, but I hold on to it. "No table is worth that much."

"This one is," I murmur.

I look up and catch him watching me, a look of raw vulnerability, hope.

"It's amazing," I force out. "I didn't know you were building anything. When did you start?"

He scratches the back of his head. "I started building in San Francisco."

"You *what?*" I say.

"The second job I had," he says. "It wasn't

369

upholstery. I was apprenticing for a designer."

In the scheme of things, it's not a salacious reveal, but it is disorienting. To realize the rift between us began even longer ago than I realized. "Why didn't you tell me?"

"I don't know. I was embarrassed."

"Embarrassed," I repeat, like it's my first introduction to the word. It might as well be. "What could possibly be embarrassing about this?"

"I've never been like you," he says. "I wasn't brilliant. I wasn't someone with a ton of goals. I've spent my first thirty years tripping through life."

"That's *not* true," I say.

"Harriet." He looks at me through his lashes, every variety of green and gray in his eyes on full display in the sunlight reflecting off the water below. "I barely got into college, and I barely graduated. And then I followed you out to San Francisco, and even *with* a degree, I managed to botch every interview I went to for jobs that would actually *pay.* If I fucked up the apprenticeship, I didn't want you to watch it happen. Saying it was another upholstery job took the pressure off, because if I lost it, I could find another."

My nose burns. I drop my eyes back to

370

the phone, the screen blurring.

"He actually didn't think I was any good," he says.

I look up.

"The designer I apprenticed for," he says. "He said I had no instincts."

I snort. "What, like you're some kind of birding dog? What an asshole."

Wyn smiles faintly. "When I left that job and went home, I was pretty sure I was done even trying. Figured I'd stick with the repairs."

"What made you change your mind?"

He eases onto the hot metal of the hood beside me. "It's hard to explain."

We're back to the push and pull, the little drips of him and then the droughts that follow.

I've never known how to take him in small doses. One taste only ever makes the thirst worse.

"Well, I'm proud of you," I say thickly, folding my arms, barricading myself from him the same way he's done to me.

His eyes return to mine. "I could make you one, if you want."

"A table?" I ask. He nods. "I don't have that kind of money, Wyn."

"I know," he says. "That's not what I meant."

"I couldn't take something like that for free," I say.

"It's going really well, Harriet," he says. "And I hardly have any expenses right now — maybe you've heard: I live with my mom?"

I laugh. "I think I remember reading that on TMZ."

He touches my hand against the hood, and god help me, I turn my palm up to his. I need to hold on to him right now, need to feel the calluses I've memorized on his palm.

"I would love to make you one," he murmurs. "I've got time, and I don't need money."

Reading my expression, Wyn says, "Or if you don't want one . . ."

"It's not that." I shake my head. "It's amazing. Seeing you like this. So happy."

He studies me for a beat before dropping his gaze on a nod. "I am. I'm really happy."

Now my chest is folding over on itself. "I'm so glad."

"You too, right?" He matches my gaze.

That seesaw feeling rocks through me. "Yeah," I say. "Me too."

"Good," he says softly.

"Why was Gloria so worried about you telling me this?" I ask.

"Because she thinks we're still together,"

he says, his gaze dark and steady. "She thinks you're still waiting for me to come back."

Back to San Francisco.

Back to me.

I'm not waiting. I've known for months he wouldn't be coming back.

So why does hearing it hurt so much?

My phone chimes, and I break eye contact, blinking rapidly as I pull it out, read the new message. "Sabrina," I tell him thickly, sliding off the hood.

His mouth hitches, an unconvincing quarter smile. "Looks like our time's up."

It already was, I think. But the pain, it still feels fresh.

28
DARK PLACE

San Francisco, California

After Hank's death, Wyn insists we don't have to postpone. He says we shouldn't lose the venue or the deposit money. But he's barely eating, hardly sleeping.

"It will be easier this way," I tell him. "I'll have more time to adjust to the residency, and then we can figure everything else out."

Months go by, and his grief doesn't abate. Mine hovers close too, always waiting to trip me up. Everything still makes me think of Hank, of what Gloria must be feeling, what Wyn must be keeping inside.

Something as innocent as a car commercial can split me open. I start taking long showers so I can let it all out without piling my pain onto his. Wyn starts taking long runs to burn it all off.

We don't paint the apartment. One weekend he offers, but between his two jobs, it's his one day off, and he looks so tired.

"We'll get to it eventually," I say.

"I'm sorry," he croaks, grabbing me by the hips, pulling me toward where he sits on the couch, burrowing his face into my stomach.

"You have nothing to be sorry for," I promise.

"I want to be better for you," he says.

"Stop," I whisper. "I don't need that. I don't need anything from you. I'm okay."

I'm not. I live in a state of terror that he won't ever come back to himself. That I've taken him from his friends and a job he liked and his family, and now I can't even give him the time he needs.

And then there's the loss of Hank, the dad of my dreams, and the guilt I feel for thinking that, after everything my own father gave up to give me this life.

The sacrifices he's made, the jobs he's hated and worked anyway, every bit of proof of his love. But he's never been a soft man. He's only accessible to a point.

The last time we visited the Connors before Hank's death, Wyn's father cried from happiness when we got there. As we were getting ready for bed that night, he gave me a tight hug and said, *Sleep well, love you so much, kiddo,* and afterward I'd shut myself in the bathroom and run the water while I cried for reasons I didn't entirely understand.

More homesickness, I guess. That lights-on-in-an-unfamiliar-kitchen pang.

Love you so much, kiddo had been such a constant refrain of Wyn's childhood that he and his sisters had all gotten it tattooed in Hank's handwriting when we went to Montana for the funeral. They said I could too, but it didn't seem fair. Hank didn't belong to me. Now he never will.

The tracks of our lives split little by little, but the moments we're together, my love still feels so big and violent it could consume me.

Every once in a while, Wyn asks if I want to look at venues or go sample cakes. He tries to be happy. I try to be enough in this small, small life I've pulled him into.

"There's no rush," I promise. "I'm so busy at the hospital anyway."

I don't want to make him celebrate. I don't want him to feel like he has to be happy when he's still acclimating to a world without Hank Connor in it.

It shouldn't have happened like this. Hank was eleven years older than Gloria, sure, but he was still only in his early seventies. And aren't seventies supposed to be like fifties now?

Sometimes we eat dinner together between his shifts. But most nights, we don't see each other until he comes to kiss me on the head while I read in bed, before taking his shower.

Sometimes when he comes back, and he thinks I'm asleep, he'll finally let himself cry, and I think, though I don't know to whom or what, *Please, please help. Please help him stop hurting this much.*

I'll make bargains with the universe: *If I make the apartment cozier. If I don't complain about work. If I make the most of the constant rain. If I need nothing from him, he'll be okay.*

We'll get through this.

One night, some of the other interns invite me out. They always do. I never go. But lately Wyn has been pushing me to.

"I won't be home anyway," he says. "You need to have friends."

"I have friends," I say.

"Not here," he says. "You need those too."

So I go out, and it's nice, fun, but I lose track of time, and when I get home, Wyn's asleep in our bed, and it breaks my heart to have missed even five waking minutes with him.

I feel guilty. I feel lost. I don't know how to fix any of it.

The next morning, when I tell him I

377

missed him, he says, "Honestly, I crashed as soon as I got home. I wouldn't have been any fun."

After that, I go out a couple of times a week with Taye, the fourth-year who's taken me in like the hospital's own feral cat, along with a couple of other first-years she's unofficially mentoring, Grace and Martin. And it's nice to have friends again, to not be so alone.

Finally, when Wyn has a full night off, he comes out to meet us at the bar down the street from the hospital, and I'm excited and nervous and a little regretful that we're spending our night out instead of at home together, but he insists it's important.

Martin, Grace, and Taye spend the whole night talking about the hospital, or else their worst professors in medical school. It's the first time I realize it's all we ever really talk about, and only because I watch Wyn zone out, recede, and I have no idea how to hold on to him, keep him here with me.

Then Martin finally asks Wyn what he does for a living, and Wyn tells him about the upholstery.

"What kind of degree do you need for that?" Martin says. I don't think he *means* for it to sound snotty, but it does, and Wyn reacts exactly how he always does to any suggestion of inferiority.

He leans into it. Jokes that he got a degree in chairs, but it took him an extra year, and everyone laughs it off, but for days after that, he seems even more distant.

My heart is screaming *You, you, you,* as if I'm watching him fall into a pit, and yet I'm immobilized, unable to find a way to reach him.

Whenever I ask him what's wrong, he takes my face in his hands and kisses my forehead, tells me soberly, "You're perfect," and we forget, for a while, about everything except each other's mouths and skin, and only later, while he lies curled around me like a question mark in bed, do I realize he hasn't given me an answer.

Then comes Gloria's fall. Her Parkinson's diagnosis, or rather she admits she's had it for years. Things have progressed more quickly since Hank's passing.

"I'm old!" she says with a flippant hand wave when we video call her. "If Hank and I had started having kids sooner, I'd still be running all around, but we didn't, and things are bound to start breaking down."

She isn't old. Older than my parents, sure, but not old enough for Wyn and Michael and Lou to have to contemplate losing their mother when they've only just said goodbye to their father.

Martin helps me wrangle a few days off from the hospital, and Wyn and I go to Montana, all three of Gloria's kids and her soon-to-be-daughter-in-law crowded into their squat little house at the end of its long drive. Wyn comes alive. He lights up, *loosens.*

And for the second time, I tuck myself into their tiny second-floor bathroom with the water running and sob into my knuckles, because I know I can't take him back to San Francisco.

Know I can't bear to be the person who takes him away from where he belongs.

When I tell him I think he should stay while his mom recovers from her fall, he studies me for a long time. "Are you sure?"

"One hundred percent," I say.

We agree he'll stick around for a month while he, Michael, and Lou work out a long-term plan.

I fly home alone. As soon as I step foot in the apartment, I feel the shift.

Somehow I know he will never live there again.

At first we talk all the time. Then we get busy. He's catching up on the repair work that his dad hadn't had the chance to finish. I'm exhausted from grueling days of scrubbing in and out to stand behind a ring of scrubbed-in surgeons and residents so thick I'm lucky if I get a glance at a scalpel. And when my intern friends bemoan that same experience over drinks, I pretend to agree when the truth is, even being tasked with a suture sounds like too much right now.

Lou has only one year left of her MFA in Iowa. Then she'll move back to Montana. Wyn tells me this like it's great news — "I'll be home soon."

You're already home, I think. I wonder if I ever will be.

Cleo texts to ask how I'm holding up with Wyn away. I feel too guilty to say anything other than a variation on All good here. How are you?

I follow Taye to happy hours and trivia nights. I join her *Bachelor* viewing party too. But mostly I fill my spare time, snuggled in bed with a cup of tea and wearing Wyn's old Mattingly sweatshirt, half watching and half sleeping through episodes of *Murder, She Wrote.*

The night before he's supposed to visit, Gloria falls again and breaks her wrist, and he has to cancel. "It's fine," I tell him. "I was honestly going to be too tired for much this weekend anyway."

We start missing calls. Sometimes I'm so tired I drift off on the couch while I'm waiting for the phone to ring. Sometimes he gets so lost in his work, he loses track of time. He's always apologetic, beating himself up about it, promising to do better.

"Wyn," I say. "It's seriously fine. We're both busy."

I'm working over Christmas, so he plans to come the week after. His car skids off the road on the way to the airport. He's uninjured, but he misses the flight. "I'll come tomorrow," he says.

Tomorrow is the only full day off I'll have during his visit, and now he won't get in until that evening. "Sure," I say. "Sounds great."

He's in town thirty-six hours, and then he's gone again.

A part of me still hopes that if I give him room, space, time, everything might be okay.

One night, after a last-minute video-chat cancellation, I decide to show up to the interns' usual happy hour spot, and Taye and Grace aren't there. "Grace had some family wedding in Monterey, and I think she took Taye," Martin says.

Taye thrives in big social settings. She's like Parth that way — so good at singling out the shiest or quietest or clumsiest person in the room and bringing them into the center of things. Probably why she took me under her wing.

I think nothing of it being just Martin and me that night. We stay for only one drink — I'm exhausted — and then he offers to drive me home.

When we get there, he insists on walking me to the door. I don't think anything of this either. Because of Wyn. How many times did he suggest we meet Sabrina at her summer internship so she wouldn't have to walk home by herself? How often did he give Cleo a ride to her car on the far side of the Mattingly campus?

On the stoop, Martin hugs me good night. Or that's what I think he's doing at first, and when I realize he isn't, I'm so shocked I freeze.

Let the kiss happen to me. By the time I think to shove him backward, he's already realized it was a mistake, that I wasn't kissing him back. He looks embarrassed.

Which only intensifies my guilt. Did I give him some kind of sign? Was I flirting with him? I don't know. A piercing pain starts behind my right eye. My brain feels like it's sloshing around in my skull.

"I'm not . . . available," I stammer. "You know that."

Martin laughs. "The furniture guy?"

I feel like I'm going to be sick.

"Wyn," I say.

"He's not here, Harry," Martin says. "He's never here anymore. I am."

I turn and run inside. I call Wyn immediately, even though it's late here, which means it's even later in Montana. It goes to voicemail. I call back, and he answers on the third ring, voice groggy.

I tell him everything, as fast as I can, poison I'm letting from my blood.

Afterward, I have to beg him to say something. When he does, his voice is hollow. "This isn't working anymore."

I want to take my plea back. I want to beg him not to say anything else.

I barely hear the rest of the call. Only snatches get through the raging of my heart. *. . . kids when we got together . . . different now . . . what's best . . .*

I don't cry. It's not real. He promised he would always love me. It can't be real.

But a deeper part of me, a voice that's always been there, tells me it was always going to end this way. That I've known since that first trip to Indiana that I would never be enough to make him happy, that I couldn't give him the kind of love *his* parents had when my only education on the

384

subject had been the one *my* parents had.

Two days after our call, my stuff shows up. No note. I don't tell anyone. I can't bear to say it.

29
REAL LIFE

Friday

Everyone is in their respective corners of the house, getting ready for the bachelorette-slash-bachelor-party night Parth and Sabrina have planned.

I should be getting ready too. Instead, my mind keeps wandering back to that dark ledge I've spent months turning away from. *Don't look, don't look, don't look.* The pain is too much. It will suck me into itself, and I'll never get back out.

Let it go, I tell myself.

It doesn't matter that I never got concrete answers about what broke us. What matters is that we broke. What matters is that Wyn's happy with his new life.

We'll make it through tomorrow, then go our separate ways. When we tell everyone we've broken up, we'll be able to say it was amicable, that it won't cost them anything.

But I *can't* let it go.

I've been trying for months, and I'm no closer to peace. Here's my opportunity — my *last* chance. It might be a mistake to get answers, but if I don't, I'll spend my life regretting it.

This is what I need from this week, the thing that will justify the torture.

I leave the bedroom, march down the hall past the hiss of running showers and old pipes creaking in the walls.

Everything feels strange, dreamlike: the time-smoothed wooden stairs soft against my soles, the prickle of cool air as I step out back, the rushing sound of the tide sliding over the rocks beneath the bluff. I cross the patio to the side gate, still open from Cleo's sudden flight of fancy the other night, and follow the path beyond it, into the dense evergreens beyond.

The sun hasn't fully set, but the foliage overhead coats the footbridge in shadow, pinpricks of mounted solar lights illuminating the path to the guesthouse.

It's like I'm moving through jelly, every step slow and heavy. Then the wood-shingled guesthouse appears, and I round the corner toward the cedarwood shower.

When I see him, it surprises me. As if I didn't come here expressly for him.

Only the back of his head, neck, and

shoulders peek over the top of the cedar walls, the breeze pulling steam out in silver wisps. A feeling of loss, heavy as a sandbag, hits me in the gut.

I can't do this, I think. *I don't want to know. I don't want to make things worse.*

I turn. My sleeve catches on a low-hanging branch, and all the moisture accumulated there spatters to the hollow forest floor.

Wyn turns, his brow arching with amusement. "Can I help you?" He looks and sounds happy to see me. Somehow it's another blow.

I waver. "I doubt it."

"*May* I help you," he amends.

"I just wanted to talk!" I step back. "But it can wait. Until you're less . . ."

"Busy?" he guesses.

"Naked," I say.

"One and the same," he says.

"For you, I guess," I say.

His brow scrunches. "What's that mean?"

"I honestly don't know," I say.

He rests his forearms atop the wall, waiting. For me to come closer or to bolt.

Now that the opportunity's in front of me, having an answer I don't like seems eminently worse than never having an answer at all.

"It's nothing," I say. "Forget it."

"I won't." He wipes water from his eye. "But if you want me to pretend, I can try."

I take another half step back. His gaze stays pinned on me.

As always, something about his face coaxes the words out of me before my brain has decided to say them: "It's killing me not knowing."

His brow softens, his lips parting in the half-light.

"Even though it's been months," I say. "It's killing me, being here, acting like everything's the same between us, and what's even worse is sometimes it's not acting. Because . . ." My voice cracks, but now there's *too* much momentum. I *can't* stop talking.

No matter how fragile, needy, broken I might sound, it's the truth, and it's coming out.

"Because you just *left,* Wyn," I say. "I never got an explanation. I got a four-minute phone call and a box of my stuff shipped to my door, and I've never even known what I did. And I told myself it was all about what happened with Martin. That you didn't trust me."

He winces at the name, but I don't back down.

"I've spent months trying to make myself

mad at you," I go on hoarsely, "for blaming me and judging me for something I didn't even do. And then I come here, and you act like you *do* blame me. Like you hate me or, worse, feel nothing at all for me. Until suddenly you act like nothing's changed. And you tell me you *never* thought I cheated on you, and you kiss me like you *love* me."

"You kissed me too, Harriet," he says, voice low, strained.

"I know," I say. "I know I did, and I don't even understand how, after everything, I still let myself do that. But I did, and it's killing me. This is killing me. Every second of every day, I feel like I'm living with a piece of me torn out, and I didn't even see it happen.

"I have this gaping wound, and no idea how it got there. It's killing me hearing how happy you are, without even understanding how I — how I —" My voice quavers, my breath coming in spurts. "I don't know what I did to make you so miserable."

His mouth judders open. "Harriet."

I drop my face into my hands as the tears build across my vision, my spine aching with the force of it when they start to fall.

The shower door unlatches and whines open. I hear the rasp of a towel being pulled from a hook and wrapped against skin. Heat billows toward me in a damp wall, and I flinch at the sudden warmth of Wyn's hands taking hold of my upper arms. I can't bring myself to look at him, not while I'm falling apart. Not after baring all the rawest parts of myself.

"Hey," he says in a quiet rasp, his wet palms scraping up my arms. "Come here."

He tucks me against his chest, the water from his skin sluicing down my arms and back. His mouth burrows into my hair. "It wasn't you," he says. "I promise it was never you. I was in such a fucking dark place, Harriet. After I lost my dad. I was drowning."

He presses me closer.

"I'm sorry," I say, voice crackling. "I wanted to help you. I didn't know how. I've never known what to do with pain, Wyn. All I've ever done is hide from it."

His hand furls against my ear. "You couldn't have done anything else, Harriet. It was never you. I just . . . I lost the best man I knew, and it was like I stopped knowing how to exist. Like the world didn't make any sense anymore. And you had this new life, this thing you'd been dreaming of for so long, and all these new friends, and — and I was greedy for your time, and I hated myself for not being happy for you. I hated myself for not being good enough or smart enough or driven enough for you."

"*Fuck* that." I try to push back from him. He holds me fast, doesn't let me go, and it makes me so angry, how he's holding on now, when it's too late. "Listen," he murmurs, "please let me say this."

I lift my gaze to his. I think of the first time I ever saw his face up close, how his features had struck me as contradictory, a rare mix of magnetism and standoffishness: *I want you close, but don't look at me.* Now he's *pure* quicksand. No stoniness. Wide open.

"I was lost," he says. "As much as I loved my parents — as much as I always knew they loved me — I grew up thinking I was a let-down. I had these two incredible sisters, who came out of fucking left field and were nothing like my parents or anyone else in our town, and as early as I can remember, everyone knew they were going to do something amazing. I mean, when I was twelve and Lou was nine, people were already talking about how she'd win a Pulitzer someday. No one was giving me imaginary awards."

"*Wyn.*" We'd been down this path too many times.

"I'm not saying anyone thought I was stupid," he says. "But that's how it felt. Like I was the one who didn't have anything going for him except that I'm nice."

"Nice?" I can't help but scoff.

Generous, thoughtful, endlessly curious, painfully empathetic, funny, *vast*. Not *nice*. *Nice* was the mask Wyn Connor led with.

"I wanted to be special, Harriet," he says. "And since I wasn't, I settled for trying to make everyone love me. I know how ridiculous that sounds, but it's true. I spent my whole life chasing things and people who could make me feel like I mattered."

That stings, somewhere deep beneath my breastbone. I try again, feebly, to draw back. Wyn's hand moves to the back of my neck, light, careful. "And then I met you, and I didn't feel so lost or aimless. Because even if there was nothing else for me, it felt like loving you was what I was made for. And it didn't matter what anyone thought of me. It didn't matter if I didn't have any other big plans for myself, as long as I got to love you."

"So that's it?" I say raggedly. "I took up all the oxygen, and you didn't tell me until I'd suffocated you. Until you didn't love me anymore, and there was nothing I could do."

"I will *always* love you," he says fiercely. "That's the point, Harriet. It's the only thing that's ever come naturally to me. The thing I don't have to work at. I loved you all the way across the fucking country, and at my darkest, on my worst days, I still love you more than I've ever loved anything else.

"But I wasn't happy after my dad died, and I kept waiting for things to feel even the tiniest bit better, and I couldn't. I didn't. And I was making you unhappy too."

I open my mouth, but he cuts across me softly, his hands gentling in my hair: "Please don't lie, Harriet. I was drowning, and I was taking you down too."

I try to swallow. The emotion grips my throat too tightly.

Wyn drops his gaze, his voice cracking. "When I went back to Montana, I could feel him."

"Wyn." My hands go to his jaw, and his forehead dips to mine.

His eyes close, a deep breath pressing us closer. "And I felt so stupid for running away from all that. For trying so hard to be different from him when he was the best man I've ever known."

"You've always been like him," I say, "in all the ways that matter."

The corner of his mouth turns up, but it's a tense expression, a wrought one. He's shaking, from the cold or adrenaline.

"I just . . ." He takes a breath. "I felt like I was failing him, and my mom, and you. I wanted you to be happy, Harriet, and the

394

Martin thing — maybe it was an excuse, but I was so low then that I genuinely convinced myself that was the kind of guy you wanted to be with. And you kept pushing the wedding off. You never wanted to talk about it. You never wanted to talk about anything, and when I saw you with all of your new friends, I thought . . . I thought you *should* be with someone as brilliant as you, who could fit into this world you spent your whole *life* fighting for."

"That's not *fair*, Wyn," I cry.

"What was I supposed to think, Harriet?" he asks, voice fraying. "When I'd have to cancel a visit, you didn't care. When I missed a phone call, you didn't care. You were never mad at me. You never fought with me. It felt like you didn't even miss me."

I break into sobs again as the reality of it hits me. That all that time and energy I'd spent trying to be fine for him, to not crack under the weight of my job, to not need anything he couldn't give — all it had done was drive him away from me faster.

"I knew you'd never leave me," he goes on, his voice like sandpaper. "Not when I was such a fucking wreck. But I didn't want to trap you. I didn't want you to wake up one day and realize you were living the wrong life, and I'd let you do it.

"*That's* why the phone call was so short. Because I couldn't have time to change my mind. *That's* why I mailed your stuff back so fast. Why I couldn't stand to have a single piece of you left where I could see it.

"Because I'm always going to love you. Because more than anything, I want you to be happy. And now you are," he says. "And I am too. Not all the time, but I'm so much better than I was, and when Sabrina called and asked me to come here, I thought I could handle it.

"I genuinely thought I would show up, and I'd see you, and I'd know you were happier. I'd know I did the right thing letting you go.

"I've worked so fucking hard on myself these last five months, Harriet, and I'm doing *well.* I'm with my family, and I'm doing work I'm proud of, and I'm on medicine."

"Medicine?"

"You asked what changed my mind about the job earlier," he says. "That's what did it. Medicine. For depression."

My throat squeezes. Just one more huge thing I didn't know about him. "From losing your dad?"

He shakes his head. "I thought it was just that. But once I started taking it, I realized

396

that had just made things worse. But it's always been there. Making everything harder than it should be. It's like . . ." He scratches his temple. "In high school, I had this friend on the soccer team. And one day, after a game, he collapsed. His chest hurt and he couldn't get his shirt off, but he wanted to because he couldn't breathe, and we all thought he was having a heart attack. Turned out it was asthma.

"Spent like seventeen years operating on fifty-five percent lung capacity without realizing breathing just wasn't supposed to be that hard. Starting antidepressants was like that for me. I felt like shit all the time, and then suddenly I didn't. And all this stuff seemed possible for the first time. My mind felt . . . quieter, maybe. Lighter."

I dash away the tears pricking my eyes. "I had no idea," I croak.

"I didn't either," he says. "I spent a lot of energy trying to be fine, and — the point is, things are finally good for me. And I thought if I came here and saw you, it would prove we were both exactly where we were supposed to be. And instead, I showed up and you were furious at me. And you know what I felt?"

"I know you're angry with me too, Wyn," I force out.

He gives a sharp shake of his head. "Relief. I felt *relief.* Because it finally felt like you cared. If you were mad at me, it meant your heart really was as fucking broken as mine is. I thought when I found a way to be happy, I'd think about you less. But instead, it's like . . . like now that the grief isn't strangling me, there's all this extra room to love you.

"But we can't go back, so I don't know what to do with any of this. I don't even know if you feel the same way, and it's killing me too. I go back and forth every thirty seconds thinking I'm hurting you just by being here, and then thinking you couldn't possibly still love me after all this time, and even if it's not real, a part of me wants to pretend I have you, but another part thinks I'll die if you don't tell me you love me, even if it doesn't change anything. Even if it's just getting to hear it one more time.

"Everything's different and nothing's changed, Harriet," he says. "I tried so fucking hard to let you go, to let you be happy, and when I see you, I still feel like — like you're *mine.* Like I'm *yours.* I got rid of every single piece of you, like that would make a difference, like I could cut you out of me, and instead, I just see everywhere you're supposed to be."

I stare at him, heart cracking open under the weight of what I'm feeling.

"Please say something," he whispers.

My eyes fill. My throat fills. I drop my face into my hands again. "I thought you didn't want me," I choke out, "so I tried. I tried to love somebody else. I tried to even *like* somebody else. I kissed someone else. I slept with someone else, but I couldn't stop feeling like I was yours." My eyes tighten against another wave of tears. "Like you're mine."

"Harriet." He tilts my face up. "Look at me."

He waits. "Please, Harriet."

It takes a few seconds to force my eyes open. Water droplets still cling to his brows. Rivulets race down his jaw and throat. His thumb grazes my cheekbone.

"I am," he says. "I am still yours."

The nail that has been driving closer and closer to my heart all week sinks home.

The pads of his fingers slide across my bottom lip. His eyes are so soft, every ginger touch pushing back another layer from my heart.

But does it even matter that we belong *to* each other when we can't be *with* each other? Our lives are immovably separate. Everything may look different than it did ten minutes ago, but nothing's changed. He's mine, but I can't have him.

My hands tangle in his wet hair, as if that can keep him here with me. His do the same to mine.

"What is this?" he whispers.

I want it to be an *I'm sorry* and an *I forgive you* and a *Promise you won't ever let me go* and a million other words I can't say.

Wyn's finally happy. He has the life that was meant for him. He has a career he's proud of, one predicated on his being in Montana, and even if he didn't, there's Gloria, who needs him. The time with her that *he* needs, time he missed with Hank. And I'm in California for at least a few more years, too deep in to back out but not so far into the tunnel as to see the light at its end.

Maybe, in another life, things could be different. In this one, this can be only one thing.

"I think," I say, "it's one last *I love you.*"

His fingers tighten on me, his breath stilling. And then, like he's answering a question, his lungs expand on an inhale and his lips meet mine.

When I let out a shaky breath, his tongue slips into my mouth. The taste of him reaches deep and loosens something I've spent months tying into knots. Need

400

stretches out in every direction, waking up my skin, nerves, blood. Wyn angles my face up, deepening the kiss, and his tongue sweeps mine, hungry, tender. A whimper rises out of me.

His hand spreads across my stomach, finding its way several inches up beneath my shirt, and my spine arcs into him, every muscle in my stomach trying to draw closer to his.

He locks an arm around me and walks us backward. His shoulder collides with the shower stall's door as he hauls me inside and knocks it shut again.

My clothes are already wet from being held by him, sticking to my skin in places, but he shields me from the water anyway as he peels my shirt over my shoulders and drapes it over the wall along with his towel. I lean back against the wall, catching my breath, as he methodically undoes the buttons on my shorts. He takes his time easing them down my legs with my bikini bottoms, and I stand there, skin prickling, breath uneven, and mind on fire. He hangs those too, without taking his eyes off me.

"Is this real?" I ask.

He reaches for my waist. "What else would it be?"

"A dream," I say.

He pulls me in against him, his warm, damp stomach sliding against mine. "Can't be," he says. "In my dreams, you're always on top."

My laugh catches as his thumb sweeps up the outside curve of my breast.

I wind my arms around his neck, and he lifts me against the wall in a smooth motion, my thighs wrapping around his waist.

I gasp into his mouth at the sudden sensation of so much of him on so much of me. The bands of muscle across his stomach tighten. My lips part hungrily under his. His hands untie my bathing suit top, peel it away, and my heart pounds into his urgent touch.

He whispers my name at the hinge of my jaw, the water spraying over his shoulders, wrapping us in its heat.

He groans, palming me in slow, intense circles as my breath quickens. His mouth glides down my throat. "Are you sure about this?" he murmurs.

I hold him tighter. He draws back to ask again, but I pull him close, my tongue slipping into his mouth, finding the bitter, bready taste of Corona and sharp tang of lime.

I reach between us and thrill at the feeling of him in my hand. His head bows into my shoulder, one of his hands coming to grip the top of the wall behind me.

"I didn't bring condoms here," he says, but neither of us has stopped moving, looking for more friction, for release. The muscles all down his back and stomach and arms and ass are rigid with tension as our hips roll together.

His hands slide roughly behind my hips, canting them up to him. "We shouldn't do this while you're upset anyway," he says.

I move my hand down him. "I'll be less upset once you're inside me."

He wraps a hand over mine, holding me still for a second, our hearts slamming together, hot water racing down us. "We don't have a condom," he says again.

Some kind of pathetic sound of dissent squeaks out of me, and he seems to forget what he was saying, pushes me back into the wall, our hips grinding together, nails skating over wet skin. He lifts me a half inch so he's right against me now. It's not enough. He grabs the top of the wall again for support as we move together.

"Harriet," he rasps against my ear. "You're so fucking soft."

"Thanks," I say, breathless, "I don't work out."

"Don't joke right now," he says. "We can

joke later. Right now, tell me what you want."

"I already told you," I say.

"We can't," he says. "I'll find a way to get some while we're out for dinner."

I laugh into his throat, catch a rivulet on my tongue. "Are you going to hang out in alleyways and wave twenties at strangers who look like they're packing condoms?"

"I was thinking I'd go to a drugstore," he says, "but I like your way better."

He draws back, his hands slowing my descent until my feet meet the wet cedar planks. Everything in me rises in protest until he turns me, lifts my hands to the edge of the wall, and lets his own slide down the backs of my arms, down my sides. One slips around my hip and between my thighs as he presses in behind me.

For a second, I can't breathe. Even my organs are too busy *wanting* to do anything else, every last brain wave occupied with the sensation of his hand. His other arm winds around me, pulling me flush against him, his mouth on the spot between my neck and shoulder.

"Was this your goal for the week?" I ask.

He bites the side of my neck. "Actually, it was to make it through the rest of the week as a perfect gentleman."

"Occasional failure's good for a person," I say.

"Is it?" he teases. "Good for you?"

I push myself back into him, pleading. *"Please."*

Wyn swears, grabs my hips, and turns me again, pinning me back against the wall and kneeling in front of me.

My joints seem to liquefy as he kisses the inside of my thigh, moves up to my center. My hips lift into the pressure of his mouth. His left palm skims up my stomach, the right moving around to cup my ass, angling me up to him.

I try to urge him back up me, but he stays where he is, the insistent heat of his mouth edging me closer to unraveling.

"Wyn," I beg.

Goose bumps erupt over his neck. He murmurs, "Come for me, Harriet."

I try to resist, to ask for more of him, but my body bows up. His name rushes out of me in a breathless plea. He drives me into a wave so heavy and dark that, for several seconds, there's nothing but sensation. No woods, no cedar shower, nothing but his mouth.

When it recedes, I slump back against the wall, knees weak. Wyn rises and gathers me into him so that my chin rests on his shoulder. The hot water pours down us as he leaves a string of kisses down my throat.

"Thank you," I say through the dreamy haze.

His smile blooms against my neck. "So polite." He sways me gently back and forth beneath the water. "The others are waiting."

"I'm not feeling polite anymore." I tip my chin back to meet his eyes. "They can wait."

"The air horn will start going any minute now," he says.

"Waiting never killed anyone," I say.

"I don't know," Wyn says. "I've felt pretty close to death this week."

"Good point," I say. "Waiting can be dangerous. We probably shouldn't."

His laugh melts into another groan. "Later. Let me buy you dinner first."

"I'm a modern woman, Wyn," I say. "I'll buy *you* dinner. I mean, if I can *afford* your dinner now that you're fancy."

"You get me a gas station hot dog, Harriet Kilpatrick," he says, kissing the corner of my mouth, "and I'll give you the best night of your life."

I close my eyes, try to hold the moment still. It's already slipping away. *One more day.*

30
REAL LIFE

Friday

While most of the Lobster Fest festivities are on the other side of town, the overflow has wound up here, at the salt-coated picnic tables on the graying Lobster Wharf, where coveralled lobstermen zigzag among the docked boats, the warehouse, and the walk-up stands.

Even after we've put in our orders, we're waiting awhile until a table opens up near the band at the dock's back corner. We slide onto the benches, and Wyn holds my thigh under the table. I set my hand over the top of his, trying to memorize this feeling.

Baskets of fries and crisp hot dog buns overflowing with fluffy lobster, heavily seasoned onion rings and fried haddock so soft that the plastic forks slice through it like it's melting butter. Corn on the cob and tragic side salads loaded with red onion and sliced radish, and blueberry lemonade in red plastic diner cups.

"I'm going to go see how much the bar will charge me to add vodka to this," Kimmy says, starting to rise.

"You might want to hold off on that," Sabrina says, with a cryptic smile. I look to Parth, who gives a my-lips-are-sealed shrug.

With a delighted yet suspicious gleam in her eye, Kimmy sinks back onto her bench.

Wyn's mouth drifts across my earlobe. It takes me a second to actually interpret what he's saying through the barrage of fragmented memories from earlier: "You think she's Postmatesing magic mushrooms to the table?"

I turn toward him, the ends of our noses almost touching. The globe lights strung overhead make his eyes glitter. "That or she's taking us straight from here to a space camp zero-gravity chamber," I say.

His hand creeps higher as he leans in. I turn to hear his whispered reply, but instead his lips meet the skin beneath my ear, a slow, soft kiss that makes me shiver closer.

Sabrina crumples a napkin as she stands. "Who's ready for the next phase of the night?"

"Space camp, here we come," I say.

We follow the residential street along the

water. Even from here, we can hear the music coming from the festival on the far side of the harbor, along with the wharf band, like the two shores are opposite ends of a dueling piano bar.

Sabrina leads us down the long, skinny footbridge across the water, the sound of Patty Griffin's "Long Ride Home" cross-fading into "It's Still Rock and Roll to Me."

"Where are we going?" Cleo asks.

"To fulfill a long-term goal," Sabrina calls over her shoulder, picking up the pace. There's an electricity in the air, a feeling of possibility.

Maybe it's emanating from Wyn and me. Maybe every time our hands link, or he tugs me into his side or pulls me to a stop and presses me back against the guardrail for a kiss while the others keep walking, we let a little more charge into the air.

"Keep up," Parth calls back to us.

Wyn brushes his lips against mine once more. "We'll have time later," he says.

Not enough, I think with a pang. How can I exorcise all this trapped, combustible love in one day? How can I stockpile pieces of him in the next twenty-four hours and then let him go, like he needs? Like he *deserves.*

I force myself to nod, and we catch up with the others.

The harbor sits in a basin, the waterfront lined with restaurants and docks, while the rest of the town rises up along curving and crisscrossing streets, wild and verdant gardens spilling over the sidewalk, tiny ferns dotting the lawns of the salt-weathered bed-and-breakfasts.

We make our way up one of these streets, past the dark windows of the Fudge & Taffy Factory and Skippy's Popcorn, with its hundred different flavors on display behind glass. They'll be open later for the weekend, but everything is already shuttered tonight.

Past the Warm Cup, we turn up a quiet side street. Easy Lane. It takes me a second to place why it's familiar: I saw this street mentioned on the itinerary. Tomorrow morning, pre-wedding, Sabrina had scheduled personalized surprises for each of us, and the address for mine was 123 Easy Lane. Which I'd noted, specifically because naming a street Easy Lane instead of Easy Street struck me as a purposefully missed opportunity.

At the end of the first block of Easy Lane, Sabrina turns us down another street. Only two buildings are still aglow: a sprawling hotel and pub called the Hound & Thistle, and a black-trimmed storefront with off-white sans serif letters across its window reading **TEMPEST TATTOO.**

Sabrina stops and spins back to us, arms thrown out to her sides. "So," she says, "what do you think?"

"Sab!" Kimmy says, pouncing on her. "You're getting a tattoo?"

"Close," she says. "*We're* getting tattoos."

No one reacts, apart from the strained smile Parth flashes and the twitch of Wyn's fingers against mine. Kimmy's gaze darts to Cleo, her grin flagging at Cleo's stunned expression.

"We've talked about it forever," Sabrina goes on, "and this is the perfect time. To commemorate our last trip to the cottage and the last ten years of friendship. Something that will always connect us."

My stomach sinks, even as my heart feels like a crazed bird fighting its way up through my windpipe.

It's one thing to accept that I might always be a little bit in love with Wyn Connor. It's another to put a permanent reminder of that on my body. Before I've come close to finding a way out of this, Cleo says, "I don't think so, Sab."

You'd think the shocked silence might've prepared her for this, but Sabrina looks genuinely flabbergasted. "What do you mean *you don't think so?*"

411

Cleo shrugs. "I don't think we should get matching tattoos tonight." Kimmy touches her arm, some unspoken sentiment passing between them.

Sabrina laughs. "Why not?"

"Because I don't want to," Cleo says. "And looking around, I'm not sure anyone else does either."

Sabrina blinks and scans us.

"It's not that," I say. "It's just . . . really sudden."

"We've been talking about this for a decade," she says.

"And we've never decided what it would even be," Wyn says.

"Who cares what it is?" Sabrina says. "It's about the bond."

"Maybe next time," I suggest. "We can pick a design tonight, and then everyone has some time to get used to it, and then —"

"I've already put a deposit down," she says. "I got the shop to stay open for us."

Cleo rubs the spot between her brows. "Sab. You should have asked us before you did that. You can't assume we'll go along with whatever you want."

"What the hell does *that* mean, Cleo," Sabrina says, hurt splashed across her face.

"She just means this is a big, permanent

decision," I say. "We all need a little time to commit to this kind of thing."

"That's not what I mean," Cleo says calmly. "I meant what I said. That she can't just decide how things should be between all of us and then bulldoze all of us to get her way."

"She's not bulldozing anyone," Parth says, stepping in toward Sabrina. "She's doing all of this *for* you all. This whole trip was for you. All of it."

"If it's for us," Cleo says, "then you'll respect my decision *not* to do something I'm uncomfortable with."

"You have, like, nineteen separate tattoos," Sabrina says. "What's so uncomfortable about this one?"

"Can we please drop this?" Cleo says, averting her gaze.

"Sure," Sabrina says. "I'll drop it. I'll drop the fact that one of my best friends keeps canceling plans and the other will barely text me back, and my dad's selling the only place that's ever felt anything like home to me, and that no one except me seems to give a fuck that we're growing apart."

She turns back toward where we left the car.

"I'll talk to her," I tell the others, chasing her down the sidewalk. When I catch up, I

413

reach for her wrist. "Sabrina, wait."

She tries to keep moving, forcing me to run to keep my hand on her.

"We *all* care about this friendship," I say. "It's just —"

She spins back, eyes damp. "Sudden?"

My heart plummets toward my feet. I don't understand why she's so hurt, but it's obvious she is. Sabrina never cries.

But she's crying now. Full-fledged tears streaming down her face, and I need to fix this, to make her understand this isn't about her.

And in this moment, the last moment I have to make a decision, I see no other way.

"It's not about our friendship," I say.

"Of course it is," Sabrina says. "You're checked out, and Cleo doesn't want to spend any real —"

"It's about *Wyn,*" I say, before this conversation can go any further off the tracks.

She stares at me, dark eyes glassy, hair frizzed with humidity.

"I can't get a matching tattoo with him, Sabrina. We're not even together anymore."

Her voice comes out small, cracking: "But it seemed like you guys were working things out."

I shake my head, trying to untangle what she's just said. "What?"

"This week," she goes on. "It seemed like you were back together."

Back together?

How could it seem like we were *back together* . . . to someone who didn't know we'd broken up?

Unless, of course, she did know.

31
REAL LIFE

Friday

"You *knew*?" I say.

She doesn't reply.

"*Sabrina,*" I snap.

She throws her arms out to her sides. "Of course I knew! Not that I heard it from you. Not like my best friends tell me a single thing about their lives these days."

It's like missing the top step, only to realize the stairs lead directly to the edge of a cliff.

I get out, "*How?*"

"Parth visited Wyn a few weeks ago."

The harbor starts to swirl around me. "Did he . . . tell him?"

"No." She crosses her arms. "Wyn went to the bathroom, and Parth was going to send you a picture of himself or something from Wyn's phone. Only when he opened your text thread, there was nothing new for *months*. And I guess Wyn had this whole long message drafted, apologizing for how things ended."

"So he read it," I say, the words bitter on the back of my tongue.

"It wasn't intentional," Sabrina says. "And not the whole thing. But enough to know what happened."

"Why didn't you say anything?" I say.

"Me? You're the one who hid this, Harry. For months you've told me almost nothing about your life, and meanwhile Cleo cancels every set of plans she makes, and Wyn wasn't even going to *come* this week until I begged, and —"

"Wait." I close my eyes, shake my head.

It can't be.

It has to be.

"That's what this is all about?" I open my eyes, lungs compressing. "This whole trip?"

Sabrina's shoulders square, her chin rising.

I think of all the moments Sabrina shoved Wyn and me together. I think of all the times she weaseled out of even a few minutes alone with me. Even on the drive from the airport, she had the music blasting and windows down so that even if *I'd* wanted to tell her about Wyn, *she* could plausibly deny hearing it.

The anger floods me now. Anger like I've

417

never felt. "This trip down memory lane? The bathroom with no fucking door? This was all — all some game to you?"

"A *game*?" she says. "Harriet, we were trying to *help* you. You and Wyn belong together."

"How could you put us through all of this?" My vocal cords are shivering from anger.

Sabrina's eyes flare, but her mouth jams shut.

"You made us bend over backward all week. You *tortured* us," I say. "How could you all do this?"

"We didn't know," comes a quiet voice.

Cleo has followed us, the light from the Hound & Thistle limning her in red gold. "Didn't know you and Wyn broke up," she says. "Didn't know this whole week was a sham."

"It's not a *sham*," Sabrina says. "We were *helping* them."

"Helping us do *what*?" I say raggedly.

"Get back together!" she replies.

"If we wanted to be together," I say, "we'd be together!"

"Oh, please," she says. "You don't know *what* you want, Harriet! You're *losing* the love of your life because you're too indecisive to just pick a wedding date and a venue."

White-hot hurt blazes out from my chest. "We're not together because we don't want to be, Sabrina! Because we can't make each other happy, no matter how badly we want to."

"Really?" she says. "Because Parth *saw* what Wyn wrote, and it sure sounds like, once again, you sat there and let your life happen to you instead of fighting for what you want."

"You don't get to decide what's best for everyone," Cleo says. "It doesn't matter how good you think your intentions were. You manipulated us. You *knew* how stressed out I was about this week, and you *knew* why Wyn wasn't coming, and you forced us all into it anyway."

"I did what I had to," Sabrina says. "Just like I always do, because no one makes even the tiniest bit of effort anymore. If I waited on all of you, this friendship would already be over, and you know it. I send the first text. I make the phone calls. I leave the voicemails. I schedule the trips, and when you cancel on them, I pitch other dates, and when you can't give me an immediate yes or no, guess what? *I'm* the one to check back in a couple days later."

"We have other things going on in our lives," Cleo says. "We can't always drop everything to relive the glory days with you."

Instantly, I can tell from Sabrina's expression that Cleo's hit a nerve, a deep one.

All my virulent anger breaks, a fog clearing enough to reveal a steep drop-off ahead. The anger's still there, but the fear is heavier, rooting through me, yelling, *Stop, stop, stop this, before it gets any worse. Stop this before someone leaves. Before you lose them.*

"Let's all cool off for a second," I choke out.

Cleo's eyes lock on to me. "I'm not angry," she says evenly.

She means it. There's no fire behind her gaze, only exhaustion, only disappointment. "I'm just not pretending anymore."

The sidewalk seems to crack underneath me, the world splitting. If I don't do something, the gap will yawn wider and wider until I can't reach them. Until I'm all alone.

"Not pretending *what*?" Sabrina asks.

"That these *are* the glory days," Cleo says. "That we're as close as we used to be, when the truth is, it's different. *We're* different."

"*Cleo,*" I say, quiet, pleading.

"Our lives are total opposites," she goes on, "and our schedules are totally different, and we don't like spending our free time the same way anymore, and Wyn's out in Montana, and Harriet's all but cut us out of her life, and you and Parth still want everything to be one big party, but it's not! There's real shit going on in our lives, and we never talk about any of it."

"I haven't cut you out of my life," I say. "We kept something from you that was so painful I haven't been able to make myself tell *anyone* about it. I can still hardly think about it — about *him* — without feeling like . . . like the world's coming apart at the seams."

Cleo's eyes are dark and glossy. "We're exactly who you're supposed to come to when you feel like that, and instead you stop talking to us, and then when things are . . . are hard for us, what are we supposed to do?"

"Oh, come on, Cleo," Sabrina says. "Don't act like you're any better. You've been dodging plans with me for *months*. As far as *I* can tell, *I'm* the only one trying to hold all this together, while everyone else would be totally fine never seeing one another."

"We've seen one another all *week*," Cleo says, "and you're just now telling us this was all some kind of Machiavellian scheme, and Harriet's just confessing she and Wyn aren't even together, and we've had *days,* and it hasn't even mattered. Because you'd rather sit in a theater for five hours, just because we *used to,* than adjust to the fact that maybe we'd all rather do something different! We're not in the same place anymore. We're growing up."

Her voice wavers. "And in different directions. And there are things we can't talk to one another about anymore, and maybe we've all been fighting it, or pretending we don't notice, when we should accept it. We're not what we used to be for one another. And that's fine."

"It's fine?" Sabrina repeats emptily.

"Things are changing. They already have. And I've never been this person who just goes along with things she doesn't want to do, but you've made it so I have to. It all has to be on your terms."

"No one's forcing you to stay!" Sabrina says. "If you want to go, go!"

Cleo looks down at her feet, a tiny fern growing up between the cracks in the sidewalk there, right between her sandals. "Fine," she says. "Kimmy and I will find a hotel for the night."

Another cold laugh from Sabrina. "So, what, you're going to *consciously uncouple* from our friendship?"

"I'm going to take some *space*," Cleo says.

"This is ridiculous," Sabrina replies. "You won't find anywhere to stay on this entire coast."

Cleo's lips press tighter. "Then we'll sleep in the guesthouse tonight."

"And then what?" Sabrina says.

"I don't know yet," Cleo said. "Maybe leave."

I have no idea how to argue with her, or if I even want to. My head throbs. Everything is all wrong.

Finally, Sabrina says, "I'll get the car." She turns and stalks down the street. I look back the way we came. Even in silhouette, Kimmy, Wyn, and Parth look rigid. They heard everything.

In a way, I tell myself, it's a relief, to have everything out in the open.

But the truth is, if I could take it all back, I would. I'd do anything to go back to that happy place, outside of time, where nothing from real life can touch us.

32
REAL LIFE

Friday

On the drive home, we're silent. Now that the truth is out, Wyn and I can't even look at each other. He won't look at Parth either, keeps his eyes fixed out the car window.

As soon as we get inside the cottage, everyone retreats, and rather than endure any more awkward or painful run-ins, I tuck myself away in the first-floor powder room.

When I make my way up the stairs, though, Kimmy and Cleo are coming down, bags in hand, bound for the guesthouse.

Cleo doesn't look at me.

Neither of them says anything, but Kimmy flashes a tense smile and squeezes my hand as we pass. A lump forms in my throat at the whine of the front door opening behind me.

I don't go to Wyn's and my room. The bubble has popped, this pocket universe collapsed. Instead, I take the kids' room. It's tidy, the twin beds returned to opposite walls and neatly made. Cleo and Kimmy left no trace of themselves here apart from the lingering scent of Kimmy's peppermint oil.

I sit on the edge of the bed, feeling the loneliness swell, not knowing whether it's pressing against me from the outside or growing from within.

Either way, it's inescapable, my oldest companion.

I shuck off my clothes and crawl into bed. I don't cry, but I don't sleep either.

The argument replays in my mind on a feverish loop until it feels like the words melt together nonsensically.

I ask myself, again and again, why I didn't tell them. All the same half-assed answers cycle through my mind until I'm as sick with myself as everyone else is.

I turn onto my back and glare up at a beam of moonlight on the ceiling.

I wasn't afraid they'd be mad at me, exactly, for how things ended with Wyn. I was afraid of their sadness. I was afraid of ruining this trip that meant so much to them. I was afraid of ruining this place where they've always been happy. I was afraid they would resent me and never say it, afraid they wouldn't like me as much

425

without Wyn, because *I* didn't like me as much without him.

I was afraid they'd ask me what went wrong, and no matter what answer I cobbled together from the rubble, they'd see right through it.

They'd know I wasn't enough.

I'm not the brilliant doctor my parents wanted me to be, and I'm not the person who could give Wyn the happiness he deserves, and I'm not the friend Sabrina and Cleo needed.

I've tried so hard to be *good,* to deserve the people around me, and I've still managed to hurt all of them.

The blankets feel too hot, the mattress too soft. Whenever I roll over, I thwack the wall.

If there were a TV in here, I'd put on *Murder, She Wrote,* fall asleep to its blue glow and softly jaunty soundtrack.

The silence leaves too much room for questions, for memories to vine around me, hold me captive.

Not just of the fight but of the *dark place,* of the weeks before and after losing Wyn. Of crying into a pillow that smelled like him, and waking up from dreams of him, my chest filled with knots. Of trying to flush him from my system with a double date with Taye, her boyfriend, and their friend.

426

Of coming home, sick to my stomach, and cleaning the apartment. As if scrubbing the grout and the condiment splatters on the kitchen cabinets could make everything about my life look different. Make *me* different.

I remember standing in my kitchen, my phone clamped in one hand, wishing there were someone to call.

That if I called my mother, she'd say, *Come home; I'll take care of you.*

That if I called Wyn, his soft voice would tell me it had all been a mistake, a misunderstanding, that he'd love me forever, like he promised.

Even if I *did* feel capable of telling them the truth, Sabrina and Parth would've *just* gotten to sleep, and Cleo and Kimmy would need to get up in a few short hours; and if I called Eloise, she'd assume someone died, because we *never* talk on the phone.

I was so close to dialing Wyn that night that I blocked his number.

And the longer I went without calling any of them, the more impossible doing so felt, the more embarrassed I was by the truth.

I spent my whole life trying to get here, and *why?* It wasn't what I pictured.

No, it's worse than that. Because honestly, I'm not sure I ever bothered to picture it.

I imagined giving relieved family members good news in hospital waiting rooms, and I pictured my own parents' happiness and pride, their faces out in the crowd at graduation, their adoring notes at the foot of the family Christmas card. I pictured a house with air-conditioning that always worked and doors that stayed open, and long dinners at nice restaurants, with everyone laughing, pink-cheeked. I imagined downtime, thoughtful gifts for my parents, the family vacations we'd never taken, their mortgage paid off. I imagined all their hard work finally repaid, all their sacrifices not only compensated but rewarded.

I imagined them thinking it was all worth it. Telling me how much they loved me.

All my life, when I thought of my future, that was what I pictured. Not a career. The things I thought would come with it.

Happiness, love, safety.

And that dream had been enough for a long time. What was school if not a chance to earn your worth? To prove, again and again, that you were *measurably* good.

One more deal I struck with a disinterested universe: *If I'm good enough, I'll be happy.*

I'll be loved.

I'll be safe.

Instead, I've pushed away everyone I love. My heart clangs in my chest. I need to outrun these feelings.

I stand and tear the sheet off the bed, wrapping it around my shoulders. The temperature drops a solid ten degrees as I make my way into the hallway, another few as I descend the stairs, but I still feel hot and stuffy.

The kitchen is a wreck. I set my sheet aside and, in my underwear, put away the dishes, loading the dirty ones into the empty dishwasher. I wipe down the counters. I sweep. I tell myself it will make a difference. That tomorrow, when everyone comes down, tonight's wreckage won't look quite so bad.

The anxiety doesn't let up. My skin feels too tight, hot and itchy. Gathering the sheet again, I let myself out back.

The wind does little to break the feverish feeling. I climb down to the bluff, and in the dark, the water seems louder, powerful but ambivalent. I imagine what it would feel like to be swept up in it, to drift across its back. I imagine being carried away from this life, opening my eyes in a different place.

Something Sabrina said intrudes on the fantasy: *You're losing the love of your life because you're too indecisive to just pick a wedding date and a venue.*

I know things are more complicated than that, but those words keep replaying, braiding in and out of what Wyn told me earlier.

I genuinely convinced myself that was the kind of guy you wanted to be with. And you kept pushing the wedding off. You never wanted to talk about it. You never wanted to talk about anything.

You were never mad at me. You never fought with me. It felt like you didn't even miss me.

I kept so much of what I was feeling from him, thinking the weight of my emotions would only drive him further from me, push him back behind a door I couldn't open.

And even after he told me that tonight, I felt trapped inside myself, unable to get the words out.

Now they wriggle in my gut, burrowing deeper, gaining ground.

As soon as I make the decision, time accordions. The steep climb up the bluff, the length of the patio, the creaky stairs, the hallway — it all blurs past and I'm standing at his door.

Knocking quietly. Maybe have been for a while, even, because the door's already swinging open, as if he's been waiting.

That would explain why he's fully dressed,

but not why he looks so surprised.

Not the way his lips part and his brow furrows as I seem to float into the room, inflated with helium-light purpose.

And it definitely wouldn't explain the packed luggage sitting by the door.

At the sight of it, a hot coal slips down my throat, hits the deepest pit of my stomach and sizzles. "You're leaving?"

His steel-gray gaze flicks back toward his luggage. "I thought that might be easiest."

"Easiest," I murmur. "How? Only like three flights leave the airport a day, and none of those departs in the dead of night."

He grabs the corner of the door and clicks it shut behind me. "I don't know," he admits.

Finally, I manage, "No."

His brow lifts. "No, what?"

"We're not done fighting," I say.

"I thought we *weren't* fighting," he says.

I step in close enough to feel the warmth radiating off him. "We're in an all-out brawl."

He looks away, the corners of his mouth twisting downward. "About what?"

"For starters, about the fact that you packed your bags up in the night," I say, pressing closer. He takes a half step back.

My voice wobbles. "And I don't want you to go."

His hands come to my hips, holding me but keeping me at a distance. "I shouldn't have come in the first place," he says. "This is all my fault."

"No, it's not," I say.

"It is," he says, insistent.

I press closer. Our chests brush. "There," I say.

"*There* what?"

"Something else we have to fight about," I say.

Faintly, grudgingly, he smiles. It doesn't last. He glances away, his brow tightening. "I'm so fucking sorry, Harriet," he says. "If I'd just stayed away this week like I said I would . . ."

I set my hands on his shoulders, and his eyes snap to mine, a current flaring in them. I push down gently, and he sits at the edge of the bed, his head tipped up to study me in the light of the lone bedside lamp. His thighs fall apart as I step in between them, my hands trailing up over his warm shoulders to his jaw. His eyes flutter shut, and he turns his face into my palm, kissing its center.

His hands come to my waist, and I slip my knee over his hip. His eyes open, inky

432

dark, and he takes my weight as I slide my other knee over his far hip, shifting over him.

"This is fighting?" he murmurs.

I nod as I sink into his lap. His Adam's apple bobs. His hands clutch the underside of my thighs, the bedsheet still caped around my shoulders. He says, "This is what you wore to fight?"

"I'm new to this," I say. "I didn't know there was a standard uniform. Do you want me to go change?"

His gaze wanders down me, considering. "Did you pack anything smaller?"

I shake my head. "Not unless you know a good way to wear a toothbrush."

"We can make do with this," he says. "Now, what are we fighting about?"

"Everything," I say.

He cups the back of my neck while his other hand drags me up his lap, fitting us together. "It's usually easier to start with something minor, and then let it slowly become about everything. At least that's how my parents always did it."

"Your parents," I say, "did not fight."

"Everyone fights with the people they love, Harriet," he says. "What matters is how you do it."

"There are rules?" I ask.

"There are."

"Like the uniform," I say.

"Like no name-calling," he replies.

"What about *honey*?" I ask.

His hands move to the tops of my thighs, slide back and forth against them, the coarse texture of his palms making my skin prickle and rise. "I'd have to double-check with Parth and Sabrina, Esquires, but I think *honey* is allowable," he says. "No jury would convict. Nothing meaner than that, though."

"What else do I need to know?"

"It's okay to walk away," he says. "Everyone says *Don't go to bed angry,* but sometimes a person needs time to think. And if you need that, it's okay, but you should tell me, because otherwise . . . ." His jaw flexes on a swallow. "Otherwise, the person might assume you're leaving for good."

I swallow too and move closer, our chests melting together. "What else?"

"There doesn't need to be a winner and a loser. You just have to care how the other person feels. You have to care more about them than you do about being right."

"This doesn't sound like fighting," I tell him.

"This information came straight from Hank," he says.

I can't help but smile. "Then I guess we'd

better trust it."

"Do you want to try?" he says.

"Something minor?" I say.

He nods.

"You load the dishwasher wrong," I say.

He breaks into a smile. "Wrong?"

"Fine, not wrong," I say. "But in a way that I hate."

His smile splits open on an exhalation of laughter. "Go on. Don't hold back."

"You fill the bottom rack too full," I say, "and the water can't get to the top rack. And you don't rinse things well enough, so even when everything does get soaped, there's still, like, full pieces of cereal stuck inside the bowls."

He fights his way back to a somber expression. "I'm sorry," he says. "You're right. I hurry when I do the dishes, and it ends up making more work. What else?"

"I don't like when you downplay your intelligence."

"I'm working on that," he says. "And honestly, the medicine helps. So does feeling good at my job."

My rib cage seems to shrink, or else my heart grows. "Good. You should be at least a fraction as proud of yourself as I am of you."

"Those," he says quietly, smiling, "are not

fighting words."

"That's because it's your turn," I say. "You're mad at me too."

"I am?" he says.

"Furious," I say.

He squeezes me to him. "Furious," he breathes. "About what again?"

Sabrina's words replay in my head: *You're losing the love of your life because you're too indecisive to just pick a wedding date . . . Parth saw what Wyn wrote . . . you sat there and let your life happen to you instead of fighting for what you want.*

My stomach flip-flops. "Maybe because of the wedding."

"What wedding?" he says.

"Ours," I say.

"We didn't have one," he says.

"And maybe you think I didn't care," I say. "Or that I was afraid to commit to you, and that's why I couldn't make any decisions. Maybe you think I was intentionally putting it off."

He swallows, murmurs, "Weren't you?"

My head swims at the confirmation, the final piece of the puzzle clicking into place, five months too late. Tears gloss my eyes.

It wasn't one moment when everything went wrong, when I failed him, when we lost each other. There were dozens, on

436

either side. Missed signs. Dropped lines.

It fucking hurts to realize it. To understand that I made him think I didn't want him.

"I was trying to be *easy*, Wyn," I choke out. "You were so unhappy. And I didn't want to rush you while you were mourning. I didn't want to *need* you when you were in so much pain, so I pretended I was fine. I was scared that if you realized what a wreck I was, you wouldn't want me, so I pushed you away."

His mouth softens, but his fingers draw tight. "Harriet," he says, all rough tenderness, the exact contradiction of Wyn Connor, funneled into one spoken word. "I always want you."

It takes me a second to get anything out. "Another thing I'm mad about . . . I hate when I hurt your feelings and you don't tell me, so I have to try to guess what I did and how to fix it. Like tonight."

"Tonight?" he asks.

"When we got back in the car. You wouldn't even look at me."

"Shit, Harriet," he says. "I was just embarrassed. About this entire fucking week. About dragging you into this situation when it turns out there was no good reason."

"But when you don't tell me what's wrong, I assume things, Wyn," I say. "And it's all I can think about. That I've messed things up."

"That's not healthy," he says.

"I know, but it's the truth," I say.

"Well, I don't like *that*," he says. "You should know you're safe with me. You shouldn't spend every moment second-guessing how I feel when I've spent eight years telling you outright."

"And *you* should have known I didn't want anyone else." My voice splinters apart, my heart going with it. "You should have known that you were it for me, from the night we met. I would have done anything to fix it, but you wouldn't fight for me. You said you would, and I believed you, Wyn. And I understand why you couldn't. But I haven't forgiven you for breaking my heart."

His hand scrapes into my hair, his mouth burrowing against my neck. "Good," he says. "Don't forgive me. Stay mad at me. Don't get over me."

"And I'm mad at you for not coming to me tonight," I say.

He tilts my chin, kissing the other side of my throat, whispering softly, "I would've made it to you eventually."

"You packed your bags," I say.

He laughs jaggedly into my skin, his hands going back to my thighs, hoisting me up snug against him. "It was bullshit," he says. "I was trying to convince myself it would be best if I left you alone. The sad thing is, I actually believe it, Harriet. But I wasn't going to. I was on my way to find you when you got here. How do you think I answered the door so fast? Why do you think I was already hard, Harriet?"

A pleasant shiver climbs my thighs. "Maybe you were doing a crossword," I say.

He kisses the soft skin under my ear. "I couldn't leave you alone. I've never been able to."

"You've left me alone for five months," I point out.

"You blocked my number," he says, his fingers tightening on me through the thin sheet. "Or else you'd know that's bullshit too. It wasn't one unsent text message that Parth saw, Harriet. It was the ones I'd sent you too. The ones you didn't reply to."

My heart flutters up through my esophagus, a giddy canary catching a breeze of cool air. His calloused hands turn my face up to his, and he kisses me deeply, coarsely.

My nerve endings light up in concentric circles that reverberate outward. Cellular fireworks. Neurological Ferris wheel spokes. My hands sift into his hair, and he flips us onto the bed, the twin sheet falling over us

439

as gently as snow. He shifts his weight back long enough for me to slough his shirt off, then stretches himself over me again, our mouths colliding, his knee dipping between my thighs. His hands roll heavily over me. My nails scrape over his warm back.

He kisses down my sternum, sneaks his tongue under the fabric, follows it with his teeth. I cry out from the relief and the simultaneous need. We arch closer. His hand works behind my back, finds the clasp for my bra, and after a brief struggle, he's pulling it away from me, tossing it out of our way, and our chests are finally pressing together, mine flattening under his. He groans. His palms move heavily over my chest, cupping, lifting me to his mouth.

The bed creaks as we move together.

He shifts onto one elbow, his other hand grating down my ribs and waist until it reaches the side of my underwear. He jerks them down my hip, and his hand skims my thigh. "I miss hearing you," he whispers against my ear. "All the little sounds you make."

Just by saying it, he's coaxed out a few more.

"We should fight more often," I say.

"I agree." He jerks my underwear down over my other thigh. I reach for the buttons of his pants, and his head lolls against mine on a groan as I slip my hand into his waistband.

"Did you find condoms?" I whisper.

"Before dinner." He fishes a strip of three out of his pocket and tosses them beside us. "I've been carrying them around all night, like some fucking teenager hoping to sneak into the bathroom at prom."

"If I'd known," I say, "we could've skipped the fight entirely."

He grabs my thigh and places it against the outside of his hip. "Please don't leave," he says in a low grate. "When this is over, don't go sleep in another room. Stay with me all night."

"I won't leave," I promise, sliding his pants down, kissing the jut of his hip.

His arm straps around my low back, and he rolls us again so that I'm on top of him. He lifts his hips enough to push his briefs down, and then I fold over him, nothing separating us now. Nothing has ever felt so blissfully good as this simple contact. He grasps my hips, sliding me over him, our breath shallowing. He pulls my wrists above his head, stretching me over him, and drags his parted lips, his tongue, over my chest.

I search through the bedding for the condoms, tear open the first one, and work it onto him. As I lift up, he takes hold of my hips, his eyes heavy and dark, guiding me onto him. His head tips back, a throaty sound emanating from him as I rise up and sink lower. He feels so familiar, so right, but after all this time, strangely new.

Our movement is slow but urgent, so intense I keep forgetting to breathe for a second too long, like nothing else is quite so necessary for my survival as this. His hands are careful on my jaw, his lips soft on mine, his tongue skimming into my mouth almost tentatively until I can barely take any more gentleness, any more restraint. I'm tired of him holding back any piece of himself.

When I tell him so, he flips us over one more time, my arms pinned above my head. Sweat slicks our skin as we become feverish, wild. I bow up under him, meeting his rhythm, trying not to come apart, not yet. I say his name like it's a spell.

Or a *goodbye* and *I love you,* a promise.

I just know my heart agrees: *You, you, you.*

We lie in a sweaty heap, Wyn toying with one of my curls, his lungs lifting and lowering me like a boat on a tide. "Do you forgive them?" I whisper.

"Honestly," he says, "I was having trouble

being mad. I know they shouldn't have lied, but . . . I don't know. It's felt worth it. To be here. To see you."

"To me too," I whisper, holding him a little tighter. Then, after another minute: "Do you think they'll forgive *us*?"

"Yes," he says.

"You didn't think about it," I chide.

"I didn't need to," he says.

I lift up to peer into his eyes. "How are you so sure?"

"More Hank wisdom," he says. "Love means constantly saying you're sorry, and then doing better."

I smile, let my fingers play across Wyn's chest. "He did okay with you, Wyn Connor. He'd be proud."

He wraps his arms tight around me. "I'm glad you think so."

Within minutes, I'm asleep, dreaming of a sunlit pine forest, the warm wood of a table beneath me, the smell of clove everywhere. And I know this place, even if I can't name it. I know that I'm safe, that I belong.

33
REAL LIFE

Saturday

Wyn left the drapes and windows open last night, and now the room is cold and bright, salt wafting in on the breeze, and bringing with it the distant squawk of herring gulls. My body feels like melted ice cream, in the best way. Bits of last night glance over my mind: hands fisting into bedding and hair and skin, ragged whispers and pleas.

And then everything that came before.

The fight. The rest of the week. Everything with Wyn.

That today is the last day of our trip.

The pleasant soreness gives way. Now I feel like I've been hit by a bus, then backed over and hit one more time at an angle. Wyn is fast asleep, one arm still draped over my ribs and one corner of his mouth lifted. My chest aches at the sight.

Usually, he's a back sleeper. We used to fall asleep curled up like this, but we'd never get any rest until he shifted onto his back. If we were fitted together like spoons, he'd always start moving restlessly in his sleep, and we'd find our way to each other in a heady, lust-crazed blur. Which was great until the morning, when we both had to get up for work or school.

He's made it through the whole night beside me, but the whole night, for us, was no more than a couple of hours.

He doesn't so much as stir as I slide out from under him. He always looks younger when he's asleep. I wonder if that's some evolutionary trait: What animal could stand attacking someone who looks so peaceful and innocent?

Okay, *I* could, but the *nice* thing would be to let him sleep.

I pull on a pair of jeans and a sweater and sneak out of the room, making my way through the silent house. As eager as I am to fix what happened last night, everyone's either still asleep or in hiding.

After a couple of minutes of aimlessly wandering the kitchen, I decide to walk into town and get everyone drinks from the Warm Cup as a peace offering.

I've often thought that the world saves its very best weather for days when you feel like everything's gone wrong, and today is no different. It's gloriously sunny, with a refreshing breeze. When the sun reaches its high point, Knott's Harbor will no doubt be sweltering. Or sweltering for the midcoast anyway, which is to say extremely comfortable when compared to the swampy summers of southern Indiana or the burning-under-a-microscope heat of July in New York City.

A midcoast summer day is the exact day you pine for in the dead of winter.

Still, after ten minutes of following the curving road, past overflowing rhododendron bushes and graying wood-shingled inns being scraped and repainted for the hundredth time, I'm wishing I'd put a tank top on under my sweater.

I'll have to find a cab back, easier said than done in a tiny village like this. Usually, Sabrina schedules our transportation, and I'm not sure how far ahead she has to do it. *If I waited on all of you, this friendship would already be over,* she said. She's not entirely wrong. Friendship with Sabrina, with this whole group, has always felt like a current I could toss myself bodily into. And that's what I'm most used to: coasting along on other people's whims and feelings.

It had never occurred to me that that could be read as apathy. That they might

446

think I just don't care. Guilt twinges through me.

The cracked sidewalk turns and deposits me in town in front of the coffee shop. Under the faded awning over its walk-up window, collecting a recycled drink carrier, is Cleo.

She stiffens at the sight of me, slowly lifts one hand.

I do the same.

For a moment, neither of us moves. Then the barista calls out, "Doug!" and the only other waiting customer nudges Cleo aside to pick up an order.

She ambles toward me with her carrier, and I meet her halfway, in front of the cheerily painted bench in front of the Italian restaurant. In between rows of cutesy red cartoon lobsters, in cutesy font, are the words *FOR CUSTOMERS ONLY!!!*

"Hi," she says.

"Hi," I say.

She lifts the drink carrier. "Coffee?"

"Then you'd only have three left," I say.

She cracks a half-hearted smile. "The salted-caramel latte is for you."

I look down at the carrier. Three very average-sized drinks, and one that's the coffee shop equivalent of a Big Gulp. "So they were out of 5-Hour Energies and Adderall, I see."

Her smile widens. "I couldn't carry five drinks. So I got one big-ass Americano for Sabrina and Parth to split, a black coffee for Wyn, and a matcha for Kim."

My chest stings. "You have our drink orders memorized."

She lifts one shoulder. "I know you."

Another beat of silence.

"You want to walk for a minute?" she asks.

I nod.

"Here." She balances the carrier on the bench and pries my paper cup out of it.

"I'll Venmo you," I say.

She winces a little. "Please don't."

We meander down toward the water, the brine in the air thickening.

After a second, I tell her, "I never learned how to fight."

She glances sidelong at me.

"Especially not with people I care about," I say. "I mean, not with anyone. But especially not with the people I love. In fact, I specifically only know how to avoid fights. Or, usually I do."

She watches me with a divot between her eyebrows.

"I don't know how fights are supposed to end when you love the person you're fighting with," I go on. "In my family, everyone always left when things got bad. Eloise would storm out, or my parents would send her to her room and then go shut themselves in opposite sides of the house, and things never got better afterward. They always felt a little worse.

"And I guess I thought . . . if I kept us from ever fighting, then everyone would stay. I was never trying to cut anyone out. It was the exact opposite. I haven't been fun to be around in a long time, Cleo."

Her brows knit tighter, an air of utter mystification to her expression. I wonder if I accidentally said the whole sentence backward.

"The point is," I say, "I'm sorry. I should have told you about Wyn and me. I should've called more."

After a moment, she looks back over the water. "I wasn't totally fair last night," she says. "I understand why you wouldn't tell us."

"You do?" I say.

She looks back at me, nods once.

"Lucky," I say. "Can you explain it to me like I'm five years old?"

She doesn't crack a smile this time. "You were in denial," she says. "And telling us would've made it all feel real. And even if it

449

is real, even if it's what you chose, you still know it's going to change everything, and that's scary. Because you need us. We're your family."

I stare at her. "Damn."

"Was I close?" she asks.

I set my drink down on one of the posts that line the water here, thick rope strung between them. "More like, *are you psychic?*" I say.

She lets out a little breathless laugh and looks back to the water sloshing against the bank. Tears glint in the corners of her eyes. "I'm pregnant," she says.

I know there must be sounds all around me — the water, the low horn of boats leaving the harbor, the lobstermen across the bay shouting back and forth, ribbing one another as they load and unload traps.

But it's like someone's clipped the wires to my ears.

When it rushes back in, I hear myself burst into tears, which makes Cleo burst into tears.

I grab the drink carrier from her hands and deposit it on the next post over. Then I pull her into a hug.

"Why are *you* crying?" she asks wetly, arms twining around me. "You're not the one who's going to have to push a squash out of her body."

"I know!" I say. "I'm just so happy."

Cleo laughs. "Me too. And fucking terri-fied. I mean, I chose this. I knew what it meant — it's not like I tripped through the door of a sperm bank. We spent *months* choosing the right donor. But . . . I think I expected it to take longer. To have longer to wrap my head around the idea of being a mom.

"But that's not how it happened. And I . . . I'm so scared I'll be bad at it."

I pull back to look into her eyes as she wipes away her tears. "Are you kidding?" I say. "You're going to be a perfect mom. You're going to be *your mom 2.0,* and — wait a second! How far along are you? How long have you known you were doing this?"

She ducks her head. "Like I said," she murmurs, "it wasn't entirely fair to be so upset about your secret."

"Apparently," I say.

"And that's why I've been hesitant to have Sabrina and Parth visit the farm," she goes on. "We already have a ton of baby shit. Kimmy's dad mails us something new every day, and I haven't felt ready to explain why we have four separate bassinets."

"Because Kimmy's dad is a baby-obsessed hoarder?" I say.

"He's going to be an amazing grandpa," she says wistfully. "I didn't even want to tell him yet, but Kimmy accidentally blurted it out. I'm only a couple months along. So many things could still go wrong."

I jog her by the elbows. "So many things could go right too."

She gives a wan smile. "I don't know what it means for us."

"It means you're going to be moms," I say.

She shakes her head. "What it means for *all* of us, Harry. If my Google searches are anything to go on, I'm going to be tired all the time and a worried wreck whenever I'm conscious. I'm already not the 'fun one' in the group —"

I snatch her hands. "Cleo! That's completely ridiculous. You are *so* fun."

"*Kimmy* is fun," she says, skeptical. "And I mean, it's why I fell in love with her. But sometimes it's hard not to feel like . . . like everyone already likes my girlfriend more than me. Even my best friends. And the more I grow into myself, the less room there might be for me."

"How long have you felt like this?"

"I don't know," she says. "Probably since I stopped drinking."

"I wish you would've said something."

"It's embarrassing!" she says. "Being jealous of your own partner? I didn't even tell Kimmy until a few months ago."

"I *love* Kimmy," I say, "and you know that. She has a lot of amazing qualities, and she's become one of my best friends. But you know what my favorite thing about her is?"

The corners of Cleo's mouth turn up. "Her banging body?"

"That's number two. Number one is how happy she makes you. When you two started dating, it felt like the final missing puzzle piece to . . . all this. Our family. But that doesn't make you any less essential. You and Sabrina are my best friends. Always. And I'm so sorry I ever gave you reason to doubt that."

Her eyes gloss, and her voice quivers. "But what if having a baby changes me? What if the gulf gets wider and wider until we don't have anything in common?"

"I don't need you to stay the same, Cleo," I say. "And it's not 'having things in common' that makes me love you. We're so different, Clee. All of us. And I wouldn't change anything about you. Like I said, you are a missing piece of my heart, and Sabrina is too. If your schedule has to change, or you start singing Barney songs to yourself, or become one of those people who post about their kids' diaper blowouts on social media —"

"You'll put me out of my misery?" she asks quietly.

"God, yes. I'll take your phone and feed it to the sea. But I'll also still love you. You're family to me. You and Sab both."

Cleo's smile fades. "I shouldn't have been so hard on her either."

"There might've been a better way to say it," I admit, "but I think you needed to get some of that off your chest. And we probably needed to hear it."

"Maybe." Cleo chews her lip. "Sabrina's pretty loyal, but when she feels wronged . . ."

"I'm not telling you to *use* your pregnancy as a bargaining chip," I say, "but I think when she finds out what you've been dealing with, she's going to understand. And then she's going to plan you a very over-the-top party, with a photorealistic baby cake and actual live storks flapping around your house."

Cleo devolves into laughter, letting her head fall against my shoulder. "I can't wait."

She laces her fingers through mine, and we stay there a little longer, watching the boats glide in and out, listening to full conversations held over megaphones as people pass one another in the water.

Everything is changing. It has to. You can't stop time.

All you can do is point yourself in a direction and hope the wind will let you get there.

Another maritime metaphor. I am truly a local's worst nightmare. But the point stands: change happens.

Two of my best friends are having a baby.

A near-painful joy flares through me. "Oh my god."

Cleo looks up. "Hm?"

"I just realized," I say, "I'm going to be an *aunt.*"

She snorts a laugh. "Harry," she says. "You're going to be a co-godmother."

34
REAL LIFE

Saturday

"She's going to be upset that I told you first," Cleo says.

"I can pretend not to know," I offer.

She gives me a look.

"Or," I say, "we can be up-front about it and talk it out."

She gives me another hug. "You sure you don't want a ride back?" She checks the time on her phone. She called Kimmy for a ride a couple of minutes ago. She'll be down to the Warm Cup any second.

"I'll meet you in a bit," I say.

First I need to find something for Sabrina. We won't be leaving this trip with matching tattoos — as it turns out, most artists won't tattoo a pregnant person, thus Cleo's true resistance to the idea — but that doesn't mean we can't find *something* to hold on to from this place.

After Kimmy picks Cleo up, I grab a

second caramel latte, iced this time, and wander past shop windows. I have no idea where to begin. I'm hoping I'll know it when I see it. So far, the best option seems to be matching T-shirts that say *GOT LOBS-TAH* on them, or matching T-shirts that say *MAINEIAC* over a lobster wearing aviators.

I follow a window display filled with lamps and cutesy tea towels around the corner, right to a window display filled with colorful buoys that have been turned into all manner of yard ornaments. I pause to let a grimy Subaru breeze through a stop sign at the next cross street, and that's when I realize where I am.

Easy Lane. The backdrop to our fight last night. Up ahead, I spot the tattoo shop on the left. My first inclination is to get away from the scene of the crime. Then I notice the glossy gold shop number over the door on my right: 125.

Number 125, on Easy Lane.

It takes me a second to figure out what's so familiar about that. When I do, I backtrack and check the number of the buoy store. 127. Wrong direction.

I'm looking for 123.

I wait for another car to pass through the intersection, and then jog across.

123 Easy Lane. The site of my *personal-*

ized surprise.

On the door, a decal reads *EARTHEN,* along with some hours of operation, but in the glare of bright sunlight, I can't make out much through the windows.

I check the time on my phone: 9:16 a.m. If I remember correctly, the itinerary said Sabrina's "personalized surprise" for me would start at nine. I waffle for a moment about going in, then bite the bullet and push the door open.

A gust of warm air meets me.

"Harriet?" a woman's voice says.

I blink as I wait out my pupillary dilation from the sudden change in light. "Yes, hi!"

I turn toward the voice, wondering if she can tell I can't see her, or anything at all, yet.

"Your space is all ready in the back," she says.

"Great." For some reason it doesn't occur to me until a half second too late that I could tell her I have no idea why I'm here. Or where here is.

My vision resolves as she leads me to the back of the shop, the floating oak shelves that line the walls coming into focus along with all the kitchenware for sale on them. Bowls, plates, cups, all in candy-colored tones that pop against the gallery-white walls.

The shop's attendant — a woman with blunt fringe, flared pants, and hoop earrings, all of which look plucked from the seventies — leads me down a hall to a room twice the size of the first one.

I pull up short, no less shocked than when I walked into the cottage and saw Wyn there.

"Feel free to take whichever wheel you want," the woman says. "No one else has space booked until four."

I still haven't managed a syllable when the bells over the shop doors ring behind us, and the seventies demigoddess says, "Let me know if you need help finding anything," and excuses herself to greet the new customer.

I stand there, computing.

The back wall is all windows, looking out onto the next street. Wooden shelves, like the ones in the front of the shop, stretch from one wall to the other, laden with bowls and vases and mugs. On the right, clay-streaked, pastel-toned aprons hang on hooks, and down the middle of the polished concrete floor sits a long wooden table, potter's wheels atop it at even intervals, stools pushed up to each of them. On the left wall, there's a long counter with a sink and a bunch of cabinets and drawers, and from the ceiling, pothos and philodendrons hang like living streamers, catching the light as the pots twirl one way, then back the other.

A lump is rising in my throat.

I couldn't have mentioned my pottery class to Sabrina any more than three times. I know this, because in general, I find talking about the class embarrassing.

Afraid people will take me too seriously, then be disappointed when they find out how mediocre I am at it. And somehow, nearly as afraid that they *wouldn't* take it seriously, that they'd brush it off with a mild *Well, everyone needs a hobby* when it feels like so much more.

Not a career — I'm not *good* at it. Something else. The place I go when I feel trapped inside myself. When I'm terrified that all my happiest moments belong to the past. When my body is humming with too much of something, or aching from too little, and life stretches out ahead of me like a threat.

In our few phone calls since I'd started the class, Sabrina asked a couple of blunt follow-up questions about it, and I gave succinct answers, then turned the conversation in another direction. It was one more piece of my life I hadn't felt ready to share before

460

this week, and yet Sabrina *saw* it, saw *me* more fully than I realized.

Because this week *wasn't* about torturing Wyn and me, and it wasn't just about preserving our delicately balanced found family either. Everything she did, misguided or not, was out of love. Out of *knowing* us and *caring* that we're happy.

I go to the wall of hooks and choose a blush-pink apron, looping it over my neck. Then I go to the drawers on the far side of the room and begin gathering supplies.

I fill a bowl with water and set it on the table along with a couple of tools, a sponge, a hunk of clay.

Not having a distinct plan before I start a project rarely turns out well for me, but I don't care right now. It doesn't matter what I make, only that I appreciate the time spent making it. It will feel good to dip my hands in mud, curve over the wheel until my back aches.

I take the stool closest to the windows and pound the clay into a ball. Then I plop it onto the wheel and flatten it with the heels of my hands.

The moment I slip my fingers into the water to start coning the clay up, calm floods me. My thoughts fritter away. I press the foot pedal, maneuvering the lump of

461

muck upward as it centers on the spinning wheel.

I lose myself in the rhythm of it.

Coning it up. Coning down.

I won't have time to glaze it before I leave Knott's Harbor, won't have room to take it home in my luggage once it's fired. I don't think about any of that.

Throwing makes my mind feel like the sea on a clear day, all my thoughts pleasantly diffused beneath light, rolling along over the back of an ever-moving swell.

My meditation app often tells me to picture my thoughts and feelings as clouds, myself as the mountain they're drifting past.

At the wheel, I never have to try. I become a body, a sequence of organs and veins and muscles working in concert.

I ease off the pedal, opening the clay. My elbows lock against my sides, thumbs dipping into the center, and as the clay whips past, a mouth widens within it. My thumbs curve under, thinning the walls beneath the lip.

The earthy smell is everywhere. Sweat pricks the nape of my neck. I'm dimly aware of an ache in my upper spine, but it's only an observation, a fact requiring no action. There is no need to fix it, to change it.

Just another cloud drifting past.

The loose shape of a bowl appears within my hands. I take the yellow sponge from the table, pressing it lightly against the bottom of the bowl, smoothing the rings. Sweat beads on my forehead now. The ache in my spine snakes through my shoulders.

I take hold of the bowl's thick lip and draw it upward, stretching the clay, coaxing it higher. When it's risen as high as it safely can, I bring my hands back to the base, funneling them, collaring the piece upward.

This is my favorite part: when I've worked the clay into a stable cylinder, when the slightest touch can shift and shape it. I love the way that everything can so easily fall apart, and the ecstasy of finding a groove in which I know it won't, without understanding the physics, the *why*. The clay becomes an extension of me, like it and I are working together.

It reminds me of something Hank told me a long time ago, about growing up on a ranch, training new horses.

He'd been good at it, apparently, and attributed that to his patience. He could wait out any bad mood. The anger of an animal didn't make *him* angry. *It helps you understand them better,* he told me. *You don't want that anger becoming fear. You want it turning into trust.*

And while there were a lot of things he'd hated about working at a ranch, he'd loved the feeling of coming to an agreement with another living thing, of understanding each other's needs, giving space when it was time for it, and pulling close when it was needed.

Wynnie would've been good at it too, he told me. *He's always known how to listen.*

At first, I mistake the sting for sweat catching in my lashes. Only when I feel the warm trails cutting down my cheeks do I realize I'm crying.

A different kind of crying from the wide variety of it I've done this week.

Not sobs. Not tears quaking out of me. A slow, quiet overflow of feeling.

I give a sniffly laugh but keep my hands where they are, shaping this beautiful, delicate thing for no reason other than my own joy.

When I look up and see him standing in the doorway, my stomach buoys, and my heart says, *You.*

Like it's summoned him here just by beating.

I rise from the stool, hands smeared with watery clay. "What are you doing here?"

The right side of his mouth rises. "Came to reenact that scene from *Ghost.*"

At my apparent lack of comprehension,

464

he says, "I woke up and you were gone."

I wipe my hands on the apron. "I went to get coffee and then I remembered the surprises Sabrina planned. Seemed like a shame to let them go to waste."

"I figured," he says. "I went to mine too."

I check the clock over the door. I've been here a lot longer than I realized. Two hours with the same vase. "How'd you find me?"

His head tilts. "You don't forget an address like 123 Easy Lane."

"Because of the missed opportunity," I say.

His smile faintly spreads. "Should've been Easy Street."

"All these Mainers," I say, "trying their damnedest not to make their towns *too* adorable."

He comes closer, peering at the wheel. "What are you making?"

"Honestly," I say, "I've barely been paying attention."

"Looks like a vase."

"You might need glasses," I say.

His gaze lifts. "Is it hard?"

"I think what's hard about it," I say, "is that you need to do less than you realize. And overthinking it and trying too hard to control it messes it up. At least in my experience."

He gives a half-hearted smile. "Life."

"Do you want to try?" I ask.

He very nearly rears back. "I wouldn't want to ruin it."

"Why not?" I say.

"Because," he says, "it looks so nice. You've worked so hard."

I snort as I cross toward the apron hooks and choose a pale yellow one for him. "It's wet clay," I say, handing the apron over. "It's not breakable."

"It *looks* breakable," he says.

"I mean, you could knock it over or collapse it, but nothing's going to shatter. And I'm not going to have time to finish it anyway, so if we put the clay back when we're done, it's no big deal."

"Is that sad?" His brows peak up in the middle. "Working on something you won't get to finish?"

"I've had a nice time."

Wyn's smile grows. "She did good, then."

"She did," I agree. "What was your surprise?"

"Kayaking," he says.

I laugh. "I love that yours was exercise and mine was sitting very still and playing with mud."

"Care to guess what Cleo's and Kimmy's were?" he asks.

"Did they go?" I say, wondering if Cleo had a chance to talk to Sabrina yet.

He nods.

"Cleo," I say, considering, "went to an agricultural museum, and Kimmy went to a hallucinogenic swap meet."

"So close. They got a couples' massage." At my expression, he adds, "You look surprised."

"I am surprised," I say.

"Why?"

"I guess now that I know couples' massages were on the table, I'm surprised she didn't send us to one too."

"I'm not," he says. "You hate being touched by strangers."

My heart keens. Another little reminder of how well these people know me against all odds, all the pieces of me I've come to see as difficult or unpleasant, the parts I never voluntarily share but have sneaked out here and there across years.

I swallow the building emotion and tip my head toward my stool. "Sit down."

Wyn slips the apron over his neck and perches, his face etched with consternation.

"Relax." I shake his shoulders as I cross to the next stool. I drag it up to his and sit. "It's like driving. Get your hands a little damp."

"Oh, I never drive with damp hands," he says.

"Well, that's your first mistake," I say. "It's illegal to drive with dry hands."

He says, "I think the laws are different in Montana."

"Don't be ridiculous," I say. "There are no laws in Montana. If you have a big enough hat, you can just claim whatever you want, and it's yours."

"True," he says. "I once owned a slew of Walmarts that way."

"Until a guy with a bigger hat came along," I say. "I'm not going to *make* you do this, Wyn. I thought you wanted to."

"I do," he says. "I'm stalling because I'm afraid I'm going to ruin it."

"I already told you," I say. "You can't ruin it. That is the whole point. Now get your hands damp." I lean forward to drag the bowl of water closer, and with a slight grimace, he dips his hands into it.

"Good," I say. "Now use your left hand to give slight pressure to the side of the vase. Your right is more for balance, to keep it upright."

He sets his palms against the structure's sides. "Now what?"

"Ease onto the pedal," I say.

He does, and because he's Wyn, he does

so beautifully. But as soon as he reaches full speed, he pushes too hard, and I dive to catch his right hand, steadying it before the would-be vase can topple. "Told you I'd ruin it."

"So dramatic," I tease, brushing my nose against his neck. "You didn't ruin it. We're just changing the shape of it."

I lean across him to put my other palm on the outside of his left hand, matching the pressure, the vase narrowing and funneling upward.

"Now we really are doing the *Ghost* thing," he says.

"Not quite," I say, "but I don't think my arms are long enough that I could sit behind you and do this."

"Definitely not," he says. "But you're welcome to sit in my lap."

"Excuse me," I say. "I'm the one in charge here. Everyone knows the person sitting in the lap is the amateur."

"So you want me to sit in your lap," he says.

"I don't have a death wish," I say.

"Glad to hear it." His gaze flickers back to the clay. Somehow, we're keeping it from collapsing or tipping over. It flares out, narrows, and flares again, wonky but standing.

I catch myself staring at him, without any

intention of replying.

When he looks up, my heart trips.

His mouth curls. "What?"

"I have to tell you something," I whisper.

His foot lifts off the pedal, his smile falling. "Okay."

I try to steel myself. I feel like Jell-O. I wish we were in the dark, on opposite sides of the kids' room. It's so much harder to say things in the light of day.

I close my eyes so I won't have to see his reaction, won't see if the world suddenly ruptures at the words: "I think I hate my job."

I wait.

Nothing.

No eardrum-destroying groan as the earth splits in two. My parents and coworkers don't come barreling into the room with pitchforks. My phone doesn't ring with the calls of every teacher, tutor, and coach who ever wrote me a recommendation letter or gave me a research position or sent a congratulations email.

But all of those things were, arguably, a long shot.

The only thing that matters right now, the only thing I'm afraid of, is Wyn's reaction.

All those sensations that tend to precede a panic attack bubble up in me: itchy heat, a tight throat, a sudden drop in my stomach.

"Harriet," he says softly. "Will you look at me?"

On a deep breath, I open my eyes.

His brow is grooved, his eyes and mouth soft. *Quicksand.*

"Did something happen at the hospital?" he asks.

My stomach sinks a little lower. I wish it were that simple, a concrete moment when everything went wrong. I shake my head.

Wyn's clay-covered hands gingerly catch my wrists. "Then what?"

"It's hard to explain."

"Will you try?" he asks.

I swallow. "It's not supposed to be about me. I'm supposed to be helping people."

"It is about you," Wyn says.

How do I sum it up? There isn't any one thing I would change. It's that for some reason, I spend ninety percent of my time excruciatingly unhappy, and the more I try to tamp it down, the more the unhappiness grows, swells, pushes up against my edges.

It's that when I'm not here, I feel like a ghost. Like my skin isn't solid enough to hold the sunlight, and my hair isn't there to dance on the breeze.

"I'm not good at it, Wyn," I choke out.

He jogs my hands. "You're brilliant."

"But what if I'm *not*," I say. "What if I've put everything I have, all my time and energy, into this, and money. *God*, the money. Hundreds of thousands of dollars in loans, some of which my parents had to co-sign because I don't have good credit, and I — I've built a life where all I do is wait. Wait for the surgery to be over. For the day to end. Wait to be *here*, where I feel . . ."

Wyn's lips part, his eyes painfully soft.

"Like myself. Like I'm in the right place."

The right branch of the multiverse, I think. *Where you're still so close I can touch you, taste you, smell you.*

"I loved school," I say. "But I hate being in hospitals. I hate the smell of the antiseptic. The lighting gives me headaches, and my shoulders hurt because I can't relax, because everything feels so — so *dire*. And every day, when I go home, I don't even feel relieved, because I know I have to go back. And I . . . I keep waiting for it to change, for something to *click* and to feel how I thought it would, but it hasn't. I get better at what I'm doing, but the way I *feel* about doing it doesn't change."

Wyn's hands tense, his eyes dropping as his voice frays. "Why wouldn't you tell me this?" he asks.

"I *am* telling you."

"No," he says roughly. "When I was there. When you needed me, and I couldn't get to you no matter how hard I tried. Why wouldn't you let me in?"

"Because I was *ashamed*," I say. "You'd followed me across the country, and things were so hard, for you and for us. I was terrified of making them worse. I wanted to be who you — who *everyone* — thinks I am, but I can't. I'm not. I never wanted to let you down."

He stares at me for three seconds, then lets out a gruff, frustrated laugh.

"I'm not joking, Wyn."

He scoots forward, and my knees slot in between his, both my wrists still cradled in his muddy hands, his thumbs sweeping back and forth, a slight tremor in them. "I'm not laughing at you. I just feel so stupid."

"You? *I'm* the one who devoted the last ten years of her life, and a lot of imaginary money, to something she hates."

"I . . ." He darts a glance at our hands. "You were in pain, and I didn't even notice, Harriet. Or I did, but I thought it was about me. I fucked up, and I lost you for it."

I shake my head ferociously. "You had bigger things going on."

"There was nothing bigger than you," he says raggedly. "Not to me. Not ever."

Blood rises to my cheeks, my throat, my chest. It's painful to swallow. "Maybe that's what made it so hard. You built your whole life around my plans. You left our friends and missed time with your family — with *Hank* — and now I can't hack it. You did all of that for me, and I'm not even the person you thought I was."

"Harriet." The tenderness in his voice, his hands, rips open all those hastily stitched sutures in my heart. "I know exactly who you are."

I look up, voice shrinking. "Really? Because I don't."

"I knew who you were before we even met," he says. "Because everything our friends told me was true."

"You mean you saw a naked drawing of me," I say.

He smiles, his hands moving to touch my jaw, neither of us bothered by the clay. "I mean that you have the weirdest laugh of anyone I've ever met, Harriet," he says softly. "And it feels like taking a shot of tequila every time I hear it. Like I could get drunk on the sound of you. Or hungover when I go too long without you.

"You see the best in everyone, and you make the people you love feel like even their flaws are worth appreciating. You love learning. You love sharing what you learn. You try to be fair, to see things from other people's points of view, and sometimes that makes it hard for you to see them from your own, but you have one. And even when you're mad at me, I want to be close to you. None of it — none of my favorite things about you, none of what makes you you — has anything to do with a job. That's not why I love you. It's not why anyone loves you."

"Maybe not," I manage, "but it's why they're proud of me. It's the thing about me that makes them happiest."

He studies me. "Your parents?"

I dip my chin.

"Come here," Wyn says.

"Why?" I ask.

"Because I want you to," he says.

"What happened to your Montana manners?"

"Come here, *please,*" he says.

I let him drag me across his lap, one of his arms roped around my back, his other hand resting on my knee, clay smudging into my jeans. "Your parents love you," he says. "And everything they do — and push you to do — is because they want you to be happy. But that doesn't mean they're automatically right about what's best for you.

475

Especially when you haven't told them how you feel."

"I feel so selfish even talking about this," I admit. "Like everything they did for me doesn't even matter."

"It's not selfish to want to be happy, Harriet."

"When I could be a surgeon instead?" I say. "Yeah, Wyn, I think it might be selfish."

"*Fuck* that," he says. "A happy potter's better for this world than a miserable surgeon."

Warmth spills across the bridge of my nose. "I'm not a potter, Wyn. This isn't something I'm making money on."

"Maybe not. And it doesn't ever have to be, if you don't want that," he says. "But that's the point. Your job doesn't have to be your identity. It can just be a place you go, that doesn't define you or make you miserable. You deserve to be happy, Harriet." He brushes a strand of hair away from the curve of my jaw. "Everything's better when you're happy."

"For me," I say.

"For me," he says, vehement. "For Cleo and Sabrina and Parth and Kimmy, and your parents. For anyone who cares about you. The world's always going to need surgeons, but it's going to need bowls too.

476

Forget what you think anyone else wants. What do *you* want?"

I try to laugh. The back of my nose stings too badly to let out a full-blown snort. "Can't you just tell me what to do?"

His arms close around me. I burrow into his chest, breathe him in, and feel my body calm. "What if . . ." I brace myself, grab hold of every last scrap of courage, and frankly, it's not all that much. I pull back enough to look up into his face, my voice whittling down to filament. "What if I came to Montana?"

His gaze drops, his lashes splaying across his cheeks. "Harriet," he says, so thickly, like my name hurts to say, and my own heart flutters painfully. Because I know him.

I know what an apology sounds like in Wyn Connor's voice.

His eyes rise, the green of them mossy and warm. The heaviness that presses into my chest threatens to crack my ribs, puncture my heart. My eyes fill up, but somehow, I find the strength to whisper, "Why not?"

"Because you can't keep doing what other people want," he says, voice gravelly. "You can't follow me, like I followed you. I won't be enough."

"But I love you," I choke out.

"I love you too," he croaks, his hands mov-

ing restlessly over me. "I love you so much."
He kisses a damp spot on my cheek, then
lets our foreheads lean together. "But you
can't follow me. I did that, and it tore us
up, Harriet. I can't let you build your life
around me. It would break us all over again,
and I *can't*. You have to figure out what you
really want."

My heart feels like it's being stretched on
a medieval rack, pulling apart bit by bit.
"What if all I really want is you?"

"Right now," he murmurs. "What about
later? When you wake up and realize I've let
you give everything up for me. I can't do
that."

Those months of watching him drown,
thrash against a life that didn't fit him, surge
back to the forefront of my mind. He'd built
his life around me, and it almost crushed
us. Starved our love until it was unrecogniz-
able.

I loop my arms around his neck and
breathe him in, one last sip to tide me over
for years to come. "I don't want to keep
feeling like this."

"It'll get easier," he promises hoarsely, his
hand brushing my hair behind my ear.
"Someday you'll hardly remember this."

The thought is searing. I don't want that.
I want any universe but that one. All the

rest, where it's him and me, scattered across time and space, finding our way to each other again and again, the one constant, the only essential.

I can't bear to let him go yet. But it's like he said.

We're out of time.

"We should get back," I whisper.

Wyn lifts his chin toward the vase, asks damply, "Should we scrap it?"

I shake my head. "Maybe they can ship it once it's been fired."

"You really want it?" he says.

I study it in all its wavy, wonky glory, my rib cage so tight I can't get a good breath, a firm beat of my heart. "Desperately."

35
REAL LIFE

Saturday

As soon as we step into the house, I know something's wrong. It's too quiet, still. Wyn and I make our way to the kitchen without seeing or hearing anyone.

"Where do you think they are?" he asks, checking the time over the stove. "They should be back by now."

"I'll see if Kimmy and Cleo are in the guesthouse," I say. "You want to see if Parth and Sabrina are upstairs?"

Wyn nods, and I let myself out onto the patio, heading through the gate at the side.

There's no sign of life in the guesthouse, but I knock on the door anyway. Where is everyone? I type into the group text as I make my way back to the patio. On a whim, I go to the top of the stairs down to the shore.

Parth sits on the rocks below, sun gleaming off his dark hair and wind rippling through his jacket. I pick my way down, calling his name as I go. He glances over his shoulder at me, then goes back to staring out at the water.

"Where's Sabrina?" I ask.

A shrug in response. It triggers a sinking sensation in my gut. I lower myself onto the rock beside him, stretching my clay-streaked legs out toward the water. "For what it's worth," I say, "Wyn and I, we're really sorry we didn't tell you."

He looks up. "You should've. But I should've come straight to you when I saw Wyn's text too."

I follow his gaze out to a white boat drifting toward one of the small islands off the coast. "I hope eventually you can forgive us."

His gaze flickers to me. "Forgive you? Harriet, you're already forgiven. You're like a sister to me, you know that? I'll always forgive you. You're family."

My heart pangs. "I thought being family just meant you have limitless time to hold grudges."

Parth scoffs and tucks an arm over my shoulders. "Maybe for some people. Not for us."

"If you're not out here contemplating how we've failed you," I say, "then why all the forlorn gazing into the sea?"

He smiles, but it fades fast. "Sabrina and I got into a fight. She walked out."

"Oh my god, Parth. I'm so sorry. This is my fault," I say. "I'll call her and —"

His arm slides clear of me, and he angles toward me. "It's not," he says. "Honestly, a part of me has been waiting for her to back out ever since we got engaged. I mean, she only agreed to get married because her world was falling apart. No matter what she said, I knew she wanted an anchor. And a part of me always expected her to run. Last night we argued, and she went downstairs to cool down, and when I woke up she was gone. Hasn't answered her phone all day."

"She's scared, Parth," I say.

He scoffs. "We're talking about Sabrina. She isn't scared of anything."

I puzzle for a minute over how to explain it. "You know what you just said to me? That we're family?"

He nods.

"Well, for you and Cleo and Wyn and Kimmy, that means one thing," I say. "For Sabrina and me, it's different. In our families, there was no coming back from fights. Her dad would rather divorce than apologize, and in my house, arguments always ended with everyone leaving. Things never got resolved; they calloused over."

"What are you saying?" Parth asks.

"Sabrina didn't run because she doesn't want you," I say. "She ran because she's scared that, in the end, she won't be worth chasing."

Parth's eyes lock onto mine, his face slackening as he takes it in. "Shit." He scrambles to his feet. "We need to find her."

"We will," I promise.

Cleo and Kimmy have just gotten back from their massages when we reach the house. They haven't heard from Sabrina either, and after we all take turns calling and texting her to no avail, we accept that we're going to have to look for her.

"You two were supposed to spend the morning together," Cleo points out. "What were you going to do?"

"I don't know," Parth says. "She'd planned it all, and there were no details on the itinerary."

"No address?" Wyn asks.

Parth stares at him. "Oh, yeah, there was an *address,* but how could that possibly benefit us?" he deadpans. "No, nothing! For all I know, she left in the middle of the night. For all I know, she's lying in a hospital bed right now!"

"We'll find her," Wyn says. "Don't assume the worst."

"This is my fault," Parth says. "I was upset about how everything went down last night, and I blamed her. Like I hadn't been totally on board. I was, completely, and when it blew up, I turned it around like I'd had nothing to do with it, and now she's *gone.*"

Cleo's eyes go distant as she retreats into thought. "We need to be logical here."

"You're gonna hate this," Wyn says, facing Parth, "but what if we called her family?"

"There's no way she'd go to them," Parth says. "She hardly tells them anything. I mean, my family's already planning a blowout wedding, and hers doesn't even know we're engaged yet."

"Then we'll look around town," Cleo says.

"We'll find her," Kimmy promises, rubbing Parth's shoulder.

"We should split up," I say.

Wyn and Parth take the Land Rover. Cleo and I use her station wagon. Kimmy hangs back in case Sabrina shows up at the house.

Most of the places we frequent on these trips are downtown, but there are also some beaches and parks worth checking, along with a couple of other towns we occasionally visit.

But when we reach Bernie's — packed,

thanks to the sunshine and the fact that it's Lobster Fest weekend — I realize a part of me was banking on finding her here, sipping coffee and watching seagulls fight over hash browns on the patio.

"We should ask the host," Cleo says, "in case they've seen her."

But they haven't. Though, to be fair, the streets are so packed with face-painted, ice-cream-cone-eating tourists that, for once, it's actually feasible that Sabrina could blend in with a crowd.

We check the Roxy Theater, ask the ticket agent (today in a porkpie hat) whether he's seen her, and when he refuses to answer with anything other than a shrug, we each buy a ticket and split up inside to check both theaters. Not there either.

We check Murder, She Read; the wharf; and the Lobster Hut, as well as the Lobster Hut's heavily graffitied bathrooms. We even check the tattoo shop on the very off chance that she's enacting some small rebellion and getting her own *wicked pissah* tattoo. She's nowhere to be found, and our next call goes straight to voicemail.

"She must've let her phone die," Cleo says.

"That's not like her," I say.

"You think she was lying about hotels being booked up?" Cleo says. "Could she have checked in somewhere?"

I pull up a search for available rooms in the area. Nary a hotel, motel, bed-and-breakfast, or hostel available in sight.

The group text chimes with a text, and we both jump.

It's only Wyn, whose number I'd unblocked again. Any luck? he writes.

None. You? I ask.

Parth's really worried, Wyn replies. He's going to call hospitals. Just to be sure.

My stomach flips. Keep us posted.

You too, he says.

Cleo's nose wrinkles as she scans our list. "That's all the usual spots. She wouldn't . . . be reckless enough to sail off by herself, would she?"

The blood rushes out of my stomach. "She's a pretty confident sailor," I say. "And I think sailing is sort of her happy place. It makes her think of her mom and when . . ."

"Harry?" Cleo says. "What is it?"

"Her mom," I say.

"What about her?" Cleo asks.

"It might be nothing," I say. "But I've got one more place for us to check."

"Stop the car!" I shriek, with such conviction that Cleo instantly obeys, right in the

486

middle of the road.

Although *road* is a fairly aspirational title for the wooded lane the GPS has directed us onto. One has to assume that there's a parking lot somewhere ahead, but parking no longer matters because (1) the little open-air chapel is visible through the trees on our right, and (2) a cherry-red Jaguar sits parked on the dirt shoulder.

Cleo hits the gas again and pulls over. We check the car first — empty — then scramble over the short stone retaining wall to hike up the hillside toward the chapel.

The damp green woods give way to a manicured garden. In its center, a pavilion of gray stone stands, ivy crawling up its left side. Butterflies move in dizzy spirals through the flowering bushes hugging the steps, the distant crash of waves the only sound.

No wonder Sabrina's parents' wedding made such an impression on her. This place is beautiful. It feels like nothing could go wrong here, nothing bad could happen.

When I start forward, Cleo hangs back. Her mouth opens and closes a couple of times. "What if she wants to be alone?"

She has a point. It's possible.

But people don't run or hide only when they want to be alone.

"What if," I say, "she needs to know she isn't?"

Cleo takes my hand. We climb the steps to the back of the pavilion.

There are a handful of timeworn pews, a flagstone floor, and a few wooden arcades on either side. Straight ahead, a stone arch frames a slice of pure Maine blue water in the distance.

Sabrina sits cross-legged before it, staring out. The whole scene is serene, down to the faint chirp of birds overhead. Then she looks over her shoulder at the sound of our approach.

I'd braced myself for some measure of awkwardness after everything, but the second we see her drawn face, puffy and red-rimmed eyes, last night's fight stops mattering.

Both Cleo and I run to her, kneel on the ground, sling our arms around her.

"You scared us," Cleo says.

"I didn't mean to," Sabrina whispers.

We peel apart, sitting in a triangle, the same way we did so many nights in our musty freshman dorm room.

"My phone died a couple hours ago," Sabrina says finally. "And . . . I guess I wanted to put off the inevitable."

"The inevitable?" Cleo says.

Sabrina draws her knees into her chest, wrapping her willowy arms around them. "The end of the trip? Goodbye? Everything's changing, and I'm not ready."

It's like someone has taken an ice cream scoop to my chest, hollowed me out.

"I wanted to put it off, but Cleo's right," she says. "We've been growing apart for years."

"Sabrina," I say. "You have no idea how sorry I am I didn't tell you what was going on."

"It's not just that." Sabrina lifts her chin. "When I found out about the breakup, I was hurt, and then after a while, I was mad, but then — I don't know. I realized it's been the six of us for so long. And the five of us for even longer, and the three of *us* before that. And it's not only that you kept this huge thing from us. It's that . . . it felt like if you and Wyn weren't together, then you didn't want us either. Like you've been phasing us out."

"Sabrina, *no,*" I say. "I promise I wasn't. I'm not."

"Maybe not consciously," she says. "But that's why you didn't tell us, right? Because we're friends with Wyn. Because our whole friendship is tangled up with your relationship, and if you two grew apart . . ."

"Wyn and I didn't grow apart." I can't get it out any louder than a whisper. "I pushed him away the same way I did to the rest of you. And it was always about me, not you or anyone else."

"But it's *not* just you, Harriet," Sabrina says.

Cleo touches her hand. "Things have been . . . complicated for me, Sabrina. That's all."

"You know," Sabrina says, watching a butterfly pirouette past, "I was really, really happy when I was a kid. My parents were happy. And then they weren't. And when they separated and moved on . . . it took a while, but they both found happiness again. Or, you know, their semi-twisted versions of that.

"With new partners and new kids. Everyone got this fresh start. But I wasn't a part of either one. I was part of *their* relationship. And once that was over, I bounced back and forth like — like a memento or something. The only thing that ever felt permanent to me, like it belonged to me, was this place." Her voice pitches higher. "Until I met you two."

She's always been so tough, and it breaks something in me to hear the vulnerability in her voice.

"I met you," she says, "and I finally belonged somewhere again."

"I felt that way too, Sab." I scoot closer.

"Me too," Cleo says. "High school was *hell* for me. I mean, I chose Mattingly because I didn't know anyone going there, and the best social situation I could dream up for myself was total anonymity. Those first few weeks of hanging out were, like, this weird out-of-body experience. I'd never had friends like that, the kind you do everything with and talk to about everything. Honestly, I kept waiting for you both to find new people and move on.

"And then one day — it was right before fall break, and we were hugging goodbye, and I realized I'd stopped waiting. Without even realizing it. I knew you were my for-lifes then. That's what my parents call each other. Because no matter what, they're always going to be family. And that's you both. The relationship can change shape a thousand times, but you're always going to be in my life. Or at least, that's what I want."

"Same," I say. "No matter what happens with Wyn, I'm always going to belong with you. I'm not going anywhere. I love you, Sabrina, and I'm so sorry I made you feel like you were just a part of my relationship with Wyn. You're a part of *me*. You're so deep in my heart that I couldn't get you out if I tried, and I don't want to. I know how lucky I am to have you. To have people who love me enough to hold on even when I'm scared to let them close."

Cleo and Sabrina each grab one of my hands, their fingers lacing into mine.

"God, I've been crying a lot this week," Sabrina manages tearily.

"Me too," I say. "The magic of the cottage, I guess."

"Same," Cleo says. "Except in my case, I think it's pregnancy hormones or —"

"WHAT!" Sabrina whirls on her, her hands jerking clear of ours to clamp onto the sides of her face in a perfect imitation of Macaulay Culkin's big *Home Alone* moment.

"Shit!" Cleo says. "I was going to tell you in a speech!"

"You're fucking serious?" Sabrina shouts.

"We're in a chapel," Cleo says.

"Oh, please. God's heard it all. But me! I've only once ever heard one of my best friends say she's motherfucking pregnant!"

"Well," Cleo says, "I'm motherfucking pregnant. Surprise."

Sabrina cackles, her feet kicking against the floor.

"And before you ask," Cleo says, "yes, I

told Harry first, but not on purpose. She ambushed me this morning, and it happened a lot like this."

"Well, as long as Harry ambushed you," Sabrina says through more breathless, shrieking laughter. "Honestly, anything else you both want to get off your chests, now's the time! I'm incapable of anger right now, I think."

"I broke your straightener in college," I tell her.

"Once I had a girl stay over who used your toothbrush, thinking it was mine," Cleo says.

"Okay, gross," Sabrina says. "I could've gone to my grave without that second one."

"I'm the one who lost those vintage Ray-Bans we used to share," I admit. "God, that's actually a huge load off."

"Oh!" Cleo chirps. "I told that one shitty poet you dated that I was a witch, and that if he ever contacted you again, I'd hex him so his dick fell off."

Sabrina touches her chest, evidently moved. "See, this is why you're going to be a great mother."

"I didn't know you did that," I tell Cleo. "If I had, I probably wouldn't have told the same guy that my dad was in the mob."

A laugh cracks out of Sabrina. "I have the

best friends."

"Best *family,*" Cleo says.

The ache in my heart is almost pleasant. It spreads through my limbs into my hands and feet, a heaviness, like love has its own mass and weight. "You know," I say, "Parth's not going anywhere either."

Her gaze averts. "If you and Wyn couldn't even make it work . . ."

I grab her face in my hands. "You're not us," I say. "You are so, so, so much braver than me, Sabrina."

She rolls her eyes.

"I'm serious," I say. "You can do this, if you want to."

Her voice is a wisp. "I do want to. He's the love of my life. I want to marry him."

"Then let's get you home," Cleo says.

Sabrina swipes the tears out from under her eyes. "Let's go home," she says with an air of relief. As if, now that she's made the decision, she's unafraid.

On our way to the cars, Sabrina throws one last look back at the chapel, the trees below, the water out ahead.

She smiles. Like when she looks back at it, all she sees is the happiness of that day she spent here with her parents, rather than the pain of what came after.

Like even when something beautiful breaks, the making of it still matters.

36
HAPPY PLACE

Knott's Harbor, Maine

A Saturday afternoon. A wedding, only in
the most technical of terms. There are
sunflower bouquets for all of us, delivered
right to the front door, and a cake that says
Happy birthday, wicked pissah on it, surrounded in real, edible flowers. At Sabrina
and Parth's expressions, I shrug. "A lot of
businesses won't do wedding stuff."

"Yes, but who allowed you to use *wicked
pissah* in this way?" she says.

"This," Parth says, "is the best birthday
I've ever had."

He wears a suit that makes him look like
James Bond On Vacation. Sabrina dons her
sailing-chic look. The rest of us sport our
Lobster Hut outfits, all rumpled from hard
wear and tight from eating well.

The photographer arrives at three thirty
to photograph us doing nothing much at all
aside from sitting around the pool in semi-

formal wear, tossing out increasingly ridiculous names for Cleo and Kimmy's baby.

When they'd told Parth and Wyn about the pregnancy, Parth had blinked, stunned to speechlessness, and Wyn had leapt to his feet and started laughing, eyes moving between all of us like he was waiting for a *gotcha.*

"Seriously?" Parth said. "There's a baby in your body? Right now?"

Cleo laughed. "Yes, it's in my body."

"This is . . . oh my *god,*" Wyn cried. "You're having a baby!"

"Someone get the fainting couch," Kimmy said. "Wynnie's going down."

He walked around the kitchen to hug each of them in turn, then looked at me, his eyes sparkling and clear, no fog. Like his first instinct when he felt joy was to check whether it had hit me too, to share it.

It made my heart soar and throb and burn with hope.

Now we're all drinking champagne and sparkling cider in the sun and pressuring our friends to name their baby Kardashian Kimberly Cleopatra Carmichael-James while a paid professional snaps photographs of us.

The wedding officiant arrives at four.

By five, Parth and Sabrina stand at the

edge of the dock, light glinting off their hair, eyes sparkling with tears, and promise to love each other always. Cleo and I wrap our arms around each other, our sunflower bouquets caught between us, and try not to sob.

By five thirty, we're flinging ourselves off the end of the dock, shrieking with laughter, failing badly at DON'T FUCKING SCREAM, then pulling ourselves out of the icy water and running up to the warm comfort of the pool.

We order pizza — no one wants to leave the house, and Knott's Harbor isn't big on delivery — and eat it with Veuve Clicquot. We don't talk about tomorrow, when we'll say goodbye. To one another, to this house, to an era of life we wish could have lasted forever.

Right now we're here.

When the sun starts falling down the sky, we bundle up and climb back down to the rocks to watch night settle. We build a fire, roast marshmallows. Sabrina burns hers to a charred crisp, and Parth patiently toasts his to golden brown.

When Wyn catches me shivering, he takes off his worn-out Mattingly sweatshirt — he's always run warm — and yanks it over my head, smiling as he ties a bow beneath my chin. It smells like smoke and seawater and him. I never want to take it off.

We light the sparklers Parth found in the garage, and we write our names in the dark, impermanent but all the brighter and more blazing for it.

This is how I used to think of love. As something so delicate it couldn't be caught without being snuffed out. Now I know better. I know the flame may gutter and flare with the wind, but it will always be there.

We talk about the night sky. We talk about the ghost of our old dorm building. The bright purple flowers that always erupted alongside the long road to Mattingly, and the broken eave over our New York apartment that let icicles grow into three-foot daggers. We talk about the things we remember, the things we'll miss.

"We'll come back," Kimmy says. "Baby needs to know about the magic of Maine."

"I don't know," Sabrina says. "Maybe next year, we go somewhere new."

Wyn's hand tightens on mine, like even the mention of next year might turn us to smoke.

And even that pain is a kind of pleasure, to feel so loved, to love so deeply.

We stay up until Cleo is nodding off against Kimmy's shoulder and Sabrina can't stop yawning, and then we say good night, like it's any other night. Like tomorrow we might wake and start the whole week over.

When we close ourselves into our bedroom for the night, Wyn and I stand locked together in the dark, my hands against the back of his neck, his head bowed into my shoulder, breathing into each other.

My body has always loved him without reservation or caution. It knew so long before my brain did, and it still knows.

His neck, his shoulders, his waist, the soft hair that leads to his waistband, the jut of his hip bones. The smooth curves of his back and the tightening muscles of his stomach. Every piece of him I've thought about, dreamed of, longed for.

"Your fingers are cold," he whispers, bringing my hand to his lips.

"Your skin's so warm," I whisper back.

Slowly we undress, find our way to each other. We don't pretend tomorrow won't come but give ourselves over fully to tonight.

A tangle of limbs and blankets. Skin sliding against skin. Fingers gripping the backs of necks, the soft parts of hips, the hard muscle of thighs.

"I love you," he says into my mouth, and I wish I could swallow it, like that would let me keep that sound forever, this moment forever.

My nose burns. My voice crackles. "Don't say that."

"Why not?" he whispers.

"Because," I say, "those words don't belong to me anymore."

"Of course they do," he says. "They belonged to you before I ever saw you. They belong to you in every universe we're in, Harriet."

I close my eyes. Try to hold on to the words. They burn into my palms.

Before I knew Wyn, I could have been okay without him. Now I'll always feel the place he isn't.

Want is a kind of thief. It's a door in your heart, and once you know it's there, you'll spend your life longing for whatever's behind it.

He knots his hands with mine, telling me he loves me in every way he can.

Only once I'm half asleep, drifting off with my temple pressed to his chest, do I hear him whisper it one last time: "I love you."

Through the gauzy layers of sleep, I hear myself murmur, *"You."*

501

37
REAL LIFE

Sunday

I wake before my alarm and turn it off before it makes a peep. Wyn is fast asleep, naked and beautiful in the deep blue of early morning.

He would want me to wake him.

But I can't stand for our last moment together to be a goodbye. I want to remember him like this, while he's still mine and I'm his.

I finish packing quietly and tiptoe downstairs.

Cleo and Sabrina are already sipping tea and coffee, respectively, in the kitchen. "I told you I could take a cab to the airport," I whisper, joining them as Sabrina fills a mug for me.

"No way," she says, "are your last few minutes in Knott's Harbor going to be with a stranger."

"Actually," I say, "my last few minutes in

Knott's Harbor will be spent with Ray."

"All the more reason to give you a ride. These could be the last minutes of your life, period," Sabrina says.

Cleo spits a mouthful of tea into her mug. "Sabrina."

"Kidding!" she says. "Is Wyn coming?"

"I let him sleep," I say.

She and Cleo exchange a look.

"I know," I say, heading them off. "But it's what I need."

Sabrina slings an arm over my shoulder. "Then that's what you get, my girl."

We drive to the airport in the Rover, and Sabrina and Cleo insist on parking and walking me inside. We linger by the security gate for a while — we're *way* too early for an airport this tiny — but I can't stand long goodbyes. Every second gets harder.

I make it through our tight group hug without crying. I keep my stiff upper lip as we take turns promising we'll see each other soon. And when Sabrina reminds me that there's room on her couch in New York anytime.

I still don't know what I'm going to do when I get back to San Francisco, and when I came clean with them about how I'd been feeling at work, they'd both been adamant that they couldn't tell me what to do either.

I need to figure out what I want.

As if reading my mind, Cleo touches my elbow and says, "There's no wrong answer."

One last hug apiece, and then we put our index fingers, with their matching little burn scars from our first trip to the cottage, together in a silent promise. Without another word, I join the two-person security line.

I tell myself I won't look back. But I do.

My best friends are crying, which makes me start crying, which makes all three of us start laughing.

"Ma'am," the TSA agent says, waving me forward, and I'm still laugh-crying in the body scanner and as I make my way down the hallway beyond it, looking back every few feet to see them wave from the far end of the airport, until finally the hall curves to the right and I'm forced to give one final wave goodbye and round the corner.

By the time I reach my gate, I've gotten it together. The seating area is empty. Any reasonable person would've shown up to this particular airport twenty minutes before takeoff, but I've left the standard two-hour window, and now I have hours to sit with my thoughts.

I pull out the book I got from Murder, She Read and stare at the first page for probably twenty minutes without taking anything in other than the words *crown molding.*

I stuff the book into my bag and pull my phone out.

My heart stutters at the image on-screen. The website I had Wyn type in for me last night is still pulled up. An oak table in a field of yellow green, wildflowers snaking up its legs, and a jagged range of purple mountains behind it.

It knocks the breath out of me. Not the image itself but the longing, the *need* it shoots out from my core. *That,* I think. *That is what I want.*

A zing of adrenaline goes down my spine.

My pulse speeds. Shivers spread, wildfire fast, across my skin.

I stand, almost laughing from the blunt force of the realization.

Wyn might be happier and healthier than he was six months ago, and I might be a little more honest about my feelings, but I *know* him, every inch. I've memorized the rhythm of his breathing when he sleeps and the smell of his skin when he's been out in the sun, and I know when he's afraid.

Maybe I didn't see it right away because I'm so unused to trusting myself. I've spent too long following everyone else's lead, placing everyone else's judgment above my own. But *now* I see it.

He's *afraid.*

He still doesn't trust that I can love him forever. Some part of him is waiting for me to choose something else. Believes that if I were given every option, he wouldn't be my pick. He might think he's protecting me, but he's protecting himself too.

He was right about one thing, though. He can't tell me what I want.

All my life, I've let other voices creep in, and they've drowned out my own.

Now my mind is strangely quiet. For the first time in so long, I hear myself clearly.

One word. All it takes to answer the only question that can't wait.

You.

I stand and grab my bag, heading back the way I came. But it doesn't feel like I'm moving backward.

It feels like the first step toward someplace new.

38
REAL LIFE

Sunday

I don't know why I'm racing through the airport. There's no plane to catch, no deadline to slide under.

This isn't my *last chance* to tell Wyn how I feel.

Instead, it's the earliest moment I can possibly get to him. I don't want to miss another minute. So I barrel down the hallway, through the security exit, my bag scraping along behind me. I almost smack into the sliding glass doors as they're opening, then trip out onto the curb, blinking against the sun, shivering at the chill.

Not a single cab idles in the pickup/drop-off lane. I pull out my phone and hammer out a search for car services in Knott's Harbor. The first number I dial gives me a busy signal.

I didn't know busy signals still existed. I let out a wordless, angry grunt and end the call, scanning the parking lot helplessly, as if hitchhiking might be a viable option.

Then I see it. A flash of red that makes my heart stop.

A car pulling into a space. A man jumping out, wind batting his sun-streaked hair around.

My lungs spasm from the shock of him, his presence always a bit more solid than anything else around me.

When our eyes lock, he freezes, the car door still ajar behind him. I seem to be floating across the lane until a car lays on its horn, letting me know I've cut it off.

I break into a jog. Wyn drifts forward too. We meet in an empty spot in the craggy lot.

"You're here," he says, out of breath.

I'm still working on regaining the power of speech.

"You didn't say goodbye," he says.

The best I can do in that moment is "I couldn't."

His brows pinch. The moment holds.

"Is that all?" I ask.

"What?"

"Did you drive all the way here to say goodbye?" I say.

He scratches the back of his head, glances sidelong toward the thicket of trees at the edge of the lot, then back to me. The corners of his mouth twist, and my heart mimics the motion, wringing every last bit of love into my veins.

"Why aren't you on the plane?" he says.

"It's going in the wrong direction."

His brow tenses on a slight shake of his head.

"You said I need to figure out what I want," I say. "That I can't keep doing what other people think is right for me."

"I meant it." His voice rattles.

"Does that include you?" I ask.

"What do you mean?" he says.

"I mean . . ." I move close enough to breathe him in, my shoulders melting with relief at his nearness. "Do *you* get to tell me what *will* or *won't* make me happy?"

His brow furrows. "I wasn't trying to do that."

"You were," I say. "And I get why. I could come out to Montana, and maybe someday I realize I want to — I don't know — get into *clowning* or something."

One side of his mouth quirks. "Clowning?"

"Or marine biology," I say. "I have to leave to study whales, or octopi."

"Closer," he allows.

"And everything could implode again," I say. "Worse than last time. So badly we

509

couldn't find our way back to each other."

His chin dips once, his voice abrading. "It could."

"You're right that I don't know what I want to do next," I admit. "I'm going to have to find some other job that I hate a little less and chip away at my loans while I figure it out. But I know what I don't want.

"I don't want to be tired all the time. I don't want to be on opposite schedules from everyone I love, or on call during dates. I don't want to be on my feet for eight hours at a time and have my knuckles bleed in the winter from overwashing my hands. I don't want to feel like I don't have time or energy to try anything new because everything I have is getting poured into a job I don't even *like.* I don't want to live my life like it's a triathlon and all that matters is getting to some imaginary ribbon. I want my life to be like — like making *pottery.* I want to enjoy it while it's happening, not just for where it might get me eventually.

"And I don't want to be across the country from you. *Or* your family. I don't want to miss a single holiday with them. I don't want to go to sleep without being able to put my feet on your calves to warm them up, and I don't want to say goodbye to your rodeo shirt, and I don't want to let you leave here without understanding that I *trust* myself on this. And you can tell me to go right now, and I will, but you don't get to think it's noble. You don't get to think you're right."

His eyes widen. "Right about *what?*"

"About all of it!" I cry. "That I don't want you! That you can't make me happy! That if I go back to California right now it has *anything* to do with what *I* want. That *you're* the lucky one in this relationship when it's obviously always been me. That Grocery Gladiators is a real game, and that it makes *any* sense to put glasses on the bottom rack of the dishwasher. You can tell me no, Wyn, but you can't tell yourself it's what *I* want. If you're too afraid, if you can't have faith in me, then tell me to go, but don't convince yourself it's what I wanted."

"Harriet," he says coarsely.

My heart teeter-totters in my chest, readying itself to fly skyward or plummet.

Wyn takes hold of my face. "I *am* scared."

A beat of quiet. Nothing but our breath and the icy wind fluttering a curl across my face.

"Oh," I breathe out.

His slight smile unzips me, vertebra by vertebra. His fingers slip back into my hair. His jaw works as he swallows. "When I woke up this morning, the bed was already cold where you're supposed to be."

His gaze lifts, so light and clear, hardly any fog.

"I would've done anything to bring you back to me for one last minute," he says. "But I couldn't, so I followed you. And if you hadn't come out here, I would've bought a ticket. And if I got inside and you were already boarded, I would've gotten on the plane. I would've waited until we landed in Boston to talk to you. And if somehow I missed you in deboarding, I would've found your next gate to talk. And as I was driving here, watching this stupid fucking plan form for how I would get to you and say goodbye in person, I realized why we can do this."

My heart whirs, lifts toward him as if pulled by a magnet. "Why?"

He smiles down at me, and it feels like a fist on my heart, a tight hug that verges on a heart attack. "Because there's nowhere I wouldn't go for you. And if you get out to Montana and realize there's somewhere else you need to be, there's nothing I'm not willing to do to make it work. I'd rather have you five days a year than anyone else all the time. I'd rather argue with you than not talk, and whether we're together or we're not, I'm yours, so let's be together, Harriet.

As much as we can. As long as we can. As soon as we can. Everything else, we'll figure out later."

"Wyn," I whisper shakily. His fingers twitch, tightening through my curls. "Are you saying I can come home?"

"I'm saying," he murmurs softly, "it's not *home* unless you're there."

My arms twine around him, my heart speeding wildly as the wind batters us. "I love you," I tell him.

"In every universe." He kisses me then, a windblown curl caught between our lips. Like it's a first and a last. The end of one era and the beginning of another.

This, I know, *is exactly where I want to be.*

39
REAL LIFE

A Monday

The day I withdraw from my residency, I call my parents to give them the news.

They are, understandably, shocked. They want to fly to San Francisco immediately.

"Let's talk this out," Dad says.

"We can help you figure out what's going on here," Mom says.

"Don't make any decisions until we can get there," Dad says.

They have never once visited me.

The irony of it all strikes me then: working so hard to earn their love and pride, and it's brought me no closer to them. If anything, I think maybe it's kept them at a distance.

"I already made the decision," I tell them. "I withdrew. But I'm going to pay back the rest of the loans myself. I don't want you to worry about that."

Mom starts to cry. "I don't understand

where this is coming from."

"It's out of nowhere," Dad agrees.

"It's not," I say. "It's taken me years to make this decision. And I already found another job."

"A job? What job?" Mom asks.

"At a pottery studio," I say.

"Pottery?" Dad sounds like I just pitched him a multi-level marketing scheme selling methamphetamine for dogs.

"You don't even make pottery," Mom says.

"I do," I say. "But it's not good. And I know that won't look very impressive on the Christmas card, but that's what I'm spending my time doing right now."

"Then *why* are you wasting your time doing it?" Dad says.

"Because it makes me happy," I say. "And I don't consider anything that does that a waste of time."

"Maybe you just need a break," Mom says.

"I want a *life,*" I say. "I don't love surgery enough for that to be mine. I want to sleep in sometimes. I want to stay up too late and take vacations with my friends, and I want to have energy to decorate my apartment and to try new things. I can't do any of that when I'm this worn-out. I know that's disappointing, but it's my choice."

"Harriet," Mom says. "This is a mistake.

One you'll regret for the rest of your life."

"Maybe," I allow. "But if I do, that's on me. And I swear, I won't let it affect you."

"Slow down," Dad says. "We'll come out there and figure this out."

"You can't come out here," I say.

"We're your parents!" Mom cries.

"I know," I say. "And if you want to visit me in a couple weeks, I'd love to see you. But I'm not going to change my mind, and there's no point in you coming to San Francisco right now, because I'm not even there."

"What do you mean you're not there? Where are you?"

Over the intercoms, an announcement rings out. My gate has been moved. "The Denver airport," I say. "I have to go, but I'll call you when I get in."

"Get in *where*?" Mom says, her voice raising in a way it never has, not with me.

"Home," I say, then clarify, "Montana."

Another silence.

"I love you both." It feels unnatural, but that doesn't mean it's not true, only that I've gone too long without saying it. "I'll call you tonight."

I get off the phone, drag my stuff over to the new gate, stopping for a Cinnabon and an iced coffee. When I slump down in one of the tearing faux-leather chairs, my phone vibrates with a text, and I ready myself for an impassioned lecture or a persuasive letter.

Instead, I find a message from Eloise. We've never been a text-for-conversation set of siblings.

Mom called me, freaking out, she writes.

I wince. I'm sorry, I write. Hope that wasn't too stressful.

I watch her typing, but then she stops. I go back to systematically dismantling my cinnamon roll.

Then her reply buzzes: UR not responsible for Mom's feelings. At least that's what my therapist says. I just wanted to check in on you bc she's convinced UR having some kind of breakdown. R U?

Eloise is the only person I know who texts in complete sentences, complete with punctuation, but still refuses to type out *are* or *you*. But that's about the only part of that text message that doesn't come as a shock.

I had no idea Eloise saw a therapist. Then again, I don't know much about Eloise, period. We never speak this openly, and I'm weirdly touched.

It might be some kind of breakdown, I write. But the truth is I don't think I ever really wanted to be a surgeon. I just liked making people proud. And the idea of the money.

Shit! she writes back, and for a minute nothing else comes through. Maybe that's it, the end of our late-in-life sisterly bonding. Ten minutes pass before her next message appears.

I should probably tell U I resented U, bc I thought U were just like them, and so they always liked U more. Now I'm realizing how much pressure U must've felt, and maybe if we'd acted like sisters sooner, things could have been different. So this might not mean all that much, but for what it's worth, I'm proud of U. And Mom will def get over this, eventually. She got over my bellybutton ring.

Really? I say.

Well, she never acknowledged it outright, Eloise replies, but she DID stop looking at my stomach and sighing. This will go better than that. I've got UR back.

I lean back against the counter as that washes over me. Thanks, I tell her. I'm sorry I didn't have yours more. I wish I had.

Don't worry about it, she says. U were just a kid. Neither of us had much say over our lives but now we do. UR doing what's right for U. That's all U can do.

I've never cried over a message with so many abbreviations in it, but I'm considering printing this text out and sticking it on the Connor family refrigerator for safekeeping. We may not have pictures of us in matching sisters' Halloween costumes, but we love each other. There's hope. If I want to be close to her, I can work at it.

Dad comes around first. He starts sending me articles about the mental benefits of making pottery, and texts about a new TV competition between ceramists.

Mom is a harder sell.

When she and Dad finally fly out to visit us in Montana, she's virtually silent the whole first day.

I take them antiquing, and on a beginner horseback ride. We hit up happy hour at a bar whose theme seems to be Hunting But Fancy, one of those new spots catering to the summer crowd by pretending to be folksy.

"Hank hated this place!" Gloria says happily as the server leaves with our order. "Wouldn't ever come with me, so I'd have to bring our neighbor Beth Anne."

Mom and Dad tag along to the beginner classes I've started helping with at Gallatin Clay Co. Dad does his best to seem inter-

519

ested, while Mom settles for simply "not crying."

Afterward, I show them my last few projects. Mom holds a bowl glazed in every shade of blue, scrutinizing it for a long time before saying, "This one's nice."

"Thanks," I say. "I made that for Sabrina and Parth."

"Your friends who just got married?" Dad says.

"Right," Mom tells him, "the lawyers."

Again, I wonder if my friends weren't the only ones I pushed away. If every time I turned the focus back to the thing about me I *knew* my parents loved, I missed the chance for them to know the rest.

We have fun at times. It's incredibly awkward at others. Then it's over, and a yellow cab is pulling up the Connors' driveway, and Wyn excuses himself so Mom, Dad, and I can say our goodbyes in private.

I go in for hugs before it even occurs to me that my family's never done much hugging. It's too awkward to take back, so Dad and I stiffly hold on to each other for a beat. Then Mom and I do the same.

Dad gets in the car, and Mom starts to follow, then turns back, crunching across the gravel. "It's never been about the Christmas card, Harriet," she says. "You have to understand."

The back of my nose stings. Some latent instinct in me believes this surge of emotion represents danger. My nervous system tells my glottis to stay open to let more oxygen in so I can sprint away. But I don't.

"I gave everything up," she says weakly.

"I know," I say. "You gave everything up for us, and I understand what that cost you, and I'm sorry —"

"*Harriet*. No." She grabs my elbow. "That's not what I mean. I gave up everything for your *father*. He wanted to keep working. He wanted to move to Indiana. And I thought if he was happy, that would be enough. It's not that I'm not proud of you. I'm *terrified* for you, honey. That you're going to wake up one day and realize you built your life around someone else and there's no room for you. It was never about the Christmas card. I want *you* to be happy."

"I *am* happy," I promise her. "I didn't come here for Wyn. I came here for me. And I don't know how this will all end up, but I know what I want."

Tears rush her eyes. She forces a smile as she pushes my hair behind my ear. "I'm never not going to worry about you."

"Maybe you could limit it," I say. "Like twenty minutes a day of worrying. Because

521

I'm okay. And if I'm not, I'll tell you."

She touches my hair. "Will you?"

"If you want me to," I say.

She nods. "I love you."

"I know," I say. "I love you too."

She nods once more, then joins my dad in the cab's back seat.

As I wave them off, the screen door creaks open. Wyn's piney scent wraps around me before his arms do, and I sink back into him. He's cut his hair short and shaved his beard, and his five-o'clock shadow scratches against my temple, followed by the softness of his mouth.

We stand, listening to the hoot of some distant owl, watching the taillights shrink.

"Hungry?" he says finally.

"Voracious," I say.

40
HAPPY PLACE

Real Life

Our home. A wooden table, a vase overflowing with wildflowers, a golden-green field. Long walks with Wyn, and shorter ones with Gloria.

Sitting on the back porch, smoking a joint with the love of my life and his mom. Getting giggly and munchy, and making brownies from scratch in a too-hot kitchen. Sleeping over in a room full of Wyn's high school soccer trophies so we don't have to drive back to our new apartment over the overpriced stationery store downtown.

Our new Save the Date stuck prominently to Gloria's fridge.

I memorize all the floorboards that creak or groan, so I can tiptoe downstairs in the morning without waking anyone, take the Jeep into town for a sugary latte for me and black coffee for them, orange cinnamon morning buns for all of us. Or at least Wyn will have a bite, and I'll polish off the rest.

I walk for a while, enjoy the bittersweet scent of whitebark and pine and quaking aspen.

There's an entire shop here for sauces, syrups, and oils. Last week, after sampling easily two dozen, Wyn and I bought a smoky maple syrup aged in charred bourbon barrels. For Gloria's birthday, we made pancakes, and when she tasted the syrup, she said, "Tastes like camping."

Then she got choked up, because camping was something she and Hank used to do. "When we were first dating and had no money," she explained. Then, after a teary laugh, she added, "And once we'd been married for decades and *still* had no money."

Wyn stood and went to wrap his arms around her shoulders, and she patted his arm as she recovered. I understood, then, the immense honor it is to hurt like she does. To have loved someone so much that the taste of maple syrup can make you cry and laugh at the same time.

And I know, if nothing else, I'll have that. I know I've chosen the right universe.

The thought breaks my heart a little for my parents. For my dad, who worked nearly every Monday through nearly every Friday at a job he didn't like enough to ever talk about, and I understand that something was stolen from him and he accepted it. Because we needed him to, or because he believed we did. And for my mom, who left behind one home to follow him and never quite found another.

I duck into the shop and buy four bottles of campfire maple syrup.

One for Parth and Sabrina, one for Cleo and Kimmy, and one for each of my parents. I want them both to have every drop.

I want them to have everything they've ever wanted.

There are times, still, when I am anxious about my decision, worry over whether my parents will ever understand it, understand me, or if I'll ever find something to be *my* thing.

And whenever I need a happy place, I still think of the cottage. Or maybe not the cottage so much as an alcove under the stairs that smells like Wyn, a sun-washed dock and Cleo asking about our other lives, Sabrina and Parth fuming over a game of gin rummy, and Kimmy singing Crash Test Dummies into a wooden spoon.

I think of sitting in a row on an extralong twin bed in a musty dorm room, silk scarves tucked into drop tiles to soften the fluorescents, watching *Clueless*.

I picture an ever-less-run-down farm in the northernmost part of New York, and the first time I held my goddaughter Zora, couldn't stop staring at her tiny fingers, the golden-brown eyes of her mother staring right back as my heart said, *Miracle, miracle, miracle.*

I revisit the drive out from San Francisco with my mom, when we finally packed up the rest of my stuff into a rented truck and hauled it out. The seedy motels we checked into, the episodes of *Murder, She Wrote* we watched while feasting on vending machine candy. So much of the trip was objectively awkward or stressful, but in my memory, those aren't the moments that loom large.

Instead, it's Mom telling me all about how she and her sister used to pretend to be witches in the woods of Kentucky, where they'd lived when they were small, grinding blackberries into mud and wild onion to smear on their foreheads, pretending it made them invisible.

It's when she asks me to tell her the whole story about meeting Wyn, and afterward, how she says through tears, *All I want is for you to be happy.*

And I say, *What about* you? *Don't* you *want to be happy?* and she looks so baffled, like the thought had never occurred to her. All that time, those nights lying awake in my little yellow bedroom making bargains with the sky, spending wishes on her joy, and now I understand.

No one else's happiness is yours to grant, Mom, I tell her. *You need to find yours.*

Eloise and I text on occasion, mostly surface-level stuff, but I'm trying again. I'm hoping.

Sometimes I cast my mind forward too. Think of the rustic ranch turned event center that Wyn and I put a deposit on, and imagine an early fall day with a bite in the air, the smell of sweet hay and dying leaves thick. I imagine our friends and family lined up before one of Wyn's tables, an antique lace cloth draped over it, blankets waiting on every chair for guests to swaddle themselves in as the sun sinks. (Or the Vegas bachelorette trip Sabrina's started booking.)

But more often than any of those places, when I need to feel safe and happy, I go home.

And no matter the weather — feet of snow or sun bleeding the thirsty fields dry — when I walk up the steps and put my key into the lock, I feel a lift in my chest, a surety:

He will be waiting on the other side, still covered in sawdust and smelling like pine.

Before I even see him, my heart starts singing its favorite song.
You, you, you.

ACKNOWLEDGMENTS

First and foremost, I have to thank the team who has been by my side for every step of this: Amanda Bergeron, Dache' Rogers, Danielle Keir, Jess Mangicaro, Sareer Khader, and Taylor Haggerty. This, like my last three books, truly wouldn't have been possible without all of you, and every day I'm grateful for you. Thank you, thank you, thank you.

A huge thank-you also to Alison Cnockaert, Anthony Ramondo, and Sanny Chiu for the gorgeous cover art and interior design, as well as to my incredible copy editor and proofreader, Angelina Krahn and Jamie Thaman, respectively.

Unending thanks also to Cindy Hwang, Christine Ball, Christine Legon, Claire Zion, Craig Burke, Ivan Held, Jeanne-Marie Hudson, Lindsey Tulloch, and the whole team at Berkley.

I also need to thank my team across the

pond, Viking, especially Vikki, Ellie, Lydia, Georgia, Rosie, and my fantastic cover designer, Holly Ovenden.

So much gratitude also to Holly Root, Jasmine Brown, Stacy Jenson, and the rest of Root Literary, as well as to my foreign rights agent, Heather Baror-Shapiro, and her team at Baror International.

Publishing can be a very transient industry, with people always coming and going, but one person who has been with me from the very beginning is my incomparable film agent and champion, Mary Pender, along with her team at UTA. So grateful to have you by my side through all of this.

So many author friends have been here for me through this (and other) books, but I especially have to thank the people I can *always* count on to speed-read for me and to talk through sticky plot points and sort out my characters' emotional logic. Brittany Cavallaro, Isabel Ibañez, Jeff Zentner, and Parker Peevyhouse: I'll never be able to thank you enough for the time, energy, kindness, and love you give to me as both friends and colleagues. As Jeff likes to say, "You're my band."

Here is where it gets tricky, because over the years, so many people have supported me and my books in so many ways, so let me just say, to every journalist, podcaster, reviewer, book club, web show, magazine, radio show, bookseller, librarian, perfumery, and writer friend who has ever engaged with one of my books: thank you. I love my job so much and am endlessly grateful to everyone who's played a part in allowing me to continue doing this.

And from a more technical standpoint, I'm only able to write books about friendship, family, and love because of the people I'm incredibly lucky to call my friends, family, and lover. Thank you for loving me and for being you.

Last but certainly not least, thank you to my readers. For everything. All of it. I'm so grateful our paths have crossed in this truly bizarre and wonderful way.

Thank you.

ABOUT THE AUTHOR

Emily Henry is the #1 *New York Times* bestselling author of *Book Lovers, People We Meet on Vacation,* and *Beach Read.* She studied creative writing at Hope College and now spends most of her time in Cincinnati, Ohio, and the part of Kentucky just beneath it. Find her on Instagram @emilyhenrywrites.

The employees of Thorndike Press hope you have enjoyed this Large Print book. All our Thorndike, Wheeler, and Kennebec Large Print titles are designed for easy reading, and all our books are made to last. Other Thorndike Press Large Print books are available at your library, through selected bookstores, or directly from us.

For information about titles, please call:
(800) 223-1244

or visit our website at:
gale.com/thorndike

To share your comments, please write:
Publisher
Thorndike Press
10 Water St., Suite 310
Waterville, ME 04901